ALSO BY CLIVE RIDDLE

Dorris Bridge
dorrisbridge.com

The Burning Z
burningz.com

The Z Tailgate

CLIVE RIDDLE

The sequel to The Burning Z

HealthQuest Publishers

HQ

HealthQuest Publishers
www.healthquestpublishers.com

Publisher's Cataloging-In-Publication Data
(Prepared by The Donohue Group, Inc.)

Riddle, Clive, 1958-
  The Z Tailgate / Clive Riddle.

  pages : illustrations, maps ; cm

  Sequel to: The Burning Z.
  Issued also as an ebook.
  ISBN: 978-0-9966646-1-5

  1. Zombies--Fiction. 2. Concentration camps--Nevada--Black Rock Desert--Fiction. 3. Football stadiums--California--Oakland--Fiction. 4. Kidnapping--Fiction. 5. Cruise ships--Fiction. 6. Fantasy fiction. I. Title.

PS3618.I39 Z83 2016
813/.6   2015956394

Printed in the United States of America.

For My Brother John

"If aliens ever visit us, I think the outcome would be much as when Christopher Columbus first landed in America, which didn't turn out very well for the Native Americans."

Steven Hawking, April 2010

"Far more Native Americans died in bed from Eurasian germs than on the battle field from European guns and swords."

Jared Diamond, Guns, Germs, and Steel: The Fate of Human Societies (New York: W. W. Norton, 1999).

Preface

Bottom Fishing

Friday, 12:05 p.m., October 29th

It was the next to last full day of the final north coast sailing of the *Pacific Duchess* for the season. The ship would arrive in San Francisco Sunday morning and switch to a Mexican Riviera route that evening. This seven-day cruise originated in San Francisco, with ports of call in Victoria, Vancouver, Seattle, and now, Astoria.

The *Pacific Duchess* Shore Excursion Tour Manager had been stationed outside on Pier 1 at the Port of Astoria since shortly after its eleven a.m. arrival, reviewing procedures with the tour coordinators who were charged with assisting passengers queue for their respective purchased excursions.

Twelve excursions were available – including four area sightseeing tours; five tastings tours of wineries, micro-brews, or local cuisine; and three outdoor activities tours including a charter fishing excursion. The tour manager assigned his own four excursion staff as coordinators for the four largest excursions, the other eight were coordinated by "volunteers" from the ship crew who presented themselves well and weren't scheduled to work in their respective departments until later in the day.

Rodrigo was the coordinator responsible for the fishing excursion. He was a Filipino waiter whose shift didn't start until prep for dinner in one of the formal dining rooms at four thirty. The tour manager had scheduled Rodrigo as the tour coordinator for the charter fishing expedition every Friday the entire season, after being badgered by Rodrigo to do so.

Rodrigo had served on a fishing crew for a season with a Scottish fishing vessel before signing on with Duchess Cruise lines. He liked to talk shop and show off his fishing knowledge with the excursion passengers as they checked in to wait for the shuttle bus that would transport them to the adjacent East Basin Marina.

Fishtoria Charters was the name of the company contracted to conduct the charter fishing excursion, advertised as a four-

3

hour adventure starting at one o' clock – with boarding beginning at twelve thirty. Bottom Fishing was the featured activity.

This afternoon's fishing excursion had sold out, with twenty slots filled. The sellout made the tour manager all the more stressed when, shortly after he touched base with Rodrigo, he received a frantic call from the charter. Fishtoria Charters' captain was phoning to cancel, as two of his three deckhands, car-pooling together, had just been in a head-on collision on their way to the marina, and were taken to the hospital by ambulance.

There were major financial incentives for Duchess's tour manager to make his excursion quota for the season. He had just met the quota, clearing his target by just a few hundred dollars. This cancellation would put him back under. The tour manager pleaded with Fishtoria's captain, stating he could provide a qualified deckhand from his own staff – a hard worker who could make them forget that they still had been one man down. Fishtoria's captain agreed, provided that the cruise deckhand would just work for tips, because he couldn't imagine they could come close to getting the paperwork straight.

Duchess's tour manager went to work on Rodrigo, who didn't have to be asked twice – but needed the tour manager to clear Rodrigo's afternoon waiter schedule. The tour manager shifted into bartering mode – the economic engine of the cruise ship crew. Similar to Burning Man, the economy below the passenger decks was not dependent upon cash. Goods, services, and favors were typically subject to trade between the crew. With one phone call, the tour manager extracted Rodrigo from his first shift with the early seating in the dining room, in exchange with granting the head waiter a comp excursion during the Mexican Riviera season.

So it was that Rodrigo checked in his twenty excursion passengers – there were zero no-shows – and boarded them, along with himself into the waiting shuttle, to be whisked off to the East Basin Marina for four hours of bottom fishing with Fishtoria Charters.

It wasn't a problem that Fishtoria was short one deckhand, or that Rodrigo was new to the boat, and a bit rusty with his former trade. The fishing season was past its prime, and there wasn't a lot of fish to be caught off the Pacific waters of Astoria Rodrigo was kept busier fetching beers and water bottles than conducting the final landing of any bottom dwellers such as rock fish, sea bass, quill back, tiger rock, yellow tail, vermillion china rock or lingcod.

Fishtoria's captain felt a little bad for Rodrigo, given that fishless passengers were notoriously bad tippers. The captain did his best to engage his guests in constant conversation, and repeatedly had everyone pull in their lines to try new spots where their luck might change.

The boat was just into its last hour, trolling some rocky structure within eyesight of the marina, when a heavyset middle-aged couple, wearing his and hers Oregon Ducks football jerseys, each yelled "fish-on" almost simultaneously. Fishtoria's captain signaled his one remaining regular deckhand to assist the lady and motioned for Rodrigo to assist her husband.

Both fish put up quite a fight. The captain shouted out he wouldn't be surprised if they were lingcod. He idled the boat, letting the two passengers reel in quite a ways before having his deckhands take over for the actual landing. The lady's fish came up first, the captain working the gaffing hook. All the passengers gathered around, to admire the catch that exceeded thirty pounds, while the deckhand prepared the fish for its final journey.

Rodrigo's fish was even larger, putting up a herky-jerky fight. The captain, wanting in on the action, took over and instructed Rodrigo to work the gaffing hook. Only Rodrigo had a close-up view of the monstrous lingcod. It was hideous and apparently diseased. Rodrigo called over to the captain – informing him he was going to release the fish.

Fishtoria's captain angrily instructed Rodrigo to do nothing
of the sort. The captain estimated the fish would weigh-in over
fifty pounds. They would land the fish, let the passenger view
his catch, and then release it, if they must.

Rodrigo shook his head, before dropping the fish into the
landing area. The passengers circling the landing area gasped
and stepped away as the fish came into view. It bore open
sores, was discolored to a gray-green tint and seemed facially
deformed.

True to the captain's word, the husband wanted to view his
catch. He knelt down with Rodrigo – the disgusting
appearance and snarling nature of what seemed to be a lingcod
didn't seem to register with the fisherman.

Fishtoria's captain, now sizing up the horrendous fish,
understood Rodrigo's initial concern. He ordered Rodrigo to
unhook the Norwegian cod jig from the fish and release it.
Rodrigo wasn't sure why he felt a wave a fear as he gripped the
lingcod's lower jaw firmly with his left hand and worked a pair
of needle-nose pliers into its mouth to extract the lure. The
fish truly did unnerve him. As he worked to release the hook,
the fish's jaw overpowered him, clamping down and biting him
savagely. Rodrigo screamed in pain, his hand and pliers still
inside the monster fish's mouth.

Before the captain could get to Rodrigo, the husband –
kneeling behind him – scooted over next to Rodrigo, grabbing
the fish's jaws, working to pry them open. In seconds, he
succeeded; Rodrigo popped backward, still screaming, his
hand covered in greenish-gray goo.

The lingcod lurched forward, sucking the husband's left hand
into its mouth. He let loose a startled cry of expletives as the
captain called for the other deckhand. Fishtoria's other
passengers, horrified, stepped backwards to the railings of the
boat.

The captain tended to the husband, pulling on him, while the
deckhand tugged on the lingcod's lower half. Quickly they
separated the two. Fishtoria's captain cut the line, got control

of the fish with the gaffing hook, then lifted the lingcod up and tossed the hideous fish back into the ocean.

Above the screams of several of the ladies on the boat, one of the passengers chastised the captain for tossing the fish overboard. "How could you put that thing back into the sea where it will infect other fish? And what if the doctors needed to test the fish when they check out these people it bit?"

Fishtoria's captain turned around, pointed at a number of the hysterical passengers, and looked his inquisitor in the eye. "Did you get a good look at that thing? Did you? I don't think you did, or you'd be thanking me for getting it out of this boat and away from your fellow passengers."

Rodrigo and the husband were both doubled over, writhing in pain, their bitten hands covered in gray and green bile and slime.

"Can a lingcod do that, sir?" asked the dumbstruck deckhand, staring at the two fallen men.

"Not any I've ever seen," the captain replied, also focused on the two. "You better grab our first aid kits, quickly, and tend to them. I've got to radio in to the *Pacific Duchess* and get their medical crew on standby, and then calm down these passengers."

I.
Black Rock Desert

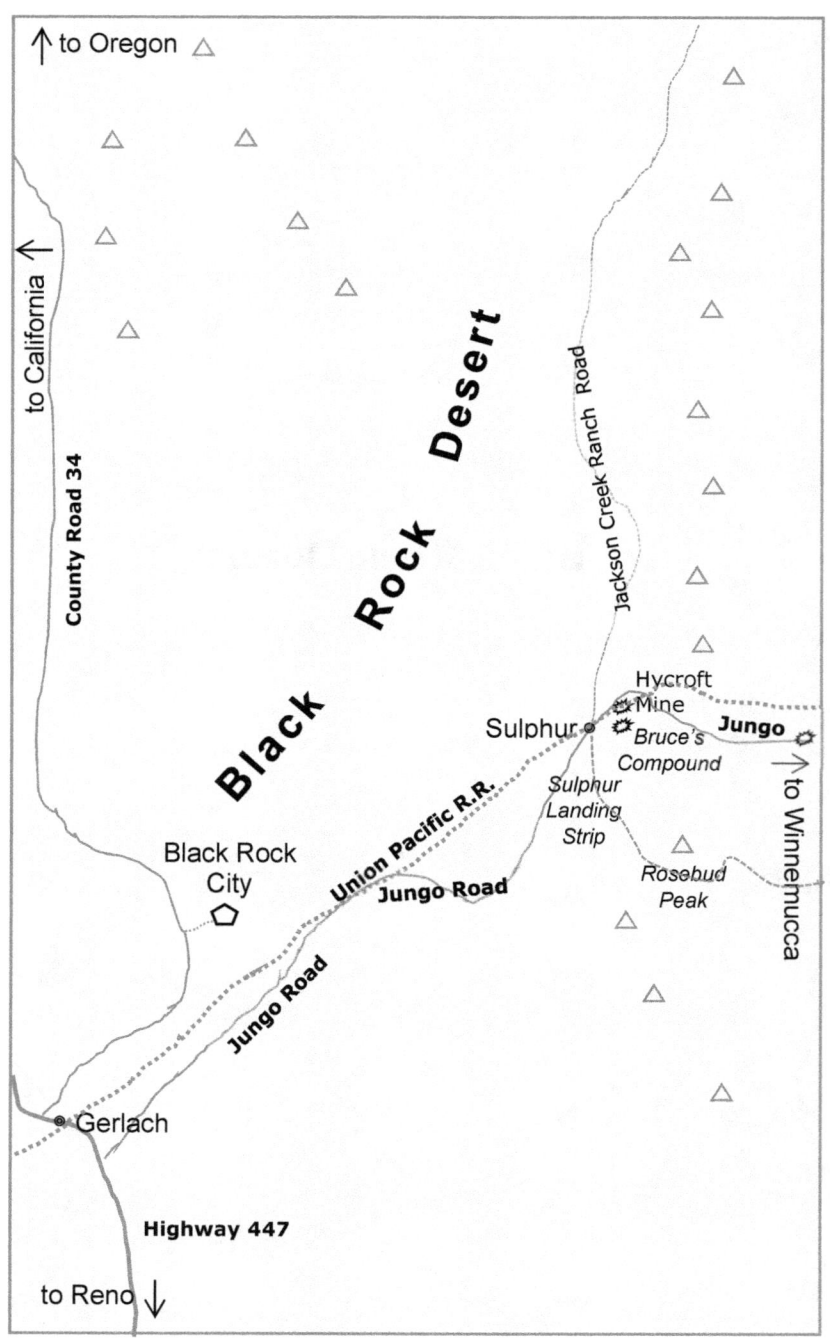

Lawyers, Guns, and Zombies

Like the star of Bethlehem, a meteor-like object appeared in in the Black Rock desert night sky, three days before the start of the annual Burning Man event. The object struck into the desert hills, firing projectiles into anyone that wandered too close. Soon the desert possessed a growing zombie population.

The temporary community of Burning Man, called Black Rock City, soon was under siege. One of the desert's frequent massive dust storms masked the zombies' arrival. A torrential rain storm followed, trapping the over sixty-thousand residents inside, as the black rock playa surface becomes an impassable sea of muck when combined with water.

Two days after Burning Man opened, during the week leading up to Labor Day, over eleven-thousand Black Rock City residents had become infected with what was subsequently called "Gorman's disease," named after Alan Gorman, the retired Air Force physician who first alerted authorities to the zombie threat. Many of the infected perished as available military, law enforcement and National Guard finally took back control and fenced in Black Rock City. The uninfected were evacuated, while those infected were to remain inside the security fences surrounding the city.

The aftermath of the outbreak of Gorman's disease at Burning Man brought about an army of lawyers that some pundits quipped matched the government response in numbers and intensity. Nearby Gerlach, Nevada seemed to have doubled in population during the two months following. Temporary quarters were secured for insurance claims service offices, private investigators, media posts, special interest groups, government offices, Indian taco trucks, and seemingly more than all those combined – branch law offices. On top of that, there were the protestors and family members, living out of cars or RVs.

The flood of lawsuits was almost immediate. Burning Man survivors wanted to recover their possessions still inside Black

Rock City. Families of those deceased or injured during the Burning Man incident sought recompense. Families of those still remaining inside Black Rock City pursued petitions ranging from declaring their loved ones deceased, to pronouncing them alive and free to exit the premises or receive visitation. Insurance companies were being sued for untimely or inadequate resolution of claims. Black Rock City LLC, the organization behind Burning Man, was suing various government agencies over their response during the Burning Man festival. Almost everyone else, it seemed, was suing Black Rock City LLC.

Rapid court orders stemming from petitioners on behalf of those left inside the Burning Man security fences, required that those inflicted with Gorman's disease be provided adequate daily supplies of water, nutrition, and protection from the elements. These orders initially prohibited use of lethal weapons by security forces inside the fences, until multiple incidents occurred with staff being overwhelmed and bitten. Guns were soon allowed back in to accompany security forces.

Then there were the end-of-times religious groups ensconced in Gerlach. Just like in nationally televised football games where one could count on viewing persons placed behind the goalposts waving signs inscribed John 3:16, televised crowd shots in Gerlach predictably had someone on the background holding a large placard emblazoned with Revelations 20:13. The verse varied in wording according the version of the New Testament in use – but a typical reading would be something like "And the sea gave up the dead in it; Death and Hades gave up the dead in them; and all were judged by what they had done." Followers – ignoring that the timeline pre-dated their belief in the age of the earth according to Genesis — pointed out that Black Rock City resided in the prehistoric lakebed of Lake Lahonton, which was once a sea the size of one of the Great Lakes. They held that this was evidence of Revelations 20:13 now taking place in a sea from "biblical times."

If responding to the seemingly endless onslaught of litigation; court-orders that sometimes conflicted; a plethora of political inquiries; proposed legislation, and religious fervor wasn't a challenge enough, then the ambiguity of jurisdiction over the many facets of the aftermath surely was.

No one in authority initially wanted to preside over the domain of zombies, but everyone it seemed wanted to share their opinion in how to handle zombie affairs. Ultimately it required a presidential executive order to name the Department of Homeland Security responsible with overall jurisdiction over issues relating to security, research, reporting, and disposition of the affected region and its inhabitants, which included coordinating the inter-agency resources of the CDC, National Guard, BLM plus state and local agencies.

The central question was, were those inflicted with Stage II Gorman's disease to be classified as living or deceased? Were they, in present form, to be considered human with inalienable rights? The Department of Homeland Security, in concert with the District of Nevada U.S. District Court and the Attorney General's Office, bought time with the pronouncement that until adequate research was completed and findings were put forth by the CDC and Surgeon General, the question would remain unanswered, leaving litigation, court orders, special interest groups, insurance settlements, estates, and proposed legislation in limbo. Any such pronouncement was still considered to be months away.

DHS did provide some operating guidance: (1) An extended radius of five miles beyond the Burning Man security fences was a quarantine zone, thus preventing visitation from families or other stakeholders; (2) Any newly discovered cases of Gorman's disease identified outside the quarantine zone were to be transported to the zone – this did occur on several occasions with straggler zombies that didn't gravitate to Burning Man after the initial meteor impact; (3) research on subjects with Gorman's disease was to occur in a designated facility in the general vicinity – no infected cases were to be transported outside the quarantine zone other than to the nearby research facility for any reason – which was necessitated after two initial zombie exports for CDC research resulted in new infections; (4) the assets inside the quarantine zone including vehicles, structures, and personal items were to remain undisturbed by security forces other than when required, to ensure the safety of personnel or inhabitants, until such time as DHS determined that inventory, transport and or retrieval of such items could safely occur; (5) the infected inhabitants would be inventoried and tagged with a GPS embedded ankle band as feasible over time; (6) security forces were to refrain from shooting infected inhabitants or otherwise using deadly force, except in self-defense – with guidelines issued regarding avoidance of engagement with inhabitants whenever possible – along with requirements for incident reports and administrative hearings whenever deadly force was deployed; (7) infected inhabitants that ceased to demonstrate signs of "life" were to be collected for research or cremation as feasible and (7) court orders requiring water, nutrition, and protection from the elements were interpreted as to necessitate daily filling of water troughs and provision of nutritive sustenance at designated stations, as well as assurance that adequate structures remained intact to provide shade and shelter from dust storms or precipitation.

The Black Rock City zombies weren't quite the same as those from legend. They required minimal amounts of water, and possessed working digestive systems. So far, the zombies had generally sustained themselves on the meager provisions provided to them. Few "expired" cases had to be collected for research or cremation. However, winter was rapidly approaching in the high desert and the first snows were expected anytime. It remained to be seen how the zombies would fare in the bitter cold.

The Air Force's interest in the extra-terrestrial origins of the meteor was dashed the day after Burning Man was secured. The globular object in the small meteor impact crater self-destructed with a small explosion when lifted by portable crane. This disappearance of evidence allowed an alternate theory as to the origins of Gorman's disease to be advanced.

Zombie Profiteers

Bruce Kepner resided in a compound he purchased in the Black Rock Desert near the ghost town of Sulphur. He placed himself in exile at that location after spending a number of years as a coder in India. His time in India had been preceded by his meteoric climb in the American dot com world, followed by the subsequent crash. After his high-profile venture-capital backed startup collapsed, he had undertaken a second dot com initiative, using angel funding from family and friends, which also failed.

Bruce had a difficult time sitting still. His wiry 5'10" frame seemed in constant motion. He paced around the outside of his trailer, waiting for Alan Gorman's arrival. He rubbed his fingers through his neatly groomed goatee and his head covered with short, jet black hair that bore occasional gray streaks.

Shortly after the meteor's fall into the Black Rock two months earlier, Alan Gorman went searching for a missing friend who had called Alan excitedly upon witnessing the meteor's descent from a distance. Alan soon found himself trapped in the basement of a nearby ranch house full of zombies.

Alan, a target shooting enthusiast, eventually shot his way out of the house, as well as two additional zombie-occupied locations as he searched for a phone to notify the authorities – being there was no cell coverage in the heart of the Black Rock. His search eventually brought him to Bruce's compound, where zombies had chased Bruce and his visiting fantasy football comrades onto the roof of an abandoned structure on Bruce's property.

Alan Gorman arrived again at Bruce's compound, a mere ten days after that first encounter, when Alan introduced himself by shooting every snarling zombie that had trapped Bruce on the roof. Now Alan was under contract with the Department of Homeland Security, and had shown up to help broker a deal on behalf of DHS. Bruce couldn't help himself upon seeing Alan, and had to share some Shakespeare.

Bruce trotted inside his doublewide trailer to retrieve his prized quote book, because it was a long passage and he didn't have it fully committed to memory. A little bemused, Alan waited patiently while Bruce thumbed through a series of pages before stopping at a particular verse, whispering the verse to himself several times.

Bruce then turned to Alan, reciting: "There is a tide in the affairs of men. Which, taken at the flood, leads on to fortune; omitted, all the voyage of their life is bound in shallows and in miseries. On such a full sea are we now afloat..."

Several hours later, DHS staff arrived to negotiate some final points and tweak the boilerplate document Alan brought with him. Before sundown, Bruce signed the papers leasing his entire property to DHS to establish the satellite research center for study of Black Rock City inhabitants inflicted with Gorman's disease under the auspices of the CDC.

Under the terms, Bruce was given a position as the onsite building and grounds manager, contingent upon successful completion of his background check, in order to qualify for requisite security clearance. Within days, additional modular structures and security fences began appearing.

DHS determined that significant onsite research needed to be facilitated, but not within the confines of Black Rock City – due to the dangers of free range Zs at every turn, as well as the peril of losing the veil of secrecy within earshot of all the National Guard and DHS subcontractors in the area. DHS also wanted some distance from the meddling throngs in nearby Gerlach.

They sought a more discreet, nearby location, where manageable numbers of test cases could be transported. Alan volunteered he had come across the perfect site – remote, private land off primitive Jungo Road, with adequate water access and utilities, some existing structures that could be put to use, and a principal (Bruce) that Alan could vouch for and who had intimate knowledge about the infected.

By late September, the center was fully functioning. The immediate confines of the structures were surrounded by security fencing. As negotiated in the lease, Bruce's seldom-used softball field remained intact, bordering the fencing. Bruce and two resident security personnel lived in his doublewide trailer. The round-the-clock shifts of other staff could take breaks in Bruce's singlewide trailer, which previously served as his office and guest quarters. One new modular unit housed the lab; the other new unit housed the resident zombies who were rotated from the vast pool of infected in Black Rock City.

The center served merely as the data and specimen collection point. All high level analysis was conducted in Atlanta and elsewhere. Each shift of two CDC lab techs, two additional security guards, and occasional inter-agency observers, commuted in a large SUV via Jungo Road from Winnemucca. Jungo Road was a reasonable unpaved, graded route from Winnemucca to the Hycroft gold mine. After that, the last few miles to Bruce's compound, or beyond to Gerlach, was a treacherous, arduous journey.

Bruce took to his new role with passion. His hope was that if the lease continued into the new year, he would be able to make a partial repayment to his family and friends who had invested in his previous failed venture.

Alan Gorman had not sought his new relationship with the Department of Homeland Security. Gorman had retired the year before as an Air Force physician. He occupied his time with a consuming hobby of meteor observation, target shooting, golf and periodic locum tenens gigs at area urgent care centers.

The day after the Burning Man incident concluded, he wrapped up his volunteer physician services when ample new medical staff arrived. Alan then accompanied his friend, the Air Force Colonel and Nellis AFB Vice-Commander, who had overseen the securing of Black Rock City during the Burning Man incident, back to the meteor impact crater. There, they witnessed the still functioning globular object explode before them, when an attempt was made to lift it away by crane.

Hours later, Alan was re-united with his vehicle and began the long ride home. He had no sooner returned to his wife, settling into a nap in his reclining chair in their Palm Springs home, when he received a call from DHS staff. Alan was told the director of Homeland Security was en route to the Palm Springs Airport, wanting to meet with Alan at the Gorman residence as soon as possible.

Soon the director sat in Alan's downstairs office, clutching a glass of the vintage port he brought and opened upon his arrival. The director had been briefed about Gorman's lower left leg prosthesis, but could not help himself from continually casting furtive glances in that direction. Still, the director could not distinguish if there was or wasn't prosthesis concealed underneath Alan's apparel.

There was ten minutes of small talk about the study of meteors – which was the dominant theme of content and appearance in Alan's office. Then, there was twenty minutes of increasing pressure, culminating in director securing the five feet ten inches retired Colonel Alan Gorman's consent to become the public face of the war on zombies, but only after the phrases "patriot" and "service to your country" were spun repeatedly into a stream of sentences.

The "z" word, the director reminded Alan – was not to be uttered again. He had consensus amongst his inter-agency group, that from hereafter those infected were to be referred to as suffering from "Gorman's disease." Alan was to be introduced to the world as the man who first identified the threat of the infection, managed to survive through the initial outbreak, and successfully alerted and convinced his government to act.

What's more, his government now called upon him to act as a senior advisor in all aspects of dealing with the disease and to promote national preparedness for any potential future outbreaks. The director confided that the president was about to take executive action naming the director responsible for addressing the various facets of this threat, and had already agreed to the director's initial recommendations on preliminary actions, including retaining Alan.

The director spelled out that what they wanted was for Alan to form a consulting firm to advise not only his department but also key components of the nation's healthcare system, local governments, and the private sector in preparedness and response options. The director expected Alan to embark on significant public speaking engagements in this regard. He provided Alan with the name of a longtime associate who would be approaching Alan to be retained as a business manager for this consulting and public speaking practice about to go viral. The director mentioned that his associate would be arranging for a book deal as part of the package.

What the director didn't say to Alan, was his pitch to the president revolved around attaching identity and ownership of the zombie incursion to someone other than within their administration. Furthermore, his pitch focused on the opportunity the outbreak brought, if painted as the product of biological terrorism and the biggest domestic threat to the country since 9/11. This, the director had no intention of sharing with Alan until he was far beyond the point of no return.

So Alan became the reluctant hero, appearing on the Today Show, the focus of multiple televised press conferences, the star witness for an initial Congressional inquiry, and the keynote speaker booked for a spectrum of national conferences on healthcare, emergency preparedness, and more. Alan quickly saw that in addition to his handlers and assistants, he needed someone of stature to join his new firm, to share the load of speaking engagements and consultations.

Alan's stories of the man in the Imperial Stormtrooper costume at Burning Man quickly transformed Bruce's friend, Conrad (Conner) Zimmerman into a celebrity. Alan shared how he met Conner and Bruce at Bruce's compound, and after they realized the infected from the outbreak would be heading toward the Burning Man event, Conner rushed to Black Rock City to rescue his girlfriend. Accompanied by Bruce, they fought off the growing swarm of infecteds when all others around them had succumbed.

Given that Conner worked in the business end of healthcare, Alan could think of no other candidate to team with him in speaking to the healthcare organizations around the country. Conner was hesitant to leave his secure and relatively anonymous hospital business development position. A compromise was reached when Alan convinced Conner's employer to let him take a leave of absence with benefits and a guarantee of employment upon his return, provided that Conner's affiliation with the hospital would be listed in all appearances.

Conner was an easy figure to recognize in those appearances. He stood six-foot-two, neither thin nor fat. His hands were large, his feet were large and his nose was quite prominent. His brown eyes exuded sadness, punctuated above by dark eyebrows and below by slightly darkened circles. His short brown hair failed to conceal his longer-than-normal ear lobes. His muscular face and neck falsely gave the impression he was an athlete.

Bruce and Conner both grew up in the small California town of Parker Creek, where Cassie also lived few a few years as a teenager. Conner and Cassie were each other's first love back then, and had recently resumed a long distance relationship as they approached age forty.

So it happened that Alan and Conner, at DHS' request, were scheduled to inspect Black Rock City on Saturday morning, the day before Halloween. Bruce, upon hearing the news, arranged a sleepover for Friday night at his new clandestine research center, also on Alan and Conner's inspection schedule. Conner made plans for Cassie to fly from San Diego to Reno and join Alan and Conner in their rental car sojourn to their first full reunion with Bruce since the Burning Man incident.

Terrorists

The DHS director, a mere week after securing the contract with Alan Gorman and parading him in front of the world, met with him again, this time at Nellis Air Force Base in the office of Gorman's friend, the base vice commander. Alan was whisked in by helicopter. The director and his entourage arrived by jet around the same time.

The tone of this meeting was quite different than their first encounter. The director was confrontational. He asked his four staff traveling with him to clear the room for a few minutes, so he could have a frank discussion with Alan and the vice commander. As soon as they exited the office, the director started in.

While the vice commander sat behind his desk, the director pulled his side chair directly facing Alan, who was seated to the left of his friend. He looked Alan squarely in the eye. "I thought we had an understanding about your little theories concerning your meteor."

Alan wrinkled his face. "What are you saying?"

The director raised his voice. "The president – your commander-in-chief — is going to appear on national television tomorrow to announce our findings thus far on Gorman's disease, and you need to be on board." He turned to face the vice commander. "You both need to be on board."

Alan and the vice commander exchanged puzzled glances. "I'm not sure —" Alan started, but was interrupted by the director.

"The president called me last night. He had been alerted by the secretary of defense – for whom I speak as well—that the vice commander had just submitted a white paper authored by the two of you regarding your extra-terrestrial theories regarding the origins of Gorman's disease..."

The vice commander broke in, raising his voice as well. "What is your problem with a classified internal document directed to my superiors that–"

He was interrupted by the director in return. "Look, no one requested you to draft or submit that paper. You of all people should know protocol. You should have asked first. So now we need you to request to recall your submission, because we're not going to have some white paper floating around internally that contradicts your commander-in-chief."

Alan again exchanged a confused look with the vice commander. "I don't understand what the issue is here. What is the president going to say?" Alan asked defensively.

"This should be no surprise to either of you. You were both copied on our preliminary report and yet you respond with your unsolicited paper," the director snapped.

"Let me get this straight," the vice commander replied sarcastically. "The president is endorsing that the meteor Alan found, whose fall was observed by his colleague and reported directly to Alan, that left a fifteen-foot impact crater, that deliberately fired projectiles triggering a disease, that so far does not match any possible earthly origin, is actually the result of a missile launched by ISIS-affiliated terrorists and that they had the capability of designing the most complex disease ever developed and launching this weaponized virus payload with a missile undetected by any branch of our armed forces or other agencies? Let alone, you're advancing this based on an operating theory not supported by any direct evidence. *That* makes more sense to you?"

The director started to rise from his side chair, before sitting back down, gripping the side arms tightly. "With all due respect, it made sense to your secretary of defense and it made sense to your commander-in-chief. I'm not going to argue the merits of our findings with either of you, because it's already been endorsed by your superiors. And I'm not going to argue the merits of your supposed theories, other than to say that, frankly, they only bear the same basis in fact as any Sasquatch or flying saucer sighting. Where's the actual witness to your supposed meteor fall? He's conveniently no longer around. Where's your supposed extraterrestrial meteor? It's conveniently no longer around. You advocate that there must be other such meteors launched at us, so where are they? Where are they gentlemen?"

Alan cleared his throat loudly. "That's the whole point. This is a big freaking planet. We need focused intelligence gathering and monitoring now that we know what we're looking for. What is the downside of the puny amount of funding required for doing just that?"

Now the director did stand. He shouted, pointing at the vice commander, "We cannot have any even minute arm of the United States of America researching a competing thesis to what is about to be announced by your commander-in-chief. Period. Now retract your report or the next visit you receive will be from your own chain of command." The director turned to Alan. "And you, I expect more from you. You of all people should know how important it is for the public to receive a plausible explanation now for this mess. You really want to go to the public with your little theory and get laughed off the stage? You want to leave this thing unexplained and consider the panic that will cause? People need answers. Your president isn't going to lie. He is going to report this as our best operating theory at this point in time. Not only that, but you can bank on ISIS taking credit for launching Gorman's disease once we accuse them. This is an answer the public will accept and support, and that will help us all to move forward..."

"And help us all mobilize even more congressional funding against ISIS no doubt," Alan interjected.

The director sat back down. "And that's a bad thing? Are you saying that's a bad thing?"

"No one is saying that's a bad thing," the vice commander conceded in a calmer tone, throwing in the towel. "Anything that helps mobilize more resources against ISIS is a good thing."

"Look," Alan retorted to the director. "I get it. We all get it. I just don't like that it's a little disingenuous. ISIS already deserves to get blown off the planet without you padding their resume like this. But I can get over that. As you said, it's not my place to undermine our commander-in-chief. But what I can't abide is that you're going to sweep the very possibility of what we're talking about under the rug. You and I both know there is some way to structure some level of research and preparedness for what we're talking about that could remain outside public visibility. Irresponsible is not a strong enough word to convey what sweeping this under the rug is. So count me out. I won't say or do anything to undermine you. But I don't need to be your front person on the war on Gorman's disease either, if this is how it's going to be. I've already retired from public service. Let's just figure out how to unwind our little arrangement and I'll just go back home to Palm Springs."

The room fell silent for a number of seconds.

The director exhaled loudly several time. "Hmmm," he repeated several times, with increasing volume. He turned again to the vice commander. "So you'll retract your paper?"

The vice commander looked to Alan. Alan nodded, sighing. "Yes, it will be retracted."

The room fell silent again. "Hmmm," the director repeated. "You really would turn your back on your country out of sheer pride, Dr. Gorman?"

"It seems to me, you're turning your back on your country out of sheer politics, sir," Alan responded sharply.

"Hmmm," the director uttered, barely audibly this time. "Alright, look Dr. Gorman, you both said you'll be team players and keep your little green men theory to yourselves. We also need you to continue to be a team player, which by definition means you need to stay on the team..."

Alan leaned back, shaking his head, his arms crossed.

"Now hear me out. I've just come up with a plan. This administration cannot advance or address any of your little theories here, but you are an independent contractor to the DHS, conducting a variety of activities outside the purview of the United States Government. Nothing is to stop you from overseeing research and monitoring in this regard." The director paused momentarily.

"What are you saying?" Alan interjected.

"I'm saying I will find a way to increase your retainer under our agreement by an amount that will more than adequately allow you to hire or outsource a couple of people to do this work and to fund the resources they'll require. But you can't involve your friend here," the director gestured towards the vice commander, "or anyone else employed by the U.S. government. And our compensation amendment to your agreement will stipulate that any research activities you conduct related to Gorman's disease will remain classified, and any staff your retain for research purposes are subject to non-disclosure agreements meeting our specifications. And it occurs to me, we should provide you the name or names of who you can consider contracting with for this task."

Alan turned towards his friend. This time the vice commander nodded. "I don't know… How much funding are we talking about and are you going to restrict what we look into?"

The director smiled. "I think we can fund you to more than make this worth your while. I must have brought my staff here for a reason. I can have them crunch the numbers and craft your amendment before we leave. And as long as you bring on board staff acceptable to us, we're not going to restrict where you look. Just understand we're not going to provide you any special access or support of any kind."

Alan scratched his cheek. "So say we find something interesting. What then?"

The director rose from his chair again. "Your agreement is that your work is classified. You tell no one. But we'll hear about, believe me. And I'm sure if it's interesting, we'll want to know."

Alan rose up as well. "So if I agree, how long is it going to take to put this in motion?"

"I see no reason why we can't have an agreement for you to sign today and names for you to contact to join your team by tomorrow." The director held out his hand. Alan paused, and then performed a half-hearted handshake.

"Now remember," the director turned to the vice commander, who was now also standing, "I want that paper retracted today." The director took a step towards the door before stopping and placing a hand on Alan's shoulder. "And one more thing, Dr. Gorman. I think your team will want to start by checking out an incident in Tobolsk, Russia. Out in Siberia. That's T-O-B-O-L-S-K."

Monitoring for Meteors

After receiving additional DHS funding, Alan Gorman had two "analysts" under contract, both working from home offices. They in turn managed disbursing funds to a series of research foundations to ensure access to targeted astronomical observation feeds and related chatter.

Both of his analytical staff were referred by the DHS director, and had been subcontracting with other agencies. One came courtesy of the National Security Agency, the other courtesy of NASA. The objective was to flag any reporting of unusual meteor activity, both current and recent past.

At the DHS director's continued insistence, they initially focused on the alleged incident in Tobolsk, Siberia. Internet chatter and international intelligence queries produced similar, sketchy sets of rumors, but nothing more. The decaying state of relations between Putin-led Russia and the U.S. left little hope for concrete, new information.

But finally, a back-channel query through the Russian Federal Space Agency produced an arranged phone call in early October between Alan Gorman and an assistant to the General Director of the Agency, who spoke a moderate level of English.

The Russian's end of the conversation was couched in hypotheticals: "If an incident like the one you described had occurred, this is what would have happened..." By the end of their twelve-minute conversation, Alan was convinced of the authenticity of the major points that had circled through the rumor mills: a meteorite fall; a globular object in the impact crater shooting projectiles into all who ventured near; the zombie-behavior of those infected; and the ultimate self-destruction of the globular object.

The big difference between Tobolsk and Black Rock City was the military response from the Ministry of Emergency Situations (EMERCOM.) EMERCOM broadcast a warning to those in the infected area to flee outside a designated radius, followed by the incineration of all those who remained inside.

For the Russian's part, the Burning Man incident was already in the public domain, except for the nature of the Black Rock desert meteorite fall. Alan alluded to the possibility that the details of their two respective attacks were quite similar.

The Russians wanted to know, despite ISIS's public affirmation that it was the source of the American attack, what hard evidence could possibly exist tying ISIS to a launch that had to at least be sub-orbital, and more likely from full-orbit or beyond. The Russians pointed out ISIS had never laid claim, or seemed to even possess the knowledge of, the Tobolsk incident.

Alan simply repeated what his president had publicly stated – that ISIS was the American government's operating theory regarding the incident, and that ISIS had now corroborated this version of events. Alan's Russian counterpart scoffed at Alan's response, and replied that they both must know they needed to keep their eyes on the sky for future objects launched from far beyond planet Earth.

The Russian's interest in the exchange of information was more directed at what was the nature of the ongoing testing of those infected with Gorman's disease, and why wasn't the Russian government or the international community given access to this information, or better yet, delivery of some of the test subjects. Alan deferred that as a consultant to, and not an employee of his government, he had no authority over or intimate knowledge of any testing of the infected, but he would certainly pass along these concerns.

The Russian ended their conversation with a warning that his government's anxiety over the unconfirmed testing program wasn't going to go away, and the Americans should expect this issue to escalate significantly. The Russian's warnings weren't unfounded. As October progressed, international protests and inquiries grew in fervor regarding America's secretive oversight of the Burning Man population infected with Gorman's disease. Russia's behind-the-scenes fingerprints were well attached to the growing global fury.

Alan's analysts so far had not uncovered any additional suspicious meteorite falls that could produce any evidence of activity meriting further research. A mid-October conference call between the two analysts and Alan elicited Alan's frustration that "It's a big planet to be searching for this kind of a needle in the haystack, let alone it was covered two-thirds with ocean, so their needle could likely be underwater."

Alan's former NASA contractor grabbed onto that statement – and stated "seriously, we've been going about this all wrong, focusing on just land-sightings. We need to – and pardon the metaphor — cast a wider net to include ocean-related activity." The former NSA analyst argued that "there was no point to engaging in such a distraction – as there would be no practical way to retrieve any such objects from the bottom of the ocean, and besides, the objects would have to be directed at land-fall targets, as they could not achieve their objectives out in the oceans."

Alan sided with casting a wider net. After two weeks, by the end of October, there wasn't much to show for their effort on land, but there was definitely measurable increase in chatter from the shipping industry and island nations regarding potential meteorite falls into the ocean during the same time frame as Burning Man and Tobolsk. Of particular interest, a number of Pacific Northwest sightings of a significant meteor fall into the ocean were recorded in social media around the same time of the Burning Man incident.

Quon Li

Quon Li was not his real name. The actual Quon Li, whose identity he assumed, was a destitute American citizen without immediate family or close friends, who matched reasonably enough in appearance. That Quon Li was now a resident in Beijing, spirited away from the U.S. by the Chinese Ministry of State Security.

This Quon Li was an operative of the Ministry — fluent in English, skilled in surveillance, a master of logistics, and a serviceable assassin. He'd arrived stateside in late September, fresh from a two-year mission in Australia. During the past month, his sole focus had been making arrangements for the securing of a shipment of zombies to be secretly transported back to the Republic of China.

After it became clear that CDC research on Gorman's disease or access to those infected would not be shared with the international community, the Chinese Ministry received the green light from above to help themselves to a few of their own test subjects. The zombie enclave at Burning Man was the only publicly acknowledged site, although there were rumors of a smaller outbreak, around the same time, in a small village a hundred kilometers from Tobolsk in Siberia.

The Ministry ruled out Tobolsk after operatives could not confirm that any infected still remained – the word was that all had been incinerated within days of the initial incident. Curious to the Ministry was rumor that the source of the Siberian outbreak was a weaponized meteor, which couldn't be confirmed, as it evidently no longer existed. Equally curious to the Ministry was the American incident produced no mention of such a meteor, and possessed a very different public explanation.

Quon Li had been a very busy man during the past thirty days. He secured two inside men – DHS subcontractors supporting the National Guard at one of the Black Rock City gates – giving them the cover story that they were going to pilfer a number of zombies for an eccentric American billionaire with pancreatic cancer, hoping to glean a cure or slow down his own disease with research on these subjects.

Quon's Ministry contacts at the Office of the Consulate General in San Francisco assisted him in lining up the shipping container, the container ship transport, and friendly regulators in the Port of Oakland. The Cosco Container Lines Americas ship was scheduled to load their container on Sunday, so the end game was near.

Li had cleared his final plans with the Ministry a week earlier. Quon could not devise a scheme to secure the zombies directly from Black Rock City within acceptable levels of risk. Once he identified the off-site research facility in the Black Rock desert, all scenarios under consideration revolved around that locale.

Initially, Quon Li operated out of Reno. Two weeks ago, he relocated his base of operations to a motel room in Lovelock. Two nights ago, he checked out for one last quick supply run and final meeting in San Francisco, driving back to Nevada in a customized transport vehicle. Upon his return to Lovelock, he rendezvoused with his two inside men, leaving them with the special cargo truck, dirt bikes, daypacks loaded with supplies, and detailed instructions.

Quon Li wasn't apprehensive about the mission as he departed on foot. His two compatriots dropped him off, twenty-five kilometers into Lake Road after the Imlay exit from Interstate 80.

Still, he *was* nervous. Nervous about returning to his wife in Shanghai once his cargo was offloaded. He had visited her only twice since leaving for Australia – with each visit limited to two days. They'd married in 1995 – had a daughter soon thereafter – their only child in keeping with China's one-child policy enacted in 1980. Their daughter died in her early twenties from injuries after being struck by a speeding motorcycle on the streets of Suzhou while Quon was in Hanoi on assignment. Since that time, he rarely walked through the doors to his home.

Quon jogged from desolate Lake Road directly toward the foothills to the west, chewing his Nicorette gum in the rhythm of his strides. He was outfitted in a padded, black jacket, size thirty blue jeans, black stocking cap, black daypack, tactical belt, and night vision goggles. His cap concealed his smoky black hair, and partially hid a large scar on the left side of his forehead.

After reaching the foothills of the Kamma Mountains, he jogged parallel to Lake Road below, bearing toward his destination near Jungo Road to conduct his final surveillance.

The Stopover in Sulphur

Conner, Cassie, and Alan climbed out of the red Toyota RAV4 Conner had rented at the Reno-Tahoe International Airport hours before, stepping into the chilly, high desert nighttime breeze drifting through Bruce's compound.

Alan had flown in from DHS meetings in Washington, DC. Conner arrived from Oakland, leaving his car at the airport there after Sacramento and Bay Area stops, concluding with a speech at a UC Berkeley seminar. Cassie cleared leaving work early – she was an analyst with a niche market research firm in San Diego – dropped off her fifteen- year-old daughter with friends for the weekend, and boarded a flight to Reno as well.

Their flights were all close to on-time, arriving within a half-hour of each other. Soon enough, they stopped by Conner's seldom-used apartment, to trade out his luggage before heading into the darkening desert, and finding their way onto the jagged, slow, bumpy ride offered by Jungo Road.

Bruce offered quite a reception upon their arrival. After they cleared the security gate, they were greeted in the darkness by Bruce his two resident security staff with chilled water bottles. Together, they all quickly toured the compound, and met the two lab techs currently on duty in their modular unit.

After they retired to the trailer, much fun was made at Conner's expense of his continued loyalty to the Raiders, who had just moved from the Oakland Coliseum this season to a new stadium. Now the Raiders were coming back to the Coliseum one last time. Their home game had to be relocated due emergency structural repairs at their new venue, and the league selected the Oakland Coliseum as their replacement location for the game. Conner had bought tickets that were offered at a substantial discount, and convinced Cassie to join him.

As Conner sat next to Cassie on Bruce's sofa, he couldn't help but feel some distance, even though their knees were pressed against each other. Conner wasn't sure exactly what was wrong, but could sense the slowly widening rift over the past several weeks. He wondered if she had PTSD from their night in the Alamo art structure, fighting off zombies, at Burning Man. Her demeanor certainly had shifted during October, and the physical distance between their homes made the growing gap in their relationship three- dimensional.

More than anything, Conner wanted to make their relationship work. Cassie had been his salvation – his motivation to stay off the bottle, other than his relapse that night before Burning Man, in this very room. The dark voice within him called out for him to order whatever his conversational companions were having almost every night on the road, in so many different towns.

Conner had struggled but maintained a sober September and October in the worst of possible circumstances. He was away from Cassie – away from home, away from the comfortable hospital system job he had been enjoying – but saddled with the temptations and downside of minor celebrity and the everyday reminders of the pain inflected by the infected Gorman's disease residents of Burning Man. It was a pain he revisited each time he gave speeches, presentations, and led Q&A sessions on that topic.

Conner at times felt the only way to rescue himself from an eventual fall into a bottle was to abandon his recent lucrative position with Alan. His recent name recognition as the savior Imperial Stormtrooper in Burning Man should be able to parlay a safe return from his leave of absence to his hospital job. Better yet, he could seek a similar position in San Diego or even remain with Alan but re-locate to San Diego.

The trouble was, Cassie hadn't invited him, and he wasn't bold enough to bring up the subject first. Instead, she just seemed to grow more quiet and troubled with time.

At other times, the rush from the high level meetings, the speeches in front of large audiences, the trade journal and even occasional mainstream media coverage held great appeal to Conner's ego. The sense of purpose in taking on an unprecedented challenge and the rising flow of income into his financial accounts were perks reminiscent of his happier life early in his career – all this so far still tethered him to Alan.

Conner's thoughts ventured away from the conversation at hand. Conner shuffled through his checklist of anxieties before noticing that the couch he and Cassie were occupying was the same one that the first zombies he encountered had reclined in that late August morning in Bruce's compound. Conner visualized the naked zombie, sitting right where Cassie was now, zoned out in front of the television infomercial just before tearing into Bruce's friend.

Time passed while the conversation wound through many turns. Suddenly, Alan's sat phone ringtone brought the proceedings to a halt. Alan entered into a lengthy conversation. Bruce and Cassie soon initiated their own discussion about Tess, concerning how she might be faring in Black Rock City as the weather grew closer to winter. Tess was Cassie's best friend, and they had attended Burning Man together for many years. Tess had been bitten by zombies during their last stand in the Alamo art structure in Burning Man. They had left her behind in a comatose state when they finally escaped.

Conner noticed it was already close to eleven thirty p.m. when he heard his name mentioned, drawing him into listening in on Alan's conversation. Within five minutes, Alan and Conner had agreed to travel by corporate jet and then helicopter, charted by Duchess Cruise Lines to their ship, the *Pacific Duchess*, positioned off the Oregon coast.

After concluding the call, Alan re-capped the conversation to Bruce and Cassie: "If this isn't horribly rude, but I'm afraid Conner and I are going to have to bail on you shortly and postpone our tour tomorrow morning. We're hoping to get back by mid-afternoon. Duchess Cruises – the ones that were in the news several times recently, for some pretty negative publicity – they want us to rule out Gorman's disease on some cases just occurring today from their stop in Astoria Oregon, allegedly resulting from a fish bite. They don't want to call in the CDC or take any action to trigger media attention if it's unwarranted, and they've had no exposure to our population. They claim to just to want to be extra cautious, so they're asking us to do an assessment, and they will bring CDC or whatever resources are necessary if we have any concerns."

Bruce and Cassie were both clearly deflated by the news. "A fish bite?" Bruce protested. "If it's such a wild goose chase, why are you going? You're always telling us that someone around the country is claiming to have encountered a zom— I mean a Gorman's disease victim, every five minutes or so."

"For one thing," Alan explained, "they are paying, pardon the expression, a boatload of money, and they need an assessment ASAP. But the big reason is that I've developed a sizeable curiosity about the spread of my namesake disease via the ocean, and the possibility of a marine reservoir host. As I've told Conner, I have a couple of analysts monitoring ocean activity, and while this is likely a wild goose chase, there's enough at stake, that we really have to go."

"But what about Conner? Why do both of you have to go?" Cassie pressed, visibly dejected.

Conner started to say something, but Alan broke in. "I'm sorry, Cassie. But they insisted, and I agreed that we need a two-man team to get in, do our assessment, and get out as quick as possible. Plus, if by some fluke we really do find something tangible there, I need Conner to corroborate our on-site assessment. I need a witness on my team, so to speak. Anyway, the charter is on its way from Reno. Bruce, I assume you can drop us at something called the Sulphur Landing Strip when they call back saying they're inbound? It's supposed to just be a click down the road."

There was no way for Cassie to hide her resentment that Conner chose what she felt was a dubious engagement, over her, especially after she flew up specifically so they could spend some time together. Conner tried to smooth things over, to little avail. He promised to call with status reports, and said they should be back mid-day tomorrow. He made a contingency plan with her to meet in Oakland, if things got really messed up, and promised, no matter what they'd enter Raider Nation together on Sunday.

Poole Waves
Goodbye

Zombies like shade. Cassie spotted her first Zs as their lead vehicle crawled through the second set of security gates in the Black Rock City Northeast entrance. She was reminded of cattle, congregated under one majestic oak tree in a wide-open pasture that you might catch a glimpse of while driving along a country road.

There stood a dozen or more listless Zs within the confines of the shady side of the dusty, dual-level pirate ship mutant vehicle, their attention scattered in every direction. If you wanted to spot a Burning Man zombie during the middle of the day, you'd find almost every last one of the three thousand, four-hundred-plus remaining Zs residing in the shade of one of the thousands of abandoned structures, mutant vehicles, camps, RVs, and art projects that served as a testament to all that was Burning Man two short months ago.

Bruce reached over from the other rear passenger seat, patted Cassie's left hand and pointed at the zombies. "You might not notice them if they weren't standing in the shade to provide some contrast. Can you believe how caked in playa dust they all are?" Cassie nodded, causing her short, dark brown hair to bob up and down; her accompanying smile accentuating the light freckles that graced her face. She now noticing the thick film of two months' worth of chalky-white playa powder enveloping each and every zombie resident thanks to countless dust storms and Zs' stumbles onto the playa floor.

"One touch of nature makes the whole world kin," Bruce added mischievously, studying Cassie to see if she recognized his Shakespeare.

The white, small lead SUV sped up slightly, progressing at fifteen miles per hour – Bruce and Cassie in the back seats, their Nevada National Guard 991st Multi-Functional Brigade escorts in the driver and front passenger seats, adorned in modified hazmat and protective gear. Hugging close behind was the water truck, followed by the sound truck.

Bruce had arranged for the two of them to take Alan and Conner's place in accompanying a scheduled morning zombie watering, which he knew would take them by the Alamo art structure. Cassie's gaze shifted from the pirate mutant ship's shade zombies as the Alamo emerged into view. She stared intently at the Alamo's open gates, then at what remained of the two-story structure at the far end. Somehow it all seemed so diminutive compared to her memory of their ordeal two months earlier.

On that Monday night during the Burning Man week, Conner surprised Cassie at her tent with a wild tale of zombies and a confessions that he'd fallen off the sobriety wagon the night before. Fearing her new boyfriend was unstable, she left him there, rushing off to join her best friend Tess out on the playa at the Alamo art structure. Soon they and a number of others were trapped in the Alamo's upstairs rooms, surrounded by a growing number of Zs. Conner and Bruce found their way to the Alamo and helped them fend off the gathering swarm of zombies. Eventually the effects of the downpour of rain, combined with the crush of zombies against the support beams, caused the upper structure to partially collapse. One by one, members of their group succumbed to their attackers. Cassie watched in horror as Conner fell into the crowd of Zs below, but protected by the Stormtrooper costume Cassie's Burning Man neighbor had lent him, Conner was able to escape and scale back up the Alamo fence to the roof. From there, he helped lift Cassie, Bruce and another woman in a Catwoman costume to safety. They also managed to bring the already-bitten Tess to the roof, where they left her when they finally made their dash away from the Alamo after the National Guard arrived.

Cassie felt a rush of disappointment as the Alamo slid from view as they made a turn and pressed on. Bruce leaned towards her, patting her arm, whispering, "Don't worry. I asked them to drive by more slowly on the way back."

Soon, they rolled to a stop in front of the long metal trough. The SUV inched forward on the right side of the trough, while the watering truck positioned itself on the left. The sound truck continued ahead more than a hundred yards, before slowing to a crawl. Cassie and Bruce could hear the dubstep begin to blast from the sound truck through their closed windows, as the truck slowly crept away from them, like some Burning Man version of an ice cream truck rolling through the neighborhood.

Within moments, a number of zombies popped up like gophers from the shade of a nearby small mutant vehicle that sported giant metallic lips that were in great need of a new coat of red paint. The Zs lurched towards the sound truck, with more stray zombies joining their parade with each few steps.

Cassie and Bruce's escorts exited the government SUV, donning their helmets, masks and grasping M16A2 rifles. The driver, the taller of the two, barked out a reminder to Cassie and Bruce to remain in the vehicle. Cassie and Bruce weren't wearing the required gear to be allowed outside. The driver hand-signaled the watering truck opposite them to pull forward several feet and then stop. The truck's passenger hopped out, opening each of the three valves positioned over the trough, allowing the truck's load to begin gushing out.

The National Guard driver remained in front of the two vehicles, while his companion took position behind the watering truck. Both continuously rotated their view ninety degrees at a time, scanning the playa with their rifle scopes. As the flow of water from the truck began to slow through the valves, the SUV driver called out, "wrap it up – Zs at twelve o'clock and closing."

The watering truck passenger shut the valves, even though the truck still had ten percent of its load left, and soon everyone was back in their respective vehicles. Their driver almost sang into his walkie-talkie, addressing the sound truck, "all done Elvis, let's head home!" The vehicles swung around, reversing their course. Looking behind into the dust clouds their vehicles were creating, Cassie could see the sound truck catching up with them. She also noticed zombie figures heading towards the trough that was shrinking in the distance.

Cassie could sense the shift in the mood of their escorts. The driver turned around for the first time, smiling while directing his attention at Bruce. "Alright, it's time for your short sightseeing excursion." The driver slowed down, letting the watering truck and sound truck pass them. Both continued making a beeline for the northeast security gate.

The SUV driver turned around again, directing his attention to Cassie this time as they approached the Alamo. "So, I'm told you two were in the thick of it out here, back then. I'll circle this structure once, real slow, and then we have to go. I'm breaking protocol as it is." The driver decided to go silent, letting his backseat passengers reflect on revisiting the trauma of that night. He nodded at his fellow escort in the front passenger seat, while proceeding to turn in front of the Alamo gates at five miles per hour.

Cassie gasped and tugged at Bruce's shirt. Four naked zombies emerged from the shade of the right front gate, advancing toward the SUV. The driver accelerated slightly, keeping the vehicle safely out of reach. Cassie studied the structure. Her disappointment returned — the dusty, sterile-looking Alamo of the present did not match her vivid memories of the nightmare-inducing Alamo of that night.

One of the images that haunted Cassie was witnessing her friend Tess go down. There had been this awful woman in their small thrown-together group at the Alamo, dressed in a tequila bottle costume, who had previously in a panicked state sent her own friend and Catwoman's boyfriend to a zombie demise in order to save her own skin. A zombie dressed in a Hawaiian shirt had lunged towards Tess and Tequila girl. Tequila girl pushed Tess into him. The zombie bit hard into Tess's left shoulder upon impact. With her remaining strength, Tess let the Hawaiian zombie have it with a two-by-four directly in the jaw. Several teeth went flying; gray ooze dripped from the zombies' mouth. The zombie fell backwards into the wall from the force of the blow. Tess collapsed where she stood. The only solace Cassie found from this recollection was that Tequila girl eventually met the same fate as Tess.

Bruce studied Cassie's reaction more than the structure at his side. He could sense her letdown, and the lack of closure their hastily-arranged tour was providing. Bruce had to visit the eerie ghost-town – make that zombie town – that was once Black Rock City, on almost a daily basis. He was jaded even to visiting the Alamo. But he knew that Cassie would experience an emotional assault upon visiting the site where they abandoned Tess on the rooftop.

Cassie softly sobbed as they rounded the corner, to the back side of the faux fort that had been inspired by the Alamo of the movie Pee-wee's Big Adventure. Cassie fought to keep her composure, staring intently up into the dust-covered, partially collapsed second story. The ladder on the back wall was still intact, that Conner and subsequently, Bruce, had scaled in order to join their cause. Not a zombie was to be seen anywhere in the upper level. Cassie took a deep breath, drawing the disappointment into her lungs, before exhaling loudly as they rounded the corner to the eastern side.

"Damn, where'd she come from?" the driver exclaimed as he suddenly swerved the SUV to avoid mowing over the zombie lady directly in front of them. Cassie jerked her head around, taking in the all-too-familiar sight now behind them. Her mouth opened, but she was having trouble sounding the words. A soft "sssss" was all she achieved. Cassie squinted, trying to best focus on what she couldn't fully comprehend.

Then Cassie watched Tess raise her arm. Cassie was sure the arm was motioning back and forth. Cassie was confused, because Tess was not wearing the Jan Space Ghost costume she was last seen in. She was fully clothed in garments unfamiliar to Cassie.

Finally, Cassie's voice found its footing. "Stop," Cassie screamed. The driver instinctively hit the brakes, but then resumed their forward motion. "What?" he snapped back at

Cassie, while exchanging glances with his partner in the front passenger seat. "What?"

"It's Tess. She's waving her arms! Stop the car!" Cassie was almost hyperventilating.

The driver shot a disapproving glance at Bruce. "No can do ma'am. I'm very sorry."

"You've got to stop!" Cassie pleaded, tears again flowing. The zombie lady began to shrink from view as the SUV slowly veered away from the Alamo, bearing towards the northeast gate.

Bruce's face wrinkled up as he looked again at the zombie behind them. "Cassie," Bruce implored in measured tone, "I really don't think that could have been Tess still at the same spot, two months later."

"Please," Cassie cried, her gaze still fixed on the zombie lady in the distance. Bruce squinted as well, giving the z another look. Bruce gasped. He wondered if it was wishful thinking, his mind playing a trick, as he was certain the zombie waved its arms. Bruce's thoughts flashed to Kubrick's and Clarke's Dave Bowman, witnessing lifeless Frank Poole's arm wave – Poole tethered to his distant pod in space — while Hal lay in wait in the ship *Discovery*.

The SUV sped up to fifteen miles per hour while Cassie sobbed. They headed toward the mutant pirate ship. The driver turned, directing his attention to Bruce, while speaking to Cassie. "I'm sorry ma'am. But we simply cannot stop on the return and we're due back at the gate. Your friend here knows this."

"Please," Cassie pleaded, turning to Bruce. Bruce grimaced, staring at his knees sheepishly. Then he gasped, remembering the pair of binoculars he had placed in the seat pouch in front of him. He grabbed them, spun around, working the zoom lever and focus dial. The Alamo fell into his sights, left of the dust cloud behind them. One more time, he swore he saw the distant zombie raise and lower its arm, before it completely faded from view as their SUV approached the northeast gate in silence.

Test Subjects

Bruce and Cassie didn't return to the compound after their watering run ride-along concluded. They stood outside his new Ford F-150 pickup, parked just outside the Black Rock City Northeast gate guard station. A cold wind whipped up a wave of dust in their direction.

To placate Cassie, Bruce volunteered to phone the lab and campaign for Tess, or whoever it had been waving at them, to be included in today's roundup for test subjects. The two on-duty lab techs were on a conference call, so Bruce waited for the call-back.

Cassie licked her lips, even though she'd just applied ChapStick minutes before. She could taste the playa dust — already adhered to her lips. She could detect the musty smell of the dust in the air, almost like a room full of sheet rock. She looked at Bruce, then at her own jeans. They both already bore smudges of playa dust on their clothing. The memory of her and Tess's first trip to Burning Man came to mind, when the greeters at the station, upon receiving her confession that the two were playa virgins, were instructed to immediately lay in the playa dust and make dust angels. She and Tess were told, "once you're out here, it gets into everything – you might as well get it over with now."

Cassie ran her hands up and down her blouse and jeans that were well-fitted to her slender physique. A small amount of playa dust rose from her clothing, but most remained firmly adhered to her apparel. Cassie recalled how she and Tess would visit the laundromat immediately upon returning to San Diego from Burning Man each year, so that the playa dust would not gum up their own washing machines. She bit her lip, frustrated with how much she missed Tess, how guilty she felt over Tess's fate, and how powerless she felt in trying to follow up on what it meant that Tess waved at them.

Cassie's thoughts drifted to Tess's fate if they managed to retrieve her and bring her back to Bruce's lab. "What exactly are they doing with all these test subjects?" Cassie asked Bruce with the intensity of a reporter.

"That's what everyone wants to know. The guys working at this gate and the National Guard, they ask us that every single time we come up here."

Cassie reached over and squeezed his arm. "Yeah? So what do you tell them – or more to the point – what's the real answer?"

Bruce chuckled. "I tell 'em the truth."

Cassie was growing impatient. She poked him in the ribs with her index finger. "Which...is...?"

Bruce laughed a moment more. "Which is, I'm under contract not to say anything, but the truth is, I know next to nothing. The truth also is, the lab techs at my place, they know barely more than me. The CDC in Atlanta, the Department of Homeland Security honchos that Alan reports to, the Department of Defense brass, they're the ones that know. The people in our lab, they get told to collect this or that specimen, to change settings on this or that equipment, to put these poor souls in this situation or that situation, to give them a dosage of certain drugs in their water or food. That's what our lab staff does, but no one from above tells them why or what any results mean. I was hoping maybe Alan was going to enlighten us, but then they took off as soon as they got here."

"So why do you work here – if they won't tell you what's going on?" Cassie pushed.

"Well, they're paying me a mountain of money to maintain everything, on top of renting my compound, so there's that. But after what you and I and Conner went through at Burning Man, I ... I just want to be where the action is, and figure at some point, answers have to start leaking out, don't you think? Don't we all want answers?" Bruce asked earnestly.

"So do you have any?" Cassie prodded.

Bruce replied playfully. "To seek the light of truth, while truth the while, doth falsely blind the eyesight of his look."

"Bruce!" Cassie admonished him, not indulgent of his Shakespeare.

"Alright," Bruce conceded, "It's just speculating, but let me share what I overheard just the day before you came when I was servicing the staff break trailer at lunch time. The two lab techs were trying to outdo each other with their guesses as to what the purpose of various tests was. They were carrying on in a joking manner, but I could tell they were just as much trial ballooning theories on each other, because really no theory can be that absurd when we're talking zombies for God's sake. I mean, who would have possibly imagined any of this before Burning Man?"

Cassie tried to get Bruce to circle back to the point. She asked slowly, raising her voice and gesturing with her hands, "So what were they saying?"

"Well," Bruce started, "not in these exact words, but after the obvious choices, like determining if they are dead or alive, what they will eat or drink, or if they dream when they're in a sleep-like state. The rest of their list included things like, could you turn them into suicide bombers; can you condition them to bite or not bite people when a signal is activated in their ankle band; do they have capacity to have sex with each other or with the uninfected; could they reproduce; could they be used to clear a minefield; what designer drugs can the pharma industry develop from them; will they respond to any schedule four drugs; can they be cloned so more could be produced without having to infect other people to do so; and most importantly, is there any way to potty-train them and is there any way to stifle their attraction to human waste?"

Cassie half-smiled and shook her head. "You know, it seems to me, Bruce, that after a month and a half of testing, maybe they've already got the answers – like if the infected should be classified alive or dead—but they're not going to tells us that until they've bought more time to run every little test they can possibly dare to think of, including tests that would not be allowed, if the infected were to officially classified as human. I just hope, if you do talk your lab into it, that we're not doing more harm than good by getting Tess out of here only by making her a lab rat."

Bruce's satellite phone rang. Cassie stared intently back into the Burning Man structure, standing tall in the center of the city, while Bruce's conversation with one of his center's lab techs commenced and devolved into an argument.

Cassie listened in on Bruce's half of the conversation.

"I'm telling you, we both saw it. Both of us..."

"No, it was not random motion. And it wasn't reaching out to grab at us. We were way too far away for that ..."

"Yes, I'm aware they have trouble with depth and spatial perception, but..."

"Listen to me. She waved left to right, not back and forth. Repeatedly, in a controlled movement. We both saw it..."

"What do I want? We're due to pick up new test subjects shortly. Let's make sure she is one of them..."

"Listen, it's simple. We'll accompany them. We can pick this one out. Your subject criteria today are broad enough that she'll qualify without your having to run this upstairs for approval..."

"We're sitting right here. They're en route. Just call them and let them know the change in plans. They can meet us here. We'll all fit up front..."

"There's not a real downside here..."

"Yes. I'll take full ownership of this if it goes bad..."

"Okay. Thanks. Thanks. You won't regret this..."

"Of course, we'll follow them afterwards on the back route. We won't be going near Gerlach..."

Bruce concluded the call. Cassie turned around, locking eyes with Bruce. She reached out, touching his right arm — not letting go of his arm or his eyes for a few moments. "Thank you, Bruce."

"Hey, this is the right thing to do. It's nothing to thank me for." Bruce raised his voice, competing with the acceleration of wind and dust all around them. "But let's not get ahead of ourselves. What we saw may or may not have been Tess. And regardless of who it is, there are no guarantees we'll find her again."

Cassie's face grew animated. "We'll find her. And it's Tess. I know it." She changed subjects, out of curiosity from what she overheard. "Why do they care about us going near Gerlach?"

They had driven through Gerlach, at Cassie's request, on the way to hitch a ride for the early morning watering run. She wanted a first-hand look after seeing so many video clips of Gerlach in news feeds during the past two months. She wasn't disappointed. Being that Black Rock City was off limits, Gerlach was the de-facto nexus of the media frenzy spawned by the Burning Man disaster. Every televised protest, press conference, and news report related to Gorman's disease had Gerlach as a backdrop.

Bruce groaned. "Yeah, I probably shouldn't have headed that way. We're supposed to keep a low profile. But it was early in the morning. You know the strings Alan pulled for you to be allowed on site at my place, and the releases you had to sign. There are people in Gerlach monitoring every car that heads up 34." Highway 34 had been closed to through-traffic immediately after the Burning Man incident. A checkpoint was set up outside Gerlach at the junction of highways 447 and 34.

Bruce started to elaborate, but the wind and dust kicked up. Instead, he yelled, "Let's get inside the truck." There they waited for the transport truck to arrive.

It took some time. Sulphur was almost thirty miles away, cutting straight across the playa.

Every five to seven days with intentional irregularity for security reasons, test subjects were rotated in and out of Bruce's research center. About one-fourth of the Black Rock City infecteds had been tagged to date, but discharged test subjects always were outfitted with GPS ankle bracelets if they hadn't been tagged already. Most were also equipped with other various wearable tech that would allow for continued measurements. Many were outfitted with helmet cams.

Even though analysts were tasked in Atlanta or other remote locations with monitoring each and every helmet cam feed to catalog the activity, Bruce, sometimes for amusement, wandered into the onsite lab trailer to scan their feed— of what they referred to as the z-channels. Occasionally, he and other staff would gather round, select an interesting zombie, then make wagers on what the z would do next or how long it might continue a behavior — like backing up and walking forward into a full length mirror repeatedly in the Loud Lingerie theme camp.

Also for intentional irregularity, sometimes the transport arrived full of infected test subjects to return, sometimes the transport arrived empty. Today brought the latter scenario – meaning there were ten infected subjects back at the center awaiting return to Black Rock City once the new crop of subjects was rotated in. The center was also inconsistent with how many test subjects were retained for each test cycle, depending on the nature of the test.

Bruce and Cassie stepped out of Bruce's pickup upon the transport's arrival. The two security staff who resided full time at the facility with Bruce emerged from the transport, both exchanging pleasantries with Cassie before paying any attention to Bruce. They had met Cassie, along with Conner and Alan, the night before.

Bruce and his two cohorts reviewed their revised game plan, while Cassie leaned against the pickup, her arms crossed. Eight new infected subjects had been requested, including the specific subject Bruce Kepner and his guest were going to attempt to spot. Everyone turned around as two National Guard jeeps pulled up to the gate alongside them, each equipped with sidearms, weighted nets, the required modified hazmat and protective gear, and the same specially constructed "zombie-collars" that Bruce's companions were also carrying. All eight of the Guard hopped out of the jeeps to join in on the discussion.

Several minutes later, Bruce and Cassie suited up along with everyone else before climbing inside the transport double cab, joining Bruce's two security staff. The transport and the two National Guard jeeps inched forward, while the Northeast Gates opened. The three vehicles sped up; clearing both sets of gates, then bore down on the Alamo.

The Desert Spy

Saturday, 8:10 a.m., October 30th

Quon Li arrived at his destination during the wee hours of Saturday morning, too late to see Alan Gorman and Conner Zimmerman's arrival and quick departure the previous might. Quon was therefore a little confused when he saw an obviously civilian lady leave the compound with Bruce in his pickup around five a.m.

Quon was settled in his camouflaged perch, chomping on his Nicorette gum, 1.3 kilometers from Bruce's compound, nestled in the Kamma foothills at forty-five hundred feet elevation. He had occupied this same nest behind a strategically shaped rock many times before. Quon had grown fond of the peacefulness of the Black Rock sunrises. He sensed a slight twinge of regret that this morning's had been his last.

Through his high-powered scope, Quon had reasonably determined the general routine, as well as the inconsistencies that occurred within the compound. During his first surveillance session, he slipped down as close to the compound as he dare go, under the cloak of moonless darkness, hiding several wireless long distance audio transmitters with directional antennas in strategic spots that relayed a signal to his present location. The sound quality wasn't ideal, but he was able to pick up the majority of conversations when desired.

Quon's inside men, Brady and Raymond, were familiar with Bruce and the two residential security staff. They conversed whenever Bruce and his companions were transporting Zs, retrieving supplies, or relaying instructions for monitoring of Zs inside the city. Brady and Raymond had never been granted access to the compound – there was not even official acknowledgement of its location. The two men had never met any of the center's other staff, having experienced just an occasional phone call from them with specific requests like "can you ask the next watering detail to reposition the center camp webcam three stand to fifteen feet south, without changing the lens angle?"

Quon had never seen guests inside the compound. He was most concerned about this wrinkle occurring on the morning of his mission. If it had been any other surveillance session, he could have texted via sat phone to Brady to confirm if Bruce and the new lady were at the Black Rock City gates and what they might be up to. But Quon was flying blind, because the two men requested the day off work per Quon's instructions and were lying in wait for the impending mission.

Quon considered for a moment whether to scrub the mission and reschedule due to this new variable. He quickly banished the thought. Brady had solid intel that the z transport would roll this morning, due to one of Bruce's co-workers letting that slip during the previous z exchange. Normally, the next transport dates weren't set in stone that many days in advance, but for some reason, this time the exchange needed to be scheduled for Saturday morning. Quon again let doubt flash through his mind. "What was the new variable involved to require the transport date to be set further in advance? Would there be added security? Was this mysterious lady with Bruce somehow the reason for the timing of the transport?"

Quon also had qualms about one of his inside men. Quon was fine with Brady, whom he initially recruited. Brady brought in Raymond, who struck Quon as a bit unstable. Quon had swept aside his concerns to this point, both due to a lack of other options as well as the knowledge that he just had to endure Raymond during the initial heist. He would be rid of Raymond after that. Still, Raymond gave Quon some pause at this moment.

Quon shook his head. He was not going to allow for such doubts to steal away the gift they had been given. He saw just one new vehicle in the compound, which he surmised belonged to the lady, and no supplemental personnel through his high-powered lens. He picked up no unusual chatter through his earpiece wired into the audio receiver. He would watch and wait, and stick to the plan.

Quon observed the small figures hauling a number of small crates from the supply shed to the lab trailer. He recognized the two onsite security staff by their height. He reflected on their fates in the hour ahead.

Quon never experienced remorse for the outcome of a mission, but he held a special sense of clarity of purpose for today's work to be done. The Americans were endangering the entire human race by not sharing information with China or the rest of the international community regarding Gorman's disease. What exactly was going on with this research during the past month? Were the American's developing a biological weapon from the disease?

Quon, of course, knew it was entirely possible his own country probably had designs beyond public health to green light an audacious kidnapping of American zombies. But he found no soul searching necessary in considering his nation's motives. If America was going to use these poor infected creatures for secret, nefarious purposes, China had no choice but to level the playing field.

Quon felt the Black Rock sun strike his face. He drank in the warm glow, after shivering through the previous hours despite his favorite jacket. Quon abandoned the lens, scanning out towards the playa beyond Jungo Road and the railroad tracks. He could see that the wind was whipping up the playa dust in the distance.

Shouting voices in his earpiece brought his attention back to his lens. Quon could see the two security staff hopping in the transport. Quon noted that no Zs were being loaded, just as Brady had been told days ago. Quon watched the transport clear the compound security gates while he reached for his sat phone. He spit out his now lifeless Nicorette gum, while he dialed Brady to inform him it was time.

Inside Black Rock City

Tess lived in the now. Her thoughts were jumbled and fragmented. She remembered bits and pieces from one day to the next. Her dreams were a different matter. She often rose from vivid episodes, featuring recurring characters and places in which she could speak, and everyone else spoke, just like the suited, masked men who arrived every day in their machines, filling the water troughs or shoveling out the piles of food on the ground.

Tess knew she was different from everyone else inside. She had no interest in the mounds of food the men in machines deposited daily. Everyone around her would grunt excitedly whenever the huge piles of food appeared. They would lurch forward as fast as their bodies would allow, pushing and shoving for position to kneel down to the mounds. They would repeatedly cup their hands into the mountains of goop, shove the drippy concoction into their mouths, while elbowing those next to them, jockeying for position.

Tess didn't possess the curiosity as to where these heaps of food came from or what was in it. She just knew it repulsed her. Tess instead foraged for her sustenance throughout the abandoned Burning Man camps. Being she was the sole scavenger, she found a seemingly endless supply of crackers, salamis, cereals, and other packaged goods to pilfer through from camp to camp. Unlike everyone around her, she was cold at night, as well as during some of the more recent days. She pilfered coats, socks and other clothing from the camps. She would discard an outfit whenever she found similar apparel that felt warmer or with colors that interested her more.

Tess did not realize her sense of smell had risen above the level of canine. She had no memory of her prior mundane, numb-nosed human-level nostril sensory prowess. Tess could sniff out packaged snacks from the most remote corners of any RV, tent, or monkey hut. The others in the city didn't have a strange odor to Tess. The men in machines did. Tess could sniff out their perspiration before they even came into view. Tess could catch the waft of exhaust from the National Guard jeeps, she could detect the god-awful gruel the machine men delivered in large mounds while it was still en route in the trucks. The one sensory odor that seemed to bring Tess pleasure – that would contort her face into a smile – was the scent of the Black Rock itself – just after sunrise, before it was corrupted by competing odors that the machine men interjected into the city.

Tess wandered endlessly each day, but always returned to the same structure at night. Tess had no recollection that the structure was called the Alamo or why it served as a nightly homing beacon to her. When darkness fell, she would sleep in the shelter of the partially collapsed downstairs room. After sunrise each day, she would hang out in the vicinity for a few hours, watching the others trudge along aimlessly, hoping to spot someone else like herself without success.

Tess noticed the ones who had been caught by the men in machines. The caught ones bore bands around their ankles and often strange helmets and other gear. Tess did her best to avoid them, and stayed away from the machine men whenever they exited their vehicles in strange outfits.

In her wanderings through the open playa inside the city, Tess was fascinated by the art structures. She didn't understand their purpose or their origins, but she enjoyed standing in front of each one, admiring how they shone in the sun, their detail and coloring.

The Temple was a favorite spot. Written words carried no meaning to Tess, so she didn't appreciate the irony of the many hundreds of notes written by Burning Man residents two months before, pinned to the Temple walls, lovingly or painfully penned to others no longer in this world. Tess would stroll through the globular Temple, intricately constructed from wooden hexagonal shapes, the massive structure towering above and surrounding her. She would run her fingers through the pinned, handwritten notes on the wall, taking pleasure from the texture of the paper.

Tess was fascinated with a theme camp full of Barbie dolls. She didn't understand what their purpose was, or remember the name "Barbie", but the dolls seemed oddly familiar. There were hundreds and hundreds of the dolls on display in strange costumes and markings. They seemed distressed. The camp contained an upright piano. Whenever Tess visited the Barbie camp, she would look around to make sure no men in machines were nearby, before touching the keys on the piano. She giggled the first time she heard the sound, before stopping, unsure why she had reacted in that way.

Tess avoided Center Camp after a couple of visits. She was initially drawn to the spot because the large, white, circus-size tent sporting giant rally flags could be spotted from a distance. Inside, the multi-colored sofas, rugs, counters and stage seemed appealing, but the place was mobbed with the others. Many were wearing ankle bands and helmets. Her first visit, she had a memory flash of being there long ago, when she could speak. The sofas had been filled with people sitting trance-like, much like they were now, but sipping from cups of hot liquid they ordered from persons behind the counters. On Tess's second visit, she spotted several odd little mounted machines, with round eye like lenses, mounted on tripods, whirring and following the motion of others as they trudged by. Tess didn't want to return after encountering the tripod machines.

Tess also avoided the dust storms. She recognized from the wind patterns when they were coming and learned to seek shelter. The others seemed oblivious to the walls of dust that would whip through the city. They would wander around aimlessly through the blinding dust the same as they would at any other time.

Tess didn't think about bathing – she didn't remember the concept of a shower or bathtub. However, she didn't like have the playa dust on her hands and arms, where she could see it, or her face, which she could feel. Whenever she passed a watering trough, after quenching her thirst, she would scrub her hands and face with the water. The others' palms and lower faces were relatively cleaner, from drinking from the troughs, but otherwise they were generally different colored than Tess – bearing heavy white-chalky layers of sediment on their skin and clothes – at least for those who were clothed.

Early on, Tess tried to use the porta-potties. She retained the memory of what they were used for. The problem was they were always crowded by the others who didn't know how to use them, but were strangely attracted to them. Soon, the men in machines arrived in large vehicles and began hauling them away.

Tess would sit on sofas during the middle of the day – many of the theme camps had old sofas situated under shade structures – while she would watch the others occasionally wander by, grunting, shuffling, and sniffing. Tess never seemed to draw their attention. She frequently came across mirrors in the camps. She would recognize herself – patting her short brunette hair with her hand – stroking her lush eyebrows above her blue eyes that seemed to speak to her, telling her to dig deeper and find questions that needed to be asked.

Tess held no specific memory of the night of the incident at Burning Man. After Conner, Bruce, Cassie, and Catwoman left her on the roof at the Alamo – bitten and seemingly comatose – she lay motionless for over a day. While infected like everyone else that had been bitten, she didn't expire and re-boot – unlike everyone else. Instead, she simply remained infected without progressing to stage II.

After more than a day, she regained consciousness, reviving little by little, but impaired from retaining most long-term memory or speech. The National Guard mop-up crew, making rounds after the security fences were installed, found her on the Alamo rooftop while they were collecting corpses under heavy guard. Seeing she was very much alive and assuming she was like all the others, they muzzled and restrained her, lowered her to the ground, released her and moved on.

This morning was exactly like every other morning for Tess, including watching the men in machines drive by on their way to a watering trough. She didn't fear them while they were moving in their vehicles; she just made herself scarce whenever they stopped.

Tess happened to notice the exquisite face of the lady driving by slowly this morning with the machine men. It was the face from her nightly dreams. She grew animated and began instinctively waving, not even sure why she was moving her arm back and forth. She continued waving long after the vehicle drove out of sight.

Retrieving Tess

After almost two months, Bruce and his two companions had z-catching down to a routine. The trick was to never take on a crowd.

When retrieving Zs from inside the compound, the special z-trailer door included an inner turnstile that would power on after the outer access door opened, then shut after one z exited. This way the traffic flow leaving the trailer was limited to a manageable single zombie at a time, to be collared.

When retrieving them from Black Rock City, the key was to pick off isolated Zs. Even though the lab staff requested test subjects from targeted areas, there was always enough leeway in the target radius to move around and snag the single Zs who hadn't been tagged already with an ankle band. Today would be trickier, because a specific z was being sought.

This had occurred weeks ago, in even a more complex setting. Back then, the lab requested an obese, easy-to-spot z, as no one near that body frame and size had been a test subject before. The supersized z, outfitted in some type of custom yellow and green striped "only-in Burning-Man" spandex, was viewed daily via the webcams planted in Center Camp, and was also caught on several z helmetcams. Unfortunately, Center Camp was a closed-in area typically crowded with zombies. The solution was to bring in two slow moving sound trucks nearby, to draw them out. Then each truck slowly led them onto a different part of the open playa like the Pied Piper. After that, it was a waiting game for them to disperse in different directions, until the extra-large yellow and green z fell into position.

Today's plan would require more improvisation. There was no fix on the target z, since she was spied some time before, at the Alamo. There was no certainty as to how friendly or unfriendly her current location would be. The lead Guard jeep could make the call to abort the targeted collar at any time, either for the day or just for the interim, in which case other Zs meeting today's criteria would be caught before returning for another attempt at their primary target.

The other wild card was a civilian was participating in the hunt. Bruce was considered a semi-civilian by the Guard, and his presence put them on edge whenever he joined his two security staff for a mission. Adding the lady into the mix, who somehow received impossible-to-get civilian access inside the city, sent the Guard's nervous-meter off the scale.

The center staff and any DHS subcontractor staff during such missions were always subordinate to their Guard escorts. The Guard only deferred to center staff regarding selection of a specific test subject, when choice was an option or during the actual collar of a test subject, once they gave the center staff the green light to do so.

The center transport vehicle was a modified Ford cargo truck with a double cab, and a cargo area containing ten small holding cells in a single row occupying two-thirds of the cargo space toward the passenger side. The remaining space was a driver side aisle, accessing all cells.

The lead jeep included the E-5 Sergeant who held overall authority over the mission. The tail jeep included an E-4 Specialist who was second in command. In their huddle with the transport crew outside the northeast gates, the sergeant, a stocky lifelong Reno resident in his late twenties with short brown hair and face full of stubble, dictated that under no circumstance was Cassie to exit the vehicle — she must assist as a spotter only from her window seat. Bruce also was relegated to remain inside to assist with securing Cassie, the onboard civilian, unless he was specially called outside by one of the Guard. The Guard's role was to protect the center staff while they captured each z, and to assist in a given collar if the staff began to lose control in any situation.

They arrived at the Alamo, circling it slowly three times. Tess was nowhere to be seen. Finally, the sergeant decreed they would apprehend isolated Zs in the general vicinity, to meet today's shopping list until they filled all seven other slots, then they would resume the hunt for their primary target—if they didn't bump into her along the way.

Curiously, the remainder of the shopping list was for women similar to Tess – between approximate ages of thirty to fifty with reasonably slender physiques. The specialist's jeep began joking that the lab nerds had sent them on a hunt for zombie cougar babes.

Slowly, the transport cells began filling up. Despite Cassie's repeated objections to the callousness of the ensuing conversation, Bruce's two companions, with both Guard jeeps egging them on, took the zombie cougar babe mission to heart, searching for the most shapely cougar-age test subjects they could find without ankle bands that happened to have wandered off by themselves.

Capturing each test subject had become a fairly standardized procedure. If the target was within a radius of one hundred meters or more that included at least five other Zs, they would pass on the target, at least for the time being.

If one to five other Zs were within one hundred meters of the target, the tailing jeep would toss its weighted throw net over the target. Then, the lead jeep would activate its sound system, crank up the techno-pop, and advance at a crawl, leading the other Zs away until it cleared the one hundred meter radius. After that, the security staff would hop out of the transport and initiate collaring the target zombie. If the zombie had no other Zs within the one hundred meter radius, the procedure was the same, except the lead jeep would stick around, minus the music.

Once the z was isolated under the throw net, the zombie would eventually manage to stand, albeit hunched, underneath the net. The throw nets included a fully weighted perimeter, plus twelve equidistant weighted balls attached around the perimeter. The z would slowly lurch forward underneath, dragging the throw net along.

When the z became upright, their antagonists would stand behind the z, lift the rear net perimeter and toss it over the zombie's head. Once the z was exposed, the two staff would advance with their z-collars – long rods with a lever-activated metal collar that would clasp around the zombie's neck. One would poke at the z, while the other attempted the collar. They would rotate if necessary, until the collar was made. Once successful, they could pull the z along forcefully with the rod, leading them up the cargo truck ramp.

When the collared z was brought to the selected open cell door, it would be pushed inside that cell to the far end. The other security staff would stand guard at the door, slamming it shut immediately after the collar was released and retracted. If somehow, the z escaped past the door, protocol was to bail from the cargo bay, while the jeep Guard joined in to assist starting over with the collar. So far, this day, that last step had not been necessary.

After one hour and forty minutes, seven zombie cougar babes sans ankle bands had been secured. The crew left the two cells toward the front cab unoccupied, filling the next seven, leaving the first cell upon entering the cargo bay open for their primary target. Tess hadn't been spotted while the other seven Zs were apprehended.

The search for Tess resumed.

After returning to the Alamo for another fruitless loop around the structure, the lead jeep slowed, signaling the transport to pull alongside and stop. The sergeant motioned for Bruce to roll down his rear window. "Hey," he called out to Bruce, "how important is it to your people that we find this one particular lady? There is plenty of fish in this this ocean of dust, you know."

Bruce lied. "They said not to come back without her. But I've got an idea."

"Good," the sergeant replied impatiently, "because we're searching for a frickin' needle in the dust, man." His jeep mates laughed at the remark, so he repeated it. "We are on a mission searching for one righteous needle in the dust."

"Seriously, I've got an idea, but you may not like it." Bruce hoped to intrigue the man in charge.

"Why is that?" the sergeant asked, smiling.

"This is why they want us to bring back this one special lady – she seemed to recognize Cassie here," Bruce nodded his head towards Cassie, "when we rolled through with the watering detail. They knew each other before, and she waved at us. I saw it, too."

"Okay, so?" the sergeant seemed unimpressed.

"So, I think she may be somewhere inside the Alamo structure, and we can't go in there. So I think she might recognize Cassie's voice and that would draw her out. You have that megaphone in your jeep, don't you?"

"Yeah, so?"

"So, I'd like for Cassie to stand outside our vehicle here, and yell out to her, and see if we draw her out."

There was a pause while the sergeant thought that through. "Why can't she just yell through the window?"

"Because I want her to see Cassie if she steps out here. That's what might draw her in."

Another pause. "I don't know. It's safer from your truck."

"Look, Cassie can get back inside if any of them step into your comfort zone."

The sergeant sighed. "Fine, but you step out with her, keep the door open, and she sprints back in and you follow right behind and slam the door whenever I say so," he decreed. "Her squawking over the megaphone is going to draw other Zs over here, so we won't have all day."

The sergeant turned around to his jeep, pulling the megaphone stashed beneath the front passenger seat. He motioned for Bruce to open the door. Bruce and Cassie hopped out. The sergeant looked her over longer long enough to make both Bruce and Cassie a little uncomfortable, then handed her the megaphone. He showed her how the detachable microphone worked, flipped the switch on, and headed back to his jeep, grinning to his men.

Cassie stood nervously next to the transport and Bruce, glancing back and forth between the Alamo and the megaphone.

"Well?" the sergeant called out to her. "Come on. The megaphone won't bite," he teased, "although your friend might." His jeep mates laughed, while Cassie continued to gather her nerve.

Finally, Cassie raised the unit up, held the microphone to her lips, pressed the button, calling out "Tess....Tess.....Tess....It's me, Cassie. Tess, it's Cassie. We've come to get you out of here, Tess." Cassie continued this for a good minute with no sign of Tess. The men in the sergeant's jeep spotted a number of Zs in the distance changing direction towards them.

"I think it's time to bail, ladies and gentlemen," the sergeant announced.

Cassie called out one more time.

"Come on, that's it," the sergeant commanded.

"I think she's inside the Alamo," Cassie insisted.

"Well, we're not going inside there, ma'am," the sergeant hollered back to her. "Now, let's go."

Cassie stared at her dust-covered shoes, feeling defeated.

"Look," Bruce shouted, pointing. There was Tess, rounding the corner of the Alamo, coming towards them at a pace slightly faster than the Guard were used to seeing inside the city. For a moment, no one did anything but gawk at Tess, dressed in a coat with several layers underneath and baggy pants. No one had seen anyone wearing garments to keep warm inside the city.

Cassie waved excitedly. Forgetting to use the megaphone, she called out to Tess again.

Tess waved back.

Jaws collectively dropped in both jeeps and in the transport cab.

"Well I'll be dipped," the sergeant exclaimed loudly. "Hey guys," he motioned over to the transport front cab, "let's get this party started." The sergeant turned around to his jeep mates. "Did you see that? Did you see her wave?"

Cassie jumped up and down with the excitement of a soccer mom watching her daughter score a goal. Bruce held on to her arm, worried she was going to sprint towards Tess.

Bruce's companions hopped out of the transport, gear in hand. They advanced towards Tess at a rapid pace. Tess eyed them, then turned around and retreated.

Jaws again collectively dropped. Bruce's two companions stopped in their tracks. No one had ever seen Zs inside the city run away from the uninfected. Quite the opposite had always been true.

"Well, I'll be dipped again," the sergeant said with more awe in his voice this time. One of his men called out that more Zs on the playa were closing in. The sergeant instructed the specialist's jeep to drive out with the music blaring and draw them away. He then called out to the security staff, who were frozen in their tracks. "This is going to be like catching a stray dog, I think. She's going to take some coaxing." He turned towards Cassie. "Okay, you win. Step a little towards her and keep calling out, and let's see if she comes back."

The strategy worked. Slowly, cautiously, Tess advanced. Cassie continued to venture towards her, a step at a time.

"That's close enough, ma'am," the sergeant barked more than once, but she continued. The sergeant was too mesmerized by what was unfolding to stop her.

Bruce began inching toward Cassie. His companions took his lead and started forward as well. Tess stopped in her tracks. Cassie turned, motioning with her left hand for Bruce's companions to stop. "Back up, some," she told them. She then turned to Bruce, motioning him forward with her index finger. Cassie turned back around, close enough to Tess as to not require the megaphone. "Tess, you remember Bruce. Bruce is with me. Remember Bruce?"

The Guard in the jeep, Bruce's co-workers, Cassie and Bruce could all see Tess clearly now. Unlike the other Zs, she wasn't snarling, grunting, or advancing menacingly with a crazed, vacant stare. She was as pale as the others, but didn't bear any open wounds or look as disheveled. Awestruck, no one tried to stop Cassie from continuing. Instead, they followed her lead. Cassie began walking backward while Tess advanced, matching Cassie's pace.

"Just give her room," Cassie called out to everyone, as she backed up. "Stay close enough to get me if something happens, but let me lead her in."

Tess was now dangerously close to all of them. She seemed to be smiling. Bruce's thoughts flashed back to when Tess planted a very long, wonderful kiss on him that night in the Alamo. Bruce had arrived at the Alamo after Conner, and managed to rescue the group out of a tight spot. But everyone was still trapped in the small upper rooms, and feeling fatalistic about their prospects. Tess proceeded to exclaim "I don't want to go down without saying I kissed, I mean *really kissed*, our hero, Bruce Kepner." Tess, still seated on the floor, uncrossed her legs, turned to Bruce, and placed a lip lock on him, stroking his goatee with her left hand, without any objections on his part.

"Tess," Bruce called out spontaneously, his voice wavering, as Tess advanced towards them.

Cassie's plan was to lead her right up the ramp. The sergeant surmised as much and deemed it way too risky. He hand signaled Bruce's co-workers to get into action. They sprang forward with the throw net. Cassie and Bruce caught Tess's seemingly hurt look, of one betrayed, as she disappeared underneath the net.

Minutes later, she was secured in the first cell.

Z-Crossed Lovers

The transport dropped Bruce and Cassie at his pickup, before quickly disappearing out on the playa, taking the direct route back to the compound. The BLM allowed the National Guard and DHS authorized vehicles to drive across the protected Black Rock lands with impunity.

Bruce and Cassie immediately disrobed their protective outer layer – the modified hazmat outfits. Bruce only wore them inside the city, because the Guard insisted on enforcing that requirement. Bruce never wore them around the compound – he explained to his co-workers that he survived a night up close and personal with a swarm of zombies without a hazmat suit – and the suits wouldn't protect you from a determined z wanting to tear and bite through the material, so he saw no need to start wearing one now. Soon the resident security staff, and then the rotating security guards and lab techs followed his lead at the compound.

The lead National Guard jeep pulled up, before Bruce and Cassie had a chance to get inside the pickup. Bruce fended off questions about Tess from the sergeant and his jeep mates — yes, Cassie and he had been with Tess that night at Burning Man; yes, she definitely had been bitten and fell into a coma; no, he had no idea why she seemed so different from the others; no, she hadn't been taken to the lab before; no, he had no idea what they were going to do with her at the lab; and come one guys, you know I'm not allowed to talk about the lab.

Bruce extricated them from the conversation as quickly as he could. He and Cassie hopped into the pickup, setting out on the same path the transport had taken minutes before. Cassie asked Bruce to again check his sat phone for any message from Conner. Despite promises to the contrary, they had not heard from Alan or Conner since waving goodbye as they boarded the chartered helicopter the night before. With no satellite phone of her own, she had been repeating her query to Bruce every half hour or so.

They cut across the playa. Bruce followed the transport's fresh tracks in the dust. The transport had to be over five minutes ahead. He didn't have a visual on them or even a dust trail. Cassie scanned the landscape – the Kamma Mountains in the distance, with the discoloration from the Hycroft gold mine at the far eastern side; the soft textures of the playa floor below. Time passed, and Tess dominated her thoughts.

Cassie's memories drifted to more than a year before, at Burning Man the first time the Alamo appeared. She and Tess stood on the second story of the structure in the middle of the day, with the bare-chested, six-pack-abs men they had met hours before, downing shots of Grey Goose that Tess's new companion brought with him. The sun began to beat down on them, and the men tried to beckon the ladies inside the upstairs rooms, with more on their minds than escaping the heat. Tess, not a veteran of hitting the bottle that early in the day, promptly leaned over the side of the Alamo, barfing up a tiny amount of the muffin she downed an hour before, and watching it land on her bicycle seat situated directly below.

Bruce cleaned his sunglasses on his tech shirt while driving with his left hand, before noticing Cassie was sobbing. He slowed to a crawl. "Cassie, what is it?"

Cassie looked at Bruce before fixing her gaze at her feet, her cries diminishing, but her breathing labored. Finally, she took some measured breaths, staring straight ahead into the playa out the window. "Sorry," she apologized in a weak voice. "I'm sorry for this."

The truck fell silent. Bruce really didn't know Cassie all that well. They were remote acquaintances growing up in Parker Creek, before she moved. They spent some intense hours in the Alamo, with Conner that night in Burning Man, as well as the next two days trying to sort things out from Bruce's compound. That had been it, until their get together started the day before. But the events of the day made Bruce feel strongly connected to her.

Finally, Bruce spoke, still driving under ten miles per hour. "Cassie, talk to me...."

Cassie shook her head, sniffling.

"Come on Cassie, you have to talk this out. What's going on?"

"I don't know... It's everything." Cassie was gasping, trying to regain composure.

"Everything? I know there's a lot of everything going on here, but help me out."

"Well, it's Tess." Cassie let out a long breath.

"Of course it's Tess. I barely knew her and I feel like crap." Bruce took his foot off the gas altogether. The truck inched along at idle speed.

"I let my best friend down. I failed her twice." Cassie resumed crying, but weakly.

"You did no such thing."

"I abandoned her that night. Now I've lured her into a trap to become a lab rat." Cassie worked herself back into a sob.

"Wait a minute," Bruce replied sharply. "I was there. Conner and I and the Catwoman lady, we were all pushing at you to leave her. You didn't want to, but we all had to. We had to, Cassie, before she turned."

"But she didn't turn," Cassie snapped. "You saw her. She didn't turn–"

Bruce interrupted. "Cassie, she's got the disease. You can see it. I know. I'm around it every day. I grant you, she's different than the others. Maybe she didn't progress as far as they did. But she has it. And you tell me how we were supposed to know she might end up differently after she was bit? You remember fighting off that never ending line of them coming up at us. Go through that as long as we did and see how you feel about waiting to see if someone bitten wakes up again human. And, Cassie, I remember you telling me later, what Conner said that got you to leave with us – that you had to think of your daughter and come back for her."

Cassie took measured breaths again, attempting to calm herself down. "It doesn't matter what we say now. It just matters that I didn't stay then and take care of her. She would have done that for me."

"Cassie, listen to me," Bruce argued. "Say best case, you stayed with her, she wakes up, doesn't bite you, and just acts like she did today. You and I both know no one would have ever let her leave that place. She has the disease. I just feel awful now, pulling strings for us to go inside this morning to see the Alamo and putting you through all this."

Cassie seemed calm, but tears still slowly rolled down her cheeks. "Let's not keep rehashing this. Just tell me, did we make a huge mistake having them bring her in to your lab? The only reason she's in the transport truck right now is we insisted on it."

"Honestly, Cassie, it's a roll of the dice. I think we did a good thing. If she really doesn't have the disease that bad, maybe there's something they can figure out to do for her. And that wasn't going to happen back inside the city."

"But they're probably going to just run experiments on her, day and night." Cassie's sobs started to return.

"We'll be there. We can speak up for her." Bruce paused, noticing Cassie's weeping was getting worse again. "Cassie, I have to think it's better for her to get this attention than to be left to her own devices out there, with winter around the corner."

Cassie's cries grew louder.

"Cassie, what is it? You said it was everything. What is it besides Tess?"

Cassie collected herself for a moment. "I think I have PTSD. Everyone's saying we all should have it after that night."

Bruce sighed and smiled. "Yeah, we might. Alan Gorman lectured me about that when he paid me a visit last time. But I'll tell you, I read up on it after that. And it seems to me, you crying and talking about this is a good thing, because what I read said the worst symptoms are when you're numb to it all."

"Like Conner?" Cassie whimpered.

"Conner? What do you mean?"

Cassie really started crying. Bruce finally put on the brakes and then shifted the pickup into park. "Is Conner the reason you're feeling like this?"

"I'm so scared, Bruce, and I keep everyday wanting to give Tess a call to talk to her about it, and then I remember she's not there. And I can't talk to my daughter about it. I can't freak her out. She's freaked out enough just seeing on the news what we went through. I have no one to talk to about this, and I fell so hard for Conner and then immediately this crap happens." Cassie stopped crying but her sniffling remained.

Bruce handed her a disposable diaper wipe from the canister he kept between the seats. He found them indispensable out on the playa. "So talk to me, Cassie."

Cassie shook her head.

"Come on, Cassie, no one knows more about what you've gone through out here, or with Conner, than me."

Cassie sighed. "I just don't know if we're ever going to get a chance. He's up here and I'm in San Diego, and he's always travelling now with Alan Gorman and all we do is Skype. But I feel like these damn zombies already took Tess away from me, and Burning Man away from me, and I'll be damned if I'm going to let them take whatever chance Conner and I had away from me as well."

Bruce smiled. "I think that says it all."

Cassie's face sank. Her hands and legs were trembling. "No it doesn't. He's just not the same. He's withdrawn. Real withdrawn. And then there's the whole thing with him staying off the bottle. It's...just...hard."

Cassie's left hand was shaking enough to cause Bruce to reach down with his right and hold it steady. "It's okay," he said, attempting to reassure her. Cassie sniffled again. Bruce turned, reached over and gave her a firm hug.

The next thing he felt was Cassie's lips on his neck, pecking several soft kisses.

Catching the Transport

The transport approached Jungo Road as they cut across the playa. Bruce's two co-workers spotted a lone figure staggering alone in the distance before them, near the junked autos. Many a hiker was found wandering these parts disoriented, but not so much at the end of October.

As they closed in, no doubt remained in either's mind. Almost simultaneously, they announced to each other, it must be a z. The transport driver eased to a stop, careful not to throw around their passengers caged in the cargo area.

He called Bruce on the sat phone, but went to voice mail. He uttered an expletive, and then redialed. This time, Bruce answered after the third ring. "Where are you, man? We got ourselves a stray z in the middle of the playa here."

"You what?" Bruce cleared his throat. "Are you sure? How close are you?" Bruce replied skeptically.

"'Hey, he's a hundred meters out or so. There's no doubt about this one, and he's stumbling away from us. Where the hell are you?"

Bruce cleared his throat again. The driver could hear Bruce's friend, Cassie, whispering to Bruce in the background. "We got delayed. We might be as much as ten minutes behind you. I have no visual on you."

"Well, hells bells, we should wait for you to be backup, but I don't want to fart around with this thing for ten minutes. Just floor it, get here faster, and we're going to collar this one now."

"Hey, sorry, man." Bruce apologized. "I'm gunning my truck now, so why don't you wait for us?"

"It's no big deal, but he's moving away towards the junked autos. We don't want to lose him. Just get here in case we need help mopping up." The driver hung up, then put the transport into drive, inching toward the rusty collection of abandoned old auto bodies near Sulphur.

"Damn, we should have kept up with them," Bruce lamented. Cassie was busy repositioning her shirt and bra while staring at the floorboard.

"Cassie, I'm sorry about this...what happened."

Cassie remained silent and staring. "Please God, do not let him quote Shakespeare right now," she whispered out loud.

"I guess the moment just got away from us. Both of us. So it was a good thing I'm sure that the phone rang when it did," Bruce continued, awkwardly. Noticing Cassie had tidied up, he gripped the steering wheel with just his left hand, while pulling his own shirt back down all the way with his right hand. He tried not to think about where his hands, and Cassie's hands, had been exploring just two minutes ago. He could hear Cassie start to softly cry again and drew in a deep breath.

"I thought it was Conner calling," Cassie blurted out after another half minute of silence, her voice trembling.

"Yeah," Bruce replied, not knowing what to say.

"I don't know what I would have said or done had that been Conner," Cassie announced, weakly. "And yet I'm so pissed off at him for not calling."

"We could call him. I've got this sat phone," Bruce offered.

"No, not right now."

Bruce heaved a sigh of relief, not wanting to deal with Conner yet after what had just happened. He squinted ahead through his sunglasses. The transport finally appeared as a distant speck near the sun's reflection off some of the metal parts strewn around the collection of junked auto bodies. Trailing Bruce was a stream of dust, as he pressed the pickup faster than he should, across the unreliable playa surface.

Bruce pushed his predicament with Cassie out of his mind and concentrated on driving. He had no choice but to slow down as the prehistoric lakebed gave way to a slight rise in elevation, bringing sagebrush, rabbit brush, rocks, boulders, a hardpan surface, and randomly strewn bottles, tires and garbage from many decades past.

The transport came into full view. Something was very wrong.

The Diversion

Quon Li positioned himself inside the rusted shell of a 1940 Packard 110 with the doors missing. Brady lay in wait, fifty meters to the northwest, concealed inside a sawed-off Chevy pickup bed, circa early 1950's. Raymond was done up in motion-picture-quality makeup and costume. He had observed enough zombies from outside the Black Rock City fences to have their gait and rhythms down.

Quon Li's plan was to hijack the transport before it reached the compound and then drive it to his own customized cargo truck stashed miles away. They would offload the zombies into his own vehicle, then he would either dispatch of or just bid farewell to Brady and Raymond, depending on the circumstances. Ditching the original transport would improve Quon's odds of eluding the ensuing search.

In planning the hijacking, Quon early on settled on the zombie diversion as the best scenario to get the transport to stop. Two weeks ago, during surveillance to confirm that the transport kept to the same return-route, he observed the vehicle pass up an overturned civilian jeep with obvious injuries on Jungo Road near the compound. Quon Li understood why the transport couldn't stop, given their secretive cargo. He determined that a stray zombie on the loose might be the only thing they would stop for.

After phoning Brady, Quon trekked to the prearranged rendezvous point, beyond the old Sulphur Landing Strip, where the playa met the Kamma Mountains. Brady and Raymond picked up Quon in the custom cargo truck, continued on the lonely dirt road, taking the turnoff to Rosebud Peak. They parked the vehicle after taking the first turn into a wide, dry creek bed that ran parallel to the road and gradually became hidden from view.

From there, they donned their daypacks and off-loaded three unregistered dirt bikes, which took them to their present location. The bikes were now hidden from view, within the maze of rusted out vehicles.

Quon Li's selection of the hijacking venue was relatively easy. He wanted the location to be near, but not on Jungo Road. Jungo itself had occasional traffic, which Quon didn't want to have to deal with. But he wanted something not far from the road so they could have ready access to return to his own stashed cargo truck to make the transfer. The small junkyard of abandoned auto bodies near the ghost town of Sulphur was perfect, as it met these criteria, plus provided ample cover when the hijacking went down.

Quon Li was veteran of enough years of missions to expect that not everything would go according to plan. Undoubtedly, a wild card would emerge. In this case, the wild card's name was Raymond.

Raymond was a native of the area, having worked at U.S. Gypsum in the company town of Empire, just below Gerlach. There, he helped turn gypsum into sheetrock, until the company ceased operations at the start of 2011 due to the collapse of the housing market. He suffered from bipolar disorder and took to self-medicating with different combinations of drugs and booze over the years. After the closure, he got by with odd jobs connected to Burning Man mutant vehicle and structure storage and maintenance. Although he had been involved in a number of shady deals, he managed to keep a clean record, allowing him to score a perimeter security detail job with a Homeland Security subcontractor shortly after the Burning Man incident. He switched to alcohol as soon as he heard of the possibility of the job. He managed to stay drug-free long enough to pass his employment drug screening.

Raymond was the same height as Quon – five foot seven, but looked shorter due to his slumping posture. He bore a crew cut, multi-colored tattoos of serpents on his right and left upper arms, was missing a right mandibular incisor, had an average build, and looked somewhat older than his age of thirty-six.

Raymond was often quiet and avoided eye contact; at other times he was overly chatty. This morning he was especially chatty, skittish, and fixated on Quon. Quon pulled Brady aside, asking what drugs Raymond had taken. Quon had specifically reminded both of them on several occasions to ensure they were sober the night before and day of the heist. Brady agreed with Quon that Raymond was definitely on something, but Raymond denied it when Brady confronted him shortly after they met up that morning.

Quon reprimanded Raymond several times as they set up for the ambush, ordering him to shut up. Raymond kept inquiring as to what the black market might bear for more zombies, beyond the ones they were hijacking for Quon's client.

Quon's plan was to hit the transport crew with fifty caliber ketamine darts, using his tranquilizer gun as soon as the crew engaged Raymond. Raymond's job was to remain evasive enough to avoid capture until the darts took effect, which could require several minutes. The hope was, in the heat of the moment, the crew wouldn't notice the dart impact. But if the crew did notice and chose to retreat towards the vehicle after being hit instead of engaging Raymond, Quon would be forced to take them out with his Glock 23, suppressed with a Silencerco Osprey 40 silencer.

After they were downed by darts or bullets, they would be loaded into the cargo bay and driven to the transfer point where they would remain in the abandoned transport. Quon was now considering adding Raymond to the back of that cargo bay once his zombie impersonation was over if his erratic behavior continued.

Quon preferred not to use the Glock. Discovery of dead bodies would escalate the level of response. Furthermore, if the crew awoke dazed and confused without much or any recollection of what had transpired, they would likely fall under initial suspicion, helping to throw the scent off Quon's trail for a while.

Brady hoped, even more than Quon, it wouldn't devolve into gunfire. He knew the transport crew – he didn't want to watch them die. Brady had never seen someone's life end and didn't want to start now. Like Raymond, he had to have a clean record to land his job with the DHS subcontractor. Like Raymond, his clean record was a result of not getting caught at minor offenses. Brady was in his mid-forties, standing a couple inches taller than Quon and Raymond. He sported short, light, tightly curled hair, a soul patch, an absence of tattoos, and a tone of skin and facial characteristics that bore out the mixture of races in his lineage – African American, Japanese, Hispanic, and Caucasian.

So Quon and Brady waited for almost an hour, in the high mountain desert, late October sun, weighing in at sixty-eight degrees Fahrenheit, while Raymond wandered around in circles – already playing the part, given it was uncertain when the transport would show.

Finally, the transport did come into view to the northwest, a trail of dust in its wake. Quon could hear Raymond singing lyrics to some stupid American rock song. "Quiet, now!" Quon snapped. "Zombies don't talk."

Quon and Brady waited silently, watching the distant dot become larger. Brady scratched his head repeatedly, out of nervousness. He didn't have to do anything until the crew was downed, unless things unraveled, in which case he was to follow whatever instructions Quon came up with. Quon had equipped Brady with a Glock, as a precaution. Quon had taken him target shooting once to ensure Brady was up to the task. Brady was not a gun enthusiast, but Quon was satisfied Brady could handle basic situations.

The silence was broken by Raymond's loud humming. Brady exhaled forcefully out of frustration. "Damn it, Raymond, shut up and get into character," he yelled to his partner. Raymond emitted a couple of loud grunts and moans, before turning around to shuffle ahead in the opposite direction.

"Get back this way, you stupid man," Quon shouted at Raymond. "You have to stay in range."

Raymond stood still for a moment, directing a stare at Quon. He then complied with Quon's directive.

Quon turned around, facing Brady. "You better hope, for your friend's sake, he gets it together now," Quon admonished.

"He's not my friend," Brady said softly enough for Quon not to hear.

The transport was now a hundred meters out, close enough to make out the details of the vehicle. It came to a stop.

"They're calling for backup. We're busted," Raymond yelled towards Quon and Brady.

"Shut up," Quon and Brady shouted back, almost in unison. "Just keep going. They'll come," Quon commanded. The transport remained still for almost two minutes, while Raymond paced around. He drifted away from Quon and Brady again.

"Come back within range. I'm not going to tell you again," Quon warned Raymond sternly.

Raymond stuck his tongue out at Quon, before complying. The transport started crawling forward at five miles per hour, aiming directly for Raymond. Quon and Brady kept low and out of sight.

"Let's see you get out here and do this, Mister Chinese man," Raymond whispered to himself, catching the approaching transport out of the corner of his eye. He slowed his staggering paces towards the auto bodies, so that he wouldn't get too close before the transport arrived.

Moments later, the transport stopped. The two crew hopped out, leaving the vehicle idling.

"What the hell are you doing out here all by yourself, little doggie?" The driver called out to Raymond in a sarcastic tone. Raymond turned to stagger forward towards the men, as any z would do. The driver held a throw net, his companion grasped a z collar and a prod-stick to keep a zombie at bay, if need be. The two closed in on Raymond.

Raymond tilted his head, grunting wildly, before stepping aside, giving Quon a clear shot at both. Raymond continued his grunting and advanced towards the men to keep them engaged. The driver was hit first, then his companion. Both noticed the dart's sting. The driver looked down at the dart stuck in his ribcage. Confused, he flicked it off. Like not recognizing someone familiar when encountering them somewhere out of context, the driver didn't piece together that they were under attack. His companion swatted at the stinging area without looking, brushing the dart off, thinking he had been bitten by some insect. They both closed into position to net the zombie.

The driver cast the net directly at Raymond, who stepped back to dodge the attempt that fell at his feet. "You ever see one duck like that before?" He called out to his companion. The driver took a step back, feeling dizzy. "Maybe it's just me. I'm feeling a little light headed."

His co-worker pushed the prod-stick at Raymond to back him up, before picking up the throw net. "Yeah, I'm feeling funny, too. Did you get bit by something just now like I did," he asked the driver, while keeping a wary eye on Raymond.

The driver stopped in his tracks. The realization set in. "Damn it, we've been drugged. I just pulled a dart out. Let's get back to the truck."

His companion dropped the throw net, reeling backwards several steps, into the driver. The z-collar and prod stick were also on the ground.

Raymond lurched forward, grabbed the throw net, and tossed it over both of them.

"What the hell?" the driver yelled, confused that a zombie could react and toss a net. He wasn't processing that Raymond was no zombie. Both men stood up inside the net, but their coordination was off, and they had difficulty trying to free themselves.

Quon was pleased that Raymond thought to use the net to keep the men from returning to the transport. Still, he kept his Glock trained on the Raymond and the two men under the net. He decided to stay out of view, hoping the darts would take effect before he had to emerge. Brady knew not to do anything until Quon advised otherwise.

Raymond continued grunting wildly, circling the net. He started pushing the two men down to the ground. The driver was becoming convinced that they encountered an intelligent zombie, who had entrapped them. Maybe the z was related to the special lady zombie they had just captured and he was trying to free her. The driver's companion kept reaching for the prod-stick in order to fight back, but couldn't hold onto it. Both men were becoming increasingly disoriented.

Two minutes later, still trapped under the net, the driver passed out. His partner lasted less than sixty seconds after that. Raymond kept grunting, while he picked up the prod stick and began beating both men with it. Quon emerged from the Packard, calling for Brady to join him. They trotted with their daypacks out to join the still grunting Raymond and then held him back from the two prone men who he'd continued to beat.

Brady noticed a new trail of dust in the distance. "Look," he called out, tapping on Quon's shoulder, "We've got company coming."

The Wild Cards

Quon's two wild cards were converging. Raymond was spinning out of control, and the pickup in the distance appeared to be the one Quon observed early the morning, with the man and civilian woman from the lab compound.

"Quick," Quon ordered Raymond, "Get those two up into the cargo bay now. Brady, grab the daypacks, then come with me up by the truck cab and get your pistol ready."

Brady grimaced. He didn't sign up to shoot people. Certainly not people he knew. They were supposed to knock out the transport crew, transfer the zombie cargo to Quon's truck, watch Quon use Venmo to send each of them their final payments with his phone, and say adios to Quon.

Quon signaled to Brady to climb up in the cab with him, tossing their daypacks inside. "We'll leave the front doors open. They will pull up around back when they don't think anyone's up here," Quon explained quickly.

"What happens to them?" Brady asked apprehensively.

"That depends on what they do," Quon answered calmly while peeking over the dashboard at the pickup's progress. "If it goes well, we take them to my truck, make them help with the transfers, then we throw them in my cargo bay with the zombies. They will have seen us, so we have to do something. That way we don't leave any bodies behind."

Quon and Brady could hear the cargo bay doors to the transport closing. "Damn him," Brady cursed, clenching his teeth, "what is he doing back there?"

True to Quon's surmise, Bruce slowed, crawled by the front cab, then continued and parked in back. "Stay inside," Bruce cautioned Cassie. Bruce hopped out, looking at the closed cargo bay. He rotated his view in every direction. It was quiet, other than for the whistling wind that had just worked up, and muffled zombie noises coming from inside the cargo bay.

Bruce called out his companion's names, while pacing between the back of the transport and his pickup. After several unanswered pleas, he pulled out his sat phone. "I don't like this. I don't like this at all," he called over to Cassie. "And where's this wandering zombie they phoned about?"

Bruce pulled up the number to dial, just as Cassie screamed his name. He turned around to find a Chinese man pointing a pistol at him, and Brady from the Black Rock City gate station standing next to him.

"Brady, get the lady out of the truck." Quon motioned with his head towards Bruce's pickup. Quon, still facing Bruce, yelled at Raymond inside the cargo bay. "Open the cargo door now, Raymond, and quit screwing around." Quon made his decision to throw Raymond into the back of his truck along with these two after they made the transfer.

Brady escorted Cassie next to Bruce. Cassie clutched her purse between her arms. Bruce turned to Brady with a puzzled expression. "What are you—"

"Shut up!" Quon interrupted, pressing his Glock against Bruce's left temple. "You don't get to talk. Either of you."

"What about his pickup?" Brady asked, tempted for a moment to jump inside and drive off in it, far away, never to return.

"Yeah," Quon replied, thinking out loud. "Let's...Let's have you get in, drive it in the middle of these wrecked cars."

Brady peeked in the Ford F-150. He saw the keys in the ignition, paused long enough to indulge one more time in the fantasy of escaping somewhere far away, before following Quon's instructions.

Bruce tried to catch Cassie's eye, hoping to provide any measure of comfort to her that he could. He now understood there had been no zombie on the loose and that his two co-workers must be inside the cargo bay with the Black Rock City zombies and Raymond. Bruce had talked much more with Brady than Raymond over the past six weeks. He had always

Black Rock Desert

thought Raymond was a bit shifty and odd. Now it appeared Raymond was in some kind of trouble with his co-conspirators.

A comment Alan Gorman made, during his and Conner's few hours at the compound the night before, resonated with Bruce at the moment. "You ought to insist on more security at your site here and during your transport runs," he told Bruce after getting a brief tour. "Feel free to use my name."

"Okay, I'm opening the cargo doors," Raymond shouted from inside the cargo bay.

Quon stepped over to Bruce, keeping his Glock trained on Bruce's head. "You and the lady are going in the back of the truck, here. Don't worry, we'll keep you separate from the infected for now. Come on, let's go." Quon took them right below the electronic cargo door that Raymond had clicked shut and now clicked back open from the inside.

The Clash's "Road to Nowhere" came to life from Bruce's pocket. Quon instinctively pressed the Glock firmly into Bruce's temple again. "What is that?" Quon demanded.

'That's my phone... my ringtone," Bruce explained nervously.

"Give me the phone," Quon demanded, with his back to the truck. Bruce reached in his pocket, the Clash still announcing a call, and handed Quon his satellite phone. Quon slid the still ringing phone in his back pocket.

Despite how anxious Cassie had been about Conner calling, Cassie was paying no attention to the phone, Quon, or Bruce. Her gaze was transfixed on the now open cargo bay door. Raymond had released one of the zombie cougar babes from its cargo cell. This one was probably in her early thirties, topless with reasonably large breasts, wearing shredded short shorts, sporting short strawberry blonde hair, and an ensemble of colored tattoos. Raymond had the zombie collar firmly clamped around her neck, while he stood several feet behind her, holding on like someone taking a walk with a dog they couldn't control with its leash.

The zombie bound right off the back of the truck, landing on Quon, causing Raymond to tumble out of the truck as well.

Quon's Nicorette gum flew out of his mouth, never to be chewed again. The impact knocked Quon's Glock out of his hand, but that was the least of his worries. The lady zombie began biting furiously into Quon's neck.

Bruce was also knocked to the ground. The lower half of his body was underneath Quon, who was underneath the zombie. While Quon screamed, Cassie stepped forward, dropping her purse and grabbing the rod attached to the zombie collar. The zombie didn't seem to notice, staying totally focused on Quon. Bruce worked his way free, grabbing onto the rod with Cassie. Together they struggled, but pulled the determined zombie off of Quon, dragging it a few feet away at a time.

"Whoa," Raymond exclaimed from behind the two of them, now clasping Quon's Glock in his left hand. "I was just going to take her for a little walk. Damn."

Quon began shouting at Raymond in Chinese. He paused twice during his Chinese rant to scream in pain. Quon started to rise, but stopped after he managed just part way, on all fours. His head was pounding and the pain was something he had never come close to experiencing.

Raymond pointed the Glock at Bruce and Cassie. "You two, just keep her right there." The topless zombie had risen to her feet again, ten feet away from Quon on the north side of the transport, her mouth, breasts and hands smeared with Quon's blood.

Brady sprinted over from the junked autos, where he had just parked Bruce's pickup. He headed straight to Quon, leaning over him to inspect his wounds. Raymond stepped right behind Brady, grabbing Brady's Glock from the sidearm holster that Quon had provided him. Brady was too preoccupied to notice until Raymond announced, "I'll just take this for safekeeping."

Brady turned around. "What have you done?" he demanded.

Raymond laughed for a moment, waving a Glock in each hand. "All I wanted to do was take one z for a walk. They've never let us handle these things, the whole time we've been working at the gate...."

"What?" Brady responded incredulously while Quon moaned beneath him.

"Look, I didn't mean for this to happen," Raymond responded, pointing the Glock in his right hand at Quon. Brady shook his head.

Quon rose to his feet, resuming a rant at Raymond in Chinese. He advanced toward Raymond, determined to take him down, not caring if he got shot in the process, given his current prognosis. Raymond took a couple steps back, pointing both guns at Quon.

"Stop there, Chinese man. I will shoot you," he warned.

Quon, bleeding profusely from the neck, collapsed to the ground.

Raymond began waving both guns wildly back and forth between Brady, Cassie, Bruce, and their zombie on a leash.

Brady stepped forward slowly before kneeling over Quon. Brady looked up disgustedly at Raymond. "I'm going to get a first aid kit out of our daypacks," he announced.

"Fine," Raymond replied. "You do that, Brady. You do that." Raymond continued pointing his gun from one target to the next, while Brady instinctively picked up Cassie's purse, taking it with him as he trotted back to the transport cab.

Raymond ordered Bruce and Cassie to reposition themselves with their collared, bloody, topless zombie, ten feet directly behind Quon. Bruce considered whispering to Cassie for both of them to let go of the zombie restraint and sprint for his pickup. He reconsidered, having no idea what Brady did with the keys, what Raymond might do with those two pistols, or if he or Cassie would really be willing to leave Tess alone with these people. It was clear to Bruce that Raymond was genuinely unstable and high on something to boot.

Quon resumed a much more subdued discourse in Chinese, directed at Raymond, while he lay face down on the ground. He again worked himself back up on all fours.

Brady returned, panting, with a daypack. He dropped it to the ground next to Quon, and then kneeled down to zip it open. Brady looked up at Raymond, again shaking his head.

"Damn it, Raymond. You have just shitted away all that money we were about to make. So now what are we going to do?"

Raymond laughed, keeping his pistols pointed at everyone. "What are we going to do?" He paused for effect then repeated sarcastically in a feminine voice, "Oh dear, what are we going to do?" Raymond went silent for a moment, studying everyone in front of him. His voice deepened. "I tell you what we're going to do. Raymond has an idea. Brady, we're still going to make a truckload of money." Raymond emitted a forced laugh.

Raymond, smiling at Brady, wiped some sweat from his brow with his left hand while still grasping the Glock. "I think we all have to say there's been quite a turn of events, here."

Nobody Loves Raymond

Quon scanned his surroundings while Brady cleaned up and bandaged his neck. He wasn't sure if he was hallucinating. Everything appeared in black and white, like the television he watched as a child. The scenery was slowly spinning, to boot.

Quon reached up to Brady with his right arm, grabbed Brady's tech shirt collar, and pulled him closer so Quon could speak quietly. "You can still finish my mission," he said.

"What?" Brady responded, hearing what Quon said, but not understanding how that was possible. "What do you mean?"

Quon glanced over at Raymond, hoping their conversation was private. Raymond had pulled the transport ramp down, while Bruce and Cassie hung on to their zombie. Raymond was now focused on them, as they pulled the snarling, bloody, topless z up the ramp, back towards her cell, per his orders.

"Get my phone." Quon gestured to his back pocket, while he rolled to his side. Brady pulled out Bruce's phone. "Not that one. Turn that one off, so they don't track it. Check my other pocket." Brady found it and handed Quon his odd looking sat phone. "Come back and get the phone from me in a minute. Make sure my truck gets to Oakland. You'll get a call tomorrow morning. They will give the green light, and you take the truck where they say in the Port of Oakland. I'm going to record a message right now. Keep jackass occupied. I'll leave word to pay you triple, okay? And they'll handle jackass. Just hand them the phone when you get there. That's your proof. Don't let jackass get this phone and get it back from me in a minute, without jackass seeing. Okay?"

Brady wasn't so sure about any aspect of the enterprise any more, but realized there was no harm in hedging his bets with Quon for now. "Okay," Brady reassured Quon, nodding his head. He finished taping the gauze around Quon's neck, then rose to approach Raymond, loud enough as to not surprise Raymond and his two pistols.

Raymond stood next to the ramp, his left side leaning against the foot of the cargo bay. His eyes were trained on the back of the zombie being led up the aisle toward her cell.

"Raymond," Brady announced loudly, hoping to drown out Quon's dictation in Chinese, "what's the plan, now?"

"The plan? The plan?" Raymond responded even louder than Brady. "Just hold on, Brady, and I'll tell you the plan." Raymond stayed focused on the activity inside the cargo bay. The zombies' grunting from every other cell had ratcheted up a notch. Cassie and Bruce were using the collar rod to push the zombie cougar babe back into her cell. Raymond gripped both Glocks even tighter in case Brady made a sudden move while his attention was divided.

Bruce instructed Cassie to let go of the rod and stand ready at the cell door. Bruce then pulled the release on the collar clamp, yanking the device back quickly while Cassie slammed the door shut.

"Alright, very nice Bruce, and what's your name again, miss?" Raymond asked with theatrical politeness.

"Cassie," she replied with contempt.

"Very nice, Cassie. Now Brady and I are going to go over our plan, so I want you get in the cell with Bruce's friends. We'll keep Bruce with us for now, because his work here is hardly over," Raymond instructed in the tone of an elementary schoolteacher in front of a class.

Cassie and Bruce looked at each other without budging. Bruce wasn't about to willingly watch Cassie enter a zombie cell without a fight.

"Cassie is it? Don't be frightened about your friends. They're not bitten – like this." Brady paused and bit into his left arm, then re-trained his left pistol on them while repositioning his right pistol towards Brady. "They're by themselves. They're just unconscious for now and all tied up. If you want to be frightened, and you should be, be frightened by the pistol being pointed at you by Raymond here. Now peek into the far cell, and you'll see what I'm talking about." Raymond paused to change his tone from schoolteacher to menacing, "and get your ass in their before I plug a bloody hole in one of you."

Raymond turned to Brady, emitting a short, troubling laugh. They watched Cassie disappear behind the cell door. Raymond shifted tones, as if he was addressing an old chum. "Bruce, get down here, man,"

Bruce stayed put for the moment.

Raymond gestured with the pistol in his right hand. "Bruce, get down here right now or Raymond's going to get grumpy."

Bruce slowly made his way out of the transport, down the ramp. Raymond gestured him to sit next to Quon.

"Thank you, Bruce. Now sit there and shut up." Raymond turned towards Brady." I never really liked Bruce, here. He was always a bit snooty, don't you think?" Raymond let out another disturbing laugh, and then pressed the external button to close the cargo bay doors, with Cassie, Bruce's co-workers, Tess and the zombies inside. "Now, where were we?" he asked Brady.

Brady lost his patience. "Jesus, Raymond," Brady exclaimed, "what happened to you? You're like, a strange dude sometimes, I'll give you that, but this isn't like you. What are you on?"

"What happened to me?" Raymond leaned forward, spitting as he responded to Brady. "Like you give a shit or have any idea? You don't like me. Nobody at that damn job likes me. You've known me like what, six weeks? We talk to each other for eight hours a day for six weeks and you think you God damn know me?" Tears started dripping down Raymond's cheeks.

Brady was ticked. He drew within a foot of Raymond, impervious to the two pistols being waved around. "Jesus, Ray. Eight hours, six days a week. That's longer than some people spend with their fathers their whole lives, man. Don't give me this bullshit. I do know you and this is messed up."

Raymond started bawling, but still pointed the Glocks toward Brady and Quon. "You think you know me, man? How come you don't know I got like, little bitty voices in my head?" Raymond stopped crying. His face turned red. He leaned forward, pressing the Glock into Brady's temple, just as Quon had done to Bruce not long before.

"You think you know me? You know I go home to my trailer and get high just so I can get through the next day at work with you?" Raymond started crying again. He stepped back, pulling the pistol away from Brady's skull.

"So I had to get a special high this morning, man, because we're gonna get seventy thousand dollars today, man. Or, for you, even more. Mister Chinese man over there, he gives us ten thousand dollars last month, man, and I'm in. I'm so frickin in. And I stayed away from meth, Brady. I always stay away from meth. My cousin Bobby, in Lovelock, man, I told you about him. It basically turned him into one of those Gorman disease dudes in the back of the truck, man. But, I had to smoke some to get through today, man. I just had Bobby hook me up once, man, just this once."

"Damn it, Ray, you're on meth?"

Raymond fell silent. The Glocks were still pointed – one at Brady, one towards Bruce and Quon. Quon had finished dictating and clutched his phone under his armpit to keep it out of view. He coughed and concentrated on remaining conscious. Bruce had a clear view of what Quon was doing. He chose to keep quiet about it.

Brady considered asking Raymond for the pistols, but then thought the better of it. "Damn it, Raymond, we can talk about all this shit later. We can't just sit out here any longer or we're all going to prison. Now what do you suggest we do, since you're the one with the guns in your hands?"

"Brady, that's the funny thing," Raymond chuckled briefly.

"What's that?"

"I have some clarity here," Raymond said, clearing his throat. "I actually have a plan, and you really have no choice but to go along."

"What?"

"See, I'd been fanaticizing this plan since after Quon told us the layout of the zombie lab. I kept thinking, there's only a few staff there. What if we knocked them off and grabbed some more zombies for ourselves?"

Brady shook his head. "What?" he repeated.

Raymond pointed both pistols at his own temples, then up to the sky. "See, seventy thousand bucks for me, maybe a hundred thousand for you...that was great when all we had to do was knock out those first two dudes, drive them to the Chinese truck, and we're home free with no one the wiser. But that snooty Bruce and his girlfriend show up, and we either have to kill them or they finger us. Either way, it's messed up. You know this means we can't stick around. No matter what happens now, our lives are done here, man. You and me both. We kill those two and stick around, somehow, some way, it will come back to us. It always does. Always, sooner or later."

Brady was listening. Raymond had a point. "And what?"

"And seventy or a hundred thousand isn't going to cut it if we have to disappear. Let alone, we ain't getting shit now that Mr. Chinese man here will soon be in zombie land. Look, I was just daydreaming before about knocking off their lab, but now we got nothing to lose. We need to make a bigger haul, and I know just how to do it."

"What are you talking about?" Brady asked skeptically, but also intrigued.

"Quon baby was getting paid some big bucks to get some zombies for his sick, rich member of the one percent. I say we can deliver the package and get his share of the money."

Brady cracked a smile. Raymond was going along unwittingly with Quon's request. "Okay..."

Raymond interrupted. "But that's not the half of it. I've been thinking, that's the tip of the iceberg. There must be countless one percenters willing to pay for one of these things, man. So we're going to go to this lab where Bruce lives, that Quon told us all about, and we're going to load up with the zombies they're holding there, and then we're going to sell them too. I know some people who have to know some people. We can make millions, Brady, you and me."

Brady gulped. He bought into some of Raymond's logic, but not the part about raiding Bruce's lab and selling zombies to the highest bidder.

Raymond detected the negativity freshly displayed in Brady's face. "Brady, it's not like you have a choice," Raymond reminded him, poking at him in the air with the Glock in his right hand.

Brady shook his head. He glanced back at Quon, who had collapsed from all fours and now lay with his stomach planted on the ground, on top of his phone. He seemed to be snoring.

Brady shook his head. "Ray, how the hell do you expect to waltz in and grab the other infecteds, load them up, get them back to Quon's truck, sneak out of here, offload them at Quon's destination, all while finding buyers for the other zombies and then handling each of those deals?" Brady stepped back towards Quon, after finishing his question, hoping to sneak Quon's phone out from under him while Raymond finished his rant.

Raymond beat the top of the right side of his skull with the side of the Glock. "I told you, Brady, I've been daydreaming this plan for days. I'll spill. So pay attention and then we should get going."

The Invasion of Sulphur

Bruce was driving the transport. He slowed as they approached the gate to his compound, situated on a private drive off Jungo Road, near the ghost town of Sulphur. There was two additional security staff that rotated each shift, along with the two lab techs on duty. One would be at the gate, the other would be stationed at the zombie trailer.

Brady was hiding in the rear cab. Raymond was seated next to Bruce, pressing one of his pistols into Bruce's side. Raymond ducked his head below the dashboard as they came into view of the gate.

Bruce clenched his jaw, holding his breath, hoping the guard for once would follow protocol and not open the gate without first checking in. Instead, the guard pressed the button to open the gates as the transport pulled up. He waved them through without looking up to notice Bruce was driving. Bruce exhaled his disappointment.

Raymond poked his head up. From the size of the trailers, it was clear to him which one housed the zombies. "Pull up there," he instructed, pointing towards the z-trailer with a Glock.

Bruce's hopes went up. There was the guard stationed at the trailer, who would be concerned that the transport didn't head directly to the holding area, bordering the fencing by the softball field. Bruce made a split decision that he and Cassie were toast anyway, and it was more important that these zombies and Tess not make it back outside the compound. He pulled alongside the trailer, his window already down.

The guard was already apprehensive, noticing Bruce was driving and not following protocol. "Where's..." the guard started to ask, reaching for his sidearm.

"CODE RED," Bruce hollered before reaching down slightly to open his door, hoping to bail out.

The guard pulled his gun from the holster. Raymond shoved past Bruce to the open window, firing a clean shot with his right hand into the guard's eye. The guard collapsed in a heap on the wooden plank sidewalk in front of the trailer. Even with the silencer, the shot taken next to Bruce's head disoriented him momentarily.

Raymond pushed Bruce down on the cab seat, shoving the Glock held in his left hand into Bruce's cheekbone. "You're lucky I still need you, man. Now get out."

Bruce stalled. He remained prone on his back on the cab seat, his head against the door, his ears still ringing from the shot.

Raymond again thrust a pistol into Bruce's face. "Damn it, move, or I swear I will execute your girlfriend the moment I get the cargo door open."

Bruce clenched his jaw again, pulled himself up, opened the driver door and jumped to the ground. He looked straightaway to the lab trailer, hoping the techs had locked themselves inside and were calling for help.

Instead, Bruce again had to exhale his displeasure. The two techs were trotting towards the transport, gawking at the fallen guard. Bruce turned to check out the gate. It had already closed. The guard was most likely back in his enclosed station, oblivious to what was going down.

Raymond jumped out of the transport and positioned himself in between the two lab techs and Bruce. He pointed his left Glock at Bruce, his right Glock at the techs, shouting at the two of them to stand next to Bruce.

Bruce thought of running. There was no way Raymond could shoot him and the lab techs at the same time. As long as the lab techs ran in different directions, somebody would make it to safety and get a distress call out. The problem was, Bruce knew these techs weren't going to do anything bold. Within moments, the point was moot; they were alongside him.

Brady watched the scene unfold from the back of the cab. Like Bruce, he considered making a run for it. Not to make a distress call but just to get away from Raymond. The problem was the dead guard added another dimension. Brady had trouble seeing how he could escape prosecution unscathed when they all got caught — as they certainly would, with Raymond in charge.

Brady pulled Quon's phone from his back pocket and rubbed the rim of it with his right thumb. Brady settled on his ground rules for the next twenty-four hours or more: (1) He wasn't going to bail out unless the situation deteriorated further; (2) He wasn't going to shoot anybody unless his life depended on it; (3) He was going to bide his time with Raymond, figuring sooner or later, he could gain the upper hand; and (4) He was sure that gathering all the extra zombies in an attempt to sell them to other interested parties was a fool's errand. He would tolerate Raymond's quest as much as he had to, until they connected with Quon's buyer, and then the cord would be cut once and for all with Raymond.

Brady noticed the sidearm on the fallen guard in front of the lab. He decided to disembark from the cab to see if an opportunity might present itself to score the weapon. He pushed Quon's phone back into his rear right pocket, next to Bruce's phone. He wondered for a moment if Quon had been devoured, locked in the first cell of the cargo bay with one of the Zs from the city. Brady smiled, recalling how much Bruce objected to having Quon placed with that particular zombie, for no apparent reason.

"About time you joined the party, Brady," Raymond quipped after Brady jumped out of the cab. "I need you to move this vehicle just a little to position it so the ramp can lead directly from this trailer door to the truck."

Brady rubbed his chin, debating how much direction he was going to take from Raymond. He decided that anything that got them out of this compound faster was a good thing. He would move the truck and then see if he could obtain the dead guard's gun.

Raymond turned his attention back to the two lab techs. "Okay, gentleman, you saw what I did to your guard here. Don't think I won't hesitate to drop both of you, here and now.

You're going to tell me what I need to know about letting your zombie friends out of this trailer and into the truck, here."

"Don't do it," Bruce warned. "He's going to kill us all no matter what we do, so don't you let these infected things out of here to start an outbreak. Don't—"

Raymond interrupted. "Never mind your buddy here, gentlemen. I'm going to let him live because I need him. I'm not going to shoot you either. I swear to God, I will only shoot you if you don't tell me about how we let them out." Raymond paused between each word, raising his voice each time.

"You won't shoot if we do this?" the lab tech closest to Bruce asked nervously.

"Don't do it!" Bruce shouted. Raymond stepped over and pistol-whipped Bruce a couple of strokes.

The lab techs both joined in a rapid explanation of the procedure involved in releasing the ten zombies inside the trailer, while Raymond kept his left Glock pressed into Bruce's shoulder.

"There." Raymond rubbed the tops of each of their heads with his right Glock. "That wasn't so bad was it?" Raymond turned around to see that Brady had finished re-positioning the truck and setting up the ramp. "All right then, Brady, would you be so kind as to get us those zombie collars and nets we took up to the cab, in case we need them, and open the cargo door? While you're at it, peek around the corner of this trailer and see what's going on with the guard at the gate."

While Brady trotted off, Raymond commanded the lab tech furthest from Bruce to start dragging the dead guard up the ramp. He then pushed his right Glock into the temple of the other lab tech and ordered him to open the z-trailer access doors, but keep the zombie turnstile shut until he gave word.

"I'm begging you," Bruce started in on the lab tech, "think about what—" Bruce didn't get to finish, as Raymond delivered another brief pistol whipping. Bruce rose back up, noticing the sidearm on the dead guard. He couldn't believe the tech dragging the body didn't spot the gun; perhaps he was just too scared to go for it.

Brady returned, eyeballing the sidearm as well. "Here we go," he dropped the z-collars and nets in front of him. "The guard out there doesn't seem to be doing much of anything."

"Okay then," Raymond started, half-singing the words. "It's party-time. Now, Brady, I have one more request. I've seen you chugging water now and then this morning, and I'm pretty sure you haven't had time to piss."

Brady looked at Bruce, exchanging a knowing glance that Raymond was off his rocker. "Yeah?"

"Well, I'd like you to piss all the way up the ramp and into the back of the truck," Raymond requested, matter-of-factly.

"What?" Brady wrinkled his face.

"Hey, Bruce here is the one who first told us about how the Zs like piss. Remember, weeks ago, he told us about it back at the gate? Then you and I walked over and peed through the fence where some were close enough and they went nuts."

"Yeah, so?"

"So, you're Hansel, your prick there is Gretel, and now go leave us a trail of bread crumbs all the way into the truck so these zombies can find their way home."

Brady shook his head, but then, eyeing the lab tech halfway up the ramp with the dead guard, eagerly went at it. Brady walked quickly up the ramp, pointing his pee away from his own feet as he took each stride. He apologized to the lab tech as he peed right past him and all the way to the back of the cargo area. The zombies in the cells began grunting wildly. Brady surmised they must be able to smell the urine. Brady heard Cassie beating on the last cell door, calling out for Bruce.

Brady zipped up before trotting to the other end of the cargo area. He kneeled down to help the lab tech lift the dead guard over the hump where the ramp met the left end of the truck. He stealthily slipped the guard's sidearm out of the holster, and pushed it into the back of his own pants, above his butt crack, concealed by his untucked tech shirt. Brady then rose, trotting down the ramp while the lab tech continued slowly dragging the corpse to the other end of the cargo space.

Raymond turned to other tech — now inside the z trailer and out of view of the truck. That tech was stationed at the control panel, next to the now-open outer access doors, overriding the turnstile to keep it shut. "Okay, your friend is clear," Raymond lied. "Now override that turnstile to remain open, and run around this corner to join us, if you want to live."

Raymond asked Brady to grab the z-collars and nets as a precaution. He yanked on Bruce, and told Brady to join them around the corner, out of view from the trailer doors. Moments later, the lab tech from the z-trailer sprinted around the corner to join them, yelling something unintelligible.

Seconds passed by, then the sounds of grunting and shuffling could be heard, as the ten zombies from inside the trailer began to exit, making a beeline up the ramp that was situated just beyond the outer doors.

"Hey," the sound of the other lab tech screaming could be heard from inside the cargo bay, "I'm still in here, God damn it!" It didn't take long for all ten zombies to rush up the ramp, while the screaming continued.

The lab tech next to Bruce, still panting from his sprint out of the trailer, stared open mouthed at Raymond. "You lied. You lied and you've killed him."

Raymond leaned forward, pushing his right Glock into the lab tech's chest. "Hey chump – I never lied. Don't you tell me I lied. He asked me to promise I wouldn't shoot him, and you know what? I kept my promise, thank you very much. You didn't think I was just going to trust Brady's trail of piss did you? We needed a bigger carrot at the end of their stick. Now come on, we need to get out of here, because we still have a lot of work to do."

A thought occurred to Bruce, giving him hope. He whispered to the lab tech, "Had you placed the ankle bands on the subjects yet?" It was standard protocol to band them just before they were to be sent back to Black Rock City. The lab tech shook his head, causing Bruce to curse under his breath.

Raymond kept them all together while they snuck up to the side of the truck to push the button to close the cargo bay. The door began to shut with the Zs seemingly content to chomp away on the two bodies provided for them inside.

The group continued together to the cab on the driver's side. The lab tech and Bruce climbed in the back. As Brady prepared to hop up, a voice rang out behind them.

"Stop right there!" the remaining security guard commanded from behind Raymond, pointing a pistol at Raymond's back.

Raymond didn't even turn around. He jumped up into the cab. A bullet whizzed by the open truck door. A second bullet pierced the door with a distinct sound. Raymond could hear the guard shouting. Through the side mirror, he could see the guard sprint toward the truck.

Raymond cranked the keys left in the ignition, put the automatic transmission into reverse, gluing his eyes to the side mirror. Raymond had driven trucks this size before on occasion at U.S. Gypsum. As he accelerated, he felt confident with his task.

Raymond could see that he was almost on the guard. Assuming the guard would bail left from the truck's onslaught, Raymond cut in that direction. He guessed correctly. He could hear the impact via his open window, although he didn't sense it all that much through the truck itself.

"Boom!" Raymond yelled excitedly. He slowed almost to a halt while shifting his angle of direction with the steering wheel. He then continued backward, until he could see the guard crumpled to the ground in front of him, to the right.

Raymond couldn't tell if the guard was alive. He stopped, put the transport in drive, and then inched forward as he studied the guard. "We're gonna make sure this dude won't be giving us any trouble, just in case," Raymond announced as he ran over the guard's legs.

"Okay, gentleman, now we have to clean up our mess," Raymond announced. "We're going to have to place this fella somewhere in the cab, because we'll need him as zombie bait when we make the transfer. So chop chop – let's all hop out and I'll help myself to his gun and check him for keys or anything else, thank you."

The Transfer

After they pulled over at the guard station to open the gate, which required over a minute of guessing and button pressing, Raymond ordered Bruce back behind the wheel. Raymond sat in the middle of the front cab, with Brady at his right side. Raymond's right leg was shaking, so he started kicking at Cassie's purse, which Brady had tossed on the floorboard. Raymond turned around every few moments, eyeing the lab tech and the dying security guard in the back.

Bruce was now as committed as Brady to stay where the action was, because Cassie and Tess were trapped back in their respective cargo bay cells, Cassie in a cell with Bruce's co-workers who were bound and still tranquilized, and Tess in a cell with Quon Li. Bruce also felt he could be the best chance at keeping the truckload of zombies in the other cells from making their way into the outside world.

Bruce considered wrecking the transport on purpose to prevent the truck from reaching its destination, as well as hopefully injure Raymond in the process. He tossed the idea aside – there wasn't much of anything to wreck the truck into, he might kill Cassie or expose her to the Zs, and there was a good chance Tess and the zombies could emerge from the wreck to scatter into the desert. Bruce decided to bide his time.

They turned off Jungo Road, drove past the dirt Sulphur landing strip, and then reached the slight rise in elevation where the playa lakebed gave way to rockier terrain. Minutes later, they entered the foothills. Within a few minutes, they entered the fold in the mountain housing the turnoff to Rosebud Peak and the dry creek bed hiding Quon's specially outfitted cargo truck.

Raymond had Bruce turn around, backing up so that the two truck's cargo bays faced each other. Raymond ordered everyone out of the cab, having the lab tech carry out the mangled, dying security guard who had been the tech's rear seatmate during the drive.

Quon Li previously showed Brady and Raymond where the hide-a-key for his truck was placed. Raymond actually asked – not ordered – Brady to grab the key and prep Quon's truck. They had verbally rehearsed the transfer procedure with Quon more than once.

Quon's cargo bay was also subdivided into enclosed cells, but with a different configuration providing just four holding areas, resulting in much more room per cell. The four cells opened off a clustered pod at the end of a narrow aisle in the middle of the bay. The interior walls were heavily padded in the hopes of preventing crippling injuries to the cargo during the upcoming drive. Brady opened the cargo door but didn't deploy the ramp.

Brady tugged on the lab tech's arm, informing him they would be loading the dying guard in the larger of the two back cells. The tech refused, saying he saw what happened to his partner when performing the same duty and that he'd rather just be shot here and now.

Brady motioned Raymond over, which meant Raymond had to bring Bruce along, to keep him close. Raymond reminded the tech that he kept his promise and didn't shoot his partner. Raymond offered a promise that he wouldn't do anything to harm them, let the zombies harm them, or prevent them from exiting the cell after they deposited the dying guard there. Besides, Raymond assured him, Brady was his partner and Brady was going to accompany him the entire way. "Or, you can sit here, not go in, and I'll shoot you here and now."

The lab tech still held out, until Raymond elaborated that he would shoot him in the thigh, and then leave him as the bait in the transfer truck when they opened the cargo bay or he could take his chances and do what was asked of him. The lab tech complied, staring at the ground.

So, the dying security guard was dragged by Brady and the lab tech into the back bay. Raymond kept his word – the tech and Brady both emerged from the transfer truck unscathed after Brady convinced the lab tech to pee around the cell area. Brady hopped into Quon's truck with the cargo bay open, then backed it into the transport until their back ends docked. As intended, their two rear bays matched up in height.

Raymond escorted Bruce and the lab tech over to the transport's control panel. He pressed the button to open the transport cargo bay door. The ten Zs from Bruce's compound that had been crammed into the transport cargo bay aisle lurched forward out of the transport, leaving the grizzled, picked over carcasses they had made quick work of during the drive. They had caught wind of the urine and dying guard. They rushed to check it out in Quon's truck. Raymond next stepped over to the outside control panel of Quon's truck and shut the door to the back cell. The zombies, too full from gorging on their meal minutes before took to just biting and gouging the dying guard.

Bruce decided this was the window to work on Raymond regarding Tess. He had been reluctant to call attention to her, but now felt time was running out and his options were limited. "Raymond, you know I'm usually not involved with these transport runs. This one was different. One of the Zs left in the transport cells is quite special."

"Oh, now you want to talk to me? Now you think Raymond is worth your precious time to talk to?'"

"Look, Raymond, I don't pretend to know anything about you, man. I just know that one of the Zs we picked up this morning from Black Rock City might even be the answer to curing this zombie outbreak. If you're peddling these things because they're carrying Gorman's disease, she's of no value to you because she's not exhibiting the final stage – she's not weaponized. But she could help research to find a cure to this thing. That's got to be worth something, Raymond. So I'm just asking you to carve out one spot, man. Leave her separate from whatever deal you've made and let us use her to maybe save like – everybody."

Raymond was quiet for a moment. "Shut up Bruce," was all he finally came up with.

Brady, standing next to them, chimed in. "Hey, if one of these things might be high value then we need to keep it separate so we can access it. It will keep our options open, maybe like a bargaining chip if we need one. Even if it doesn't pan out, we need options."

"Shut up, Brady," Raymond responded, waving his pistols. Brady and Bruce again exchanged glances. Raymond was looking even more unhinged. Raymond pushed his right Glock into the lab tech's chest. "We're on the clock here. We got to unload these other zombies one at a time, and we've got Bruce's girlfriend and the transport drivers to deal with, and they'll probably be waking up soon. Brady, you need to separate the two trucks again."

Brady tried to convey contempt in his silent stare at Raymond. He overcame the temptation to access the pistol nestled in his rear pants, which were tight enough to hold the gun in place. Brady followed Raymond's instructions.

Raymond stood between Bruce and the lab tech. He cracked a smile, held up his right Glock, and began rapidly alternating pointing the pistol at each of them. "What am I to do with the two of you? Eenie, meenie, miney, moe..." Raymond continued this for a minute.

"Raymond!" Brady appeared behind them, the trucks now separated. He brought the z-collars and the nets with him, dropping them at his feet. "Come on, let's get this done. These two can work the collars, and we can use the nets if we need to."

"Hold your horse, Brady boy. I'm deciding some things here." Raymond resumed pointing his right Glock at Bruce and the lab tech, silently this time.

Brady had run out of patience. "Raymond, we've got to move it here. They're going to be putting choppers in the sky looking for us anytime now."

Raymond nodded his head. "Okay," he responded, before pointing his right Glock at the lab tech's upper leg and firing a round. The tech screamed as he crumpled to the ground. Bruce and Brady exchanged a startled glance.

"Raymond!" Brady admonished him.

"Hey, I have one too many people to keep track of, and now I don't need to worry about this guy doing anything that upsets me." The tech took to cursing while he clutched his leg.

"So here's the deal," Raymond began speaking excitedly. "We need a few more infected if we're going to maximize our score, here. We're putting Mister-one-good-leg-left in the next cell with the two tied-up drivers and we'll add one of the smaller lady zombies to the mix. They should be able to manage to avoid getting totally devoured by just one smaller z, but they'll get bitten I'm sure. Then we put all but one of the other Zs in the third cell, along with Quon, if he hasn't turned or been eaten already. And last of all, Bruce baby, we'll put you and your girlfriend in a cell by yourselves with your special zombie, who is sharing a cell with Quon right now. If you're wrong, you'll be more livestock for Brady and me to sell. I guess if we find Quon all munched on, we'll know you're in for a tough time. If you're right, and she doesn't infect you both, we'll see that we have something of value."

The lab tech wasn't paying attention to Raymond's final solution. He had removed his shirt, using it to apply pressure to the wound and reduce the bleeding. Brady and Bruce again looked at each other.

"So Bruce, you're going to help us do all that, and quickly now, and then you get your girlfriend and favorite zombie all to yourself. And if that doesn't motivate you, then I can always take out one of your legs too, my friend." Raymond turned to Brady. "And Brady, don't you worry about those choppers. No one knows these back roads like Raymond. I'll get us out of here without getting spotted."

Thirteen minutes later, Brady and Raymond were rolling down the road – Bruce, Cassie and Tess being thrown back and forth between their padded walls as Raymond rounded each turn.

II.
Pacific Duchess

Pacific Duchess

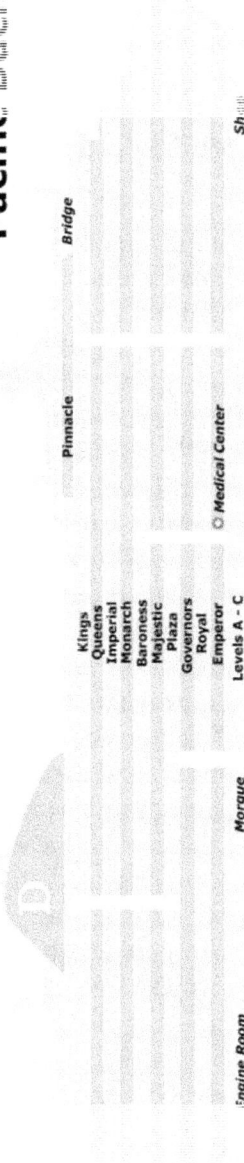

Bridge

Pinnacle

Kings
Queens
Imperial
Monarch
Baroness
Majestic
Plaza
Governors
Royal
Emperor

Levels A - C

○ Medical Center

Shop

Morgue

Engine Room

The Morgue

The *Pacific Duchess* had a guest capacity of twenty-five hundred, serviced by 1,060 crew. The ship was 950 feet long, two hundred feet high with seventeen decks, and had a tonnage of 108,000. The ship contained fourteen lifeboats, six tenders, and two rescue boats.

It featured four pools, nine whirlpool spas, six showrooms and lounges, three main dining rooms, eight specialty restaurants and grills, an atrium, a spa and fitness center, children's and teen's centers, a sports deck, wedding chapel, casino, library, internet café, art gallery, and several boutiques.

The ship also had a morgue. While all major cruise lines contain a morgue within the bowels of the ship, there is no uniform standard for their size, layout, or capacity. The *Pacific Duchess* morgue, down in Level A, was not a room – rather it consisted of a sliding stainless steel door that opened to three individually refrigerated body-size vaults. The brown horizontal vault doors, stacked on top of each other, were situated three feet deep inside the morgue area. When not in use, the morgue served as a storage area for janitorial supplies.

Both fish bite victims, Rodrigo, the Duchess crewmember that filled in as a deckhand on the Fishtoria charter, and the bitten excursion passenger, had just been pronounced dead. A medical center nurse, designated as the morgue attendant, immediately made a call down to Level A, requesting the 3rd engineer to have someone activate refrigeration to two of the vaults and to clear out the stored supplies in the morgue.

The medical center protocol was to transfer the deceased to the morgue as rapidly as possible to avoid encounters with other ship passengers visiting the medical center. The staff placed Rodrigo in a black body bag and positioned him on a gurney in a separate bay. None of the medical center staff had ever met or seen Rodrigo before, but the death of a fellow crew member struck a personal chord with each of them. They waited for the confused and distraught wife of the deceased fishing passenger to conclude her time alone with her departed husband, then prepared him in the same fashion as Rodrigo.

By ten twenty p.m., the nurse designated as the morgue attendant, and the janitorial aide on duty accompanied the gurneys holding the two cadavers down to Level A.

The deceased passenger's wife, minutes after the transfer, decided her husband's body should be shipped home by other means from Astoria, and that she wanted off the ship to accompany him. She was escorted to the morgue area, where the bodies were being held just outside the vaults. She was accompanied by the volunteer ship chaplain and a member of the Excursion Tour staff who was assigned responsibility to serve as a care team support liaison in such cases.

Upon arriving at the morgue at ten forty-five p.m., the group discovered the sliding door open, blocked by the attendant sprawled on the floor. The nurse attendant lay face down, in front of the body vaults, moaning, bleeding at the neck and arms from bite wounds, her matted hair stuck to the bloodied floor inside the bay of the morgue. In front of the sliding doors, the metal gurney previously holding Rodrigo was unoccupied. His body bag lay on the floor beneath the gurney.

To the left of the sliding door and the attendant, the other gurney still held the body bag of the fallen charter fishing passenger. The body inside was thrashing about. The passenger's wife froze in her tracks, unable to speak or move. The support care team member stooped down to the floor to examine the fallen nurse lying halfway inside the morgue bay.

The volunteer ship chaplain, a tall Baptist minister in his mid-thirties, rushed to the gurney holding the thrashing body bag. He hastily unzipped it, making a snap judgement that the passenger had been declared deceased prematurely. The Fishtoria passenger emerged, sitting upright, and clutched the chaplain by the throat before yanking the chaplain down on top of him and tearing into the minister's throat with his teeth. The two fell to the floor, the gurney crashing on top of them.

The support care team member abandoned the attendant. She lunged over to pull the gurney off the two men and assist the chaplain, only to suffer his same fate. The fish bite victim's wife began to shriek unintelligibly upon seeing her husband rise up halfway from the moaning tangle of bodies. He crawled over the chaplain, care team member, and gurney until he cleared them. He rose up, his teal patient gown smeared in blood. He slowly approached his shrieking wife as she backed up against the wall. He embraced her and began gouging his teeth and fingers into her left arm while she collapsed into a heap on the hallway floor, still shrieking.

The care team support member collected her wits, pulling herself out of the tangle with the chaplain and the gurney. She clutched her neck, applying pressure with her palm to slow the bleeding. She staggered over to the wall phone opposite the sliding morgue door and made a frantic call to security, before collapsing back to the floor.

Minutes later, the mid-section of Level A was abuzz with activity. Medical center nurses attended to the chaplain, care team support member, morgue attendant, and the fish bite passenger's wife, while they were prepped for transfer up to the medical center on level four, known as the Emperor deck. Janitorial staff cleaned up the area around the morgue. Security staff combed the hallways searching for previously assumed deceased fish bite victims. Soon, aided by video feeds, security had announced they located and trapped their suspects in a mechanical HVAC air handling room.

No one thought to wonder about the trail of blood leading down the hallway away from the morgue area, before it was mopped up by janitorial staff called to the scene. In the heat of the moment, no one thought to question the whereabouts of the medical center area janitor, who at the end of his shift accompanied the nurse attendant down to the morgue to assist with placing the bodies in the vaults. The two security staff standing guard at the Level A mechanical HVAC room door didn't think to pay attention to the pleas for help coming from inside, having been told that the two occupants were experiencing hallucinations.

The PR Problem

Cruise lines were currently in the news, and not in a good way. The current cruise-related media feeding frenzy commenced when another cruise line's deranged passenger murdered other travelers in two separate cabins on that ship before taking his own life. With the media pump primed, Duchess Cruise Lines proceeded to suffer through separate high-profile situations during three consecutive weeks.

Duchess's travails started when the *Caribbean Duchess*, whose passengers included the Robertson family of Duck Dynasty fame filming an episode onboard the ship, experienced a major outbreak of norovirus. The following week, the *Mediterranean Duchess* had over one hundred crew conduct a work-stoppage in protest of deteriorating work and cabin conditions, which was highly publicized via Twitter. The protesting crew were all forcibly escorted off the ship at the next port of call – in Barcelona – in a televised spectacle. The week after that, the *Grand Duchess* made international headlines while sailing around Scandinavia when two large wealthy groups—one from Russia, one from the Ukraine – had an escalating series of heated encounters, culminating with a cocktail lounge brawl that spilled out into adjoining areas, drawing in various other passengers who were struck by one side or the other during the melee. Numerous major injuries resulted from the brawl, but the eventual show of force by ship security, caught on cell phone video, produced a fatality and many nearby passengers not involved in the fracas were roughed up by the ship enforcers.

Duchess was now operating in crisis communications mode. Every ship had been issued an urgent priority set of new protocols requiring immediate reporting of any potential media situation to its applicable regional corporate office, in Seattle, Rome or Sydney. The regional office would assume complete decision-making authority relating to the event until its closure.

On this basis, the Seattle office began calling the shots for the *Pacific Duchess*, while they were still in port in Astoria. Crisis management was triggered when the excursion's charter fishing boat captain called the *Pacific Duchess* shore excursion tour manager. The charter captain informed him they had cut the excursion short a half-hour to head back to the marina. A passenger and Duchess crewmember had become seriously ill from a fish bite, with both requiring immediate medical attention.

Donald Wadsworth, the senior vice president for North American Operations, personally assumed command after the incident was reported. He ordered both victims to be transported back to the ship medical center, as opposed to local medical facilities, where Duchess would lose control over the situation and subsequent publicity. Shortly after six p.m., Rodrigo and the bitten Fishtoria passenger were both secured in the ship's medical center.

During their initial work-ups, both patients exhibited significant pain, inflammation around the wound, and skin discoloration. Lab results provided nothing conclusive. By eight fifty-five, the ship's medical director requested both victims be transferred to Columbia Memorial Hospital in Astoria, due to their deteriorating conditions and his lack of a diagnosis. His request was denied by Wadsworth, who countered that the local twenty-five-bed hospital did not offer the level of tertiary services required to warrant the move. Instead, he arranged for a telemedicine consult with their corporate medical director.

Around nine forty-five, as a result of the online consult, Wadsworth was overruled by the corporate medical director, who ordered for transfer arrangements to be made immediately. The transfer was cancelled just after ten when the second of the victims expired within minutes of the first. By ten twenty p.m., they had been transferred to the morgue.

The *Pacific Duchess's* scheduled departure from Astoria was eleven in the evening. This late departure was timed for the distance the ship needed to travel to arrive in San Francisco

Sunday morning, as well as to accommodate several of the onshore excursions that included offsite dinners and music. Donald Wadsworth consulted with the ship captain, and decided that the ship's departure would be delayed from eleven until midnight, but the gangways would be closed to passengers at eleven. This way the disembarking of the deceased and his wife could occur after that time, out of the public eye.

At ten forty five p.m. the group accompanying the deceased passenger's wife arrived at the morgue. Minutes later, a distress call from a member of the group was placed to security.

At eleven-ten, a heated conference call debate transpired between the corporate medical director, Donald Wadsworth, and ship's captain regarding if these new victims should be transferred to Columbia Memorial, if Astoria law enforcement should be called upon to assist in securing and offloading the previously assumed deceased patients, and if experts should be brought it to determine if they were infected with Gorman's disease.

Wadsworth and ship's captain scoffed at the suggestion of Gorman's disease. Googling Wikipedia as his source, Wadsworth argued that all the evidence so far pointed to something materially different: a fish bite versus human transmission, the considerable distance from the Burning Man site, the much shorter duration of time elapsed from the bite until being pronounced deceased, and the longer period of time involved after being pronounced deceased until re-awakening.

Wadsworth contended that it was more likely the men had encountered an exotic poisonous fish, the ship medical director had incorrectly pronounced them dead, and the effects of the poison were hallucinogenic, causing the victims to behave in their bizarre, violent behavior. The corporate medical director rebutted that he was as qualified to advise about the ship's navigation as Wadsworth was to be offering his clinical opinions.

Wadsworth reminded his adversary that the fate of their company might rest with how they handled this situation if the media were to pick up on it and sensationalize it inappropriately. It was Wadsworth's position that since the two original fish bite victims seemed to have physically, if not mentally recovered, and had been secured in the mechanical room, and since new casualties were receiving treatment in the medical center, it was in everyone's best interest that they proceed as planned to San Francisco. From there, all the victims could be transferred to the best available tertiary care. This would allow for media containment and control of the situation.

He further argued that with the passage of time, the original fish bite victims would come down from their hallucinogenic state and could then be secured and treated, providing a safer scenario than attempting to offload them from the ship now, in their present agitated state.

After additional argument over the capabilities of the ship's medical center versus Columbia Memorial in Astoria, Wadsworth acquiesced to determine the real-time condition of the new victims. If they were deteriorating rapidly, he agreed not to stand in the way of an immediate transfer. They patched the ship medical director into the call, who provided the good news that the new victims were all sutured and had stabilized. They continued to experience pain and were lacking a diagnosis, other than the trauma from the bites, but were not exhibiting the other symptoms or deterioration of the first two victims.

With this report, the corporate medical director threw in the towel, and dropped his opposition to the midnight departure, even allowing that perhaps Donald Wadsworth's poisonous fish hypothesis might be conceivable. However, he won the concession to attempt to discreetly bring on a private consultant asap to rule out Gorman's disease. He had attended a lecture by Alan Gorman several weeks before and picked up his business card. The wheels were set in motion for Rachel Darst, their PR executive, to contact Dr. Gorman.

Ground Rules

Alan and Conner touched down at the Warrenton-Astoria Regional Airport, stepped off their chartered Eclipse 500 six-seater corporate jet, and were greeted by Rachel Darst on the tarmac. Rachel was Duchess Cruise Lines' North American director of communications, based in Seattle. She was considered quite attractive, even in her usual, no-nonsense corporate attire, even in the wee hours of a Saturday morning.

In her early thirties, she was a consummate professional and took pride in her appearance – her whitened teeth, her short, styled brunette hair, her piercing blue eyes that required no corrective lenses after her LASIK procedure, and her almost model-thin waistline.

Rachel had likewise chartered a flight to Astoria in order to escort the men during the second leg of their journey, via a chartered Bell Jet Ranger helicopter. The chopper flight didn't take long; the *Pacific Duchess* disembarked shortly after midnight, more than an hour behind schedule. After clearing the Port of Astoria harbor area, the ship headed directly for international waters – twelve nautical miles off shore, to accommodate a short session of casino gambling.

Rachel spent most of the duration of the short flight talking, while Conner and Alan nodded politely, listening on their headsets. Just before they boarded, she asked them not to discuss their mission or Gorman's disease during the flight, as the chopper pilot would hear whatever they discussed over the headsets.

Instead, Rachel talked about Duchess's spate of recent bad publicity, wanting to be sure Conner and Alan were sensitive enough to how Duchess needed to approach the current problem at hand. She reminded them that cruise ship snafus in the news were cyclical, and many might fly under the news radar when cruise problems weren't the topic du jour.

Just before landing, without bringing up their subject matter, Alan pushed Rachel to confirm their return arrangements. Over the phone they had discussed the chopper sticking around for a couple hours in case their assessment wrapped up quickly. Worst case – if they confirmed presence of Gorman's disease — was they would stay with the ship until it reached port in San Francisco early Sunday morning. Rachel agreed that was the plan, but ominously informed them they would be going to an orientation meeting as soon as they touched down to review the ground rules for their engagement.

Alan was instantly agitated over Rachel's tone of voice and choice of words but reserved a reaction until this all important meeting of theirs took place. A little over ten minutes after takeoff, they stepped off the small helipad – hidden from view from the ship's public vistas at the bow (the fore end) – and proceeded directly to a small conference room off the captain's quarters.

Joining Conner, Alan, and Rachel at the six-person conference table in the middle of the night was the ship's captain, chief engineer, and chief of security. Pleasantries were not even exchanged as they introduced and seated themselves. A loud voice emerged from the black, cylinder-shaped speaker situated in the middle of the table. Senior vice president Donald Wadsworth introduced himself, explaining he was calling from his Seattle residence.

"So, Dr. Gorman, and I didn't catch your assistant's name so forgive me. I wanted to ensure you are fully versed in our ground rules of engagement before you perform services on our behalf, which we are paying you quite handsomely for, I might add. We just need you to tell us what we already know – our patients are victims of some exotic poisonous fish bite and not Gorman's disease."

Alan Gorman stood up from his chair. "Excuse me?" he replied indignantly.

"Who's talking?" Wadsworth snapped. "You need to say whose speaking."

Alan turned to Rachel, ignoring the voice booming through the speaker. "What is he talking about – 'ground rules of engagement'?"

Rachel addressed her boss through the speaker. "Dr. Gorman is asking about the ground rules of engagement." She turned towards Alan. "We emailed you the document right after our phone call. You replied that you received our email and agreed to the engagement."

Alan grew even more defensive. "I didn't see an attachment to your email. What are you talking about?"

"Look, it's no big deal," Rachel replied in a more conciliatory tone. "But the email did clearly refer to the attachment, and given our media relations crisis, we are extremely sensitive in this regard, as I mentioned during our flight. So, let me just review these items with you to make sure we're all on the same page before we start with your important work at hand."

Alan sighed, not attempting to conceal his irritation. "Fine, please review your items with us."

Wadsworth interjected. "Look gentleman, I'm assuming that was Gorman, but you've got to state who is speaking."

Alan crossed his arms, turned towards Conner and raised his eyebrows.

"That was Dr. Gorman, sir," Rachel responded. "As I was saying, we need to repeat our corporate need for confidentiality and security of the nature of your visit. If word leaked out regarding why you are here, it could potentially put Duchess Cruise Lines out of business. So we have to insist that you sign our non-disclosure and confidentiality agreements in person and that we collect your phones during the duration of your visit."

Alan stood up, motioning for Conner to do the same.

"I'm sorry, Ms. Darst, for any misunderstandings and to have wasted each other's times, but there is simply no way we are parting with our sat phones, and from the sound of your senior vice president here, we are not going to be compatible working with you. We'll just show ourselves the way out, get back on your helicopter, and head home with no hard feelings."

Wadsworth's voice boomed through the speaker again. "Excuse me gentlemen, but we have paid a small fortune to fly you out here, which you agreed to without batting an eyelash.

We are paying you a lot of money simply to tell us something we already know – that our cases are not Gorman's disease. Where I come from, a high priced consultant such as yourself is expected to be a man of his word and honor his agreements. And for the fee you are collecting, you damn well shouldn't have a problem with any of this."

Alan bristled. "Listen, sir. We've never met before, and in the one minute we've gotten to know each other, you've mentioned that you're paying us a lot of money at least five times, and that basically, we need to do exactly what you say. Well, guess what? We're feeling a little ambushed. It seems a little ridiculous to expect us to work without our phones, and no amount of money is worth putting up the arrogance I'm sensing here. Gorman's disease is a serious matter, and when you're ready to take it seriously, I suggest you bring in the CDC and see if they can address your concerns. They will do it for free, I might mention, since you're so worried about the money you're spending." Alan patted Conner on the shoulder. "Come on, Conner," Alan motioned with his head for the two to exit the conference room.

Another voice interjected from the speaker. The corporate medical director introduced himself "Dr. Gorman, Conner Zimmerman, I beg you to just let us confer for a moment while you step outside, and please re-join us momentarily to resolve this amicably. I apologize for the obvious misunderstandings that have developed, but I'm sure we all agree it would be a terrible waste for all concerned if your trip out here was for naught. Please do indulge me and give us just a few moments."

Alan relented, now that a fellow physician was involved. After the two left the room, the medical director launched into a tirade that Wadsworth had been so disrespectful, so suddenly, to the man that Gorman's disease was named after. He questioned out loud, that if Wadsworth and Rachel were truly committed to corporate public relations in the current environment, how could they mishandle relations from the get-go with a man of Alan's stature?

Donald Wadsworth wasn't about to share with anyone his personal agenda: that if he'd agreed to allow the ship to be assessed for Gorman's disease by the most esteemed consultant in the field, but then the consultant ultimately walked off the job on his own volition, he'd avoid any complications their assessment might produce, while still having been on record as approving their engagement.

But Wadsworth knew he could only push things so far without calling his leadership into question. The medical director was unusually articulate in reminding all of them why they needed Alan and Conner on board and provided a reasonable compromise to propose.

When Alan and Conner were called back in the room, the medical director did the talking. "Gentleman, we are so sorry we got off on the wrong foot. We apologize if we seem overly blunt about our requirements, but we're sure you understand how devastating the media has been for us the past month."

Alan and Conner nodded.

"So," the medical director resumed, "I am sure it wouldn't be an issue for you to sign any confidentiality or non-disclosure agreements, and the real concern for you is the use of your satellite phones and that we treat your work here seriously and with respect. So please rest assured, we would have not have brought you out here under these conditions if that weren't the case. We think we have a workable solution for you. Please understand, we've already shut the Internet and outside phone lines down on the ship, and we really do have a corporate requirement with collecting your phones. But if you simply left them with Rachel, who will remain by at least one of your sides at all times during your presence here, you can ask her to use your phones at any time should the need arise, as long as she is available to be witness to your conversations. We apologize for the inconvenience that will cause, but we hope you understand how difficult our situation is at the moment, and how sensitive this matter is for us. Given the probability that Gorman's disease is not present on this ship, we have to ensure every protection against it becoming public that we brought you here to investigate the possibility."

So it was that Alan and Conner surrendered their sat phones on the *Pacific Duchess*. The security officer gave a quick status report. Discussion ensued regarding how Alan and Conner would handle their assessment. Five minutes later, Alan and Conner exited the small conference room, stepping outside to confer privately before proceeding with their task at hand.

The Last Friendly Words

Saturday, 2:12 a.m., October 30th

Conner and Alan stood out on the lower open deck in front of the bridge on the fore side of the ship, having exited the captain's conference room, an area off-limits and out of view to the public. The small helipad containing their chartered chopper sat fifty feet ahead, closer to the bow. The wind registered mightily on this end of the ship, carrying the ocean's aroma. Rachel Darst waited for them in the glass interior hallway to the captain's quarters, allowing them a private conversation.

"Well, what do you think? What the hell have I gotten us into this time?" Alan asked Conner, loud enough to penetrate the sounds from the outside of the ship. Alan chuckled nervously. He had grown to like and appreciate his younger partner and was beginning to feel guilty for taking Conner away from Cassie. He had sensed, as of late, that Conner was having some relationship difficulties with her and knew that Conner had hoped this weekend would help set things right.

Conner didn't mention Cassie in his response. "Did you notice the captain never said a word? He just nodded along with Rachel and that corporate dick. I think we're either wasting our time or in big trouble here if that Wadsworth guy is calling the shots and not the ship's own captain."

Alan took a step closer to Conner, to be able to hear him more clearly. "Well, in their defense, they have to be a bit nuts after all they've been through the past month. I've never been on a cruise ship before – don't care about cruise ships, don't pay attention to anything about cruise ships. And even I've picked up on their name in the news over and over as of late."

Conner dropped that concern for the bigger question on his mind. "What they describe so far sounds similar, but with differences to what we know to be Gorman's disease. Could your theory about a marine version explain the discrepancies?"

Alan had briefed Conner during their chartered jet flight to Astoria on his thoughts regarding the possibility of additional "meteors" like the Burning Man drone falling into the ocean. The social media postings of the Pacific Northwest meteor around the same timeframe, brought to Alan's attention by his analysts, were the primary reason he agreed to board the *Pacific Duchess.*

Alan nodded. "Clearly, these cases didn't contract Gorman's disease from Burning Man. So I would think you either have to buy into their exotic poisonous fish theory that has these two fish bite victims tripping out or consider a Gorman disease infected fish theory. And both sound equally implausible. So here we are."

"So here we are," Conner repeated. "And where do we go from here?"

Alan yawned. The late hour was starting to sap his stamina. Conner couldn't help but yawn and stretch as well. Alan glanced over to see Rachel Darst staring at them from inside the well-lit, windowed corridor outside the captain's conference room. "In the hope that we rule out Gorman's disease and get you on this chopper in the next few hours, we'll want to split up. I should go to the medical center, see the patients, check the charts, and interview the doctor and staff. I will ask Rachel to track down this charter fishing boat captain and have him talk to me on the phone. You, my friend, can have the pleasure of visiting the morgue, interviewing available staff down there, and find a way to get a peek at the two patient zeroes they have locked up in that room down there."

"I think we also need to think ahead for these ding-dongs, in case things go south," Conner cautioned. "You heard their security officer in our briefing at the end. They have fifteen total security guards, with half on duty and even less during graveyard shift. They removed their only firearm that was locked in the captain's quarters from all their ships after the bad publicity hit. And they have twenty-five-hundred passengers, with a preponderance of seniors that aren't exactly fully mobile or in fighting shape, plus over a thousand crew that speak who knows how many different languages and might not be able communicate quickly and effectively in a pinch. If there is an infection and it goes bad, this could make Burning Man seem minor league."

"Yeah," Alan agreed. "If things go bad, time will speed up, not slow down, and they don't have a plan for something like this. My guess is they're going to keep Rachel with me, and they're not going to let you go down to the morgue alone. They'll send their security officer with you, and you can talk to him about that. But fortunately, that's most likely just a precaution and we'll find some other explanation for their troubles here."

Conner looked up into the nighttime sky before scanning the private area of the ship they were occupying. He had grown to view Alan as a mentor, older-brother figure, and good friend during the past two months. He shook his head before speaking. "You know, this is my first time on a cruise ship as well. My wife and I had a cruise scheduled for a number of months out, when she passed away." Conner had previously shared with Alan how his pregnant wife died suddenly from a hyper-aggressive streptococcal bacterial infection, so many years ago — sending him on his downward trajectory. "I think if I remember correctly, it was even with *Duchess*."

Conner shook his head again. "You know, we never got the chance to take a real vacation together, I was always so into my corporate position. I think about the best we did was take a long weekend at Disneyland and that kind of thing."

"Disneyland." Alan laughed. "My favorite ride with my girls was always the Pirates of the Caribbean."

"Yeah," Conner smiled. "Me too."

Alan grinned mischievously, "It's funny we bring that up, because I can't help but think of that voice warning you as your little boat is about to descend down the tunnel. Perhaps that voice is speaking to us now, too, before we descend to the bottom of this ship. Do you remember the words?"

Conner chuckled and shook his head.

Alan deepened his tone. "These be the last friendly words ye'll hear, Conner."

The Croatian

Just as Alan predicted, the security officer accompanied
Conner down to Level A. Level A contained two redundant
engine rooms; compartmentalized mechanical rooms relating
to the ship generators and electrical system, HVAC, the water
filtration system, wastewater system; solid waste disposal;
piping, cabling and ducts; storage rooms; a shop; restrooms;
and the morgue.

The engine and certain mechanical rooms were three levels
high. Levels B and C were functionally mezzanines in selected
sections, which housed larger storage areas, additional
mechanical rooms, some crew support areas, and offices.
Passengers were not allowed in Levels A to C. The fourth deck
wasn't referred to as Level D; the fourth deck and above had
fancier monikers standardized throughout the Duchess fleet
and not in perfect alphabetical order– such as the Emperor
deck on level four.

Conner and the security officer descended the crew-only
stairs that began on level six – called the Governors deck. The
security officer had introduced himself previously up in the
conference room. His name was Ranie Navarro, a stout, five-
foot seven-inch, ruddy-faced, crew-cut forty-year-old Filipino
in standard white cruise ship uniform, with two and a half
epaulettes on his shoulder bar. He appeared to be no-
nonsense, speaking only when spoken to. It struck Conner as
odd that the man had no curiosity – no questions to ask –
regarding Conner's mission.

While they descended the series of flights of stairs, Conner
asked how many of his staff was on duty at the moment. Ranie
replied that seven of his fifteen were currently active. He
pointed out that normally there were five on duty during the
graveyard shift, but he held over two that were assigned to
guard the mechanical HVAC room with the fish bite victims.

Conner suggested he consider pulling some of the other staff
back on duty and assign a couple to the medical center in case

the new victims underwent a similar reaction as the fish-bite victims. Conner further suggested that after they toured the affected areas in Level A, they sit down and map out a security plan in case they were facing a Gorman's disease type of infection.

Ranie answered curtly that they had already discussed that possibility with their corporate office and had determined there wasn't a credible threat. His orders from the corporate office were to assist Conner and Alan with their assessment but not to take any additional measures in response to a supposed threat of Gorman's disease as to not unnecessarily cause undue panic with the crew and, ultimately, the passengers. He reminded Conner to be careful not to discuss Gorman's disease in presence of other crew that had not been briefed about Conner and Alan's visit.

Conner pushed back that he had to interview various staff in order to conduct his assessment. He assured Ranie that he would show discretion in his choice of questions, but the questions had to be asked. This caused some visible discomfort with Navarro, who stopped on the next to last flight of stairs, stepped a few feet back, reaching Rachel Darst on the walkie-talkie. He spoke in quiet tones that Conner couldn't decipher but returned stone-faced, remarking that the questions could be asked but only with caution.

They arrived in Level A and proceeded through the labyrinth of narrow passageways. Conner marveled at all the massive pipes and conduit encasing cabling — painted white with banded color coding to indicate systems — lining the hallways, occupying all visible real estate. Mechanical humming and whirring, while not overbearing, was never far off as they traversed the passageways. Every thirty feet or so, they seemed to arrive at another open watertight ovular doorway, compartmentalizing different mechanical system areas with a side passageway winding into the interior of the ship. Several hallways were lined with barrels or boxes along one side, other corridors were unobstructed.

They arrived at the morgue. A single janitor was waiting patiently in the hallway for their arrival. The short, frail young Filipino almost sprinted up to Ranie, welcoming him to this part of the ship.

Conner approached the janitor at a brisk pace, arms outstretched to greet him. "Hello, my name is Conner. We're investigating what happened here." Conner pointed to the morgue. "Do you mind if I ask you a few questions?"

The Filipino janitor looked towards Navarro for permission to talk. Ranie nodded. The janitor bowed out of habit, then replied softly, "No problem, sir. How can we help you?"

Conner assumed a reassuring tone. "We are just here to report on what happened to the victims that came down to the morgue. Were you here when they were attacked?"

The janitor looked to Ranie for permission to answer. He nodded, so the janitor smiled and replied. "I was not. I think only people up now with the doctor were here at that time, sir. But I was here soon after that."

Conner returned the friendly smile. The janitor kept his nervous gaze focused on Navarro. "So, can you tell us what you saw when you got here?"

The janitor again turned his attention to Ranie, waiting for approval before speaking. After the nod was signaled, he replied. "Security got here first. You can talk to them. They're both guarding the bad guys now. They call me in to clean up. When I got here, I see the lady. The one who keeps company with passengers with troubles. She called for help from that phone right over there." The janitor pointed to the wall phone across the hall from the sliding morgue door. "She's lying underneath the phone, all bloody. I look straight across, and there's another lady and man lying underneath a gurney and they're all bloody too. The two nurses got here right after me. One starts tending to the two on the floor across from me. The other nurse notices a lady, a passenger, on the floor on this side of the hall, just down there."

The janitor pointed down the hall another fifteen feet. "The nurses get on the phone for more help," he continued. "They ask me to help them until their people arrive. They have the two security help them too. We each stay with a person and clean them up, and hold down gauze on where they bleed. Then their help arrives, and security leaves to go look for who did this. I start cleaning up. There's blood everywhere. The nurses and their aides, they take everybody up to the medical center. So I'm by myself. I can hear people yelling down the corridors."

The janitor pointed down the interior passageway that turned toward the stern another twenty feet ahead. "Another one of your security comes by and tells me to stay in this area and phone if I see anything. I think they forgot about me, because I've been here a long time," he added. "That was hours ago, and I've cleaned up everything up and down until this area is spotless. I called my boss on that phone, and he said if security told me to stay here, I had to stay here until they said I could go. So I wait and wait, and no one comes by. Which is weird. Where is everybody? There are not a lot of us down here, but somebody walks by now and then. I was getting spooked. I'm very glad you came by now." He turned his attention to Ranie. "Can I go?"

Conner broke in before Navarro could answer. "First, can you show me exactly where everybody was lying on the floor, and where else you had to clean up any blood?" The janitor, eager to please, proceeded to take them to the exact spots where the victims had been. He escorted them down the interior hallway all the way to the turn, pointing out where bloody footprints and handprints on the wall had been. He showed them the nearby closet containing a wash basin where he stored the mop, pail, and cleaning supplies for this sector.

Conner asked what happened to the gurneys that the bodies were on that came down to the morgue. The janitor looked at Conner blankly. "There were no bodies in the morgue. The morgue is empty. These people got attacked before they were bringing bodies down to the morgue is what I assumed when I got down here. There were two empty body bags lying by the gurneys, but they were all bloody. I called upstairs and they said to properly dispose of them. The gurneys they used to take the patients upstairs."

Ranie didn't want a conversation to continue about bodies in the morgue. "Thank you. Thank you so much for your help. You are relieved now. I'm sure your shift was over hours ago. You can let your boss know the ship is secure and we thank him, too, for your help."

"Wait," Conner protested. "I may have more questions."

"We can find him in his cabin if you do. Now let's let this poor man call it a day." Ranie patted the janitor on the back and gently pushed him away. The janitor was more than happy to quickly disappear.

Conner turned to Navarro. "You know, I'd think you'd have some questions for him. And I'd think you'd have some protocol here not to rush in and clean up a potential crime scene before you had a chance to conduct an investigation and preserve any evidence."

Ranie replied without emotion. "My staff was first on the scene. We saw what we needed to. If you knew anything about running a ship like this, you'd know that for health, safety, and orderliness, keeping it spotless is a first order of business. Now, what do you need to see next?"

Conner sighed. He pointed down the corridor. "Doesn't the trail of bloody footprints and handprints that were once headed down this way concern you? Have you traced their entire route before you trapped them in the HVAC room? What if they attacked someone else along the way that you haven't found? Have you taken a roll call of who is on duty?"

Ranie turned to directly face Conner and assumed a formidable presence. "Look, sir, I know your background is not in security. Don't pretend you know how to do my job. We hired you to do an assessment if your disease is here, not to ask questions about securing my ship. Now, let's get on with your assessment."

Conner didn't back down. He shook his head slightly. "You don't get it. These issues are one and the same. If there is a member of your crew lying somewhere, out of sight down these corridors, in theory, they could be infected and they're not secured. What is your comfort level that the path these men took, before you contained them, is fully accounted for and that your crew down here is fully accounted for?"

Navarro tightened his face. "I don't answer to you. But we don't need to concern ourselves with that. We reviewed video feeds tracing their route right up to when they were apprehended."

Conner sighed his skepticism. "Okay then, let's go check these fellows out."

Ranie guided him through a series of twists and turns down the narrow hallways surrounded by green and white tubing, with occasional tall or long cylinders in between. Conner was thoroughly turned around, with no idea how to find his way out. They quickly arrived at the double doors to the mechanical HVAC room in question, with Navarro's two staff standing stern-faced in front of each door, with a long beam wedged between exterior pipes and the lower part of the door and adjacent walls helping to secure the door shut.

Ranie introduced Conner to his men. Before Conner could commence with any questions, a bleating cry in another language rang out from behind the doors. A couple of short sentences were repeated.

"What language is that?" Conner asked Ranie, recognizing that it was Eastern European, but uncertain beyond that.

"Croatian," Navarro replied matter-of-factly. He confronted his two guards angrily. "Has there been yelling like that since you first called me?"

The guard on the left nodded. He had been on the walkie-talkie with Ranie when they witnessed the two men run into the room. The two guards shut and secured the HVAC room doors, trapping them inside. The yelling commenced then, which they reported to Ranie, telling him that nothing intelligible was being shouted. He instructed them to ignore it, as they must be high and hallucinating.

Conner could tell it was a single, hoarse voice in a pleading tone. "What is he saying?" Conner asked Ranie.

"He is begging for help. He wants to get away from the other person in there." Ranie replied in an aggravated tone. He turned toward his men. "Why didn't you tell me what he was saying all this time?"

The guard on the left spoke up again, slowly, almost cowering. "We don't understand what he is saying. It's just gibberish, isn't it?"

"No, it's not," their boss answered angrily.

"Croatian?" Conner repeated. "Neither of those two men was Croatian, were they?"

"No they were not," Ranie answered loudly. "The fishing passenger was American. The crewman was Filipino." He confronted his men. "Tell me again, when you saw them running in the room, were they running together or could one have been chasing the other?"

The guard on the left again answered in the tone of one who has been accused but professing innocence. "Boss, you know that it all happened so quickly. It's hard to know for sure. There was some distance between them, but not much. They weren't really running, just kind of walking fast and strange, and one of them was limping, I think."

"We need to get a look into there," Ranie announced.

"There is no video feed into the room?" Conner asked hopefully.

"Not in the mechanical rooms. We'll have to get a videoscope and slip open some venting down the hall," he replied.

"What about just talking to them in there, for starters?" Conner suggested.

"What?" Ranie responded, unsure what Conner was getting at.

"You understand Croatian. Can you speak it? Can you ask if he speaks any English? You could ask what's going on in there, who he is, and what the other guy in there is doing."

For once, Navarro didn't dismiss something that Conner had uttered. He proceeded, in broken Croatian, to ask Conner's questions. Ranie quickly learned the man claimed to be a refrigeration/HVAC engineer who spoke almost no English.

This was his first cruise ship, having just joined the crew two weeks ago. He had been called down to ensure the morgue was activating properly, and was on his way back when he came across this crazy man who chased him. He fell over and twisted his ankle, trying to get away, and was pursued into this room. He climbed up the tubing and wedged himself out of reach from the snarling man below. At some point, when he was repositioning himself to keep the weight off his ankle, the snarling man managed to reach his right leg and bit him. Now he felt weak and sick. He was thirsty and didn't think he could stay awake much longer.

After gleaning this information the best he could, Ranie pulled Conner aside away from his guards, to explain what he had just learned.

"Do you believe him?" Conner asked, hoping the answer was yes.

Ranie now bore that body language conveying Conner was an ally, not an adversary. "I do," he replied. "He gave his name, which is easy enough to check out. We need to get a videoscope and figure out how we're going to get him out of there and see if his assailant, who from the way he described him must be the passenger, is still a threat."

"That's not our biggest problem," Conner remarked.

Ranie paused, but then understood Conner's meaning. "Yes, we have to find our crewman that was bit by the fish. His name is Rodrigo. And this means he's still on the loose."

Rodrigo on the Loose

Friday, 10:28 p.m., October 29th

Rodrigo awakened inside the body bag. He lay on the gurney just outside the open morgue bay. The zippered bag constrained him to very limited movement. The nurse attendant had just slid the door open and examined the top vault for a moment, to ensure it had been emptied of storage items. She turned around when the janitorial aide accompanying her let out a startled yelp.

The body inside the first bag was thrashing about. Grunting could be heard from inside. The janitorial aide stood frozen behind the animated bag, grasping the second gurney that was parked just behind the first. The aide looked down quickly at the body bag on the second gurney, but detected no movement.

The morgue attendant let loose an expletive and leaned over the first gurney to open the bag. She thought about the reaction she would soon receive when she carted Rodrigo back upstairs to the medical center to inform the doctor he had incorrectly declared his patient deceased.

After she unzipped the bag, Rodrigo sat upright immediately. She leaned over to help pull the body bag all the way off of his shoulders, not noticing his skin pigment had altered to a grayish tone. He grabbed her forcefully, pulled her to his chest, and began ripping into her neck with his teeth. After several bites, he pushed her away. As she crumpled to the ground, he bound off the gurney, tripping onto the floor, as the body bag still embraced his feet.

Rodrigo thrashed about, finally freeing his legs. He crawled for a moment on all fours, vomiting a mixture of bile and blood onto the floor. He then arose, clothed in his now blood-soaked, teal patient gown, noticing the terrified janitorial aide standing behind the second gurney. Rodrigo advanced toward the man, almost reaching him before the aide regained his composure, and turned around to sprint down the passageway toward the starboard side calling for help.

Rodrigo followed in pursuit, leaving the bloodied morgue attendant and his fish bite companion – who hadn't re-awoken yet – behind. Rodrigo wasn't capable of running, but he was able to effectively maneuver down the passageway, grunting as he progressed. He snagged his leg on a loose edge of sheet metal sheathing from a section of ducting, slashing his calf. Only a small amount of grayish, thick, oily fluid emerged where red blood should have appeared.

The janitorial aide, hollering as he sprinted down the passageway, turned around while running forward full speed, to see if Rodrigo was still behind him. He banged his head hard against the upper white-painted piping as the corridor took another turn. He paused, stunned for a moment, before collapsing, unconscious.

Rodrigo soon caught up with his quarry. He leaned down and then settled in on all fours, biting into the aide's left arm. After tearing out a small portion of flesh the size of a half-dollar, he looked behind the aide, noticing a lower bank of pipes with considerable open space above and below them. Rodrigo was attracted to their warmth, condensation, and the oily grit on the floor beneath them. Rodrigo began to drag the aide out of the corridor and into the lower piping with him.

Rodrigo was soon prone on the aide, to the side of the corridor, taking deeper and deeper bites into his left arm. The aide awoke briefly from the pain, terrified. Trying to escape his captor on top of him, the aide banged his head hard into the piping just above their heads a second time. The aide did not resume consciousness. Rodrigo continued methodically consuming the aide's upper left arm from just below the shoulder socket. Strands of ligaments, tendons, and arteries dangled as Rodrigo finished off the aide's bicep.

Rodrigo started to bite at the elbow joint, but grew frustrated with the amount of bone in his way. Rodrigo's urge to continue gorging on the arm dissipated. He began smearing the blood leaking from the aide onto his fingers and then licked them.

Rodrigo noticed the aroma of the oily floor below them. He began to rub the blood on the floor into a nearby oily puddle with his right hand and drew his fingers back to his lips, licking them. Rodrigo continued this ritual for considerable time, eventually forgetting about the aide and crawling off to lie directly over the puddle of oil where he smeared his hand back and forth between the nearby pool of blood and the oily puddle.

A couple of hours passed in this fashion. Rodrigo finally noticed footsteps pass by, along with the sound of whistling. Rodrigo crawled out of the piping and back into the corridor, his once teal patient gown now completely soaked in blood, condensation, and oil. He abandoned the aide, who would eventually expire from his wounds and re-animate as well.

Rodrigo stumbled after the whistling man. The whistler turned around, sensing someone behind him. Assuming from appearances that Rodrigo had just been in an accident, the man exclaimed an expletive, before rushing forward to assist Rodrigo. He instructed Rodrigo to let him help walk him to the staff room, where they could call for the medical center to come help. Rodrigo grunted in response, while the man positioned himself to Rodrigo's left. He pulled Rodrigo's left arm around his shoulder and placed his right arm around Rodrigo's shoulder.

They took a series of steps forward this way. Rodrigo would lean in without much force, trying to bite into the man's chest, but each time they took a step, Rodrigo's head would bounce back out of the way. Finally, Rodrigo leaned in harder, but in doing so, he pulled them forward suddenly, and off balance, sending them both to the floor. Rodrigo fell sideways, his arm rubbing the grease off a recently over-lubricated linkage joint.

The man let out another expletive and scolded Rodrigo to watch his step more closely. The man pulled the grunting Rodrigo up and resumed their positions with Rodrigo on his right. Rodrigo was now fascinated by the greasy gunk on his right hand – too distracted by its aroma and consistency to resume attempting to bite into his companion for the moment.

Rodrigo licked his right hand over and over while they took several more steps forward.

The man finally noticed Rodrigo's finger-licking. He stopped in his tracks, shaking his head, demanding to know what Rodrigo was doing. The man's yelling caught Rodrigo's attention, causing him to abandon his oily fingers. Rodrigo turned into the man, pile-driving him to the left side of the corridor, as if he were performing a takedown on a wrestling mat.

The area they landed in was clear of any overhead piping for several feet, but contained lower green tubing just above the deck. The man fell into the lower tubing, banging his head hard, stunning him. Rodrigo landed on top of him and sank his teeth into the man's cheek before both slid off onto the floor behind the tubes, against a wall and out of view of the corridor.

Rodrigo commenced with a similar sequence of events as he had with the janitorial aide, only he was focused on consuming the left side of the man's face and neck instead of an arm. The man never had the opportunity to scream, first stunned by the blow to his head by the pipe and then robbed of the opportunity to produce sound, as Rodrigo bit all the way through his check and chomped down hard on the man's tongue.

After considerable more time passed, Rodrigo emerged to take down several more solo victims, one-by-one in the thinly staffed sectors of Level A, leaving each to expire after they eventually bled out and then re-animate after less than a half hour later.

No one else knew yet that Rodrigo was still on the loose.

Putting a Bow on It

Alan Gorman sat patiently in the medical center lobby, its front doors locked for the night many hours before. He thumbed through the patient charts just handed to him, while he waited for the ship's medical director to finish with another round of examining the four morgue biting victims.

Rachel Darst stepped across the room toward Alan, announcing she had their man on the line. Using Alan's sat phone, she had been tracking down the Fishtoria charter boat captain at Alan's request. She apologized again for waking the man in the middle of the night and handed Alan the phone.

"This is about the incident with the tour today, again?" the Fishtoria captain asked, groggily. "I've spoken at length with your medical center physician and the excursion manager several times, you know." The captain would have been rude at this hour with almost anyone else besides the cruise ship.

Alan stood and began pacing in front of Rachel. She had sat down by him in the blue, molded plastic lobby chairs, nervously playing with strands of her short, brunette hair. "I'm sure you have, and this won't take but a minute, I promise," Alan began. "I am an outside doctor the ship brought in to deal with this case, and I just have some quick questions. Did you actually see this fish bite either of these men, and is there any chance that someone still has the fish in their possession?"

The Fishtoria captain cleared his throat. "I saw them both get bit, right in front of me, and believe me, we tossed that fish overboard. It was the most disgusting lingcod I ever laid eyes on. It was discolored. It had open sores. Its face looked hideous, and it was a big freaking lingcod. Not a record fish, mind you, but it had to be over fifty pounds."

Alan stopped pacing. "How certain are you it was a lingcod? There is some talk here that it might have been a more exotic fish, one that is poisonous."

The Fishtoria captain let out a chuckle. "What, you think we have lionfish or pufferfish in the Pacific Northwest?" He chuckled again. "You don't even want to know how many years I've been fishing these waters, and what we caught today, that was a lingcod. The ugliest, scariest lingcod I've ever seen in all my years, but a lingcod it was. Diseased with something weird, for sure, but a lingcod. There's no debate about that."

"You're absolutely sure?" Alan asked.

"Look, doctor. That was a lingcod. Now is that all?"

Alan paused. "Actually, there is something else. We need to find out if there's more fish like that in your waters. I'm hoping I could pay for a charter with you to cover the same area and try to catch another one like that and keep it this time."

The Fishtoria captain laughed one more time. "There is no freaking way you could pay me enough money to go after a fish like that again. And I already have a private party chartered not that many hours from now this morning."

"Look, first off, this is an important health and safety issue that could be really critical. And second, I'm sure we could pay you enough to make it well worth your while. I'm sure knowing what you know now, you could take proper precautions if you landed another one. And, if you're going out there tomorrow anyway, what makes you think you wouldn't accidently catch another one anyway?"

"Because I'm sure as hell not going to do any bottom fishing anytime soon, that's how I know I don't have to catch another one anyway," the Fishtoria captain answered, this time with a forced small chuckle. The conversation paused for several seconds, before the captain asked, "But, for the sake of argument, if we were to go after this Moby Dick of a lingcod for you, how much money might we be talking?"

The medical director stepped into the lobby. Rachel stood up. Alan signaled the doctor with his hand that he was wrapping up the call. "Look, I have to go now. But I'm going to give someone on my staff your number, and they will call you and set something up that will work for you."

Before the Fishtoria captain could reply, Alan hung up. He turned to Rachel, confirmed that she'd heard his end of the entire conversation, and pulled up his analysts' email from his contacts. He asked her to relay his request to commission the Fishtoria for a charter in search of another strange lingcod, even if it was way above market rate.

The medical director, Dr. Hernandez, introduced himself before motioning Alan to sit back down in the lobby chair. Hernandez was exhausted after the rush of adrenaline the previous hours had brought. He sat down next to Alan. He was currently the only medical center physician aboard ship. With the repositioning of the *Pacific Duchess* to the Mexican Riviera beginning Sunday, his one staff physician disembarked in Seattle, their previous port of call. Another staff physician would join him for the Mexican Riviera tour of duty when they reached Long Beach, the first stop after San Francisco.

"Alan Gorman, it's an honor to meet you in person, even at this late hour," Dr. Hernandez began. "I certainly know why you're here. I spoke with our corporate medical director several times about this during the past few hours, so I can see why we would bring you in to rule out Gorman's disease. But, I don't share his concern that anyone here contracted the real deal. This is just too different from everything you and the CDC have published on the disease. Mind you, it's humbling for me to call the time of death on two men who obviously aren't. And just as bad, I still don't have a good diagnosis for them or our patients here, as you can see in the charts."

Dr. Hernandez cleared his throat and continued. "We should have transferred those two men to the hospital in Astoria. That should be obvious by now; we wouldn't have these four patients on our hands. And now, I tell you what we should be doing. We should be hightailing it back to Astoria, or to the nearest port of any size, or even start loading these patients onto your chopper a couple at a time. Even though they've stabilized, they belong in a hospital, not here. I'm hoping you can impress that upon our Mister Wadsworth, or whoever you're talking to, because no one listens to me. Maybe you can threaten them that you'll call the CDC if they don't do that."

Alan smiled and patted his fellow physician's wrist. "I don't envy you, what you've been through today. But calling the CDC isn't a threat. It's a requirement once this second round of victims was bit. But first things first. We have to finish our assessment to be able to have something to report to them."

"But you don't have enough to link this to Gorman's disease," Dr. Hernandez responded defensively.

Alan shook his head. "Doesn't matter. Let's say for argument's sake this isn't Gorman's disease. It still, on its face, requires the CDC be contacted. Especially because you don't have a diagnosis."

The medical director nodded, conceding the point. "What we need is to get our two patient zeroes restrained and back up here so we can pinpoint what's going on with them. That's where the real action is."

"I'm with you there," Alan agreed.

"But I'm told the plan is to leave them locked in the room down in Level A until we hit San Francisco," Hernandez complained.

"That's standard protocol for security with someone who is a clear threat to others or who has conducted a material infraction of the law. We sequester them in available quarters until port is reached," Rachel interrupted, walking over to them, having just completed her requested call for Alan. She had been half listening to their conversation during her call.

"And what if they die in there, for real this time?" Dr. Hernandez shot back at Rachel.

"And what if the only way I can finish my assessment is to have a look at them?" Alan added.

"Look," Rachel responded to Alan, "as much as we'd all like to get you back in that helicopter, if you're adamant about examining those two men, you'll most likely have to wait it out and see them after we get to San Francisco where those two can be offloaded properly."

Rachel reached over and patted the medical director's wrist, as Alan had done moments before. "And I am sure our security is going to monitor the two of them, and if their health deteriorates again, we'll be notified."

Rachel stepped back, crossed her arms, and adopted a sterner tone. "I overheard you talking about the CDC, Dr. Gorman. We had an understanding that we'll contact CDC per standard protocol, which is after we reach port in San Francisco, as long as you don't find direct evidence of Gorman's disease. I just want to make sure you're not saying something different here, because that would be a problem."

Alan sensed the irritation he experienced earlier in the captain's conference room, seeping into the medical center lobby. "Ms. Darst, let's stop reminding me about your corporate position on this matter every few minutes and worry about these patients and your passengers and crew. I can't tell you at what point we need to contact the CDC until we finish this assessment, which I'm trying to do. And in theory, we can wait to file a report until you reach port and keep this whole thing under your media radar. But this could go a lot of other ways too. It's just too early to tell, okay?"

An awkward silence ensued.

Rachel had been taught that in negotiations, at the end of a long silence after a request is made, the next person who speaks loses. She was determined to wait it out, and let Dr. Gorman make a concession.

More silence.

Finally, Dr. Hernandez broke in. "Hey, what is the next step here? I'm just in a watchful waiting mode with these patients, really. There's not much going on with them right now."

Having not been the first to speak, Rachel saw her opportunity. "Well, if that's the case, I assume you want to take a quick look at these patients yourself, Dr. Gorman, and if you don't have anything conclusive after that, I suggest we raise Ranie, our security officer and your man Mister Zimmerman, and see if they have anything to report, and we take it from there. You know, despite your healthy pessimism, Dr. Gorman, I'm liking our chances for you to wrap this up, and put a bow on it — allowing you to get home and us to just report a bizarre fishing incident to the CDC after we make port Sunday morning."

The Bow Unravels

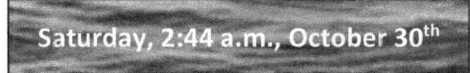
Saturday, 2:44 a.m., October 30th

Alan finished rounding the four patients with Dr. Hernandez. He was stumped. They clearly experienced a negative reaction to the bites from the Fishtoria passenger. But enough time had passed and they certainly hadn't degraded rapidly as in a classic Burning Man Gorman's disease case.

Alan noted that the two patient zeroes, Rodrigo and the Fishtoria passenger, did rapidly decline before being declared deceased. It was possible those two had re-animated after clinical death, as in a classic Gorman's disease case, but the time for reanimation – if that's what it was — took longer than back at Burning Man.

Alan was not ready to concede anything for now, given his theory that these cases may have been generated from a marine source bearing a different branch of Gorman's disease, with separate characteristics. He also knew that he wasn't going to establish anything conclusive during his time on the ship, even if he stayed on until they reached San Francisco.

Alan was leaning toward doing just that – staying on to file a report with the CDC after they came into port and follow through on the case after that– but send Conner back to Sulphur. He wanted Conner to have a fighting chance of mending whatever fences with Cassie that he needed to mend. Alan had taken quite a liking to Conner, despite Conner's lapses into sullen silence for periods of time. Alan hoped Conner could find peace. Knowing what a center of gravity his own wife was all his years in the service, Alan saw Cassie hopefully as Conner's solution for whatever demons that continued to haunt the poor man.

Alan smiled and motioned Rachel – who had been dogging his every step during the rounds – back into the lobby. "Alright, Ms. Darst, I think we're at that point in your little plan where we can track down Conner and your security officer and see if they have anything to tell us about our two biters down there."

Rachel was elated. She sensed from his tone of voice that a corner had been turned with Alan Gorman. She couldn't wait to call her boss, Donald Wadsworth, after they connected with Ranie Navarro, and give Wadsworth the good news so everyone could get some sleep. She would remind her boss that the CDC was going to be infinitely more lenient with them in any follow-up when the CDC received word that Duchess had brought Alan Gorman in on their own volition.

Rachel Darst had an inherent intensity since she was a teenager. She grew up in Tacoma, Washington, received undergraduate and graduate degrees at U.W., married and recently divorced in Seattle, and had been with Duchess since receiving her Masters. She had anchored herself in the Seattle area since college to be near her ill mother in Tacoma. Her mom recently passed away after an unusually long battle with lung cancer. An only child not close to her father — he left them while she was in middle school — and childless herself, she was ready to abandon Seattle and start fresh someplace with less rain. The Silicon Valley or the L.A. basin came to mind. She just wanted to get a successful crisis management tour of duty completed with Duchess, and she would have her recruitment firm put her into play.

Rachel pulled out from her small, triangular purse the walkie-talkie that Ranie provided. She repeatedly paged Ranie to no avail. She phoned Ranie's office. She was tempted to contact the captain's quarter and have Ranie paged over the ship-wide speaker system, but thought the better of the request, given the late hour.

Rachel ran her fingers through her hair, trying to decide what to do. She was so close to putting this crisis to bed. She worriedly thought of the hook to a song her mother – a Paul Simon fan — used to sing out loud when she was a child: 'the nearer your destination, the more you're slip-sliding away.'

Alan Gorman plopped into a lobby chair, absorbed with once-again reviewing the two patient zero charts. Rachel quietly stepped up behind him, rubbing him lightly on the right shoulder for just a moment. "Dr. Gorman, if you don't mind, I'm just going to run to Ranie's office and try to catch them. They're not picking up when I've tried to reach them."

Rachel barely registered with Alan, who was lost in thought considering the possibilities with Rodrigo's lab results. "Okay," he replied, not really noting her message.

Rachel stepped out of the lobby, exiting out the back door from the treatment bays. The Duchess ships have a standard layout, so she was able to quickly navigate herself to Ranie's office on the same level at the other end of the ship –aft.

Ranie Navarro's door was locked, but she could hear a muffled conversation inside. She pounded on the door. No one answered. She banged again. This time, the door open quickly, with Conner greeting her, and closing the door behind her just as rapidly once she stepped inside.

Before Rachel could start in with asking for a status update — so she could hopefully close the books for now on the site visit — she became curious with what held Ranie so captive in front of the widescreen display with twelve different rotating video feeds. Ranie had set Level A feeds to fill the giant monitor. Another guard stood inches away to Ranie's right, just as fixated on the video screen. Conner, too, was focused on the monitor, paying Rachel no attention.

Rachel was about to speak up, when Ranie exclaimed, "Look, there's movement again behind the pipes. Someone is just out of view there." Ranie pointed excitedly at feed number four. "You see? Someone's back there."

"What is this?" Rachel asked with apprehension. No one answered.

"Perhaps one of their coms are out, and they're on task," the guard to Ranie's right suggested.

"Just watch. The movement seems too random to be doing any kind of job," Ranie said. Everyone in the room leaned forward, witnessing someone coming in and out view between some large vertical pipes. They seem to be rotating around the pipe, almost embracing it. It appeared a man was repeatedly rubbing his right hand around a joint seal, then bringing his hand to his face."

"What is he doing?" Conner asked slowly.

Suddenly the man stepped out in full view. No one bothered to answer Conner's question. Ranie cursed before leaning into the monitor to gain a better look. Before them stood a man missing his upper left arm, other than the humerus bone and small patches of tissue. The lower left arm dangled without purpose. The man was covered in dark fluid, most assuredly blood, perhaps mixed with oil or other substances.

Navarro lifted the file from his desk, opening it to consult a picture inside. He looked again at feed number four on the monitor. "That, my friends, is not Rodrigo. I'm not sure who that is, but it is definitely not Rodrigo." He turned to his guard. "Go down there. Wait here—" Ranie pointed to the location in video feed three. "—where I can see you. I'm sending two guards to join you. Then we'll check this fellow out." Ranie grabbed his walkie-talkie, giving orders hurriedly.

Rachel tugged at Conner's short-sleeve shirt. "What is going on?"

"It seems the patient zeroes bit by the fish weren't both locked in the HVAC room. One was, but the other man, trapped in there with him is some poor Croatian mechanic he was chasing. And the Croatian's been bitten. So the other one – this Rodrigo – we came up here to Ranie's video feeds, to look for him. He's still out there somewhere. Ranie checked in with the 3rd engineer on duty to ask him to roll call everyone active in level A. Eight crew on duty are missing. Two more have been badly bitten. Plus, they figured out an aide is missing that helped take those two down to the morgue in body bags. And it looks like we just found one of the missing right here." Conner pointed to video feed four.

Rachel took a step back, speechless. She closed her eyes for a moment, focusing on her breathing, drawing in and exhaling deep-measured breaths. "I'll be right back," she announced. She stepped outside Ranie's office to call her boss.

Back in the medical center lobby, Alan finally noticed that Rachel was gone. He set down the two patient charts, calling out her name, to no avail. He then vaguely remembered that she told him she was leaving but couldn't recollect where or for how long. Alan wandered out of the lobby into the treatment bays, wondering if she had stepped into there. He was startled to see a beehive of activity.

Dr. Hernandez caught Alan's entrance out of the corner of his eye. "Dr. Gorman," he called out. "Thank God you're still here. Is your license to practice still valid?"

Alan paused momentarily, taking the scene in. Two nurses were each laboring with separate patients. Dr. Hernandez was attending to a third. "Yes. Yes, it is," he finally blurted out.

"Out of the blue, they just started to crash, one by one. Can you get in here and take over those two on that side?" Hernandez pointed to the two bays opposite him.

Three minutes later, their fellow nurse serving as the morgue attendant expired, despite Dr. Hernandez's resuscitation efforts. Within ten minutes time, all four were dead. After the medical director made the final call for the volunteer chaplain, the last to die, Hernandez sat down in the nearest molded plastic chair against the wall, overwhelmed. He shook his head. His two nurses both started to cry. "What the hell is going on here?" Hernandez exclaimed to Alan.

Both nurses sat down as well, exhausted. Alan leaned against the bed in the bay bearing the expired wife of the Fishtoria passenger. He scanned the room, observing the four bodies. "I'm afraid we don't have much time. I think, somewhere in the range of twenty to thirty minutes—"

Alan was interrupted by loud banging on the back door to the treatment bays. A nurse rushed to open the door. A security guard burst in, addressing the nurses. "We need you down in Level A. They tell me we have several crew just found in bad shape needing suturing and more. They're real bad."

Alan and the medical director looked at each other. Alan could sense that Hernandez and his nurses were losing their grips. "I'll go down there," Alan volunteered. "How about one of you come with me?" Alan asked both nurses. The older of the two wiped her forehead and said she would go.

Alan turned to the security guard. "You need to stay here and help them lock up these bodies. You need to store them in a small, secured room, pronto, but can you tell her," –Alan pointed to the older nurse – "where we need to go to?"

The security guard gave directions before starting to argue with Alan, not understanding why they would need to waste time securing the bodies of the deceased patients. Alan grew frustrated and stepped up to Dr. Hernandez. "I better go down and check out your crew below. But you have to get him—" Alan pointed to the security guard. "—to help you lock these bodies up. I hate to tell you this, but you've got a different kind of strain of Gorman's disease here, and we can't predict exactly what's going to happen with them."

Hernandez shook his head, overwhelmed. "Dr. Gorman, just because they all just expired unexpectedly doesn't provide this is Gorman's disease. They—"

Alan interrupted him. "You want to sit right next to them and find out for sure? You need to secure those bodies," Alan warned him again, before exiting with the older nurse. He followed her aft to the crew stairwell, where they descended from the Emperor deck to Level A.

They wound through the same maze of narrow hallways, continuing to face aft, following the route that Conner and Ranie had traversed earlier. Alan, like Conner before him, had no idea where they were in relation to the rest of the vessel. Following the nurse through one ovular doorway after another, they soon arrived outside the morgue.

Directly in front of them were two bloodied crewman, writhing on the floor – the most recent of Rodrigo's attacks. The two security guards Ranie had just sent down were sitting on the floor beside them, next to a number of bloodied rags. The nurse rushed to the two wounded men on the floor. She kneeled down and opened the kit she brought with her.

While the nurse prepped the bite wounds for both crewman, Alan talked with the guards who brought the victims to the morgue from two different points in the solid waste treatment area. They explained that they chose bringing the fallen men back to the morgue area, because they assumed it would be a better set up for medical purposes until transfer up to the medical center could be arranged. They also confirmed that a number of crew was still unaccounted for. They pressed Alan for what he knew about what was going on. Alan said he would share what he could after the two victims were stabilized.

Alan informed the guards that the medical center was full, and he preferred to find someplace a little more secure to hold the fallen crewmen for now. He asked if they could stay a few more minutes to help make that transfer, but first go find some type of rolling carts they could use to transport the two victims. Alan sutured both men on the floor quickly, while the guards ran down the hall to retrieve two carts.

After the suturing was complete for both the wounded, who were groggy and incoherent, Alan pulled the nurse aside, speaking quiet enough so their conversation wouldn't be heard by their patients. "Listen," Alan began, "I don't know what you've been told or how much you've overheard upstairs, but I assume you are familiar with Gorman's disease?"

The nurse nodded.

"Well," Alan shared, "we appear to be experiencing an outbreak of a new version of the disease in real time. The victims upstairs that just expired? They are going to go stage two. These gentlemen here will eventually do the same. There are evidently more victims scattered down here somewhere. It is not safe for you and I to be treating them out in the open — and it's not safe for them to be in an unsecured area where they might progress to stage two. Stay close to me and let's get them moved somewhere safer when the guards return. After that, I've got to get ahold of security and your captain. There needs to be some ship-wide measures in place."

The two guards returned with carts. "Where is a room down here that can be locked that we can take these patients to?" Alan asked upon their arrival.

One of them half-chuckled. "The storage areas are all way too small or way too big. And the problem is, they're all jammed full. There's no such thing as empty space down here. But I have something in mind."

The guards helped transport the two victims to the engine department shop, adjacent to the water distillation tanks, just beyond the wastewater treatment system, further aft. As they offloaded the two victims on the floor, one of the co-workers received a call on his walkie-talkie. They were informed another fallen crewman had been found and were asked to transport him to whatever staging area they had come up with.

Alan remembered that Rachel had his phone. The nurse had no walkie-talkie on her. Alan tasked her with searching the shop for a staff phone to track down Ranie Navarro, so he could implore him to get Level A secured. His two patients seemed less alert and had worsening vital signs than the four did upstairs shortly before they crashed. Alan figured there wasn't a lot of time until he would be facing the same outcome.

Back on the Emperor deck, Rachel Darst concluded a three-way conference call with the ship's captain and Donald Wadsworth. In her previous call to her boss outside Ranie Navarro's office, she shared the devastating news that an outbreak of some kind was occurring in Level A. She was instructed to track down Ranie to confirm the current status. Ranie didn't answer her walkie-talkie pages, so she contacted the captain, asking him to pull rank and get Ranie to talk to her. A minute later, a very curt Navarro informed her there were a number of attacks in Level A, and at least one new perpetrator as well.

Rachel checked in with the medical center to learn all four patients had just abruptly passed away within minutes of each other. She immediately set up the three-way conference call. Wadsworth had requested her to exclude the corporate medical director from the conversations going forward, being they were no longer discussing individual patient issues but rather ship-wide concerns.

Wadsworth made his position clear. They needed to maintain maximum authorized speed and get the ship to San Francisco asap, as opposed to planning for any assistance or partial evacuation en route. Since the activity was contained to just Level A, he instructed the captain to seal the levels below the Emperor deck off until it was secured.

Wadsworth reminded Rachel and the captain of his maxim, that a problem made public at sea is ten times as bad as a problem made public at port. It was their job to ensure these actions stayed under the passenger's – and thus ultimately, the media's radar — until they reached port. They needed to avoid the media circus of television helicopters hounding their ship for the next day on the open sea, broadcasting to network and cable news, like their sister ship experienced with the Duck Dynasty fiasco.

The captain's order to seal Level A, plus the B and C mezzanines, came quickly. The security guard who dropped in on the medical center — who Alan implored to help secure the four deceased patients — was ordered below to assist with the protocol involved in closing off the lowest levels. He left Dr. Hernandez and his remaining nurse to their own devices.

Hernandez, not buying into Alan's urgency in the matter, had not yet even placed the patients into body bags. Instead, the doctor went to his phone, trying to track down Alan and his other nurse down in Level A to advise them they would be on their own with the patients down below. He quickly pulled his remaining nurse in, having her look up different intercom stations in the Level A directory.

Dr. Hernandez pulled a wipe from the counter and mopped his brow below his balding head. He was starting to perspire. He sighed, homesick for Albuquerque, where he left his ex-wife and teenage daughters after the hospital didn't renew his emergency medical group's contract to staff their emergency department.

By the time Hernandez and his nurse noticed the sounds coming from their deceased patients in the treatment bays, two were already upright and a third was waking. The nurse instinctively ran towards them, stopping just feet away from the first two when she changed her mind. She backed up a number of steps, until she bumped into the bed of the waking third patient – the chaplain. The chaplain embraced her, pulling her onto his bed, biting hard into her shoulder. They both fell off the bed onto the floor. The chaplain rose up, still on top of her, vomiting a small quantity of blood and bile onto her upper body, before resuming with her shoulder.

The nurse screamed for Dr. Hernandez's help. Sizing up the situation, he determined he needed a weapon to defend himself. He darted over to the bins next to the fourth treatment bay with the one patient that had not yet awoken – the care support team crew member. He searched the bin and broke open the sanitized seals until he located and removed a scalpel.

Hernandez slowly advanced toward his nurse on the floor. The other two zombie patients had joined the chaplain. All three had descended on the nurse – the chaplain had torn through the upper part of her smock and continued to rip the flesh of her right shoulder with his teeth. The other two – the Fishtoria passenger's wife and the nurse morgue attendant— each clutched a separate thigh, biting and tearing through her pants and into her flesh. His nurse's screams began to weaken.

Dr. Hernandez considered quickly maneuvering around them to the left to make his escape out the back door or simply retreating into the lobby and locking the door. Frozen momentarily, his inner voice told him he must rescue his co-worker. But then, he rationalized, if Alan Gorman was correct and this was some version of Gorman's disease, his nurse was toast already.

Hernandez didn't get the opportunity to decide. The fourth patient – the care support member — arose behind him. She lunged at his upper body, biting him on the left arm as they teetered, off balance, and then fell forward. The medical director, clutching the scalpel in his right hand, landed with the scalpel protruding into his neck, piercing his juggler. He bled out quickly.

Thomas Crapper

Ranie Navarro had been employed with Duchess Cruise Lines for four years, including the past two on the *Pacific Duchess*. A native of the Philippines, he served with its military police for a decade before stepping down to take a position with Soliman Security, in order to be at home more with his two daughters. The time at home deepened the distance with his wife. By the time his daughters were getting ready to leave home, so was he.

The past four years away from the Philippines, away from home, Ranie flourished. For the first time, he loved his job. He continued to support his wife financially, if not emotionally. He enjoyed the other Filipinos on board, even if there was constant turnover in the crew. He could imagine staying on with Duchess until he had to retire from duty.

Ranie set up temporary shop in Level A in the engine control room. For the moment, it was being shared with the 3rd engineer, junior 3rd engineer, 1st engineer, and Conner. One of Ranie's guards stood watch outside. The noise from the main engines dominated the outside area; it would be impossible for the guard to hear any Zs approaching. He would have to rely upon staying alert and scanning his surroundings for movement.

The control room contained two wings of consoles, with four stations each. Every station contained double monitors and a special keyboard and input console. In the center, where the wings met, was a bank of mimic panels with system diagrams, lighted push-buttons, digital display readouts, and a phone. A bank of three-foot-high windows provided views into the online engine room on the forward and portside walls. Gauges, an additional phone, and a door were placed in both other walls.

The 1st engineer received notice of the impending sealing of Level A and managed to sprint from his cabin to the crew stairwell, clearing Level A with less than thirty seconds to spare. The 1st engineer, not fully briefed on their zombie problem, wasn't pleased to be sharing his area with outsiders.

After witnessing the bloody, wild-eyed one-and-a-half armed aide on the video feed, receiving word the four patients upstairs in the medical center had expired, and tabulating a mounting casualty list, Ranie shifted gears. He was a firm ally and believer in whatever advice Conner could dispense.

Ranie stood up to give an overview of the events leading to this point and a current status report to the 1st engineer and others in the room, along via speaker phone to the management team upstairs in the captain's conference room. Ranie cited the terminology that Conner had just shared with him – there were two stage one infected cases under Dr. Gorman's care in the shop at the other end of Level A, with a just discovered third case en route. That left seven missing crew assumed to be stage one. Another stage one case was trapped in a HVAC mechanical room with one of the original stage two cases. The second original stage two case was still wandering Level A undetected, along with a new stage two case that was spotted briefly on video.

Ranie provided an inventory of able-bodied staff remaining in Level A. In addition to those around the control room, Dr. Gorman and a medical center nurse had just contacted Ranie from the shop, he had two guards still outside the HVAC room holding the two infected men inside; two additional guards were transporting the third patient to Dr. Gorman; six additional engine department staff and a new janitor just starting his shift were still performing duties elsewhere on Levels A, B and C, but were being recalled for safety precautions.

Rachel Darst, seated up in the captain's conference room, interrupted Ranie near the end of his briefing, via the speaker phone. "Excuse me, Ranie, but our stated policy as of this time is that it is premature to refer to whatever malady this is as Gorman's disease until such time as we receive a full and final report from our on-board consultants, as well as our on-board medical director, and receive confirmation if appropriate from the CDC after we make port in San Francisco. It is still entirely possible these incidents involve some other yet to be determined or diagnosed cause. We have to stress, to all listening, that we cannot prematurely refer to this as Gorman's disease and cause undue panic among the passengers and crew, who are perfectly safe in the upper levels of the ship. We have exercised an abundance of caution by sealing you off with a small crew to maintain operations and secure the area down there, and we have every confidence we can re-open Level A within a few hours after you've given the all clear that we're secure."

Ranie bit hard into his index finger as he listened, seething. He thanked everyone, promising to provide another update in twenty minutes, before hanging up the speaker phone. The 1st engineer spoke up. "Ranie, let's never mind about what to call this. I'm sold that we don't want our crew on task out there if it isn't safe. So what do we need to do to secure this area?"

Ranie stepped behind Conner, seated in the right wing of consoles, and patted him on the shoulder. "Gentlemen, let's listen to the one man here who spent an entire night fighting off these things. Conner, share your experience with everyone here."

Conner glanced around the control room. Raising his voice, he said, "Look, what you need to know is, once you are bit, there is no hope. You have stage one, and you almost immediately lose your capacity to fight back. Once you die and progress to stage two, all you want to do is bite the uninfected, sometimes eat the uninfected, and nothing can fully stop you or kill you except penetrating your brain with a bullet or a lethal-enough sharp object. Stage two don't attack other infected. If they're agitated and on the prowl, you'll get tired long before they will. On the bright side, stage two cases have no higher brain function, they don't run, and they don't make plans. Sometimes they go into a sleep-like dormant stage for long periods of time. You can distract them. Loud noises will attract them. If there's protective gear available, you might be able to dress yourself to reduce the risk of getting bitten."

The 3rd engineer broke in. "So we have zero guns on this ship. Will Ranie's guard's Tasers stop them?"

Conner shook his head. "I'm told they experimented Tasing test cases with the infected population still at Burning Man. Tasers weren't effective."

"So how do we defend ourselves? Like, what are the rules of engagement here?" The 3rd engineer turned to direct his questions to Ranie. "Can we, as Conner here says, ram a sharp rod through their skull?"

"I don't think we can," Ranie replied, and the 1st engineer nodded in agreement. "You just heard management inform us they aren't willing to classify this as Gorman's disease yet, so we can't proactively injure our co-workers. We just plain can't attack them unless it comes down to self-preservation at that moment in time. Instead, we need to develop a plan to distract, lure, and lead them into an area where we can trap and secure them."

"That all sounds fine until one of the Gormans jump out at you. I'm gonna self-preserve, if you know what I mean," the 3rd engineer continued.

"Whoa," the 1st engineer jumped in. "I think we all need to dial it down. Ranie, I know we just heard upstairs tell us to secure this level, but we need to really think this through. If we even try to do what you're saying – to lure and lead them into a trap – something won't go according to plan. That is a given. The A level wasn't designed for conflict. The next thing you know, we could inflict inadvertent damage, creating any number of scenarios triggering system failures that could result in this ship being dead in the water. We have these levels sealed off. These few Gormans running amuck down here can't cause too much damage unless we let them. We need to go slow, secure the immediate area here, think this through, and stay safe."

Ranie sighed. "I understand your concern. But know this: If these Gormans keep picking us off one by one, they are going to seriously outnumber us. If we can't kill them, they're going to just keep coming and coming and wear us down, as Conner warned. And at some point, you will lose control of operating this vessel down here, and this ship will be dead in the water anyway. So, you're the ranking officer here. We'll secure this area first. But we are going to have to make a plan to lure them elsewhere after that, if we all don't want to be waking up as Gormans by tomorrow morning."

"'Wait a minute," Conner chimed in, glancing around the room. "What are you talking about... 'Gormans'? Does Gormans mean what I think it does?"

Ranie laughed. "That's what people call them in the Philippines after it made the news. That's what everybody here on the ship calls them, when we talk about it. Your American government keeps saying in the news not to call them zombies. You should be happy." Ranie laughed louder. "Unless your name is Alan Gorman."

Conner shook his head. He had not heard the term before, and was certain this would be news – unwelcome news – to Alan. Everyone but Conner in the control room laughed nervously. Ranie proceeded to talk through how they could better secure the area and asked Conner questions on how effective various ideas would work against the zombie Gormans.

A brainstorming session ensued. Ranie lamented that his anti-piracy gear – including throw nets, fire-hose nozzles, and anti-traction mobility denial system — was stored many levels up. However, several protective suits were in storage nearby. Sealing off a number of interior passageways was discussed, once they accounted for other staff. Someone needed to say focused on the rotating Level A video feeds via the console monitors. It was decided that all crew would stay in the control room except when critical maintenance was required, and then, two additional persons would accompany the person performing the task for protection.

Two engine department crew and the janitor, out on assignments in the lower levels, having been recalled via walkie-talkie, arrived within the span of a couple minutes. Three other crew that had checked in during the last roll call did not make it back and were added to the missing list. The last one to arrive, the night shift electrical engineer, sprinted into the room cursing in Spanish. He kneeled over, directly in front of Ranie, to catch his breath.

Ranie cut short their idea session. "What is it? What happened?" he asked the panting engineer.

"Gormans. Two Gormans. I think they were the lady wiper and that kid," the electrical engineer blurted out in a mild accent. He was referring to the two of the missing crew still unaccounted for. "They definitely Gormans now. They didn't see me. They both following something up B corridor back aft."

Ranie ran his fingers through his hair. "They just may be headed toward Alan Gorman or our guards stationed outside the HVAC room with the infected inside. And my two guards are still returning from dropping the third victim with Alan Gorman. So what are they following?" Ranie had the 1st engineer show him how to access the rotating Level A video feeds on his monitor.

The phone in the middle of the console wings rang. The 3rd engineer answered. "Speak of the devil. It's Alan Gorman. He wants to talk to you." The 3rd engineer pointed at Conner.

Conner stood up and took the phone. He exchanged quick hellos with Alan before Alan got straight to the point. "Can you get an outside line on your phones? We can't, and Rachel Darst has our sat phones. It's time to call in some help, I think."

Conner shook his head out of habit while answering. "I checked, and no lines down here have outside access. And just so you don't feel bad about not having our phones, they tell me the sat phones never work down in this level anyway."

"So we have to convince someone up there to make the call?" Alan asked, knowing the answer.

"That's about right," Conner chimed in. "But listen, Alan, watch yourself. Someone here said there's a couple of stage two maybe headed your way, and it sounds like they are new – not the ones being tracked already."

"Why not?" Alan laughed sarcastically. "The more the merrier."

The 3rd engineer, still standing next to Conner, butted in, elbowing Conner. "You going to tell him about Gormans?" he asked Conner, laughing.

"What was that?" Alan responded, overhearing the remark.

Conner decided he might as well let Alan know, if he didn't already. "It seems, Alan, in these parts and elsewhere around the world that heard about Burning Man, they refer to the stage two cases as Gormans."

There was momentary silence – followed by, "Gormans...you don't say. I guess it was a matter of time," Alan said.

"I guess now you know how Thomas Crapper felt," Conner offered light-heartedly.

The remark elicited a short chuckle from Alan. "Actually, Conner, did you know Thomas Crapper didn't invent the flush toilet? He just improved upon it."

That brought a smile to Conner's face. "Well, you didn't invent zombies either—"

Ranie interrupted, shouting to everyone. "Crap! I count four of the things going by the camera. Look, they're chasing my guards. They've abandoned the rolling cart and they've reversed course, sprinting back down the corridor. I think they're heading back to Alan Gorman. Damn, I lost them..." The video feeds were rotating on his screen. The next feed displayed outside the HVAC room holding the original stage two Fishtoria passenger and his Croatian victim. "Where are they? Where did they go? My guards outside the room are gone." Ranie's voice lost its calm demeanor. He grabbed his walkie-talkie, calling out for his men.

"Did you hear that?" Conner asked Alan. "I better let you go. You may be getting company."

"See you," is all Alan said, hanging up.

Conner stepped over to the video feed monitor, while Ranie tried to hail his men on the walkie-talkies.

The phone rang again. The 3rd engineer answered. "Ranie, it's that lady and the captain. They want a status report."

Dr. Hernandez's House Calls

Saturday, 4:08 a.m., October 30th

The medical center slipped through the cracks. Alan Gorman assumed the security guard that arrived at the medical center, just as Alan left, was sticking around to help ensure the deceased patients were locked away before they progressed to stage two. Alan, Ranie Navarro, and everyone else in Level A had become focused on their own plight. The disposition of the expired medical center patients was not brought up.

But the security guard was called away to assist with protocol in sealing Levels A-C, and was assured that the medical center situation was under control. With Ranie down in Level A, the guard was subsequently assigned with occupying Ranie's office and monitoring the video feeds for the Emperor deck and above. While the video feeds monitored the medical center lobby, they didn't extend into the treatment bays.

Rachel Darst phoned the medical center to check in after the lowest levels were sealed but wasn't overly concerned when no one answered. She was told that staff there often didn't pick up the line when they were busy. She quickly became preoccupied in facilitating her boss's communication with the captain and others regarding Level A.

Per protocol, the captain had been informed as soon as the medical center patients passed away. The chief engineer, on behalf of the captain, left a voice mail for the medical center. He informed them that with Level A being sealed, they would need to have the deceased patients transferred to an alternative refrigerated location since the morgue would be unavailable. His message to Dr. Hernandez advised that staff would be arriving shortly to facilitate the transfer to the alternative location. The captain had the chief engineer also mention that just in case of the slim possibility that Alan Gorman was on to something with these cases, they should ensure the patients were secured inside their body bags.

The chief engineer, summoned back to work when sealing Level A was first discussed – with all his on-duty staff now cut-off from him — had another refrigeration/HVAC engineer awakened from his cabin along with a utility man. He charged them with identifying an alternative morgue location and handling transfer of the bodies. It took considerable time to locate a smaller walk-in refrigerated area that was removed from public view, inform the affected department head, and coordinate transfer of food and beverage currently stored there to another area.

It was after four a.m., by the time the two men completed these tasks and made their way to medical center, which wasn't responding to their calls. No one answered the door to the back entrance, so the engineer swiped his badge through the card reader mounted next to the door in the hallway. He pushed the door, only to have it bump into something after opening halfway.

The banging at the door attracted the zombie doctor and his four zombie patients. The zombie nurse slithered behind them on the floor, her upper legs having been consumed by the others before she bled out. The mob grabbed the door as it opened. The five zombies proceeded to overwhelm the engineer and his helper. The door remained ajar, propped open from where the utility man collapsed on the ground after being bitten. Soon the zombie nurse reached the door, crawling on her stomach over the utility man while her companions bit away at him.

The refrigeration/HVAC engineer cried for help as the attack started, drawing two crewmen to respond who had been en route to their shared cabin. As they approached the bloodied engineer and utility man, the zombies rose up, abandoning their current prey, to pursue the new crewmen. The new crewmen reversed course, and ran down the corridor to the elevator banks with the zombies on their tail. Only the crawling zombie nurse remained with the initial victims. Her right bicep and shoulder were shredded – pieces of muscle and veins dangling loosely– causing her to have great difficulty in trying to accomplish much with her prey.

The other five zombies in pursuit, including Dr. Hernandez and his four patients, scattered as new targets presented themselves in the elevator banks and stairwells. Hernandez – his sliced neck displaying the wound now coated with congealed grayish-thick-oily fluid – entered the elevator door as soon as it opened on the Emperor level, revealing its two Romanian cocktail waitresses in their twenties. They were returning to their cabin from partying elsewhere with their bartenders after their lounge closed.

Dr. Hernandez cornered them both, biting one in the face and one in the shoulder. After that, they weakly tried to fight back while the elevator door closed. They remained at the Emperor deck — level four – for almost a minute with the elevator doors closed. Hernandez continued biting and bloodying both women until the elevator was requested two levels higher. There, the door opened to three disbelieving crew who'd been heading back to their cabin from late night kitchen prep.

Dr. Hernandez – his upper body now drenched in blood – turned around, abandoned the two young women, and bounded at the three now-panicking men. He caught one just outside the elevator door, tackling the man. Hernandez crawled over his prey, and sank his teeth into the man's lower back, which had become exposed from his shirt lifting during the fall.

The man was overwhelmed with a flood of horrible sensations. Sharp, intense pain radiated from the bite wound in his back. He felt all at once severely nauseous and dizzy. A rushing sound filled his ears. His vision began to blur. The room began to spin and his thoughts became jumbled. The man's two companions lunged at Dr. Hernandez, trying to save their friend. They managed to dislodge the doctor, but were both bit in the process.

One of the bitten rescuers managed to rise to his feet, despite the pain, nausea and disorientation he was experiencing.

Hernandez advanced as the man backed up toward the stairwell. As the zombie doctor reached out, touching the man for a split second, the man fell backward. The man's back hit the side railing immediately. He then bounced forward, careening freakishly on his head, breaking his neck.

Dr. Hernandez's short attention span didn't stay centered on the man with the broken neck, sprawled on the stairs, soon to expire and join the corps of zombies. Hernandez was now on the march, following a frightened woman who had just arrived on that scene. She sprinted down to the corridor for the portside crew cabins, with the zombie doctor ambling after her.

Reports of the attacks quickly were called up to the security office, where Ranie's guard was stationed. He hadn't caught the initial encounters on the video feeds, as he was focused on a phone call with Ranie down in Level A. The guard asked Ranie to call the bridge to inform the captain of this new development, while he ran downstairs to assist.

Ranie ordered the guard to stand down, reminding him that someone needed to be the eyes and ears, monitoring the video feeds for the rest of the ship. Instead, while Ranie called the bridge, he wanted his man to dispatch every remaining guard to the Emperor through Governors decks. All guards not on shift had been already recalled to duty when Level A was sealed.

The medical center zombies were scattered throughout the crew corridors in these three levels. As a number of crew opened their cabin doors upon hearing a commotion in the hallway, they would find a comrade under attack down the hall – and suffer the same fate if they ran to help. The count of bitten crew lying in the corridors was growing quickly– most too weak, disoriented, and ill to move very far from where they'd fallen.

Six off-duty busboys, hearing a ruckus outside, emerged from adjacent cabins and spied the chaplain zombie down the hallway. The chaplain was pinning a female Casino blackjack dealer, who had just left a romantic tryst with a fellow casino worker, against the wall. The chaplain bit a large chunk out of her left cheek. The half-dozen busboys gang tackled the chaplain, pressing him to the floor with their knees and hands.

Within sixty seconds, the chaplain emerged from the dogpile. Four of the six busboys were bitten, the other two assisting their fallen friends. The chaplain continued down the hall after a new target.

Ranie was losing his temper. He demanded that the captain order an alert for all crew not on shift and for all passengers to remain in the quarters until further notice, and for the Coast Guard to be hailed with a request for assistance.

Through the speakerphone upstairs, Ranie could hear the captain consulting with Rachel Darst before replying that both requests of that nature required Donald Wadsworth's approval under the new protocols. Rachel chimed in that they needed more information before presenting a matter of this magnitude to her boss. It would be best if Ranie's guards could assess the situation in person and then report back. She reiterated they could not take such drastic action based on second- and third-hand reports. They would evaluate the request after the guards could report on a first-hand encounter.

Ranie slammed down the phone. He called his guard in the security office, asking him to stay on the line and give him a real time accounting of what was viewed on the video feeds on the Emperor through Governors decks. Ranie only had access to Level A video feeds.

Ranie's upstairs guards assembled on the Plaza deck stairwell next to the crew elevator, one level above the Governors deck. Ranie issued an order over the walkie-talkie for his nine guards to split into three groups, each taking a level and sticking together – focusing on ordering any crew or passengers in public areas to their quarters, identifying and relaying locations of any victims and attackers, and attempting to avoid any direct single confrontation or provision of assistance, until a rapid overall assessment could be made.

The nine guards descended the stairwell.

Down in Level A, Conner tugged on Ranie's shoulder and pointed at the Level A video feeds. Minutes before, two of Ranie's guards had retreated to join Alan Gorman and his nurse in the shop. The shop was now surrounded by the Level A zombies outside the room, near the distilled water tanks.

Upstairs on the bridge, Rachel Darst ducked out for a moment, while they awaited word from Ranie on his guard's assessment of the lower decks. She knocked on the side door to the captain's guest room, where the charter helicopter pilot was cooling his heels. Upon his answering the door, she inquired how much time they had before he must leave in order for him to make it back to Astoria. She advised him to start making preparations for the two of them to fly well within the hour.

Applause for Conner

Just like that, Conner Zimmerman had time on his hands, while everyone else swarmed around him, engaged with activity. Duchess Cruise Lines did not appear to require any additional assessment pertaining to the presence of Gorman's disease on their ship.

Ranie Navarro was pre-occupied with coaching his guard upstairs, in managing the com, and the video feeds throughout the rest of the ship. The 3rd engineer commandeered Conner's spot, monitoring the Level A video feeds. The zombie threat had migrated forward — to Alan Gorman's end of Level A. Now, the control room crew had the opportunity to settle in and ensure the engine department operations hadn't been compromised.

The 3rd engineer announced that the two Gormans had escaped from the HVAC room. The beam wedged between the pipes, holding the doors shut, eventually were jarred loose by the occupants; the guards were no longer outside to re-secure the beams.

Ranie overheard this and halted his phone conversation with his guard upstairs to correct the engineer — one was a Croatian who had just been bitten and hadn't progressed to stage two. The 3rd engineer rebutted that something must have happened to the poor bastard between then and now, because he was clearly a Gorman, wandering with his friend down the hall.

The 3rd engineer provided play-by-play, reporting the path of the two Gormans – they were making a beeline forward where their compatriots already were milling about. The 3rd engineer also spotted the two missing HVAC room guards. They were both lying still on the floor near the wastewater treatment area – both apparently bitten and partially torn into.

Conner sat at the end of the right wing of consoles, rubbing his forehead. His thoughts became random as he tuned out the conversations surrounding him. He realized he hadn't eaten since a breakfast of one lightly buttered bagel on Friday morning. He instinctively reached for the countless time into his front right pocket for his sat phone, before remembering it resided with Rachel Darst upstairs. Conner bit into his lower lip, wishing he could call Cassie as promised.

Conner scanned the room, noticing how quickly the people — who shortly before were united in their cause for survival – were now absorbed into the details of their daily jobs, like motorists, who having slowly passed a grisly wreck, resumed speed without giving the misfortunate souls in the smashed vehicle another thought.

Conner's thoughts turned to death. He lowered his head, running his fingers down each side of his face, and remembered how much he missed his own parents. They vanished from his life abruptly in a head-on car wreck shortly before his pregnant wife's death. Conner considered his unborn child he would never meet. He reflected on the sea of death he swam through in Burning Man two months prior. Had the Burning Man experience changed him? Cassie had hinted her concerns that it had subdued his spirit.

Conner next dwelled again on how he pissed away a decade and a half after his wife's death, starting in a free fall into alcohol followed by endless years of the bottom that he hit, without rising back up. Conner licked his lips thinking of a drink at that very moment, and with it memories of the sensation in his head growing light and heavy, tingling and untethered all at the same time. The desire never seemed very distant.

Conner closed his eyes and exhaled every cubic inch of air he could muster. He had viewed his life, until recently, as being in three acts: his traditional, small town, happy but uneventful youth; his rapid but short-lived personal and professional ascent after college; and finally his prolonged, numbing, defeated existence without meaning. Was there to be an act four? During the past year, he had grown to believe so, finding sobriety and then finding Cassie. But then he found zombies, and with it, rough, unravelling edges to his optimism, even as his fortunes improved and minor celebrity was bestowed upon him.

Conner could suddenly feel the sway of the ship at sea, even on the bottom deck of a vessel this large. Had they just hit a rougher patch of ocean or had he simply been pre-occupied before? He raised his head to peer out the windows surrounding the control room. He was still a little confused by the layout on Level A. He arrived with an expectation he would be descending into a cavernous, gargantuan machine city. Instead, there it was an endless maze of compartmentalized system components.

Suddenly, Conner stood up with resolve. He had the epiphany, that his past was a different life that he simply possessed a shared memory of, and the course of his new life – with or without Cassie — was completely undetermined. Perhaps he had the zombies to thank for helping wipe the slate clean. It was time to forge ahead and discover that new life – as short as it might be, given the present circumstances.

Conner stepped over to Ranie, who was in a lull in his ongoing conversation with his guard upstairs. "I'm not needed here anymore. I'm going to find my way to Alan. I know they can use my help there."

Ranie let his guard upstairs know he would call him right back. He set the phone down, and clutched his new ally's right arm. "You can't do that. You of all people know how unsafe that is. Besides, I need you as an adviser right here."

Conner smiled for a moment, before leaning in so he could speak a little more softly, keeping the conversation to just the two of them. "I'm sorry. This is something I have to do."

Ranie was having none of it. "I have two good guards protecting them. And no one between here and there made it through the corridors without being bitten. With everyone who is missing, we are way too short staffed to send anyone with you and keep the ship running. Plus, even if you make it there, you'd have to get through that crowd of those things gathering around where your friend is holed up. And as you said, once you're bitten, that's it. We can't help you."

Conner's mind was made up. "Look, two months ago, I was trapped on a roof, surrounded by the infected until Alan Gorman arrived and saved me and my buddy Bruce. I owe him this. They are stuck in there with those three bitten patients who are going to progress to stage two sometime soon. I also have an idea how to lure and trap these zombies, as you were saying we needed to do. I'm going to go. I, of all people, know what I'm getting myself into. But I could use your help, first. I'd like to get one of those protective suits over what I'm wearing and whatever other gear there is to reduce the chance of getting bit. I'd like whatever we have that I can give Alan to restrain his three patients before they turn—whatever sharp tools or objects I could use as weapons. I could sure use a walkie-talkie. And I'd like that old boom box sitting in the back of the room, if it works."

They argued some more. Ranie felt Conner's quest was foolhardy. But eventually, Ranie relented. He knew Alan and his guards could use the help. Perhaps Conner could really lure the infected away. Conner wasn't a Duchess employee and wasn't bound by the same rules as Ranie, so he would have more flexibility in dealing with his attackers. They could send two people partway with him and take care of some nearby issues that needed tending to.

While wireless was too unreliable in Level A, with all the thick compartment walls and machinery, Ranie did have a plug-in com that connected to a walkie-talkie so Conner wouldn't broadcast as much noise as he made his way aft. Ranie drew Conner a quick map of the Level A layout and offered to have someone monitor the video feeds to report what was ahead as he worked his way through the vessel.

Conner soon emerged wearing a helmet, elbow pads, knee pads, and boots, with a protective suit over his street clothes. He inserted a walkie-talkie into his side pocket, with a cord running up to his left ear supplying his com piece. Conner wore a nylon backpack with water bottles to deliver to Alan, packets of nylon ties and duct tape to strap around the infected's wrists or ankles, and the grease-covered, battery operated boom box complete with CD of the Eraserheads. He carried two tools specially selected by the 3rd engineer – a special welding hammer and a fireman's axe. The engineer had spent time sharpening the edge of the axe until he had honed it razor sharp; he warned Conner to be careful handling it. The hammer was the engineer's personal customized welding hammer made of good tool steel, longer and heftier than most. In addition to the usual chipping hammer, the other end was fashioned into a long spike, sharpened to a point.

The group around the console broke out in applause as Conner ventured outside the control room. "See?" Conner yelled underneath the helmet, trying to be heard over the engine noise and testing the com plugged into the walkie-talkie. "They know this is the right thing to do."

"Ha!" Ranie responded through his walkie-talkie. "Don't ever let applause fool you. I'm sure the gladiators in Rome received a nice round of applause right before the lions were released."

Conner headed down the corridor with the guard and junior 3rd engineer. The din of the engine noise enveloped them. They would escort him to the forward end generator compartment. They had been given a laundry list by the 1st engineer of seven items to check on while heading back.

Ranie picked up the phone to contact Alan Gorman before he called his guard upstairs back. Ranie informed Alan that Conner was on the way over, and they would keep Alan apprised of his progress. Alan implored Ranie to talk Conner out of doing so – he would never get through the group of infected milling outside the shop; Alan didn't have an exact head count, but it was around a dozen. Ranie whistled; that number was higher than Navarro had thought. Ranie let Alan know he was preaching to the choir, but Ranie couldn't convince Conner otherwise and Conner had already left.

Conner waved before disappearing around the first corner.

The Zombie Census

Conner slowly wound his way down the corridors. Ranie relayed Alan's zombie head count in the shop, trying to talk Conner into returning. Conner was undeterred. Ranie turned over the walkie-talkie to the 3rd engineer to give Conner status reports to let him know when each video feed ahead looked all-clear. Ranie soon became too pre-occupied in helping direct his guard upstairs as all hell had broken loose above.

Conner progressed to the forward generator room and bid his two companions farewell. Their short journey had been uneventful. Conner rushed past the next two online generators and the HVAC units. The level of mechanical noise emitted in that area was unsettling; he certainly wouldn't hear a zombie lurking around. He had to be careful with his breathing not to steam up his helmet visor.

"Hold there," the 3rd engineer held him advised over the com, as Conner reached the inboard passageway that turned toward the morgue. "Okay Conner, be as silent and still as possible," he continued. Conner stopped in his tracks, listening to the hum of the mechanical rooms now well behind him.

Down that inboard passageway, towards the starboard side, another corridor began near the morgue, bearing aft toward the staff stairwell and elevator. The two fallen security guards had been spotted lying motionless on the floor there some time ago, in a pool of blood.

Now, one of these guards had risen, slowly ambling back towards the morgue. "Conner, I don't want to send you forward if this Gorman could end up flanking you from behind. You can still retreat back to me from where you are now if need be," the 3rd engineer explained.

The new zombie continued back in Conner's direction, step by step, sniffing in the air, touching the railing provided in that corridor with its right hand. Behind it, the second of the two guards rose to its feet. The first guard turned around, hearing the commotion, as the second guard slipped and fell in the surrounding small puddle of blood. The second guard rose again, grunting. Both guard's shirts were torn to shreds, revealing sizeable areas missing flesh and muscle around their arms and ribs.

The first z-guard turned back toward the second. Soon both were facing aft, toward Conner. "Stay put a little longer, Conner. Now you've got two Gormans to deal with, and let's figure out where they're headed, so they don't end up trapping you. In fact, now might be a good time to abort, given these two have been added to the mix," the 3rd engineer suggested.

"I'm still all-in," Conner replied, "and just waiting for the all-clear." He used the time to think through his plan for the boom box. Minutes ticked by.

The 3rd engineer spied the two zombie guards making their way past the sealed off stairwell and elevator area, and through the solid waste and wastewater system corridors. Finally, the z-guards connected to the corridor that would dump them off with the corps of zombies gathered around the shop, next to the distilled water tanks. "Okay Conner, you're good to go, I guess," the 3rd engineer gave Conner the go-ahead to proceed down the parallel portside corridor, with some trepidation in his voice.

Meanwhile, Alan, the two security guards, nurse, and three patients were holed up in the shop which consisted of two large worktables in the middle, with cabinetry containing tools and parts lining the edges. The patients had been placed on the worktables. There was one window near the door, which they took turns peering out to see what the zombies were up to outside. They monitored the conversation between Conner and the 3rd engineer over their walkie-talkies. They now knew two more infected were headed their way.

The dilemma for Alan and his companions was they were caring for three infected patients that would eventually become adversaries. The shop contained plenty of power and plumbing tools and spare parts and included welding equipment, which none of them knew how to operate. They hadn't located any rope, cords, or other useful items to restrain the three patients. Their only hope would be to use one of the power tools or a large pipe wrench to inflict blunt trauma on the patients when they turned, if it came to that.

The 3rd engineer in the control room pressed Alan for an accurate zombie head count outside the shop, but with the one window, it just wasn't possible to produce a number with confidence. The best he could do was to continue to estimate around a dozen.

Conner had an uneventful passage to the fore end of Level A. "Okay, Conner, these two Gorman guards just reached the entryway to the water tanks," the 3rd engineer informed him. Conner was in a parallel corridor following the portside hull. He had had just reached stairwells to the B and C mezzanines that bordered the water distillation area. The tanks occupied all three levels, but catwalks for the B and C levels overlooked the interior of the water tank area on the starboard side.

"You need to find a safe vantage point to get a first-hand fix on what all these snarling Gormans are up to outside the shop, Conner," the 3rd engineer advised.

"I'm all for that. What do you suggest? Conner responded.

"Well, if I were you, and I'm glad right now that I'm not, I would quietly climb up to Level C. You should see an open metal stairwell near the hull coming into view that is out of their line of sight. You just need to avoid being spotted once you reach the catwalk above," he told Conner.

Conner successfully made it up and halfway across the catwalk. Far from the engine, generators, and HVAC, it was quieter in this portion of the ship. Conner had to be careful to step gingerly as he traversed the catwalk – no easy feat in his outfit and weighted down with his gear. Once Conner obtained his optimum viewing position, he checked in with the 3rd engineer.

"Okay, Conner, now let's see if you can do a better job of counting these things than your buddy Doctor Gorman attempted to do from his window. I know it's a challenge if by chance the number gets higher than you can track using your fingers, but we have every faith in you," the 3rd engineer teased.

It wasn't easy counting zombies. They didn't stay still, wandering aimlessly around the outside of the shop and the tanks. They would frequently bump together en masse. Every time Conner was close to feeling he had accounted for all of them, they would gravitate together again, causing him to lose track of one or more. Finally, after more than five minutes up on the Level C catwalk, Conner had a number that he was sticking to – thirteen, including the two latest zombie guards joining the party.

"Thirteen? Are you sure Conner? That's three more than we were hoping for, because it means three of our missing crew are still unaccounted for and could be still loitering somewhere over on our side," the 3rd engineer complained.

After filing his head count, Conner continued across the catwalk in the open area before entering the storage areas and mechanical rooms in that sector of Level C. Conner reached the stairwell on the starboard side, receiving an all-clear to descend aft from the 3rd engineer viewing the video feeds.

Conner had no intention of taking on alone all thirteen of the zombies below. He would proceed into battle accompanied by the Eraserheads and a boom box.

Because We All
Have Things to Do

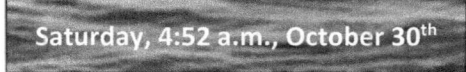
Saturday, 4:52 a.m., October 30th

It all fell apart quickly. The nine security guards – three assigned per floor, on the three decks housing nearly all the crew – did not succeed in their mission. All were bitten before they could complete their sweep of their respective decks in order to report an assessment. Several checked back in via walkie-talkie with the guard in Ranie's office after they were bit. The common denominator from their reports was that anyone out in the hallways was a goner. The only safe persons were those not awake or choosing to stay within their cabin.

The problem relayed to Ranie was that the zombies – or Gormans, as the guards referred to them – could not be stopped. They were slow and stupid, but they were relentless, and there was no weapon the guards could improvise to put them down. They had stabbed a few Gormans, beat them over the head with blunt objects, Tased them, thrown everything within arms-reach at them or in their path, but they just kept coming. Sooner or later, each guard went against orders – trying to help someone in harm's way – and were bit themselves.

Ranie's anti-piracy tools weren't much help. Each team had a throw net and put it to use. But after each group downed a couple of zombies with the net, none were willing to retrieve it to use again – given a couple of snarling, biting Zs were underneath. The fire hose nozzles would only be practical for use on the top deck.

There was one anti traction mobility denial system — which held great promise. The system backpack was strapped on a guard in one of the teams. Encountering several Zs down an interior passageway, the guard laid down the powder and water streams on the carpeted surface in front of him, while the team backed up.

The zombies advanced, slipping and falling hard into each other once they reached the treated surface. The problem came

171

when a passenger heard the commotion from her cabin, stepped outside to see what was happening – then slipped immediately and fell into the middle of the tangle of zombies on the carpet. The Zs bit her – and seeing her cabin door ajar – began crawling into her room while dragging her along.

One of the crew tied to come to her rescue, slipping into the mess as well. Then three Zs came around the corner behind them, cutting off their rear escape route. Trapped, soon the entire team was bitten, including the guard bearing the mobility denial backpack.

In the aftermath, Ranie finally gained an audience again, via speakerphone, with the captain's team on the bridge. He no longer inserted a tone of respect into his voice. He was angry beyond caring about his career prospects.

"Damn it, I can't do it from here. You've restricted our phones to in-house calls only. But I will get one of my remaining staff to make the call if you won't. You have to call in the Coast Guard *now* and coordinate a rescue. You have to send a general announcement on the ship for everyone to stay inside their cabin or seek shelter inside the nearest fully enclosed area until further notice. This needs to happen before people start waking up for breakfast and strolling around the ship. And I hope you've thought about the fact we no longer have the staff available to serve them breakfast anyway. You have to do this now, not five minutes from now. Now!"

"Calm down, Ranie," the captain replied, impatiently. "We are getting this under control. We—"

Ranie interrupted. "Under control? You do not have this under control, you hardly—"

"Mr. Navarro, thank you for reaching out to us, but now it's out of your hands," another voice interrupted. It was Donald Wadsworth, who Rachel Darst had patched into the call. "With your being out of pocket to the rest of the ship, we've discussed this, and relieved you of your other duties so you can focus on securing Level A. The captain has just ordered your guard to vacate your office on the Embarcadero deck, for safety purposes, and join the bridge under the captain's command. I have just ordered that everything be sealed from the Governors deck below. This will contain the crisis that unfortunately spread from the medical center. We have notified some essential personnel still in their crew cabins to report immediately upstairs before the decks are sealed. That is occurring now, and then we'll be secured from the Plaza deck and above within minutes."

"Never mind all that," Ranie implored. "Have you called the Coast Guard?"

"We are considering all options, and we'll circle back to that in time," Rachel Darst responded. "But first we need to evaluate the impact from sealing the decks before we talk about contacting the Coast Guard, and having to slow the boat to coordinate any actions."

The captain interjected, "Right now, most everyone above the Plaza deck is still asleep in their cabins. We are set at maximum speed toward San Francisco, where the safest off-boarding of this many passengers could occur. We stop the ship for any rescue operation, and we can't off-board our passengers fast enough or safely enough. As long as you can keep Level A secure enough to maintain ship operations, with the remaining crew down there, we feel that is our best option for the moment."

"We also have to consider panic among the crew or passengers that would further compromise their safety," Wadsworth added. "Right now, they aren't agitated above the Plaza level. If we broadcast an incoherent report based on the very limited information we have of an incident with too many unknown variables, we will fuel a panic we can't control. We are containing the damage and have to roll with things as they are for now. We'll race to port and make the best of it."

"Damn it, all of you!" Ranie exploded. "Don't you think our crew below Plaza deck is a bit agitated? Don't you know how many of them are injured and infected at this very moment? We are so short staffed with healthy people now down here in Level A, and it is unsafe to leave this control room. Your 1st engineer here tells me he can't guarantee he can keep you going at maximum speed, and we may reach the point where we become dead in the water."

"That's news to me," the chief engineer broke in. "We can have that conversation offline, and we haven't crossed that bridge yet."

"Listen," Ranie shot back. "That's not all. You think for a minute that our crew you are sealing in, who have sat phones, aren't already posting or calling somewhere about what is happening? You think our passengers in the decks above them aren't going to hear about it? You think that one or more of these infected people won't leak up through the stairwells before you can seal off decks below the Plaza level? You can't keep this quiet, if that's what you're trying to do. You need to call the Coast Guard and call them this instant. And you need to give our passengers fair warning to stay inside."

It was quiet on the phone line for a moment. Donald Wadsworth finally spoke. "Mr. Navarro, thank you for your impassioned feedback. It has been duly noted. Now, having said that, we're going to break off this call now, because we all have things to do and we don't want to keep you from focusing on keeping your area secure."

The Energizer Bunny

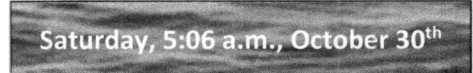

Saturday, 5:06 a.m., October 30th

Conner reached the bottom of the metal stairs without attracting attention from the zombies around the corner that were hanging around the shop and water tanks. He tiptoed back aft down the corridor, to the fire-safety door. Behind that door was the wastewater system.

It was unclear why the zombies had been drawn to this end of the ship. Conner speculated perhaps with their heightened senses they were attracted by the wastewater system, and as well as the potable water, and then were drawn a little further to the shop once they sensed there were people inside.

Conner had the 3rd engineer remind him of the route back to the shop. He checked the fire door, making sure he knew how to properly seal it. Then, without pause, he set the aging, greasy boom box down, set the volume knob to the highest level, pressed play on the CD, and retreated to the fire door, latching it. The four-and-a-half-minute song "Ligaya" track one on the Eraserheads CD blared from the speakers as he retreated through the wastewater area.

Peering out the shop window, Alan Gorman relayed to the 3rd engineer, who in turn informed Conner that his ruse worked. Within two minutes, every zombie exited the area around the shop and water tanks and headed down the corridor that led to the wastewater system and the Eraserheads. Conner traveled as fast as he could, given his outfit and equipment, circling the back way, to the portside access for the shop and water tanks. The 3rd engineer teased him for being outfitted in a helmet, pads, protective suit, and duct tape without ever having encountered a zombie. Just in case, Conner still had the fire ax in his right hand.

Then the music dragged for a second—and stopped.

The zombies were in various locations inside the corridor when the music died. They milled around momentarily until they heard Conner sprinting into the water distillation area.

The straggler zombies, the last to enter the corridor, turned around and reversed course.

Conner traversed around the front two water tanks, the pumps and pipes, until he reached the platform leading to the staircase on the other side where he had snuck down five minutes before. In Conner's dash past the water tanks, he banged against a set of pipes, loosening the connection to his walkie-talkie com. He no longer could hear the 3rd engineer.

The open fire door to the entryway of the corridor was ten feet ahead. Conner had sealed the corridor at the other end; his objective now was to trap them inside by sealing this fire door as well. Several zombies were advancing toward him from just inside the corridor. Conner decided the opportunity to lock up all thirteen zombies was too good to pass up. He pressed ahead.

Conner dropped his fire ax and grabbed onto the fire door latch, pulling mightily to swing it shut. It closed on two different zombies' arms. He leveraged his feet against a nearby vertical pipe, pushing on the door with all his might. The zombie arms were still extended past the door seal – one revealing a hand and wrist, the other an entire forearm. Conner could feel the tug of war with the door start to sway in the zombies' favor. Several more must have reached the door inside and joined the push forward.

The door started to extend outward several more inches. A third zombie arm came into view. Conner knew if the arms grabbed anything for leverage, the door would burst open. He could feel his left foot start to slide. He considered abandoning his cause and sprinting back to the shop. Before he could act on that impulse, he heard sound of feet racing toward him.

Within moments, one of the guards from the shop was by his side, pushing against the door. The guard, a strong but skinny young man from Dehradun, India, dug in with determination. The zombie's forward momentum halted.

"Conner!" a voice called out. It was Alan, unable to keep the guard's pace due to his left leg prosthesis, catching up. "What happened?" Alan asked, panting as he reached them, helping push against the door.

Conner was also huffing and puffing from the exertion against the door. "The boom box went dead. Where's the damn Energizer Bunny when you need him?"

They were at a stalemate at the fire door for the moment. Several more zombies must have reached the door from the other side, joining their surge to counter Conner's additional help. Conner eyed the fire ax at his feet. "Do you two think you can keep your position if I let go for a minute?" Conner gasped out.

"Sure," Alan shouted, thinking Conner was gassed and needed to rest his arms momentarily. Instead, Conner released his hold on the door, reached downward, grabbed the fire ax and shifted position so he stood to the right of Alan and the guard. Conner judged that they were both clear of him by a safe enough distance, so he swung away. His ax became firmly planted into the wrist of one protruding hand. Conner pushed against the door and pulled back on the ax. The hand was still hanging on by a few tendons. The wrist started to withdraw inside the door and the sliced hand dropped to the floor.

Conner next took aim at the forearm still wedged in the door. He sliced heavily into the limb, more than six inches below the wrist. The ax caught in the arm but didn't sever the bone. Conner pulled back hard on the ax. In doing so, he helped the zombies' momentum, aided by the push of additional Zs reaching the door from the other side.

The door swung open far enough for the zombie with the lacerated forearm to begin pushing his entire body through. Conner took another swing. This time he connected with the zombie's skull. The ax stuck into the Zs forehead, causing it to slump downwards. Unfortunately, the zombies behind him had too much forward momentum, even with Conner rejoining the push against the door. The fire door extended further outward.

"Let's bail," Alan commanded. All three stepped back and bolted towards the shop. Conner was last. He could feel zombie arms clinging onto his backpack, pulling him down. Conner fell forward with a zombie on his back. Conner rolled to the side, wishing he still had his fire ax that was imbedded in another zombie's skull. The zombie dived at his legs, biting into his right knee.

"Conner!" Alan shouted, having turned his shoulder to catch sight of his fallen comrade.

Conner winced, and then pulled back his left leg, kicking the zombie several feet away. Conner rolled again and rose to his feet, just ahead of two more zombies on his heels.

The Tiki Lounge

While nearly all passengers are sound asleep after the bars and casinos closed, there are always a few roaming the ship not ready to call it a night until the sun pierces the horizon. The lingerers hang out in various corners, particularly on the Plaza deck and the top level, the Pinnacle deck.

Minutes before the Governors deck was sealed off, Dr. Hernandez and two zombie friends were once again loitering in the elevators — this time in the public elevators going down to the formal dining rooms on the Governors deck. The zombie doctor and his cohorts chased several crew down the starboard corridor from the crew stairwell, passing by the crew cabins. Their prey stopped a number of times along the way to knock on crew cabin doors, hoping someone would answer and provide them refuge.

No one at any of the cabin doors answered their pleas. The constant starting and stopping at the series of cabin doors allowed Dr. Hernandez and friends to keep pace. Soon the panicked crew reached the foyer for the two dining rooms, where they ducked into an empty elevator just stopping at their floor. They anxiously pressed the button for the Plaza level just above. Hernandez reached the elevator just as it was closing. The doors bumped into his outstretched arms, then returned to their original position. Hernandez and friends entered for the quick ride up one floor.

The three zombies all ganged up on one of the crew, biting away. The other two crewmen beat on Hernandez and the other two attackers, trying to pull them away. After the elevator door opened at the Plaza level, while they were yanking on the three Zs, everyone fell in a heap outside the elevator door. The other two crewmen were soon bitten in the tangle of bodies.

A drunken middle-aged lady, clad in peach-colored slacks and a drink-stained white sweatshirt emblazoned with an image of Seattle's Space Needle, stepped up to take the elevator. Witnessing the scrum of bodies, she emitted a barely audible yelp before turning around to escape through the starboard corridor, heading forward. Dr. Hernandez and the other two zombies rose up, abandoning their current prey to stalk the drunken lady. The three bitten crew all managed to crawl from the elevator foyer to the dark, small portside lounge, hoping to use the lounge phone to call for help. They eventually passed out there, after making one call to security that wasn't picked up.

The drunken lady stumbled and fell just outside the largest Plaza level lounge. After two attempts, she managed to get upright and take cover inside the lounge area. By this time, the Hernandez zombies caught up enough to spy where she had taken refuge. They soon entered the lounge – themed as a tiki room.

The zombies began wandering through the darkened tiki lounge, stumbling into chairs as they searched for the Space Needle sweatshirt lady. She was hidden underneath a corner table, having difficulty controlling her breathing. As Hernandez approach her table, she panicked upon seeing his approach. She quickly crawled back out, rose up, only to be tackled by Hernandez into the large planter of fake ferns, tonga statues, and other foliage next to the table.

A young couple, having something more than a necking session in the other side of the closed lounge, ceased their activities, and called out through the darkness, asking what was going on and threatening to call security. The couple each shared a cabin with their respective families, so the closed tiki lounge provided a venue for their shipboard romance.

While the couple hurriedly restored themselves to a fully clothed state, the other two zombies bore down on them. Hearing and seeing their assailants almost upon them, the boyfriend valiantly rose up in front of his young love to protect her. The muscular young man — able to have buckled up his Levis but still shirtless — was able to push the first zombie over a chair, sending it to the floor. He picked up another chair and pushed it into his other attacker, forcing the zombie backwards.

His girlfriend, her blouse only fastened by two buttons – both in the wrong slots – followed right behind the young man while he fought their way out of their corner table. He continued to send the second zombie reeling backwards with the chair. She saw an opening, in between the other chairs, leading toward the dance floor in front of the small stage.

The girlfriend thought she had made her escape when the zombie that had been bowled over on the floor reached out and grabbed her ankle from behind. The zombie's grasp was strong enough to bring the young lady to a halt, before falling into the table in front of her. Seeing his girlfriend in peril, the shirtless young man turned with his chair toward her. He smashed the back of the chair into the floor zombie's head, causing it to lose it grip on his fallen girlfriend.

The boyfriend turned quickly, knowing his other assailant would be right on him. He quickly pushed the zombie square in the chest, driving forward with his legs, until he sent the z toppling over another table. He turned back towards his girlfriend, just as she screamed. The zombie on the floor had managed to crawl forward while she was extricating herself from the table and chairs she had fallen into. She felt an intense sharp pain in her left calf as the zombie sunk its teeth into her.

The boyfriend forcefully kicked the floor zombie in the head, knocking a couple teeth out of the z, separating it from his young love. He rushed forward, quickly pulling her with him, to make their escape from their crazed attackers. While both zombies started crawling over fallen chairs back towards them, the young man pulled his dazed companion toward the wide opening of the tiki lounge into the corridor.

He was almost home free. As he pulled his girlfriend past the long planter full of faux greenery, the blood-drenched zombie Hernandez rose up from on top of the now unconscious drunken woman. Hernandez had chewed off the left side of her face, so that her skull, cheekbone, jawbone, and forehead all protruded through and oozy mush of skin and tissue.

The young man didn't see Hernandez coming until it was too late. Hernandez lunged forward, biting him in the left arm. He lost his grip on his girlfriend. He was still upright, managing to strike a right blow into Hernandez's left temple, separating the two men.

The shirtless young man then dropped to the floor, grabbing his throbbing left arm. Everything grew blurry. The room started spinning. Hernandez and his friends were just getting started.

Blame Management

Rachel Darst had been monitoring social media and was preparing to comment on a handful of posts just made from crew with sat phones on the ship. The captain's general quarters were the only place left on the ship allowed to have an Internet feed.

Rachel suddenly became aware of the mechanical thumping outside the captain's conference room, but assumed it had to be something else. Still, she rose up, abandoning her laptop. Rachel entered the interior glass hallway to the captain's quarters in time to spy the helicopter rising away from the helipad.

She turned and burst through the exit to the outer, lower deck. It was too late. The chopper was already close to a hundred feet above her. Rachel let loose a string of profanities before rifling through her small purse to select her sat phone, packed in between Alan and Conner's.

Rachel stayed outside so that no one else could hear her call to her boss. She ignored the cold and the strong breeze. Donald Wadsworth picked up after the first ring. Rachel spoke loudly, to compensate for the outside noise. "The chopper just up and left without me. There must have been some kind of screw-up. I was right up here, ready to go. How do we get him back here, sir?"

There was silence on the other end.

"Sir, how do we get him back here?"

Finally, he spoke. "Rachel, I am so sorry, but that was my call. We had to send him back now or our costs could double. Now, I know you were saying you were wrapping up on what you could accomplish there on site, but frankly, Rachel, I need your presence there for the duration. You and the captain are the only ones who appreciate our situation, and I need your eyes and ears there onboard to guide us through this."

Rachel mouthed a string a silent profanities. "Sir, don't you think it would be better for me to get back on that chopper, head to San Francisco, and start working proactively on our public response before we make port? This is quickly spinning out of control and we need to shift gears."

"How so? We've just sealed off the lower levels. Now we can start to mop up."

"Sir, everything was sealed off from the Governors deck down, but we're starting to get reports of incidents on the Plaza deck and even higher. I don't think we sealed it in time."

"Is that confirmed?"

"No, which is why I didn't bother to call you immediately. But we need to be prepared for the possibility it will get confirmed very soon. And that's not all. I just spotted several tweets, an Instagram, and a YouTube post from our crew stuck down below, and it's not good."

"What are they saying?"

"It's spotty, just some grainy pics and confusion. But it's going to snowball. You need to know — several minutes ago, I watched a video feed setup in the bridge, scanning the lower decks. There are people strewn all over the hallways. No one is tending to them. I saw two men come out of their crew cabin to see what was going on and they were attacked right on camera. It looks like we're not doing anything about it, and this just isn't going to play well. Criminal charges can come from something like this."

That got Wadsworth's attention. He paused for at least five seconds, before his pronoun use altered. "Look, Rachel. You know I have supported everything you, the captain and corporate medical director have put forth to this point. Even bringing in those supposed expert consultants. You know, everything was under control, until they arrived. And look how long they've had now and still haven't given us a final report to go on. We're going to have to make it clear that a failure on their part deprived us of the actionable intelligence we needed during this critical period of time."

"Sir, I'm not sure that—."

Wadsworth cut her off. "Rachel, with things changing as fast as you say they are, it's clear to me that I've made the right decision keeping you on-site. We have to adjust our crisis management protocols to reflect what's really happening now anyway. You are going to have to officially represent Duchess's corporate interests onboard, as in reality you have been for the past several hours due to my being remote. And the captain is going to need to assume official responsibility in all phases of ship decision-making in this crisis, as in reality he has been performing that role anyway."

"Sir, what are you saying?" Rachel feared she knew exactly what he was saying – or rather, rehearsing.

"Rachel, there is no point in including me from this point forward on the decisions you two have developed. You can just send regular status reports when you have time. I'll concentrate on looping in corporate counsel and document what has transpired up to now."

Rachel stared angrily at the clear, star-filled night sky – soon to surrender itself to daybreak - before responding. Her boss was clearly in full blame management mode, if one read between the corporate lines.

"Sir, with the captain officially bearing full responsibility here, my presence on board may not be as necessary as you might think. I still am of the opinion I can best serve our interests by bringing that helicopter back here and setting up an advance team in San Francisco."

Wadsworth sighed. "Rachel, you of all people should know how bad it will look publicly if our corporate representative bailed on the ship at this point. Think about that. Now, I know you must be beating yourself up that little bits of news is leaking out, because social media is your issue to manage. I'm sorry that you weren't able to control that better. But you need to not let that get you down when we need you at full strength."

"Sir, I did not—"

Wadsworth cut her off again. "And I have to imagine you're second guessing the decision you and the captain put forth to delay any announcement in the middle of the night because of the likely confusion and chaos. It's hard to make those decisions when your consultants and others aren't getting you information in a timely manner. Your security officer managed to trap himself down in the Level A, where he hasn't able to step up to the plate like we needed him to. So, if the captain wants to revisit any of these decisions, based on what you know now, maybe you need to decide to alert the Coast Guard, or probably make some ship-wide announcements or robocalls before people start waking up, or make calls to organize some kind of response team with the crew in the lower decks so they can start securing things on their own and set up some casualty collection points."

Rachel had so many things to say, she didn't know where to start. Finally, she opened with, "Are you saying we should proceed with those items? We should bring in the Coast Guard?"

Wadsworth now wanted desperately to wash his hands of the *Pacific Duchess* and wrap up the call. "I'm just trying to help you think things through for a moment. Those are the captain's options. You talk to him. I don't want to keep you. I'll message him right now to make sure he knows what we've talked about."

They said their goodbyes. Rachel knew her boss was preparing to throw her under the bus, once he worked out the finer points. She fought back tears. She had never cried on the job and wasn't about to do so now.

Rachel stared at her phone, which illuminated the dark, windy outside deck. She briefly considered tossing it into the sea from where she stood. Instead, she placed it into her triangular purse, back in between Alan's and Conner's. She had heard nothing from the two men in some time, and wondered what had become of them, down in Level A.

The Bite in the Knee Cap

Saturday, 5:20 a.m., October 30th

Alan resumed toward the shop door when he saw Conner back on his feet, limping, but slightly outpacing the zombies behind him. The guard inside the shop, another Filipino, yelled for all three to hurry up as he held the door open. The Indian guard stopped at the door to look behind for Alan and Conner. They both came into view, rounding the corner of the last water tank. A trail of lumbering zombies was close behind.

The two guards shifted their position, standing inside the shop while holding the door open. Alan arrived first, Conner two seconds after that. The first zombie made it to the door as it was closing, with the group inside. The z managed to grasp the shop door jamb tightly with its right hand, preventing the door from shutting all the way.

Alan and the Filipino guard shoved against the door as the Indian guard sized up the situation. Inspired by Conner's previous attempts to remove protruding zombie limbs, the Indian guard bolted over to the cabinets that he previously rummaged through, containing the power tools.

Conner's knee buckled. He collapsed to the floor. The nurse quickly emerged from behind the shop tables containing their patients, and came to Conner's aid while eyeing the zombie hand in the door.

Alan and the Filipino guard could feel the door slowly edging in toward them. Other zombies must have joined the push against the door. The zombie hand wiggled further inside. Alan grunted, clenching his jaw while pushing his right shoulder into the door, frustrated that they seemed to be playing out the same scenario they had just faced minutes before at the fire door to the corridor.

The Indian guard returned with a power metal saw. He plugged it in the floor outlet near the door. He advised the other guard and Alan to slide further right. He pressed against the left side of the door with his right knee, raised the saw and

187

activated it, before carefully approaching the zombie hand as to not saw into the wall. The wrist was too embedded in the doorjamb to make a clean cut at that spot. Instead, he sliced just below the knuckles. He accidently nicked the wall with the saw, but managed to sever the upper half of the zombie hand.

The remaining stump, having lost its grip, spurted out thick, grayish oily fluid, while retreating back outside the doorjamb. The shop door slammed shut, with a set of dangling zombie fingers loosely attached to severed bone, lying on the floor below.

Everyone turned their attention to Conner. The nurse was already removing his backpack, while instructing him to shift from his side and lie on his back. Alan kneeled down and inspected Conner's right knee. His duct-taped knee pad had shifted slightly left. A vertical tear was evident on the right side, penetrating through the duct tape, knee pad stretch cloth, protective suit and Conner's jeans. Alan could see evidence of blood, slowly seeping through the torn apparel.

Alan was filled with dread. Now on his knees at eye level with Conner, he examined his patient. Oddly, Conner seemed coherent. "Conner, talk to me. Tell me what you're experiencing right now." The nurse began expanding the tear, shifting the knee pad downwards, until the entire knee was fully exposed. The two guards stood to the side, both leaning over to see exactly what was happening.

Conner winced again with pain, "My knee stings. It really stings. Can you take off my shoes? I just want to feel the ground one more time with my bare feet." Conner loved the freedom of being barefoot. If he was going to die now, it would be with his shoes off. The nurse smiled, and gently removed his sneakers. Conner thought of Cassie. An intense sense of regret jolted him, as he considered that he would never see her again.

Alan stared into Conner's eyes. The amount of dilation wasn't that alarming. Alan shifted to inspect his now exposed knee. The wound was fairly precise. There wasn't evidence of discoloration around the wound or bite-marks. "Conner, talk to me. Are you dizzy? Are you nauseous? Can you keep your eyes focused?"

Conner paused, gulped, looked down at his knee and up at Alan. "Is this what being zombie-bit is supposed to feel like?"

"What do you mean?" Alan asked with apprehension.

Conner exhaled loudly. "I mean, it really hurts where I got bit, but other than that, I'm not feeling that different. And I can see just fine."

"Could he be immune to the biting?" the Indian guard asked, wide-eyed.

The nurse, cleaning the wound had a different take. "I hate to burst your bubbles, here, men, but I don't think anybody got bit. Take a look here, doctor."

The nurse scooted over, handing over her medical kit, allowing Alan to inspect the wound close-up. "Well, I'll be," Alan exclaimed. He dived into the medical kit, and went to work on Conner without warning. Conner shouted out in pain. Moments later, Alan tossed a thin, sharp broken-off metal strip into the near-by trash can. "It appears, Conner, you fell into something that sliced into you when that infected fellow took you down. But fortunately, your little knee pad did the trick. The only thing that penetrated your crazy costume here was that metal shard."

The Indian guard whistled, leaning over to allow Conner to slap him a high five. Conner weakly obliged.

The nurse began laughing.

"What?" Conner and Alan both responded, almost simultaneously.

She picked up Conner's left sneaker and began to force it back onto his foot. "And here I was thinking I was honoring your last wish."

Conner winced and chuckled. "I thought that's exactly what it was."

The nurse laughed harder. "My Dad's favorite movie was on television all the time - *Little Big Man*. He had me watch it with him more than once. And this old Indian, he goes off and lies down to die. Then it starts raining. And he asks Dustin

Hoffman, 'Am I still in this world?' And Dustin Hoffman says 'Yes, Grandfather.' And the old Indian just groans. And that's what you reminded me of just now, when you realized you didn't feel any different, you could see just fine, and you didn't get to die in your bare feet."

The nurse even made Alan Gorman chuckle. "Let's suture you up, Connerman," Alan announced. "I think we're talking just a few stiches here. And while I'm doing so, why don't you tell us what presents you brought us in your backpack here?"

Conner invited the Indian guard to open the backpack. The water bottles were a big hit. The nurse stashed several for their three patients on the worktables, in case any regained consciousness. Alan was more excited with the ties and duct tape.

Alan explained to everyone that the medical center patients expired around four hours after being bitten, but the problem was, there was not a firm fix on what time their current patients were attacked. All three, back when they were more lucid, were able to say that they had been bitten awhile before being discovered, which was two and a half hours ago. Alan added that there were undoubtedly individual variables at play too, but they might be expected to expire anytime between now and an hour and a half later.

All they could do now was wait, while the zombies loitered outside the shop, and bring out the duct tape and ties when the time came.

The Coast Guard

The captain, untethered from Donald Wadsworth, made a general announcement at five forty-five for all passengers and crew to stay inside their cabins until further notice, or to seek the nearest secured indoor area if their cabin wasn't nearby. He advised this measure was due to an ongoing security threat throughout the ship, without providing additional explanation.

Robocalls were made to crew cabins – seeking volunteers to phone into the bridge about assisting with nearby collection points for the injured, and advising all crew to hide from, and not to engage anyone appearing agitated, non-verbal, and with skin discoloration or open wounds.

The captain also contacted the Coast Guard. He was put in touch with the Sector North Bend Air Station. He was evasive, not sharing details about a Gorman's disease epidemic or anything of that nature. Instead, he asked for support in securing the lower decks of the ships due to a series of uncoordinated attacks among the crew that didn't involve use of weapons, but still had inflicted a wide number of injuries and even some fatalities.

The captain acted on Rachel Darst's advice, that the longer they kept a lid on the words 'Gorman's disease,' the better off they were. It was possible the Coast Guard would punt jurisdiction to the CDC if that were the case, and the ship might get quarantined. The captain planned on providing a more enlightened briefing once the Coast Guard arrived.

The captain's hope was to keep pressing south, with the local Coast Guard security support, so that he could clear Oregon and reach the Eleventh Coast Guard District starting at the California border. The chances of being allowed to continue to San Francisco in some fashion would be greatly enhanced once they were in California's district.

The Sector North Bend Air Station dispatched a MH-65D Dolphin helicopter, equipped with two pilots, a flight mechanic, six enforcement personnel, and one rescue swimmer. The rescue swimmer was requested after the muster station incident. The plan was for the helicopter to drop the enforcement personnel, proceed north to rescue the overboard passenger, and then return to the ship.

The muster station incident occurred as a result of the five forty-five general announcement. As predicted, some passengers didn't understand the message – either being disoriented from being woken from their sleep, actually sleeping through all or part of the message, or not understanding English, Spanish or Japanese, the three languages in which the message was provided.

A number of these passengers assumed they needed to report to their muster station due to the emergency, as they were trained to do by staff during mandatory drill that occurred in the opening hours of the cruise. One of the muster stations was in the Duchess Theater, back aft, which occupied three levels, from the Plaza deck up to the Baroness deck. A group of passengers arrived at the Baroness deck level, clad in their lifejackets. They were irritated that staff wasn't present yet.

Upon opening the starboard side theater doors, they were confronted by Dr. Hernandez, causing all to scream and scatter in every direction. The zombie doctor followed a number of them through the Baroness deck starboard double doors, leading to the outside wooden-floor walkway. Hernandez made a beeline for the railing, sensing something primal in the ocean spray misting from below. Directly in his path was a man with a shaved head, who had only partially donned his lifejacket on the way to the muster station. The zombie doctor reached out to grab him, but only managed to snag the life jacket, damaging the built-in beacon during their struggle, while inadvertently slipping into one of the jacket's arm holes, leaving it looping around his grotesque arm. The man with the shaved head sprinted away screaming.

Next in his way was a middle aged woman with a severe limp. He caught up to her and pinned her against the railing. Hernandez attempted to bite away, but kept sinking his teeth into her lifejacket. As she struggled to get free and he wrestled to keep control of her, she went overboard, which was witnessed and reported by several passengers, as they fled.

Dr. Hernandez, still tangled in the life jacket from the man with the shaved head, watched her connect with the waves below. He found the sensation of the ocean spray irresistible. Hernandez hoisted himself over the railing, unintentionally clutching the life jacket, unnoticed after everyone in the vicinity fled the scene.

The logistics took a little time, but eventually the Coast Guard chopper departed from North Bend, not far from Coos Bay, bearing north to intercept the *Pacific Duchess*. They touched down at the ship's helipad at seven twenty. The six maritime enforcement specialists reported directly to the bridge for a briefing. The chopper returned to the air to rescue the overboard woman.

Four minutes into the briefing, the ranking specialist, an MEC – referred to as a chief – cut off the captain's discussion to sum-up what he had taken in so far. "Pardon me, sir, but let me get this straight. What you are describing doesn't come close to matching your distress call. If I didn't know any better, this sounds just like to me that you have an outbreak of – what is it called?– that Gorman's disease onboard here, just like out in Nevada. And we're not equipped for that. You need the CDC out here and some experts. There are like, a bazillion laws protecting those people infected out there in Nevada, from what I understand. I have to radio North Bend about this before we can set a foot off of your bridge, sir."

Rachel Darst, who several of the specialists couldn't take their eyes off of, spoke up. "We are so very sorry for any misunderstandings, but our information here is changing as fast is it can get reported up to the bridge. And how exactly would you try to describe this in a thirty second distress call? But to your point, we did bring in experts as soon as we identified the initial victims and made available every resource; they just failed to get things under control in time."

"Experts? What experts?" the chief asked.

Rachel paused. The captain jumped in. "Our corporate office brought in Dr. Alan Gorman. He came in on a chopper over five hours ago."

"You brought in the man they named the disease after? Why isn't he up here in this briefing?"

Rachel remained quiet. "He and his associate unfortunately were caught down in our Level A when we sealed off the lower decks, and now they're trapped in a room, surrounded by the infected," the captain answered.

"So you can talk to him?" the chief queried.

"Yes, I suppose so. It's been awhile since we spoke, but there is an in-house phone where they're situated."

"Then I want to talk to him. Now, before I check in North Bend. Get him on the phone," the chief insisted.

Rachel spoke up. "Sir, they really don't have access to current information. We haven't found the need to consult with them as of late, and frankly, we're not so sure we would recommend relying on their expertise. Look where that got us."

"They told you everything was alright? They said there was no Gorman's disease on board here?" the chief asked.

Rachel started to answer but the captain broke in. "That's not exactly the case. I think what Ms. Darst is trying to say is—"

The chief list cut him off. "Let's not get into all that. There isn't time. Let's just get him on the phone."

The chief engineer dialed the shop. The Indian security guard picked up the phone, yawning. As tired as he was, he didn't want to go to sleep. An hour before, the three patients expired, after which they were each administered nylon ties to the wrists and ankles, and copious quantities of duct tape to restrain them. They had since reanimated, were highly agitated, and were the subject of constant surveillance from the shop's other occupants.

Alan Gorman came to the phone. They spoke for less than a minute, when the chief decided he'd like to take the call in private. He put Alan on hold, and asked the chief engineer how to make that happen. He was shown to the small conference room. They spoke for several minutes, after which the chief emerged, requesting to have another call made. He spoke next to Ranie Navarro, upon Alan's recommendation.

Ranie had his hands full in the engine control room, taking over monitoring duties previously filled by the junior 3rd engineer. The 1st engineer had been sending staff out periodically on maintenance missions, with one person assigned to perform a task, and two to stand watch. Shortly after six a.m., the junior 3rd engineer, Ranie's security guard, and the janitor were ambushed by the zombie Rodrigo, who had never wandered across the ship toward the water tanks and the shop, with the others. The aftermath of the attack was caught on video. Ranie exited the control room with improvised weapons to subdue Rodrigo.

Ranie never got the chance. He was intercepted by two missing crew zombies that were hanging out near Rodrigo. Ranie barely made it back safely to the control room, with not just the two zombies in tow but also Rodrigo, who rose up to join the pursuit. The outside of the control room was now being loitered by Rodrigo and his two companions.

Over the phone, Ranie provided confirmation of what Alan Gorman had shared with the chief. When the call was concluded, the specialist radioed Sector North Bend. Afterwards, he requested to convene the other specialists in the small conference room. Soon they emerged to address the team in the bridge.

"Alright, here is the deal," the chief began. "This is going to take a minute, so listen up. We have received some conflicting information here, and we don't have time to sort through things very democratically, so we're going to have to just go with how I have read your situation. CDC Atlanta needs to be contacted asap, and Alan Gorman needs to be their point of contact, but he can't access an outside line. One of you up here can call the contact person he provides you and then supply a person to relay the conversation using a second line. For now, you can continue on your present course while the CDC determines if a rescue operation at sea is to be coordinated, or if we are supposed to make port somewhere, or if we are to be quarantined and ride this out. You're going to make a general announcement right now that better informs these people what's going on and why they can't venture outside of their cabin or a safe area, and that you will have no services for them for an extended period of time."

The chief paused to take a breath and continued. "We are going to act solely as responders for your passengers and crew and not directly engage your infected population. We will shepherd any uninfected not in their cabins to the safest possible locations. We will help collect infected stage one victims, as Alan Gorman describes them, to enclosed areas that can be secured. We will abandon any of these duties temporarily to avoid engagement with the stage two infected. We are authorized to take kill shots with the stage two infected, but only when under attack and as the only alternative available in self-defense. I understand you've basically lost your ship security force over the past number of hours, so right now, we are all you've got. But we are all North Bend could spare, and it will be determined if Sector Humboldt Bay will fly in a crew to add to our numbers as we progress. In the meantime, it is possible we may ask you to organize a group of crew volunteers to take direction from us in providing support. They wouldn't be put in harm's way..."

The chief stopped. He was being hailed on the radio. After a brief conversation, he shared the report. "I have good news. The woman who went overboard was recovered. She wasn't bitten, and wasn't injured, but she of course is suffering from hypothermia, although her prognosis is optimistic. It's been decided to take her directly back to emergency facilities on shore instead of the ship, given your circumstances."

Dr. Hernandez drifted into the Pacific Coast shipping lanes, right arm wrapped around through the damaged life jacket. Unseen when he fell, unseen when the Coast Guard chopper was in the vicinity, he licked the salt water as it lapped into his face.

Saturday Morning on the Pacific Duchess

Saturday, 7:28 a.m., October 30th

The biggest problem, the Coast Guard chief and Ranie Navarro agreed, with most any crisis situation, was the people who won't listen. There were plenty of those people on board the *Pacific Duchess*.

On the top, open deck – the Pinnacle deck – there were no signs of danger, so an increasing number of passengers were straggling in, as word spread, to eat in the buffet dining rooms. Enough crew had reported early in the morning for the breakfast shift before the lower decks were sealed and prepared the morning's culinary lineup. They assumed that since they were in an enclosed area, they were following the captain's directives close enough. Trained to be responsive to passengers, they didn't turn away those who straggled in.

The Coast Guard chief insisted that Ranie's authority over *Duchess* security throughout the ship be reinstated by the captain. The chief was given a *Duchess* security walkie-talkie so he could communicate directly with Ranie, Ranie's guard in the bridge, and Alan Gorman's group. The chief tasked the bridge guard to stay glued to the video feeds and continually report over the channel what he was seeing.

As the chief went over final plans with his five personnel, the bridge guard broadcast his first report. The Pinnacle deck was starting to fill with passengers. The chief's plan to go straight to the sealed decks and tackle the worst problems first was derailed. Instead, he decided everyone would go up to the Pinnacle deck and work their way down. His orders were that the group could split into two units of three – one taking the portside and one the starboard side – but they must always stay relatively parallel and be on the same deck.

The group filed up the closest stairs to the Pinnacle deck. They encountered several individual passengers along the way, whom they ordered back to their cabins. The chief shook his head when they arrived on top. The late October early morning air was cold and crisp. Ahead he spied a breakfast line extending out the portside dining room door, into the open area, housing one of the clusters of pools and Jacuzzis. The passengers were dressed in sweatshirts, jeans, pajama pants, robes – looking as if nothing unusual was going down.

He grabbed the walkie-talkie, ordering the bridge guard to make an announcement directed at the Pinnacle people. Moments later, it was broadcast that the Pinnacle deck dining room was closed and all passengers were to immediately return to their cabins. Few passengers left the line, or their dining table, to comply. As the Coast Guard started to advance toward the dining rooms, one of the specialists noticed a couple sleeping in the first of two portside raised Jacuzzis.

Stepping closer to order them to leave, he noticed the Jacuzzi water was discolored. On further inspection, it became clear that one of the couple was a man, clothed with a tattered shirt, and open wound, and gray skin coloration, seated next to a another man in a swimsuit who appeared to be passed out.

The Jacuzzi zombie, eyeing the chief for the first time, rose up and grunted, climbing out but slipping and falling on the wet steps that descended to the ground from the raised Jacuzzi. The zombie rose up, a broken arm – bone protruding through the skin - while the chief stepped back.

"Come on," the chief ordered his men and anyone else out on the open deck, "Let's get inside." Screams and panic erupted on the open deck as the passengers in line, or otherwise outside, mobbed the dining room doors. Despite the heavy jostling, almost everyone made it through the double set of doors before the zombie. An elderly man, behind the guards and the zombies, continued towards the doors after everyone else made it inside.

The guards, stationing themselves in the foyer, noticed too late, the nicely dressed man in his late eighties calling out to everyone. The zombie heard him, turned around and took him to the ground in an instant, sinking its teeth into the man's neck. Two specialists opened the glass doors with weapons raised, seeking to take a kill shot.

The chief had them stand down, reminding them it was too late for the old gentleman. He instructed four specialists to remain guarding the doors, while one accompanied him outside. He stepped out, grabbing the large four-foot-high round brown plastic trash receptacle outside, close to the outer dining room doors. With assistance of the other specialist, they turned the receptacle upside down to empty it, before running up behind the zombie.

The zombie was kneeling down, leaning over, biting away chunks from the elderly man's neck. Before the two men could reach the z with the receptacle, it rose up, apparently catching a whiff of ocean spray in the breeze. The Jacuzzi zombie followed the spray to its source. While the ocean spray misted through the railings below its waist, it was thwarted by the long sheet of Plexiglas fastened above the railing. The zombie pounded on the clear sheet while the two men from the Coast Guard arrived behind it and shoved the trash receptacle all the way over the zombie.

With the chief leading, they pushed the receptacle down and dragged the zombie trapped inside over to the outdoor bar, situated toward the starboard side of the dining room doors. Improvising, the chief inspected the storage cabinets below the bar, which were emptied nightly of the beer ice chests.

He grabbed a push broom, opened one set of the cabinet doors, and knocked the receptacle over so that its top lined up to the opening in the cabinet doors. The grunting zombie crawled out into the three foot high, four feet deep cabinets. The chief closed cabinet doors before running the broom handle through the cabinet handles. He grabbed a sharpie from the bar shelf, scrawling "Zombie Inside" on the largest of the white cabinet doors.

The chief strode back to the Jacuzzi to check out the other man still in the water, while the specialist tended to the fallen elderly man. The middle aged man in the Jacuzzi was slumped over, bearing several large open wounds around his chest and arms. The man's skin was also discolored, the wounds slimy with grayish oily fluid instead of red blood. As the chief stood over him, the zombie's eyes opened. Startled, the chief took a step back. The swimsuit zombie reached out toward him through the Jacuzzi railing. The other specialist jumped up, leaving the already unconscious elderly man and joined the chief behind the railing.

The swimsuit zombie struggled to get out of the Jacuzzi, slipping repeatedly as it grabbed onto the railing. The chief considered Tasing him, but didn't act on the impulse, thinking it would surely electrocute him. He understood his rules of engagement were to only take zombies out if it was in self-defense. He scanned the area, looking for a means to subdue the z before it managed to fully emerge from the Jacuzzi. He spotted the rope netting covering the swimming pool for the night. He instructed the other specialist go to the other end of the pool and help him remove the netting.

The swimsuit zombie finally pulled itself out of the Jacuzzi and crawled down the steps. It made a beeline for the outer railing as the first zombie had done before. It pushed against the Plexiglas, trying to thrust itself into the ocean. Moments later, the two Coast Guard specialists threw the netting over the zombie, and then used the netting to pull the z to the ground.

The chief shook his head, wondering what to do now. Taking the butt end of his rifle, he knocked the zombie in the head, then decided to go ahead and Tase the thing through the netting. He quickly learned that Tasing had little effect on the z. After causing the zombie to pause for a moment, it turned towards the railing, trying to squirm underneath it, oblivious to the net and the two Coast Guard specialists standing over it.

The chief shook his head again in disgust. He considered the amount of time they were wasting on these two Jacuzzi zombies when there was ship full of trouble on every deck they should be sorting through. He instructed the other specialist to keep knocking the zombie down with a rifle butt while he made a quick call. He grabbed his walkie-talkie, repeatedly requesting Alan Gorman to get on the line. Soon, Alan responded.

"Tell me more about these things, Dr. Gorman. Tell me what you would do if you were me, with just six of us to try and restore some order to this entire damn cruise ship."

They spoke for over two minutes while the other specialist continued butting the zombie away from the railing. The chief concluded his conversation, stepped over to his comrade, signaling his subordinate to step back away from the netting. The chief lifted his rifle, aimed it directly at the zombie's forehead, and took the kill shot. He turned to the specialist, "We're going to re-write our rules of engagement. Now let's figure out what to do with this corpse and where to secure the poor old man back there."

The chief scanned around the open deck area. From the portside passageway, winding around the mid-ship enclosed area, which contained the elevators and stair well he and his men had ascended, he spotted a new zombie – a lady in crew attire, shuffling slowly toward them. He signaled his comrade to go dispatch her.

The chief hailed the bridge guard on the walkie-talkie. "You better retract our previous command. Tell these people to stay put if they're already in an enclosed area that can be secured. Even on the top deck there's several of these things wandering loose. We're putting these people in harm's way having them move around."

The six specialists descended level by level, informing every passenger and crew they engaged to secure themselves in the nearest available room with locking doors. But elsewhere around the ship, passengers and crew continued to venture out - sometimes without incident, sometimes with a close call, other times being chased into hiding in a new location, or resulting in lying prone on the floor, disoriented with agonizing pain, blurred vision, severe nausea, significant blood loss, and a body riddled full of open wounds and missing flesh.

The vexing problems for the Coast Guard specialists were what to do with the infected victims that hadn't turned, and the stage two zombies roaming the ship with seeming impunity. Alan Gorman advised the chief that job one needed to be corralling the stage one infecteds into secured rooms before they turned to stage two. Armed with a master key card that could access all cabins provided to him by the bridge guard, they identified unoccupied rooms. They pulled nearby infected inside, then marked the rooms with improvised warning signs. The zombies, they attempted to avoid, but took kill shots when confronted.

The chief soon put a stop to the shootings, with the realization their ammo was not going to get them through much of the day. He instructed his specialists to switch to their knives, which would require piercing a sweet spot in the skull.

They split into their two units, sweeping the long hallways in the Monarch deck — the tenth level — when one of the units was ambushed by three zombies that had been standing in a dormant-like trance behind the gallery of art for sale on display in the wide transition portside corridor. The Zs quietly emerged from behind the tall panels in the middle of the corridor bearing gaudy paintings of dogs playing poker, Elvis, and seascapes with lighthouses. They surprised the specialists, managing to bite one in the arm before the skirmish concluded with all three Zs receiving a blade to the skull.

CDC Atlanta got back to the *Pacific Duchess* captain, who conferenced the Coast Guard chief in via his sat phone. The CDC recommended an at-sea rescue, but only if the ship could be secured enough to allow passengers and crew safe passage to muster stations and lifeboats. The chief, kneeling over his fallen, bitten comrade, next to panel of paintings that toppled during the scuffle, replied that it wasn't an option in the foreseeable future. The CDC next asked about heading to the next feasible port. The captain advised that tenders would be required anywhere before San Francisco, which would require the same process as boarding the lifeboats for an at-sea rescue. CDC was adamant that neither scenario could be attempted unless the ship could be adequately secured.

The *Pacific Duchess* sailed on towards San Francisco, waiting for confirmation that a larger contingent of Coast Guard would be dispatched from Sector Humboldt Bay.

The Coaster

The privately held coaster contracted exclusively with COSCO Canada, a division of one of the world's largest full service intermodal carriers, owned by the People's Republic of China. The coaster was a smaller-sized shallow draft vessel, designed for short sea shipping. The coaster transported cargo that had been carried by one of COSCO Canada's gigantic container liner vessels to Vancouver, and then delivered each shipment nonstop either to Victoria, Seattle, or Oakland.

Included in the coaster's small crew were two communications specialists, arranged by the Chinese Ministry of State Security. Their unofficial job duties were to conduct surveillance up and down the Canadian and U.S. coastline. Their official duties were to blend in with the crew, assist with cargo when in port, and keep their unofficial job duties and the true purpose of their equipment unnoticed by the rank and file crew, and any inspectors in port.

The coaster was bound for Oakland. Before six a.m., one of the communications specialists picked up the distress call to the Coast Guard from the *Pacific Duchess*. Messaging back to the Ministry, he passed along instructions to the coaster's captain to follow the route of the cruise ship, within surveillance range.

The coaster communications specialists, monitoring the Coast Guard helicopter dispatches, had to request the coaster captain to reduce speed at seven twenty-three, so that they didn't end right on top of the Coast Guard rescue operation for the woman who fell overboard. Around seven thirty, after the rescue was completed but before the coaster resumed normal speed, they scanned the area ahead with high-powered binoculars, stumbling upon sighting another person with a life jacket.

The coaster captain wanted to contact the Coast Guard about the second person they had missed. One of the communications specialists, messaging the latest developments, had to relay a different request. After being alerted to the unusual distress call, an analyst back at the Ministry searched for social media chatter relating to the *Pacific Duchess*, and found a handful of very interesting posts. Acting on a hunch, he recommended the coaster rescue the overboard passenger themselves. It was apparent that the *Pacific Duchess* had no idea this second passenger was missing, and the man – if still alive – might have key information to share about what exactly was going on in the cruise ship. The analyst's superior approved the recommendation, passing along the instructions to the coaster.

The coaster brought itself to a halt. The ship carried two small lifeboats, one also designated as the rescue boat. Three crewmen were lowered in the motorized open rescue boat. In minutes, they reached a man, partially wearing a life jacket, bobbing up and down in the cold, open ocean water. The boat approached up close, but stopped short of hauling in the man. Instead, one of the crew radioed back to the captain.

The conversation was in Chinese, but basically passed along that there was no way the crew wanted to pull the partially submerged man barely clinging to a life jacket onto the boat. The man, with an odd grayish skin discoloration was snarling and groaning menacingly, and had a strange discolored open wound on his neck.

The captain, concerned about bringing an apparently diseased and potentially dangerous man onboard his ship, thought that perhaps his initial approach — to defer the rescue to the Coast Guard — should be followed. He again had his request passed along by the communication specialists. The captain was overruled, with the news being relayed to the rescue boat crew.

Circling in close, all three crew cringed. The man didn't seem to want to be rescued. One of the crew commented that he more seemed like a shark than a man, and didn't appear to be bothered by the ocean temperature in the least. They began referring to him as 'shark-man.'

One of the crew came up with the idea to use their telescoping water rescue pole hook, to snag shark-man's arm and life jacket, and then just tow shark-man at a slow speed back to the ship. It took a few minutes to snag the life jacket and position him so that he was facing backwards behind the boat while being towed.

The coaster captain wasn't happy with the crew's plan nor with the time it consumed while they returned to the ship at a crawl. When they finally arrived at the ship's starboard side, they faced a string of Chinese obscenities until the captain took a good look at shark-man. Agreement was reached, that they would pull shark-man up with the ship's cargo boom, hooked around the life jacket and arm. After the man was onboard and restrained if necessary, the rescue crew would secure the rescue boat and climb onboard with the chain ladders extended over the side.

Everything went according to plan, until they tried to restrain shark-man once onboard. As soon as he was on deck, shark-man rose up and fell several times before getting a firm footing and began lunging at the crew. He was eventually restrained and tied down — his mouth sealed shut with duct tape — but not before two crewmen were bit in the process.

Back home, the analyst and his superior at the Ministry took a keen interest in the rescued man. They directed the coaster communications specialists to focus their attention on monitoring their new passenger, and his two victims, and to keep the Ministry apprised as to their status.

Saturday Afternoon on the Pacific Duchess

Saturday, 1:35 p.m., October 30th

By the time the three Sector Humboldt Bay Coast Guard helicopters arrived shortly after one thirty in the afternoon, chaos reigned throughout the *Pacific Duchess*. Despite ongoing announcements for all to stay inside their cabins or a secured area, a continual stream of passengers and crew chose to do otherwise. Their fates were varied.

A number of bitten passengers and crew had been carried – some by the North Bend Coast Guard, some by volunteer crew — to currently unoccupied cabins or to designated secured casualty collection points on the Plaza deck, including the two premium restaurants. Still more were strewn in every corner of the ship, unattended. Some were taken into occupied cabins by good Samaritans. With the passage of time, more and more of these infected had turned stage two.

The chief leading the North Bend Coast Guard unit watched his ranks dwindle down to two, including himself, as they descended deck by deck. Originally hoping to restore order above, then venture into the decks below the Plaza level that housed the crew, he abandoned that objective, instead stalling at the Plaza level. He and his remaining specialist were now providing protection for the remaining *Pacific Duchess* crew in the ship operations center, who were managing the overloaded in-house phone communications system and several other key functions.

The ship announcements never acknowledged Gorman's disease, fearful that would add to the state of onboard panic. Instead, passengers and crew were advised that the ship had been overrun by an undiagnosed, contagious, and potentially lethal condition that caused victims to suffer dementia, bite, and infect others they came into contact with.

Of course, many passengers and crew saw things for what they were – and began referring to Gorman's disease being present on the ship. While public Internet had long been taken down, social media posts by those with satellite phones continued to trickle in. The first media inquiries arrived in Rachel Darst's laptop and sat phone around eleven a.m. She began waging a two-front battle – one with the media, being as evasive as possible, stalling for time and the other with her corporate office, as she read continuing missives from her boss, finding fault with how she, the captain, Alan Gorman, the corporate medical director and basically everyone but himself, had handled the situation during the past eighteen hours.

Perhaps the oddest observation recorded on video in one social media post, was one of the Zs lunging over the railing on the Baroness deck, and disappearing into the ocean. Rumors began passing around the ship that this had occurred several times.

The Coast Guard commanding officer for Sector Humboldt Bay waited hours for CDC Atlanta to provide a pronouncement, confirming if they were facing Gorman's disease or some other malady onboard the *Pacific Duchess*. Gorman's disease required sign-off by the Department of Homeland Security, and triggered a series of laws and regulations governing encounters and treatment of those inflicted.

Adding to the complexities facing the commanding officer were reports from the Sector North Bend's chief specialist on-site, informing his command of each fallen specialist; advising them of their eventual determination to use lethal force on a number of the infected — perhaps violating various Gorman's disease regulations and their own rules of engagement in doing do — and his overall assessment of the gravity of the situation.

The CDC, in assessing an exit strategy for the ship, had come to face the "garbage barge" scenario – the Mobro 4000 barge in 1987, loaded with trash from Islip, New York, that was refused entry to dispose of its contents in South Carolina, Mexico, Belize and elsewhere, before having to return to its point of origin. As the CDC provided full disclosure on the nature of the medical emergency faced by the passengers and crew of the *Pacific Duchess*, California ports from Eureka on down wanted nothing to do with hosting an emergency disembarkation — meaning hours and hours of red tape would have to be waded through if the CDC were to override local and state authority. So the ship pressed on towards San Francisco. A one thirty p.m. rough census pulled together by Ranie Navarro, polling various personnel still available throughout the ship, put the estimated total zombie population at around three hundred, with a similar number infected with stage one.

Three Coast Guard Sector Humboldt Bay MH-65D Dolphin helicopters dropped off seven enforcement specialists per chopper. The contingent of twenty-one proceeded to the bridge for a briefing, as the North Bend squad had done before them. The captain of the *Pacific Duchess* tired of participating in blaming Alan Gorman for their travails. He had personally experienced enough of Donald Wadsworth's barbs during the past several hours, and was cc'd as Wadsworth and Rachel Darst continued to hurl blame at each other. He left it to Rachel Darst to provide her version of corporate spin on the events leading to this point.

The chief Humboldt Bay MECS enforcement specialist listened politely for two minutes, before interjecting and wrapping up their time with the captain and Rachel. He had already been briefed via radio from his North Bend counterpart regarding the onboard politics at play. Like his North Bend comrade, he secured a ship walkie-talkie and introduced himself to Alan Gorman and Ranie Navarro still stuck below.

Alan and Ranie both encouraged the Humboldt Bay chief to be more liberal in use of deadly force on the Zs. Alan reminded him that at Burning Man — before all the laws and regulations protecting those infected with Gorman's disease were put into place — that is exactly what the National Guard, military, and local law enforcement did to bring Black Rock City under control.

The Humboldt Bay chief replied that he was duty bound to avoid lethal force until all other avenues were exhausted. He adopted the same basic plan and path as the North Bend specialists had taken before him, keeping the entire team on the same level, starting at the Pinnacle deck and working their way down.

They quickly encountered their first z in the men's restroom on the Pinnacle deck, located in the stairwell and elevator foyer, separating the forward and aft set of pools and Jacuzzis. After securing the zombie with ties and duct tape, they proceeded to the next level – the Kings deck, with confidence. That confidence was quickly shattered.

Split into four groups of five, with their chief rotating between the groups, they split and swept the long, narrow cabin hallways in four quadrants — portside and starboard, forward and aft. The group sweeping the starboard forward quadrant was confronted by two male zombies, rounding a jog in the hallway, as they progressed forward. The group retreated, as their protocols were to avoid engagement when possible. They soon found the hallway heading aft was occupied by a teenage female zombie advancing toward them. Trapped in between, they elected to subdue all three Zs in hand to hand combat. They successfully tied and gagged the three Zs, but two of the guards incurred deep bites in the process.

The group in the portside aft quadrant was sweeping their hallway without incident, until coming across two stage one infected housekeeping crew victims, barely conscious on the floor, in an open bay interior housekeeping station. Looking for an unoccupied room to store the two victims in, they knocked on a nearby interior room cabin door. No one answered, so they radioed the chief that they needed his cabin access card.

The chief sprinted away from his current group, soon arriving with the key card. After opening the door, the chief stood back to allow the specialists to carry the two bitten staff inside. With the cabin door shut, the last two specialists heard a noise in the bathroom, after setting down the second housekeeper on the queen double bed next to the first victim.

One of the specialists opened the door to the small bathroom, to determine the source of the bumping sounds emanating from within. A middle aged zombie lunged out, grasping onto the specialist who had opened the door, sinking her teeth into his cheek, tearing away skin and flesh until his jawbone was exposed. The second specialist managed to tackle and subdue the z, while separating it from his fellow specialist.

By two fifteen p.m., a third of his contingent already bitten with progress much slower than anticipated, he contacted Alan and Ranie again, asking for advice and ready to re-write the rules.

The Family From Twin Falls

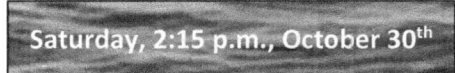
Saturday, 2:15 p.m., October 30th

The husband was beyond aggravated. There was a dearth of information forthcoming from *Duchess* about the events around the ship. Things had been relatively quiet outside their interior cabin on the Queens deck. He, his wife, and only son were having a hard time understanding what all the fuss was about.

They had thoroughly enjoyed their cruise up until this day. They had never been on a cruise before. The husband had been building up his vacation fund with monthly deposits for over two years, so that the three of them could finally take the cruise they had talked about for almost a decade.

The husband had snagged a sale price of $699 each for per adult, and less for their son. They couldn't afford the cruise price for ships sailing earlier in the season. He was a merchandising supervisor at Walmart in Twin Falls, Idaho; his wife was a part-time bookkeeper. They had to pull strings to get their son out of middle school and coordinate their vacations. They drove the entire way to San Francisco to catch the cruise.

During the week, they had eaten in the formal dining room every night. The husband ordered multiple entrees, as did their son. Before dinner, the parents took Jacuzzis with a bucket of beer on ice. After dinner, they attended shows in the Duchess Theater. The son spent the afternoons in the teen camp, making a number of new friends, while the husband and wife attended high tea and bingo. They strolled through the downtowns of each port of call, all being cities they had never traveled to before.

Everything had been perfect. Up until this day.

The husband and wife both were brought up to go by the rules. When they woke up to the warning announcement to stay in their room, they did just that. The ship television channels offered no detailed explanations. Their phone calls to various ship departments went unanswered. Poking his head out the door, the husband conversed with their neighbors who decided to head up to the Pinnacle level for breakfast. The husband and wife agreed they would obey the captain's broadcast request and stay in their room.

Hours passed. The three were getting hungry and cranky. Information from the ship was not forthcoming. Poking their heads into the hallway, things were eerily quiet. There was no sign of their housekeeping staff or any other staff for that matter. A few times they heard bizarre sounds out in the hallways. They would wait for the noise to subside and then poke their head out to find just an empty corridor.

At a quarter after two, the son could no longer take being cooped up. "I am not going to watch another stupid episode of *The Big Bang Theory* on this little television even if you chain me to the bed," he announced to his parents. He had long ago tired of watching the limited number of ship television channels in their small cabin. "I know some of the guys must be up in the teen room. The ship isn't really enforcing a lockdown," he informed them, authoritatively.

"You are not going to the teen room," his father replied, annoyed. The son had been repeatedly threatening to go up to the teen room, only to receive rebukes from both his parents. His mother stepped the small cabin bathroom. His father picked up the phone off the desk in front of the mirror, attempting to call the ship operator. Seizing the opportunity, the son bolted out of the room.

Hearing the door slam, the husband turned around to see his son was gone. He hung up the phone. "Can you believe your son just out and out disobeyed a direct order from us? Now he's going to get us all in heap of trouble. I'm going to go get him, and make him rue the day he started smart-mouthing us like this," the husband called out to his wife, who was still in the bathroom. He grabbed his Duchess key card to the room, and rushed out the door without putting his shoes on.

The husband looked fore and aft in the interior hallway. There was already no sign of his son. He assumed the boy would be headed straight to the teen room. He trotted around the corner to the staircase. He then jogged up one flight of stairs to the Kings deck. At the top of the stairs he turned to the portside corridor, heading aft toward the teen room.

Just down the narrow corridor, he ran into two rifle-bearing Coast Guard specialists. Beyond them were several bloodied, snarling people in torn attire, with their backs to the specialists. Further down the corridor, the husband could see his son, being held protectively by another Coast Guard specialist. There were two more of the creepy, growling, smelly people behind them.

"Go back to your room, sir, right now!" one of the Coast Guard specialists ordered the husband.

"I can't do that," the husband explained. "That's my son down there."

Everything unfolded rapidly after that. The specialist guarding his son produced a pistol, firing a kill shot into the forehead of one of the Zs behind him. He took aim at the other z, missing his mark with the next two shots, hitting it in the jaw and grazing its ear. The z behind him was almost on him. The three zombies in front of him were closing in fast as well.

Two rounds were fired by the specialists next to the husband. All three zombies were struck by the bullets, but the specialists didn't have the angle to connect a fatal shot. The Zs weren't fazed by the bullets that struck them. After that, the specialists had to hold off firing, as the three zombies were getting too close to their companion and the boy.

Sprinting forward, the two specialists drew their knives. Their companion fired a shot into the head of the remaining z in front of him. He let go of the boy. "Run," he commanded the son. The three zombies caught up to both of them, with the two other specialists right on their tail.

"Hey, I'm right here," the husband called out to his son.

Amidst the tangle of specialists and zombies, the boy slipped through unharmed and sprinted to his dad. The Zs were preoccupied with the larger adults.

The husband raced toward his son and embraced him momentarily. "Thank God you're okay," the husband blurted out, his voice quivering. They turned as they heard the anguished scream of the specialist who had been protecting the son. They watched him crumple to the ground after being bitten. Stepping back, the other two specialists began to mow down the three remaining upright Zs with their rifles. The husband and son both recoiled with each shot.

Suddenly, the husband yanked his son's arm and starting sprinting back toward their room. They turned the corner to the stairwell on the Kings deck. The noise of the gunfire had drawn two additional zombies in their direction. The husband literally ran into one of them. It grabbed him and bit him savagely in the right shoulder.

The husband fought through the stabbing pain, clutching onto the other z so it wouldn't lunge at his son. Both zombies proceeded to focus on the husband.

"Hurry," the husband commanded his son. "You sprint to our room and when your mother lets you in, keep the door locked and don't come back for me." Then everything became blurry for the husband.

The son didn't listen to his father. The boy stood ten feet from the carnage, screaming. The two specialists bound around the corner. They positioned themselves behind the two Zs that were tearing into the husband, planting their knives into the backs of each Zs skull. The zombies collapsed on top of the boy's dad.

The son began sobbing. One of the specialists put a hand on the boy's shoulder. "Son, we'll come back and attend to your father. But he's infected now, and you can't stay with him. We'll take you back to your room. But we need to move it."

The boy composed himself enough to guide them back to his room and his mother. He never saw his father again.

Jail Break in Level A

Everyone at their two respective ends of the Level A was exhausted and sleep-deprived, despite both groups rotating to take short naps. Alan Gorman and Ranie Navarro had both grown beyond impatient, and wanted to break out of their confined areas, subdue the zombies that had imprisoned them, and get on with their lives. Conversing back and forth, they agreed upon a plan, with Conner volunteering to reprise the role he assumed that morning when he made his way to Alan's shop.

Time was running out. The 1st engineer was adamant that unless they could soon resume specific maintenance tasks throughout the various systems, the ship sooner or later would become dead in the water. The chief engineer in the bridge agreed the engine speed needed to be reduced fifteen percent, as an interim measure. Engine failure, power outages, loss of running water and sewage management, all were growing possibilities. While there was a redundant engine and generator, switching to those systems required maneuvers outside the control room, which was now surrounded by six zombies – including the zombie Rodrigo his two accomplices, plus the three crew ambushed by Rodrigo and friends at 6 a.m., who had subsequently turned as well.

The other concern was that they were seriously understaffed to maintain operations. Accessing the engine department staff directory, Ranie began phoning applicable crew cabins in the Emperor through Governors decks. He reached a number in their cabins who were willing to risk making their way to Level A, if one of the sealed stairwells could be opened long enough. Ranie asked them to wait for a call when they were ready to put that into motion.

Back in the shop, the three former patients – now zombies – ominously thrashed around, restrained by nylon ties and duct tape. All three had maneuvered off the work tables onto the floor, where they continued to roll around, trying to make contact with the shop's uninfected occupants.

The door exiting the shop continued to be surrounded by the rest of the Level A zombies in their area, preventing Alan's group from disposing of their three Zs outside the shop. Alan was trying to live within the Gorman's disease regulations as best he could, but he was tempted mightily to execute the three with the shop power tools while they had the opportunity.

There was also the rising demand for a ship doctor. Various passengers had called in non-Gorman's disease related medical emergencies from their cabins. Alan dispensed some telemedicine via the house phone, but several of the situations demanded some on-site evaluation. These cases also required access to the medicine and supplies located in the Emperor deck medical center.

The two guards in the shop conducted a more thorough inventory of the cabinets, stumbling upon replacement batteries for the boom box. The plan was hatched, again featuring the grease covered boom box. Conner, feeling healed up enough from his knee wound, donned his makeshift zombie protection gear including pads and helmet, duct taping the tear in his suit near his right knee. He tossed the batteries into his backpack. The shop contained another fire axe, which Conner selected as his weapon of choice, keeping it in his right hand.

The com piece connecting to the walkie-talkie was damaged during the previous scuffle with the zombies outside, and Conner didn't want to risk the noise from the walkie-talkie giving away his location to the Zs. He took his walkie-talkie in the backpack — leaving it off, but available – should an urgent need arise.

A wall ventilation grate had been discovered by the guards near the back corner of the shop, in a gap between the wall cabinetry. Peeking through the thirty-inch square grate, they could see it opened directly outside the shop, behind the first water tank.

Everyone stacked items against the shop window so the zombies couldn't see what was going on inside. The guards unfastened the grate manually with screwdrivers, while Alan and the nurse banged on the door and yelled, as a diversion. Moments later, Conner crawled out, slipping behind the water tank unnoticed. The guards re-attached the grate, then removed the obstructions from the window, so events outside could be monitored and they could distract the zombies. Everyone inside the shop continued to bang on the doors and walls to keep the Zs focus in their direction.

Conner slowly snuck around the back of each water tank. He reached the metal staircase on the starboard side. The corridor was just beyond the staircase, where he had previously chopped off a zombie hand and put down another z with a fire ax to the skull.

Conner couldn't continue down that path, because he had previously sealed the fire door at the other end of that corridor, with the boom box still residing inside that fire door. Conner had to backtrack to open the fire door from other end and get the boom box working again.

The first part of Conner's mission went without a hitch. He climbed stairs to Level C, traversed the catwalk to the portside undetected, then made a turn forward, until he took a staircase back to Level A, well out of view of the zombies and the shop. Conner remembered enough of ship's layout to find his way back to the sealed fire door.

Alan, the two guards, and nurse continued to keep the Zs around the shop occupied. Their plan was to exit, once they saw all the zombies head to the corridor, after Conner-the-Pied-Piper started the music back up at the other end. They planned to follow from a safe distance, before sealing the Zs inside the corridor with the fire door from their end, after the zombies were all the way inside. They would then re-unite with Conner and make their way to toward Ranie and the control room up forward, to take on the handful of Zs at that end of the ship.

That was the plan.

At the other end of that corridor, standing at the edge of the wastewater system area, Conner worked the fire door open.

The boom box lay in front of him on the corridor's walkway. To Conner's surprise, several feet in front of the boom box, remained a groaning z, its left foot and ankle hopelessly wedged and stuck between two vertical pipes running floor to ceiling next to each other.

The zombie lunged toward Conner but fell to the ground, its face less than a foot from the boom box. The thought crossed Conner's mind, that they should have attempted another zombie count out the shop window before he embarked on this quest. Conner shifted the fire ax to his left hand, then edged forward and grabbed the handle of the boom box with his right. He pulled it away from next to the snarling z on the floor, with its left leg slightly lifted up – its left foot still caught between the pipes.

As Conner drew the boom box in, clutching it to his chest, he first noticed a second z still in the dark shadows of the corridor, behind some piping. It was squatting in a trance-like state, ten feet or so beyond the z on the floor. Conner's commotion jarred the zombie out of its stupor. It rose up, snarling, charging directly at him. Conner didn't have time to seal the fire door shut.

The Chicken
and the Pig

Saturday, 3:25 p.m., October 30th

Rachel Darst grimaced and took the phone call from Donald Wadsworth. They hadn't spoken since well before six that morning when he arranged for the chartered helicopter to leave without her. He dispatched a flurry of emails into the late morning, building his documentation of how events had transpired, in concert with the Duchess General Counsel. He then settled into a several hour nap.

Somewhat refreshed, Wadsworth continued focusing on positioning to minimize Duchess' and his own legal exposure, as well as identify steps to protect their assets. Along those lines, Wadsworth realized there was no one on the ship available for him to address the latest item on his checklist. He felt he had no choice but to reach out to Rachel.

"Rachel," he began, "I can only begin to imagine the trauma you and everyone else aboard that ship is going through. And I realize, without the opportunity for us to communicate face-to-face during the course of the morning, we have been forced to electronically exchange conflicting viewpoints on the events that have transpired and how we are to address them going forward. But I just want you, of all people, to be rest assured that despite any healthy disagreements we're experiencing as we struggle to get through this, my professional respect for you – and the company's respect for you - has not wavered. Your commitment to Duchess in our time of need is unquestioned and is immensely appreciated."

Rachel wasn't swayed. She cleared her throat and thanked him in a flat voice.

"I've just spoken to our president, and it is your commitment to Duchess that I'm afraid we must call upon again, Rachel," Wadsworth continued.

There he goes again talking about commitment, she thought. Every time Rachel heard that word, it evoked the memory of her boss, repeating the phrase like a doll with a pull string of an oft-told business fable that he falsely claimed to be his own: "It's like when you ask the chicken and the pig to help out for a breakfast of bacon and eggs. The chicken gets involved and we have a nice omelet. But the pig, he's the one that shows true commitment."

"What's this about?" Rachel cut to the chase.

"Well," Wadsworth paused for a moment, hoping to put things in the best light possible, "this is a very sensitive request. You especially will appreciate the public relations sensitivity here. You see, given the preponderance of day shift staff on your ship is stuck below the Plaza deck, we have no one in accounting. No one. As I'm sure you're aware, during the last full day of the cruise, we finalize and queue credit card processing for the outstanding balances on all passenger accounts for all charges they have rendered while onboard the ship. Now, given the present circumstances, Duchess will suffer a mammoth public relations black eye if passengers go to the press, complaining about our insensitivity and tone-deafness if we subsequently and knowingly charge their credit card after all the suffering and losses that were experienced onboard."

"Okay, I'm following." Rachel filled her boss's void in conversation.

"Alright," he resumed. "The problem is, especially in light of the losses we will undoubtedly incur from this fiasco when everything is tallied up, Duchess has no choice but to charge the balance due on these accounts, if we wish to survive. Like that or not, we have a duty to our shareholders to ensure our survival. Now, I've discussed this with the president, and we've determined our best course of action is to run the credit cards today. That way, passengers won't see charges hit their cards days after they're off the ship, and we can claim the processing was automated before this incident snowballed."

Rachel sighed, not sure how this was going to lead to her demonstrating commitment. "Alright, I understand the logic."

"So Rachel, I've just called in some staff to our business center in Seattle. We can process the charges from here. But there is literally no one in accounting onboard to initiate transmitting the pending transactions to the cloud, so we can access them. Not only that, this is a sensitive request. We don't want our crew spreading word that in the midst of everything going on, that all we were worried about was getting the credit cards processed, so we can't ask anyone on duty on Plaza level to do this for us. It needs to be handled quietly and confidentially."

"So what do you want me to do?" Rachel asked with dread.

Wadsworth exhaled loudly. "Rachel, I need you to know how much I and the president appreciate your taking this on for us. I'll patch you in with someone here who can give you some detailed instructions, but not too complicated I'm told. It shouldn't take but a few minutes to do. The main issue will really be just guiding you to the right workstation and providing you the logon credentials. But as you know, this means you're going to have to leave the captain's offices on the bridge and make your way to accounting on the Plaza level."

"Sir, that's exactly my concern. You know it isn't safe down there. People have died—and worse—down there," Rachel reminded him.

"Rachel, there's no doubt that it takes a special person to go outside their comfort zone to do this for their company. But even though we need some stealth when you do this, we can still have the security guard up on the bridge first monitor the video feeds with you for an optimal moment to go and then accompany you down. We just don't have to tell him the real reason for the trip. You can check in with the two Coast Guard men guarding our operations and communications staff down there. I'm sure you could be successful in talking one of them into escorting you to the workstation while you leave our security guard back with the other one. The Coast Guard won't know that he's taking you to accounting. He can just be led to believe we're backing up critical passenger information to the cloud, which is sort of the truth anyway. Then you can go back up front and have our security guard escort you back up to the bridge. You could be in and out in less than ten minutes."

Rachel was silent, thinking through her options. Should she refuse? Should she propose some alternative? Should she ask to think about it? Instead, she jumped in with a reply. "Okay, I'll do it."

Rachel felt, as the day progressed, it became clearer that Duchess was toast as a company. No company could probably survive the publicity nightmare that would unravel as the details of the day became public. Her boss and the president were only deluding themselves in tending to the weeds of their problems.

But unlike others in the corporate level at Duchess whose careers were vertically locked in the cruise industry, as a relatively young, attractive, ambitious public relations executive, she could horizontally shift outside the industry and beyond whatever taint the word 'Duchess' on a resume might bring. Avoiding burning bridges with the Duchess executives would help with a reference someday. If demonstrating commitment to the company, by putting herself in harm's way for ten minutes, would prevent anything bad being said about her during reference checks for her next position, she was willing to do so.

Rachel was patched into Wadsworth's business office manager. Wadsworth then called the captain and security guard on the bridge, to request that the guard accompany Rachel on an important, unexplained mission.

Everything went uneventfully, zombie-free and according to plan — just as described by Wadsworth — including the Coast Guard chief pulling rank over his companion, so he could accompany the lovely Ms. Darst back to a workstation to transmit information to the cloud. The entire process took less than ten minutes from when they left the bridge, just as advertised by her boss.

The return trip was another matter. Two floors up in the central stairwell on the Baroness deck, Rachel and the guard encountered an elderly lady in matching, white-striped sweat suit and pants stained with blood, sprawled upwards on the staircase before the landing. She had been very recently bitten

— as Rachel and the guard didn't see her when they descended ten minutes before.

"Help me," the elderly lady gasped, weakly raising her hand toward them.

Rachel looked away from her, grasping the guard on his left wrist. "We can't do anything for her," Rachel almost whispered. "We need to keep moving."

The guard stopped in his tracks. "No, we need to take her to a secured room. That's my boss's standing orders."

Rachel tugged harder on his wrist. "Please, you were told to escort me back. You can come back down here afterwards, if you want. But you need to get me back up to the bridge, now."

The guard shook his head. "This will just take a minute. If we leave these people out, not only is it a bad, bad thing to do to another person, but eventually they will just become another one of these snarling Gormans."

Rachel looked at him oddly. She had not heard that term. "Please..." she implored, taking a step upwards.

The guard shook his head. "Won't you help me?"

Rachel let go of his wrist. She shook her head. "I'm sorry. I can't. You go ahead, and I'll head back on my own."

Rachel bolted upwards before the guard had a chance to argue any further. He leaned over, patted the hands of the wheezing, elderly lady, and assured her he would take her someplace safe.

In between each deck, the stairwell took one flight up to a landing, where the next flight reversed direction to the next floor. Rachel made the turn on the landing, just above the fallen woman, and sprinted up the flight towards the next level — the Monarch deck.

At the Monarch level, blocking Rachel's path was an obese younger man in his twenties with an ill-fitting, button-up shirt, sweat pants, and sandals. The left side of his face was mostly devoid of flesh – only grayish tissue and bone remained. He hissed, stepping towards her, down the stairs. Rachel realized he was probably the one who had attacked the elderly woman just below.

Rachel, screaming, turned around, darting past the guard who was kneeling to lift the bitten, elderly woman on the stairs. Rachel froze as she approached the bottom. Another zombie, a teenage girl, had emerged, entering the stairwell. They were trapped.

Rachel retreated again, heading for the guard, positioning herself directly behind him, while he locked arms with the obese man, attempting to keep him out of biting distance. They stood directly over the elderly woman.

Rachel could see the zombie teenager almost upon them, coming up the stairs. While the guard occupied the obese z, tussling with him, she scooted past them with her back against the wall, holding her breath the whole time. She felt a rush of relief and she reached the Monarch deck, made the turn, and started the next flight.

Behind her, she could hear the anguished cries of the guard as the teenage and obese zombies sandwiched him and began tearing away at his arms. The guard collapsed directly on top of the elderly woman, while the zombies lowered down to their knees and continued feeding.

Rachel didn't consider the guard's fate. She was focused on completing this flight of stairs, where she would need to switch over down the portside corridor towards the private area accessing the bridge. Engrossed in thought, considering where she needed to head to next, she ran directly into the embrace of a male zombie still outfitted in a housekeeper's crew uniform.

The zombie housekeeper bear hugged her, before biting deeply into her neck. After taking a second bite, the z dropped her, distracted by a passenger's scream just above them. The woman passenger sprinted back up the stairs with the housekeeper zombie in pursuit.

Rachel collapsed on the staircase. She felt dizzier and more nauseous, than she had ever imagined was possible. Her thoughts started to fragment, while her vision began to blur. An odd thought popped into her head. She no longer had to worry about her job. The unanswered media calls and emails, the social media posts that needed attention, the plan for a prepared statement or press release – they no longer mattered. Despite her intense pain, the thought caused her to weakly smile.

Time passed. She wasn't sure if it was seconds, or minutes, or hours. Her mouth was parched. She felt almost overwhelmed by her thirst. Rachel sensed someone talking. There were two men standing over her.

"Help me," Rachel pleaded, stretching her hand toward them, hoping they could bring her a cup of water.

"Sorry," one of the men answered matter-of-factly, before disappearing with his companion.

The Return of the Eraserheads

Saturday, 3:31 p.m., October 30th

Conner needed to improvise. The zombie that emerged from the shadows of the corridor was quicker than what he was accustomed to. Carrying the boom box with his right hand, the fire ax with his left, Conner wasn't quite as nimble. Breathing underneath his helmet seemed to wind him more than usual. He retreated into the wastewater treatment room. The zombie remained right on his heels.

Ahead, Conner spied stairs to Level B and C mezzanines, overlooking the treatment tanks. He considered ascending the stairs, but was worried the z was too close, and would bite into his legs as he started to climb. There was also the problem that both his hands were occupied.

Instead, Conner ducked under the railing, lining the walkway. Conner headed straight to the first wastewater treatment tank, the z still on his tail. As he reached the tank, he leaned over, setting the boom box down in mid stride. Minus the boom box, he was able to pick up the pace enough to add a few more feet of distance from his pursuer.

Conner circled around the tank, which required hurdling intake pipes. He then made his way to the adjacent tank, rounding it while sidestepping more intake pipes, before retreating to the unit housing the pump, behind the tanks. He repeated this circuitous path until his zombie pursuer fell back enough to be at the opposite end, behind the pump, while he was next to the first tank, near the walkway.

Conner's mind raced between his options. Should he take the fight to the z with his fire ax? Should he race back to the corridor containing the zombie with the foot trapped in the pipes? Should he go climb the nearby stairs? Conner scooped up the boom box with his right hand, deciding on the stairs option.

Conner easily climbed out of harm's way before the zombie reached the staircase. Conner stood at the Level B mezzanine, set down his fire ax and boom box, and watched the z trying desperately to figure out how to snag Conner up above. First, the z stood below, outstretching its arms, grasping into the air with Conner directly in its line of sight. Then the z next tried to climb the stairs. It managed to rise several steps before losing its grip and falling to the floor. It began repeating this process ad infinitum.

Conner sat down, cross-legged on the mezzanine walkway, removed his helmet and backpack, and the eight size C batteries within. He changed out the batteries and tested the CD player one more time. The Eraserheads sprang back to life momentarily before Conner pressed the stop button. Conner remained cross-legged, and began tossing the old C batteries at the Zs forehead. He connected three for eight on his throws.

While pitching batteries to the z, Conner formulated his plan. He concluded that he needed to take this z out of the game. If he continued on his mission with this z on the loose, the problem could literally come back to bite him in the butt. Conner left the boom box on the mezzanine, donned his helmet, and descended the stairs with the fire ax in his right hand.

Conner halted two-thirds down the metal stairs, his feet just out of reach of the zombie's outstretched arms. Holding onto the stairs with his left hand while taking a few more steps downward, he used gravity and his upper position to his advantage and swooped down, solidly connecting the fire ax into the Zs forehead.

Conner hadn't fully learned his lesson from his previous zombie forehead-fire axe-encounter. Once again, the axe didn't separate from the Zs skull after impact. With the axe stuck in the z skull, Conner lost his balance. He tumbled to the ground, side by side with the zombie, both of them on their backs.

Unfortunately, his axe hadn't fully penetrated through the bone. The z was still very much functional. It rolled over, the axe stuck firmly in its forehead, and lunged at Conner. Conner wheezed, the impact on the walkway literally knocking the air out of him. Conner instinctively raised his right leg, attempting to block the zombie's attack or kick it away.

The zombie grabbed Conner's leg in mid-air and sank its teeth into Conner's knee. After bracing for the lethal bite, Conner noticed that a z had once again only connected with his knee pad. The thought flashed in his mind that sooner or later he was going to run out of luck if he kept tempting fate.

Conner recoiled his leg and kicked again, sending the z back toward the stairs. Conner rose to his feet, continuing to gasp from the impact of his fall. The zombie, still sporting the fire axe in its head, regained its balance and went on the attack. The two became entwined back on the walkway, having grabbed each other's wrists, like two high school wrestlers sparring and seeking a takedown.

The zombie reminded Conner of a snapping turtle, as it leaned forward, jaws in motion, biting into thin air while they tangled. Conner decided that he needed to do something bold before the z managed to successfully land a bite somewhere that mattered.

Conner butted his helmet into the Zs jaw to keep it from biting while he reached in with his right arm. Conner grabbed the fire ax and pulled back. Unfortunately, he simply pulled the zombie into him, close enough to be slow dancing. The z snapped its jaws at Conner again, connecting with only his helmet.

Their re-entanglement provided Conner the leverage he needed to pull the fire axe from its forehead. As the zombie started to lower itself, instinctively heading for Conner's lower neck with its jaws, Conner managed to remove the axe, raise it in the air, and strike again. The axe missed its mark, connecting into the Zs right eye, but not sticking.

Conner yanked the axe back. The zombie's head seemed to rotate almost as much as a baseball park giveaway bobble head doll. It leaned forward, attempting to sink its teeth somewhere into Conner's upper body. Conner desperately lowered the axe into its head again, managing to connect into the previous wound.

This time did the trick. The zombie fell backwards, axe-in-skull, no longer in the fight. Conner raced up the stairs to retrieve the grease-covered boom box. Upon his descent, holding the boom box by the handle in his left hand, he reached down with his right and grabbed the axe out of the Zs skull.

Conner hurried back to the fire door beyond the wastewater treatment area. He set the boom box inside the corridor's walkway, close to the snarling z trapped inside, its foot still wedged tightly in between the vertical pipes. He pressed play for the CD. The Eraserheads launched into track one at full blast. Conner stepped back, sealing the fire door, with the boom box and Eraserheads still inside.

The Battle of the Control Room

Conner hopped on the walkie-talkie to let Alan and Ranie know phase one of their plan was good to go. Alan, the nurse, and two guards watched through the shop window while the zombies loitering around their shop door began to peel away, honing in on the source of the loud music blaring from the distance.

After a couple minutes, only one stubborn zombie remained, pressing its face into the window. The z, a one-time member of the engine department crew, didn't seem like much of a threat. Almost all the flesh was missing from one of its arms, and the other was not in much better shape. Certain that the rest of the Zs had left the shop area, the four agreed it was not worth waiting any longer.

The Indian guard opened the door, before quickly stepping back with the others. Within moments, the skeleton-armed zombie lurched inside the shop. Somehow, the presence of an additional z in their midst, agitated the three zombies tied up on the floor even more. Their groaning grew louder, creating a strange resonance through the duct tape binding their mouths.

The Filipino guard stepped forward nervously holding the cordless drill rummaged from the shop cabinets. The Indian guard advanced with him, grabbing the Zs intact left hand, stepping on its left foot, while the Filipino guard activated the drill, raising it to eye level. The Indian guard yanked back on the z, keeping its open mouth away from his Filipino comrade, who pressed the drill with all his might into the zombie's forehead. Seconds later, the z collapsed in a heap, thick greenish-gray oily residue emerged from the drill hole.

Soon, the four had managed to confirm the Zs were inside the portside corridor with the Eraserheads. They sealed the fire door off from their end. Minutes later, they reunited with Conner, still in his zombie-gear outfit, near the morgue. The

Filipino guard traded him weapons – cordless drill for fire axe — as Conner agreed to take the lead, given he was the most protected in their march towards the control room. Conner stopped to also provide the guard with the welding hammer he had been carrying in his backpack, before donning his helmet.

Most of the tools from the shop were of no use as they required plug-in electricity. The Indian guard held a knife found in the shop drawers, Alan clutched a pipe wrench, the nurse had a long, sharpened screwdriver. Alan, in possession of the other walkie-talkie, advised Ranie when they were getting close to the control room, with Rodrigo and five fellow zombies surrounding it.

Once Conner and Alan's group entered the noisy engine room area, all six Zs turned and staggered towards them. The Zs probably didn't hear them but could smell their arrival. Ranie and the 3rd engineer waited a few moments, before opening the door and exiting the control room, each with a crowbar they had rummaged from the area. The two of them were all the 1st engineer was willing to spare from their understaffed operation.

There was considerable trepidation from Ranie, the 3rd engineer, as well as the Filipino and Indian guards. They were about to attack fellow crewmembers they had worked side-by-side with just the day before.

Conner stepped up his pace, hoping to pick off the lead zombie before all the other Zs caught up. The Battle of the Control Room began.

Conner reached the first z, planting the cordless drill into its forehead just as it started grasping him with both arms. The drilling required several seconds to do the trick, during which time, the next zombie caught up and grabbed onto Conner's left arm while Conner drilled the first zombie with his right. "A little help, please," Conner called out.

The Filipino guard stepped forward, striking the fire axe into the second Zs face. The force of the blow knocked the second zombie backwards, sending it to the ground, although it was very much still moving.

Conner removed the drill from the first Zs head then pushed its lifeless body back into the pack of the other Zs. From the rear, Ranie and the 3rd engineer each took a turn swinging their crowbars into the back of the head of the tailing z. The first blow didn't seem to faze it; the second blow knocked it to the floor.

The sudden pile up of three zombies on the floor – one dead, the other two rising back to their knees— caused confusion, as Conner and his group in front, Ranie and the 3rd engineer in the back, tried to track all the movement. The zombie Rodrigo tripped over one of the Zs on its knees, sending Rodrigo to the ground as well, several feet off the walkway.

Rodrigo rolled away from the group, peeling back into the shadows of the piping, where he had spent so much time that day. Rodrigo held on to a vertical pipe, pulling himself up, eyeing the pileup back on the walkway. For the moment, he was unnoticed.

Conner grabbed onto the left arm of the one of the two Zs still standing. Alan caught up with Conner. "Here you go," Alan hollered through the din of the room's machine noise, as he grinned and grasped its right arm. Both steadying the z, Conner pressed the drill into its left temple, quickly rendering it lifeless.

"Doctor Gorman," the nurse standing behind them screamed as she witnessed one of the Zs crawling forward and bite into Alan's leg. Alan, nonplussed, kicked it back a couple of feet, before lowering his pipe wrench into the top of its skull, flattening the z for a moment. The nurse smiled as she noticed Alan's prosthetic lower extremity as his pant leg raised up during the kick.

The Indian guard took on the one remaining standing z, sending his blade into its eye. The zombie staggered, but didn't fall – with the knife still stuck in its eye socket, the eye now squished and dangling out to one side.

Conner turned his attention to the standing one-eyed z and pushed the drill into its temple. After removing the drill, he grabbed onto the knife handle, as the zombie collapsed. He flicked the knife to rid it of the eyeball still attached to the blade, before returning it the guard.

Ranie and the 3rd engineer continued working on the tailing z on the ground, beating its head with the crowbars. "Die you stubborn, stubborn stupid Gorman, die," Ranie hollered as he worked the crowbar until its skull cracked wide upon, and the z ceased to move.

The Filipino guard focused his attention on the remaining crawling z, dropped the fire axe into its head, but mostly missed the mark – just removing its left ear and slicing its shoulder at the base of its neck. "Here," Alan exclaimed, offering his assistance, pressing his prosthetic leg down on the Zs back. Alan immobilized the z while the Filipino guard swapped weapons, shifting the spiked welding hammer to his right hand. The Filipino planted it firmly into the zombie's left temple, rendering it lifeless.

Rodrigo had slowly advanced up the side of the walkway, squeezing through the piping. He emerged next to the nurse, who was standing at the end of the scrum of the battle. Rodrigo bit into her shoulder from behind as he tackled her to the floor.

The others didn't see it happen - they were assessing the pileup of zombie bodies amongst them – except Ranie who caught the attack from the corner of his eye. "No," he cried out, sprinting past all of them with his crowbar.

It happened quickly. Everyone turned as they heard the nurse scream and fall into the walkway. Rodrigo grunted as he bit into her while Ranie moved past them. Ranie reached down to pull Rodrigo off the nurse, then raised his crowbar to strike Rodrigo in the head. Rodrigo, on his knees, lunged forward into Ranie's legs as Ranie struck down, causing him to miss his target.

"I have had enough of you," Ranie yelled at Rodrigo. Ranie, knocked backwards a few steps, recoiled his crowbar, striking Rodrigo across the face, sending the zombie back on top of the nurse. Conner, caught up to them, leaned over Rodrigo – who was already resuming taking another bite into the nurse – and pushed the drill firmly into Rodrigo's left temple, ending it all.

Everyone fell silent. Ranie dropped his crowbar, which clanged onto the walkway. He then collapsed on the walkway, moaning. Conner reached him first, while Alan began to examine the bitten nurse.

"What's wrong?" Conner asked Ranie.

Ranie drew in and let out two measured breaths. He leaned over and lifted his left pant leg. The discolored wound was evident. Deep bite marks had broken the skin in his calf. "It bit me. I could feel it right away. It bit me when it dived at my legs."

Conner set the drill down next to Ranie, and then kneeled down to inspect Ranie's leg.

"It was an honor working with you, today, Conner Zimmerman. I came to realize you are a good man, and had people listened to you and Dr. Gorman from the start, all of this might never have happened," Ranie told him, weakly.

Everyone else had gathered behind Conner. Alan left the nurse, working his way around the huddled group, to inspect Ranie.

"Ranie, I'm so sorry," Conner began, looking away at the zombie carnage behind them. "I just—"

"No!" Alan cried out.

Ranie had picked up the cordless drill and placed it against his temple. He activated it, pressed it in, and slumped over.

The Secretary
Checks In

Saturday, 6:47 p.m., October 30th

By late afternoon, the world found out about the *Pacific Duchess*. Social media began to blow up with various accounts, followed by reports from major news outlets, concerning a Gorman's disease-like outbreak aboard ship.

All that the media had to go on were isolated sat phone posts and calls from frightened crew and passengers, holed up in their cabins. The Coast Guard, CDC and Department of Homeland Security only would respond that an official statement would be forthcoming.

Duchess only issued the following 133-word statement from its Seattle office: "We deeply regret to inform the family and loved ones of the passengers and brave crew of the *Pacific Duchess*, that the ship has experienced a serious outbreak during the last day of their voyage that has affected hundreds onboard, and that there have been fatalities. The Coast Guard has responded to distress calls and has placed personnel onboard the ship. Detailed information, including the nature of the outbreak, is still subject to official confirmation and is not available at this time. Further updates will be coordinated through the respective agencies of the United States government assisting Duchess in handling this crisis. Please direct your thoughts and prayers to those onboard the ship, and know that Duchess Cruise Lines is dedicating every available resource toward the safe return of those onboard the ship."

Once it was clear the media had broken the story, and the corporate statement was released, the captain of the *Pacific Duchess* saw no point to continuing an Internet blackout on the ship. He ordered general Internet service and outside phone service to be restored, within available capacity. With Rachel Darst having disappeared, and Donald Wadsworth tending to other matters, the captain anticipated no immediate pushback for doing so.

The CDC, Coast Guard, and Department of Homeland Security were having great difficulty arriving at an exit strategy for the ship. Resistance from state and local agencies in California to taking in the ship was no longer the primary obstacle. The CDC concern had shifted to preventing the outbreak from reaching land. Isolated reports from the ship of infected passengers diving into the ocean were discomforting.

For now, the path of least resistance was to continue sailing to San Francisco. The CDC was leaning toward quarantining the ship in the San Francisco bay without allowing it to dock, and arranging when feasible for passengers to be tendered to a suitable quarantine location where they could be processed and cleared. Alcatraz was mentioned as a possible location.

Sailing the *Pacific Duchess* the rest of the way to San Francisco had become much more feasible after the Level A was cleared of zombies during the mid-afternoon. A coordinated effort, supported by the remaining Coast Guard personnel, allowed a number of volunteering engine department crew from the Emperor to Governors deck cabins to quickly make their way from the crew stairwell to Level A, which was unsealed long enough for them to descend.

Conner Zimmerman and Alan Gorman crossed the threshold in the other direction, returning to the medical center under Coast Guard protection. The Coast Guard cleared the facility of Zs in advance. Alan agreed to take on any non-Gorman disease emergency patients, when escorted there by the Coast Guard. His first two patients were Coast Guard specialists who needed patching up.

The Coast Guard had an easier time of it once the Department of Homeland Security issued an authorization for them to use deadly force on those with stage two infections at any time deemed necessary – not just in self-defense. Zombies still roamed numerous corridors and public areas of the ship; the Coast Guard wasn't equipped with sufficient ammunition to take them all down and was also concerned with limiting how often they fired their weapons in the midst of thousands of passengers and crew.

But the remaining Coast Guard was able to more adequately protect themselves as they moved about the ship, and passengers and crew became more or less compliant with staying inside their cabins or secured areas. This allowed the Coast Guard to concentrate on relocating infected stage one passengers to enclosed areas and to conduct specific rescue missions.

The biggest problem was the number of cabins that had taken in infected stage one victims, despite a growing number of public announcements not to do so. Sooner or later these bitten people turned – and attacked the others inside the cabin– converting a growing number of cabins to become zombie occupied. The challenge for anyone outside was to determine if behind a given cabin door was an empty room, a room of frightened, uninfected passengers or crew, or a roomful of Zs.

The Secretary of the Department of Homeland Security tracked down Alan in the medical center while Conner was taking a catnap in one of the treatment bay gurneys. Alan took the call from the medical director's desk, wondering what exactly had become of Dr. Hernandez as he picked up the phone.

The director had Alan give him a quick briefing of everything that had transpired aboard ship from Alan's perspective. The secretary proceeded to raise trial balloons for Alan's reaction, of how terrorist activities may have fit into the events of the day.

"Unless your terrorist is a fifty pound lingcod, I'm not seeing it," Alan replied.

"About that lingcod…" The Secretary shifted topics. "What exactly was your thinking in chartering that boat in Astoria today?"

"What?" Alan replied confused. He had forgotten about trying to commission the Fishtoria charter to catch another lingcod like Rodrigo's.

"It's a good thing I actually reviewed my status report from your staff today. Evidently they commissioned a charter for you, and they caught a diseased lingcod per your request. What's that all about anyway?"

"Well, sir, the thought was we could track down an actual reservoir host for what caused our outbreak."

"We've taken possession of it. I just wanted you to know."

"Now just a minute. I thought we agreed earlier that—"

The secretary cut him off. "Alan, this isn't all I called you about. We definitely need to further debrief about how this relates to our Gorman's disease population up at Black Rock City. But there's the other reason I'm calling. There was some kind of a kidnapping there today. We're about to publicly acknowledge it – or may have done so in the last few minutes — hoping the publicity will flush out whoever is behind this. A small truckload of infected population has been taken, along with some of the staff at the research facility. I understand you and your associate were just there last night."

Sunday Morning

It had been a long night. The zombies wandered the corridors, groaned from inside cabins, filled secured larger areas where stage one infected had been gathered throughout the day. Zombie corpses littered spots where the Coast Guard had swept through without the time or opportunity to remove their grayish, hideous bodies. Occasionally, an unnoticed person infected with stage one would expire – reanimating a short time later to join the other Zs wandering the ship. A current rough estimate was that at least seven hundred of the thirty-five hundred-plus passengers and crew — one in five — had become infected.

The most dangerous place onboard all night were the crew levels from the Emperor through the Governors decks. The Coast Guard dared one sweep through the area to escort engine department crew down to Level A, and escorted various other crew that were reporting to work in the higher levels. After that, the zombies had the run of the crew corridors all evening. The remaining crew, still afraid to report to duty, learned to stay inside.

The *Pacific Duchess* eventually was anchored in San Francisco Bay. A swarm of media helicopters buzzed the periphery, working around the Coast Guard helicopter that was enforcing a no-fly-zone over in the immediate area.

Two Coast Guard cutters and an array of smaller Coast Guard vessels surrounded the ship. New Coast Guard enforcement personnel lined the Pinnacle and Baroness decks, shooting on sight any stage two infected approaching the railings, attempting to dive into the bay.

Duchess tenders were lowered one at a time. Several hundred Coast Guard and National Guard troops, clad in full body protective gear swept the ship, one deck at a time, escorting small groups of passengers and crew appearing to be uninfected, to the tender boarding area. From there, they would be taken to Alcatraz – now closed to the public — for quarantine processing.

The ship was fairly void of conversation. An eerie hush had come over the *Pacific Duchess* during the past half-day. The sounds of the surrounding Coast Guard activity, the choppers overhead, the whistle of the ocean breeze were what comprised the ship acoustics, along with the continued drone of zombies moaning from certain sectors of the ship.

Conner and Alan had been escorted to the bridge early in the morning, well before they reached the bay. There they found their sat phones still in Rachel Darst's triangular purse. They had taken no pleasure in learning of Rachel's demise.

Conner had been beside himself since learning the night before of the kidnapping at Burning Man. His calls to Cassie and Bruce continued to go to voice mail. While Alan Gorman spent much of his time giving briefings in conference calls, Conner spent his time phoning anyone he knew that was connected with Black Rock City, trying to glean what had happened. There had been no sighting of Cassie, Bruce, the other co-workers, or the kidnappers.

No one he contacted at Black Rock City could provide much useful information, other than sharing that, before they disappeared, they had picked up a new group of study subjects. The group included a female they had spent considerable time targeting, who seemed to display some unusual characteristics for an infected person. Conner speculated that since Bruce managed to get Cassie inside Black Rock City, and they were targeting someone infected, it had to be Tess.

An occasional burst of gunfire interrupted the quiet on the ship. It had occurred enough times since anchoring that no one looked up any more when it didn't originate in the immediate area. Sometime the shots were to stop a zombie from jumping overboard. Other times, there was still a zombie in a public area, needing to be taken down.

Conner and Alan were waiting outside the captain's conference room for yet another debriefing conference call with various officials. Conner glanced outside the Plexiglas full length window, overlooking the helipad and beyond. The San Francisco Bay looked majestic. It was a gorgeous fall day – not a cloud in the sky – no haze or fog hovering anywhere.

Conner shook his head. "What do you think this all means now?" he asked Alan.

"What?" Alan didn't understand what Conner was driving at.

"It this it? Is what just happened on this ship a one-off occurrence, like Burning Man – or is this someday going to become the new normal?"

Alan shook his head as well. "Did I tell you that the Astoria fishing charter found another fish similar to the first, and DHS has already confiscated it? Or have you seen the news feeds on your phone this morning? DHS is pitching this as terrorism, which Duchess must love, because it might get them off the hook. They're claiming the kidnapping of some of the infected at Burning Man and the outbreak on this ship may be related to the same terrorists. DHS wants to sweep what's really going on under the rug, so they can pitch terrorism, yet they want us to keep digging." Alan paused, looking out into the bay as well.

"But to relate that to your question," Alan continued, "consider we now know there are more fish out there like the one that started this mess. Consider there are now a few of the Burning Man population perhaps released into the wild. And consider that the infected on the ship, instead of having a passion for porta potties and human waste, seem fascinated with oil and grease and are driven to jump into the ocean. What happens to the ones who have managed to escape the ship?"

"So you're saying this may become the new normal." Conner half stated, half asked.

The captain interrupted their conversation as he wandered up to open the conference room door. He was also to be a participant on the call. Smiling with some satisfaction, he informed them that Donald Wadsworth had just been brought in for questioning up in Seattle, accompanied by his lawyer.

Alan's sat phone rang. Conner and Alan looked at each other. It wasn't quite time for the call. It was an executive assistant to the Secretary of the Department of Homeland Security. The conversation lasted less than a minute. Alan turned to the captain and Conner. "There's been a change of plans. Conner and I have been cleared from going through the quarantine process, and a chopper is already en route to pick us up. Evidently, some kind of incident has just erupted at the Oakland Coliseum parking lot. There's a concern about Gorman's disease, and we've been requested asap as on-site advisors."

Conner's mouth opened in disbelief. In his obsession, during the past twelve hours of trying to find out any information about the kidnapping, he had forgotten about the Raider game that he and Cassie were supposed to attend. "Could this get any weirder?" was all Conner could ask.

Alan thought back to when they first boarded the ship, less than thirty-six hours before when their visit was viewed as a simple public relations precaution. He thought about his time in the bowels of the ship, locked in the shop with the infected, that they had to tie up before they turned. He considered his time in the medical center – he wondered what ever became of Dr. Hernandez. "I would say no," Alan replied to Conner, "but aren't you afraid that it could?"

Out in international waters on the Pacific, the Chinese coaster turned from its previously charted course to Oakland. The crew was informed they would be rendezvousing within the day with another ship, which would the pick up the three men sequestered down below — the passenger they had rescued and the two crew who had fallen ill. After that they would return to the Port of Oakland to drop the crew and cargo.

Dr. Hernandez was headed east.

III.
Oakland Coliseum

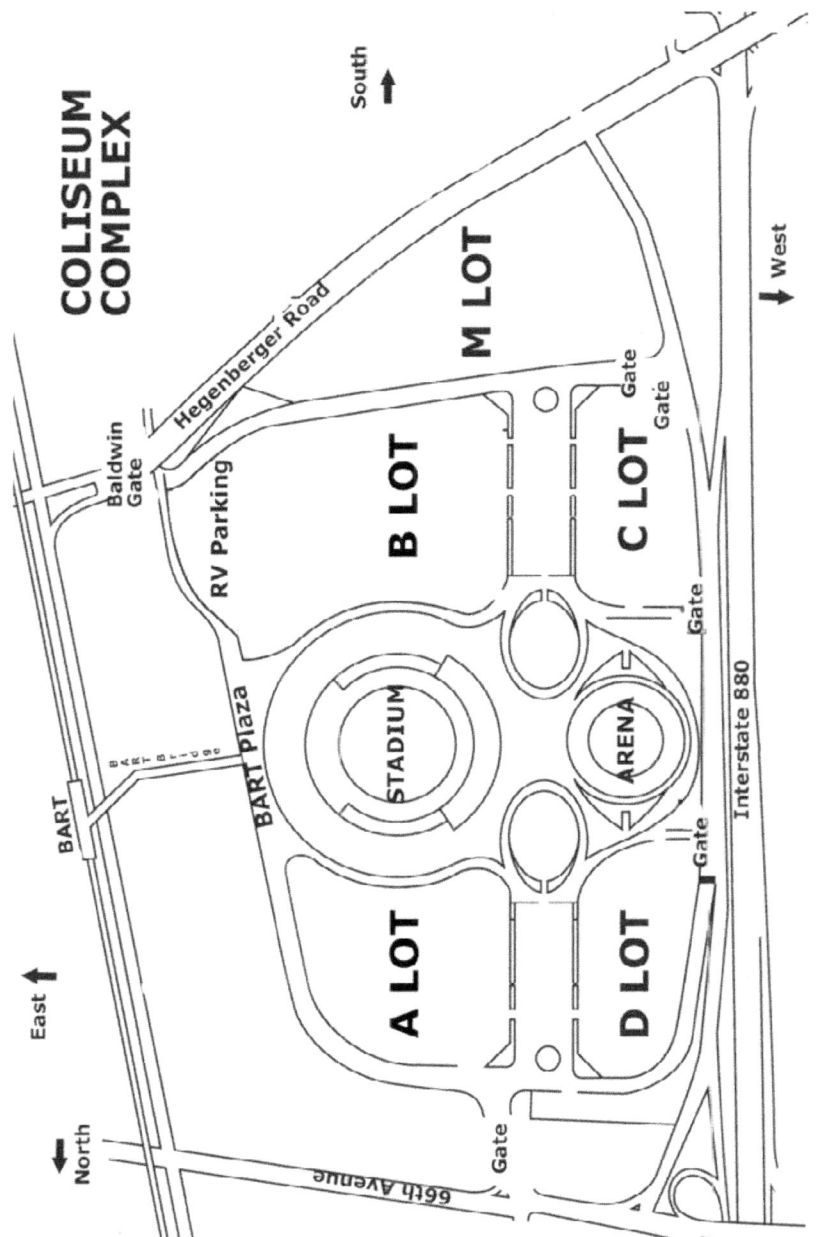

COLISEUM COMPLEX

South

East

North

West

BART

Baldwin Gate

Hegenberger Road

BART Plaza

RV Parking

B LOT

M LOT

STADIUM

A LOT

ARENA

C LOT

D LOT

Gate

Gate

Gate

Gate

Gate

Gate

Interstate 880

66th Avenue

245

Zombie Flatulence

Bruce, Cassie, and Tess had been tossed around their padded cell for four hours in the back of the cargo truck driven by Raymond and Brady.

Tess seemed terrified as the drive progressed. She clung to Cassie, her blue eyes darting around wildly. Each time a turn was made, sliding or throwing them against a wall, Tess would scoot or crawl back over to Cassie once the vehicle straightened out – clutching tightly onto one of Cassie's arms.

Tess's clothes were still covered with white, powdery playa dust from Black Rock City, now smudged all over Cassie's clothes and arms. Even Bruce bore patches of the pervasive white powder from when he bumped into Tess from time to time in their cell.

Before they were thrown into the cargo truck, Bruce had overheard Raymond and Brady discussing driving to Oakland. He could tell they weren't getting there via the freeways by their relative low speed and how bumpy the ride had been. Bruce's bigger concern, until they reached their destination, was if their driver – unbalanced and on meth – would crash the vehicle, particularly if they were spotted by law enforcement and a chase ensued.

Cassie spent her time soothing Tess. Cassie stroked Tess's brunette hair, caked with playa dust and longer than Cassie remembered from two months earlier. Cassie spoke softly to Tess, initially in an adult monologue, but gradually Cassie simplified her comments to those similar one might give a beloved pet or a baby.

Bruce and Cassie engaged in active conversation the first hour – speculating as to their route, their destination, their ultimate fate, their possibilities for escape, and their captor's motives and capabilities. They also speculated about Tess — right in front of her – discussing how much she could understand, her mental and physical state, if it was possible that she might regain what she had lost. But as time wore on, their dialogue wore down.

The first two hours of their ride had been extremely bumpy. The last two hours had been much smoother. Four hours in, Cassie began to cry. It commenced with mild sobbing, but soon escalated. Tess seemed to sense and empathized with Cassie's melancholy. Tess began to pat Cassie's right hand. Tears began to stream from Tess's face as well.

"What is it?" Bruce finally asked.

"My daughter," Cassie blurted out. "I don't think I'm going to get to see my daughter again. There is so much of her life I was counting on sharing." She paused, trying to regain composure. "She's just a teenager, and she needs her mother to be there for her. Her father – my ex — and she just don't seem to connect. She has so much going on right now, you know? I can't believe I was so selfish to leave her this weekend. And she's been so busy lately. I didn't get the chance yesterday to tell her how much I love her."

Bruce scooted over next to Cassie's left side, while Tess snuggled her on her right. "Cassie, we'll get through this," he said with conviction. "We got through this two months ago, and we'll get through this today."

Their cell in the cargo truck fell silent. Cassie leaned her head on Bruce's shoulder. Through the thin, padded cell walls, Cassie and Bruce could hear the periodic moaning of the zombies next door. Then, in an especially quiet moment, they could hear the unmistakable sound of one of the zombies passing gas, loudly and protracted.

"Huh," Bruce spoke up, "I didn't know zombies could fart." Cassie smiled. Then Tess smiled.

Suddenly, the truck slowed down, taking wide turns, and several short stops. Finally it rolled to a complete stop. The engine shut off. Bruce stood, and began stomping and yelling, hoping to attract someone's attention, wherever they were. Cassie joined in. Tess rose up as well, once Cassie did, slowly lifting and lowering her right leg – imitating Cassie – without much effect.

A Hit off the Pipe

Saturday, 5:35 p.m., October 30th

Raymond escaped the Black Rock Desert undetected. He took an indirect route on dirt roads, around Rosebud Peak, eventually connecting with Pioneer and then Lake Road, until hooking up with Interstate 80 at Imlay. Four hours after they departed, they rolled into Reno.

Raymond took the Keystone Avenue exit in Reno, driving several blocks until he found an independent self-service station without much business. Brady got out to pee and top off the gasoline tanks, while he consulted the detailed glove box maps Quon had provided. Raymond remembered that there would be a California Border Protection Station in Truckee on I-80 that they needed to avoid.

Raymond selected a route where they would turn off at Verdi, take Henness Pass Road to Highway 89 North, connecting with Highway 49 at Sierraville. After that, they would follow the winding Highway 49 all the way to Auburn, where they could hook up again with I-80.

Raymond pulled a large baggie from the small daypack he had thrown into the cargo truck at the start of the day. His high was rapidly wearing off. He pulled out the glass bubble pipe, leaned down towards the floorboard, and fired it up, taking several quick hits after it crystalized. Smoke filled the cab momentarily.

Raymond scooted over to the passenger side, rolling down the window before putting his pipe away. He decided Brady should drive – both so he could keep an eye on him, as well as to avoid driving while he experienced the rush of his new high.

Brady ran up to the passenger side, looking agitated. Raymond waved him over to the driver side. Brady hurriedly worked his way around the front of the truck, hopped in, and turned on the ignition. "Damn it Raymond, didn't you hear them making noise in the back of the truck? We're lucky to get out of here before someone else pulls up. No more stops between here and Oakland." Brady looked his companion over,

248

sensing the change in Raymond. "Crap, Raymond. You got high again while I was out there, didn't you?" Brady put the truck into drive, slowly exiting the station.

Raymond didn't answer the question. Instead, he informed Brady of the route they needed to take to avoid the inspection station, speaking so rapidly that Brady had to ask him to say it again more slowly. As they got back on the freeway, Brady turned up the AM radio volume. They had been scanning the news stations for any mention of their heist.

"This is weird, man." Raymond began scratching his face while talking. "You know they had to have discovered what we did hours ago. Why are we not on the news, man?"

"You want us to be on the news?"

"I'm not saying that, Brady. I'm not saying that at all. I just don't get what's going on. Are they like, trying to keep this a secret, so no one knows they screwed up? And what's with this thing on the news about a cruise ship with people attacking each other, like its Gorman's disease? Are they like just planting that story to cover up what we're doing?" Raymond started coughing.

"You heard what they said. Those are just rumors about the ship on Facebook and YouTube and stuff. They're waiting for official statements, and I bet the truth is way different from crap people say on their iPhones. We shouldn't be worried about some stupid ship or what else is on the news. We should be worried about what choppers are overhead on this freeway. I'm sure everybody in law enforcement knows about what we did, so we have to be more careful, that's for sure, Raymond. I'm glad you let me drive." Brady looked Raymond over, who was drumming the seat rapidly with his right hand in concert with his right foot tapping the floorboard.

"Yeah, me too, man. This way I can start better planning how we're going to going to unload these other zombies after we sell the first batch to the Chinese. And I wonder if old Bruce is right, and if they haven't been bitten by the one he was talking about, we can get the mother lode for her, huh?"

Brady didn't argue. He had long ago settled on his play. Quon's Chinese contacts would take Raymond out when they rendezvoused in Oakland. Brady would take his payday from the Chinese and let them decide what to do with all the extra zombies, and Bruce and his friends.

"But don't you worry," Raymond continued. "You and me are partners, man. We will split everything fifty-fifty. All that money, fifty-fifty, even though I'm the man with the plan, here. And that's not all, Brady. I'm going to get us home free. When I'm done figuring out who we're calling on to get these other zombies to market, I'll start working on our exit plan, so we can get out of the country."

Brady eyed Raymond stroking one of his pistols with his left index finger, while he continued tapping furiously with his right hand and foot. "Raymond. Let me ask you something. You told me you'd been daydreaming about your plan for a while. But did you plan on taking Quon out the way you did or did that just happen?"

Raymond laughed. "Yeah, that just happened. Before that, I was just fantasizing. But maybe my subconscious helped direct me to have that zombie land on poor old Quon Li. I don't know, it just went down real fast. And then, I just seized the moment. And it's a damn good thing I did too. If we had stayed back there, we would've been picked up and in jail for sure, right now. That's damn straight."

"So, when you shot the guard back at the research place – Bruce's property – had you ever killed anybody before, Raymond?"

Raymond suddenly gripped his Glock pistol tightly. "Yeah, well, no. Not really. I've messed up some dudes in fights before, but no. No murder and mayhem on my account until today. Once I realized we're beyond the point of no return, I just decided we have to go for it, you know. We don't really have a choice. Kill or be killed, man. And you know what's funny, Brady? I don't feel bad about it, not in the least. Do you?"

Brady stared ahead at the freeway. His thoughts turned to the pistol hidden in his pants that he hoped not to use, and Quon's phone hidden in his pocket that he most certainly hoped to use. "Raymond, I don't know. I wish it could have come down differently, but I suppose it's all too late for that.

"You know what, Brady? Maybe you'd feel better about it if we stopped later on and you took a couple hits off my pipe, man. I'm not big into meth, but I'm telling you, it has saved the day, today."

"We are not stopping, again, Raymond. We've got to stay focused and not call attention to ourselves, you know?"

"Fine," Raymond replied, scratching his face again. "Be that way, but know that I offered."

Brady eyed Raymond and his pistol. He looked back up the road, watching for the Verdi exit.

Auburn

By the time they reached Auburn, at nine twenty p.m., Raymond was falling apart. They became the lead story on KCBS 740's seven o'clock CBS radio national news roundup, and continued to remain the lead, each half hour. Starting with the seven thirty edition, Raymond and Brady were specifically named as persons of interest, based on video surveillance footage from the research facility on Bruce's property.

Beginning with the eight o'clock edition, a Homeland Security spokesperson acknowledged that the *Duchess Cruise* ship off the coast of California did appear to have an outbreak of Gorman's disease. They stated the department was operating under the assumption that the Black Rock desert kidnappings and the *Duchess Cruise* ship incident were potentially related and were a product of a terrorist attack. The DHS spokesperson added that they were investigating if the named persons of interest had ties to ISIS or other terrorist organizations.

Once they heard their names on the radio, Brady and Raymond quickly realized they might be tracked by their cell phone activity. Brady handed Raymond his smartphone; Raymond removed the batteries from Brady's and his own device. Raymond rifled through the cab. He found Bruce's and Cassie's phones and removed their batteries as well.

They began to worry that some of the other staff in the back might have mobile devices on their person. While there was no concern about these being used – everyone but Bruce and Cassie would have long ago turned into a z – their devices still might be trackable once the authorities pieced together who all might have been commandeered in the kidnapping. Raymond was becoming increasingly stressed, thinking about how some of the new zombies in the back might be giving away their location, and there was nothing he could do about it.

Raymond wasn't concerned about how to connect with Quon's people at the Port of Oakland. As he had previously explained to Brady, when Quon had them prepare Quon's cargo truck that morning, Raymond spied a slip of paper with a detailed location at the Port of Oakland, as well as a phone number. Raymond later watched Quon place the slip in the glove box. When they arrived at the cargo truck to transfer the zombies, Raymond retrieved the slip, which was still residing in his pocket.

But while Raymond felt he knew how to find Quon's people, he devolved into a verbal meltdown because he no longer had the means to call Quon's number, written on the slip in his pocket, to confirm when they would be arriving. More importantly, he couldn't call any prospective leads to shop the extra zombies. Brady tried to pacify him for the time being, suggesting they could stop at some point and use a pay phone to make some calls. Raymond wasn't consoled – the numbers he wanted to call were saved in his contacts, and he hadn't bothered to search and write them down before pulling his battery.

The radio news bulletins started running a request to the public asking assistance in spotting the two men, stating their pictures were being run on television and on the DHS website. It was broadcast that the two were likely in vehicle large enough to transport close to twenty hostages, and were most likely heading to a major Northern California urban area, such as San Francisco, Oakland, San Jose, or Sacramento.

Pulling into Auburn on Highway 49, Brady spotted an empty twenty-four-hour self-serve car wash. He convinced Raymond it would be wise to pull in and quickly spray the vehicle to lose the tell-tale desert playa dust accumulated all over the truck from the initial part of their trip.

As Brady hopped out to place coins in the receptacle for their stall, he thought about sprinting away and leaving Raymond with this mess. Brady dismissed the idea and instead, he began digging for quarters in his pocket as he realized that as much as this had blown up, his best hope now was to ask the Chinese to take him with them on the ship.

Brady ignored the muffled cries for help and zombie moaning, emanating from inside the cargo area.

Brady returned to the cab to find Raymond smoking the small remainder of his meth in the pipe. "Damn it, Raymond. Knock this shit off. We have enough going on right now."

Raymond finished, coughing for a moment as the smoke dissipated, while gripping one of his Glocks tightly. "Yeah, I get it. I just need this to cope right now, with the whole damn United States of America coming after us."

"We need to re-route getting to Oakland," Brady stated authoritatively. As he unraveled, Raymond slowly was ceding control of their mission. "We need to stay off the interstate, and even these state highways as much as we can so we can avoid highway patrol."

"Yeah, that makes sense, Brady." Raymond set both pistols in between his lap. He began rubbing the top of his right hand with his left. He didn't stop.

"So, Raymond, I need you to help navigate. Quon left us these detailed maps." Brady pulled out the pages focusing between Auburn and Manteca. "We're going to take Auburn Folsom Road, which becomes Folsom Boulevard, up to County Road E2, and take that south." Brady continued to guide Raymond through the route that would take them to Stockton, before cutting over through the delta towards the bay area. Brady unfortunately could tell not all of it was sinking in with Raymond, whose mind was now spinning into other realms.

Brady shook his head, started up the cargo truck and pressed on. He had no choice.

Arriving in Oakland

The backroads took time to traverse. After finally reaching French Camp, Brady drove down farming roads into the delta, until he hooked up with County Road J4. He next cut across Marsh Creek Road past Mount Diablo to Concord, Ygnacio Valley Road through Walnut Creek, and eventually St. Mary's Road in Moraga. They continued to Pinehurst Road and descended down Shepard Canyon Road through the Oakland hills.

It was two in the morning. Brady was struggling to fight off sleep. Raymond had long ago become useless – fidgeting, talking nonsense, becoming lucid only when another news bulletin mentioned their names.

Brady was overwhelmed at the concept of being the subject of a national manhunt. Saturday had been intended to go down very differently. Quon should have been the one driving the cargo truck, and Brady should have received his payout half a day ago, with no one the wiser.

Brady related the escalating hole that Raymond had primarily dug them in to be like many of his trout fishing escapades on the East Walker River, far south of Reno on Highway 395. After seeing others land some massive fish, he would grow determined to stay until he caught one. After a few hours of being blanked, he would be tempted to leave, but felt he had to stay, now that he'd invested three or so hours into it. Half a day later, he felt he had no choice but to remain, with the same rationale, but lamented he had not left after the first hour when not so much was at stake.

Brady now wished he had bolted right when everything went south – after Quon was bit. Even if he was caught after that, he would not have been around when anyone was killed or transported across state lines. But now, he was invested.

Brady cringed from embarrassment, knowing his mother in Reno would have seen his name in the news on television Saturday evening or that his born-again sister – his only sibling – in Pocatello, Idaho, would only now learn just how far Brady had sunk. He seethed at his own shortcomings for causing either of them the pain he must now be inflicting. Brady wasn't worried about how his friends would view his notoriety. His friends were really just acquaintances.

Brady weighed the severity of all his past transgressions against those incurred during the past day. In his youth he bought and sold marijuana. Once he stole a car and drove it around for three days before abandoning it across the street from the Carson City police station on a dare. He shoplifted regularly in his twenties. More recently he had fenced stolen goods through Craigslist on occasion. He had been in his share of bar room brawls. How did that kind of record evolve into the events of the past day? Brady had no answers.

But the more pressing question on Brady's mind was where were they going to cool their heels until he heard from Quon's contacts via Quon's special phone hidden in his pocket? The two a.m. CBS national radio news broadcast on KCBS, informed listeners that Raymond and Brady were still at large – possibly in the bay area — and the Duchess cruise ship suffering the Gorman's disease outbreak was possibly headed for the San Francisco Bay for quarantine.

Brady came to the Warren freeway – State Highway 13 – and turned on Mountain Boulevard, which served as a frontage road. Raymond, brought out of his stupor by the national news, turned around in the cab, looking for something new to rifle through. He grabbed Cassie's purse. He listed each item out loud as he lifted them from the purse: wallet with California driver's license, keys, tampons, an Altoids tin, a Starbucks gift card. Raymond paused for dramatic effect before announcing the next item with a raised voice: "Two tickets to the Raider football game for Sunday, October thirty first, one oh five p.m."

The commercial break on KCBS ended, causing Raymond to quiet down. Although many of the news items repeated themselves each half hour, the lead local news story was new: a line of cars had already formed leading up to the Oakland

Coliseum parking lot gates, which wouldn't open until eight a.m.

When the Raiders played full time in the Oakland Coliseum, cars weren't allowed to queue up for the parking lot gates until six. But with the Raiders coming back for just the one game, no procedures were put into place to monitor or enforce the rule.

Brady took it as some kind of sign that the Raiders news story ran immediately after Raymond mentioned the tickets in Cassie's purse. "That's it, Raymond. We're going to go cool our jets waiting in line for the Raider game. No one will be looking for us there, I guarantee you. We can just peel out of the line when it's time to go to the port, or if we're already in the parking lot, we can just exit when we need to."

"Raaaayders!" Raymond called out loudly – as did many Raider fans in the Coliseum parking lot during their tenure at the stadium.. "Let's do it, then, Brady."

The Once and Future Oakland Raiders

Depending on the decade, they were a team of destiny or dysfunction. They were one of the most storied franchises in the National Football League – revered and reviled. One of the original American Football League teams in 1960, they suffered through horrific seasons and attendance, until Al Davis arrived at age thirty-three to become one of the youngest head coaches in professional football history.

Al Davis turned the team around before leaving to become commissioner of the AFL, helping to pressure and orchestrate the merger of the NFL and AFL. After the merger was announced, he returned to the Raiders as a partner and general manager. Within a number of years, Davis maneuvered to get full operating control of the Raiders over the other limited partners. He remained the patriarch, principal owner, and public face of the Raiders until his death in 2011.

After Davis' arrival, the Raiders were one of the winningest professional sports franchises over a two decade span, including three Super Bowl appearances, two Super Bowl victories, and eleven league or conference championship appearances. The team took on the rebellious personality of their owner and gained a reputation as a place that veteran players down on their luck could come to and revive their careers in an atmosphere that allowed for free spirits and a motto of "just win, baby."

The Oakland Raider fan base was intensely loyal and as hard-partying as the players. Their sense of betrayal was equally as intense when Al Davis successfully sued the NFL to allow him to move the team to Los Angeles in 1982. But Davis quickly grew as unhappy with his Los Angeles Coliseum surroundings as he had been with the Oakland Coliseum.

Within five years of his move, the team was already rumored to be shopping for a new home, and even returned to Oakland for a preseason football game. Davis negotiated with multiple venues in Southern California and Oakland during the late 1980s and early 1990s, leading an *L.A. Times* sportswriter to suggest the team and stadium don roller skates. Finally in 1995, Davis struck a deal with Oakland to return to the Oakland Coliseum, with an expansion of the stadium and additional luxury seats.

The jilted Oakland fan base welcomed the Raiders back with open arms, resuming their rabid relationship. It was tested as the team fell on hard times after their return, before a brief winning respite during the coach Jon Gruden years. But as Al Davis aged, it became more difficult to for persons of stature to co-exist in his shadow.

He drove Gruden out after the 2001 season and began a coaching carousel of hirings and firings that lasted until Davis' death. Appearing in the Super Bowl after the 2002 season – losing to Gruden's Tampa Bay Bucs with a Raider team that Gruden assembled – the team didn't experience a winning season again for well over a decade.

Yet the Raider fans – known as Raider Nation – persevered. They were as loyal as ever despite the on-field losses and back office dysfunction. The Black Hole of the Oakland Coliseum – the south end zone seats – maintained their notoriety. Raider Nation developed a league-wide reputation as the most-costume-clad fan base in the league and perhaps the most dedicated pregame tailgate party crowd.

Rumors of the Raiders once again relocating began swirling over Raider Nation's heads within a decade of their move back to Oakland and accelerated after Al Davis died in 2011 - with his son Mark assuming ownership control. Relocation rumors continued to escalate with each passing season.
Finally, the trigger was pulled to relocate to a new stadium. Then, just as in the 2014 season, when the Buffalo Bills had to relocate a home game to Detroit due to a massive snowstorm, the Raiders had to reschedule to a new venue for a home game this season.

A major structural snafu with their new stadium was discovered mid-season, requiring extensive work. Fortunately, a bye week and an away game followed allowing repairs to begin, but completion was not feasible in time for the home October 31st game. The NFL and the Raiders agreed to relocate the game to the Coliseum – which had still not been shuttered – and the Oakland Raider Nation fan base was given access to significantly discounted tickets.

So another tailgate was in the works for the costumed Raider Nation – on Halloween – for a National Football League contest with the Once and Future Oakland Raiders.

In The Queue

The cargo truck finally settled into the line for the oversized vehicle lot behind the Baldwin Gate. Initially, Brady pulled the vehicle into the main line on Coliseum Way, off of Hegenberger Road, but was quickly informed by the partying passengers milling around outside the vehicles in front of him, that his truck would never be allowed entrance at that gate, as it was oversize.

Brady was directed to the Baldwin Gate entrance, where the RVs were lined up. Not wanting to call undue attention to himself, he complied. After circling back around the Coliseum complex, Brady arrived at the more subdued Baldwin Gate crowd, where most of the more experienced RV tailgaters were sound asleep inside the vehicles, pacing for the long tailgate ahead.

Brady encountered only one small group awake outside their RV, who took it upon themselves to give Brady counsel. They advised him that he was fortunate to be attending this game, because previously, when the Raiders were based in the Coliseum, you could not enter the Baldwin Gate without a prepaid parking pass. But for this special game, it was announced you could just pay the seventy-five dollar oversize vehicle fee upon entrance.

Brady asked for suggestions on where to park once inside so that he could exit again before the game started, if he needed to, without getting trapped inside by the other vehicles. He was advised to head toward the stalls just inside the gate, which the RVs in line wouldn't be as interested in, given they wanted to be closer to where the action was.

Brady discovered a custom switch for the radio to play through speakers in the cargo area. He shut the engine off, but turned the radio to FM and kept the sound system going at a tolerable level, hoping to drown out any pleas for help or zombie grunting from the back. Raymond was wide awake, but not plugged into the surrounding world. He rocked back

261

and forth, alternating between mumbling, humming, and announcing selected expletives in various tenses and forms.

Brady felt reasonably certain that the call from Quon's people wouldn't arrive for many hours, and that Raymond had settled into a fairly harmless state, so he decided to get a little shuteye. Brady briefly once again entertained the idea of bailing – leaving Raymond to deal with the situation – but dismissed the thought, as he decided his best play was to take the payday and hopefully escape the country with the Chinese.

Brady did puzzle through how he would explain the presence of Quon's phone to Raymond. He decided that he'd announce that he just discovered it at some point in the morning. He also considered for a moment if he should use his hidden pistol and cross Raymond off his list of problems – but he couldn't bring himself to kill another person, let alone his concern over calling further attention to what was going on in their truck.

So Brady shut his eyes, leaned back, and soon was snoring. Raymond stayed awake in his meth induced state of mind, flipping around channels on the FM stations, with the music piped into the cargo cells.

In the back, Bruce, Cassie, and Tess's throats were parched. They had not had any water since Saturday morning. Bruce speculated as to what it meant that they had come to a stop and the engine shut off, with no subsequent activity. FM music began pulsing through the cells. He spied a small speaker mounted near the roof. The stations began to change every other minute, offering a spectrum of genres.

Bruce and Cassie called out for help for fifteen minutes or so, to no avail. They finally gave up – their voices cracking, the radio muffling their appeals. They picked up no sounds from the outside offering them any encouragement. During the drive, their conversations had grown more fatalistic. They both had come to the conclusion that when they emerged from the cell, they would be offered up as zombie bait or shot. Tess seemed to pick up on the air or resignation surrounding her. Her face developed a pout.

Bruce recalled a bar room debate with his friends in Winnemucca – long before Burning Man, when they were turned into zombies. He and his friends argued over drinks regarding how they preferred to die, given the choice: knowing the moment was coming in half a day or so or to suddenly bite the dust unexpectedly. Bruce's friends chose unexpectedly, which, as it turned out, was their fate. Bruce chose to have some notice, which, as it turned out, was to be his fate.

Bruce considered if he had put his last few hours of life to good use. Had he confessed any great sins? Had he tried to leave a note behind? Had he attempted to ease the pain and suffering of those he was with? Had he reflected on the mistakes he had made in life? He afforded himself a pathetic smile to accompany his answers of no.

He leaned his head against Cassie's in silence, reflecting on his business failures with Vinopalooza.com and Joggen.com; his failures at relationships during his time in India and at home; his choice to live in seclusion as a hermit in the desert. He had recently hoped the research facility at his compound would be the opportunity to get the life back on the track that he lost in his twenties. Instead, he now reasoned, it was about to become the death of him.

In the darkness, Bruce imagined a sign hanging over the door to their cell wall bearing Dante's inscription, popularized in Disneyland's Pirates of the Caribbean: 'Abandon Hope, All Ye Who Enter Here.' As usual, a Shakespeare quote came to mind next: The miserable have no other medicine but only hope.

The air was stuffy and dusty in the back, but quite chilly. Bruce, Cassie, and Tess huddled together in the darkness, Cassie in the middle. Tess continued to cling to Cassie like a frightened child. One at a time, they nodded off, despite the deluge of tunes from the speaker above.

The Call

Sunday, 8:47 a.m., October 31st

They were inside the lot. Brady slept fitfully, waking up for good a little before seven, as the RVs around him sprung to life. The Baldwin gate opened at eight — to the minute. Brady pulled the truck inside and parked at a stall near the gate, as recommended. He nervously scanned the activity all around him.

Raymond never slept, instead playing with the FM radio the remainder of the night – twice reaching over to start and run the truck for a while so the battery would not run down. Raymond's high wore off by morning and he had no opportunity to binge – his supply was gone. He was tired and felt very strange. He heard a cry for help penetrate the cargo truck walls. He cranked the radio volume up, drowning out any hope Bruce or Cassie held of catching someone's attention.

Brady stepped outside the truck, turning around to take in the scene in the Coliseum parking lot. There was activity in every direction – tables, BBQs, chairs, pop-canopies, outdoor bars, of all sizes and shapes, many customized with Raider logos — emerging from the nearby RVs. The distinct smell of lighter fluid on freshly lit charcoal was in the air. Brady directed his gaze west, away from the RVs. The parking lot was filling fast. No one, it seemed, wanted to be denied the opportunity for one final tailgate at the Oakland Coliseum, particularly when the football tickets had been made available at the last minute for bargain basement prices.

Raymond finally took notice that Brady was outside the cab. Raymond rubbed his brown, crew-cut hair and stuck his index finger in his mouth, fiddling with his gums where his tooth was missing. It occurred to him that he had lost control of the mission to Brady, during his meth high and it was time to wrest it back.

Raymond wanted to obtain someone else's cell phone and call the number he found in the cab for Quon's contact. It was time they got down to business. He took one of the Glock pistols and placed it inside his daypack. He grabbed the daypack, hopped out of the cab, and decided to get in Brady's face.

Brady had grown impatient. Even though the hour was relatively early in the morning, he could not stand the suspense any longer. Knowing they were the object of a national manhunt was a crushing weight on his psyche. He couldn't bear to sit in the lot for hours more, wondering if the next person who strolled by might recognize their pictures being displayed on televisions and smartphones.

Brady pulled out Quon's secure phone from his pocket. There was only one number entered into the contacts. He hovered his index finger over the dial button. Raymond stepped up from behind – unannounced – grabbing Brady's left hand that clutched the phone. Brady, startled, turned and instinctively almost struck Raymond. "What?" he cried out to Raymond instead in an annoyed tone, pulling his hand and the phone away.

"I thought we didn't dare turn on our phones because we'd get located," Raymond stated in an accusatory tone.

"Oh, yeah, this." Brady stumbled momentarily, shaking the phone up and down with his left hand. "I just found this phone in the cab, rummaging around, while you were out of it. I think it's Quon's phone, so I'm gonna dial the one number in it and see if we can get things moving."

Raymond paused momentarily, before again grabbing at the phone. Brady yanked it back, out of reach. Raymond considered pulling his Glock out and taking command, but thought the better of it, as he surveyed the growing crowd of tailgaters in the periphery. He watched Brady press to dial, then hold the phone to his ear. Raymond stepped forward. He debated if he should get nose to nose with Brady, pull out the Glock, then put a bullet in his brain.

Brady held out his right hand, signaling Raymond to stop in his tracks. He pointed at the phone. Someone was answering. Raymond swooped in close to listen.

"Hello?" Brady started, unsure of what else to say, hoping the voice on the other end would start with good news.

There was silence at the other end of the line. Raymond leaned forward, touching Brady, pressing his ear almost into the phone.

"Hello?" Brady repeated himself.

"Please identify yourself," a voice with an Asian dialect boomed from the phone.

Brady stated his name. Silence followed. He repeated his name.

"Listen very carefully, Brady. We received Quon's last communication. But since that time, the situation has changed. We no longer require the merchandise. You need to abort the mission. Walk away from the merchandise now and don't contact us again."

"What do you mean you no longer require the merchandise? We are here. In Oakland. We're ready to deliver. What about our money?" Brady shouted into the phone.

"The deal is off the table. Walk away and don't contact us again," the voice repeated.

"Wait. Let's talk about this. I need you to take me with you," Brady pleaded.

The call terminated. Raymond grabbed the phone out of Brady's hands, oblivious that no one was at the other end.

"Damn it you stupid Chinese-shit-for-brains. We want our money and we want it now. You hear me?" Raymond yelled into the phone. He carried on for thirty seconds, before acknowledging they had been hung up on. He pressed dial. No one answered. He hung up, and tried again, repeatedly. Raymond dropped to his knees, holding the phone. "Noooo!" he screamed.

Brady looked around, hoping Raymond had not caught the eye of those nearby. No one seemed to notice. The crown behind them was wrapped up in setting up tailgates. Brady looked up at the sky, rubbing his hands into his short curly hair, and then scratched his soul patch with his right hand. "So it comes to this," he exclaimed out loud. He shook his head at Raymond, who was fiddling with the phone.

"Hey, this is a blessing in disguise, Brady o' Brady," Raymond called out to him. "We have a phone we can use without getting traced. I remember now a couple of numbers to call. I can get the contacts I need from them. And I can call the number I found for Quon and see if it's any different. We're going to make even more cash, Brady. Even more." Raymond turned his attention back to the phone.

Brady shook his head again. He, for one, was going to listen to Quon's people. He turned his back on Raymond and walked away toward the ramp up to the stadium and the BART bridge. He had no intention of returning.

Quon's contacts took measures to have Quon's phone remotely disabled after the call. They hadn't shared with Brady the reason for their scrubbing the mission; they had already arranged for delivery of Dr. Hernandez and the two crewmen he infected.

A Raider Tailgate

Tailgates at the Oakland Coliseum are divided into half –
the north 66th Avenue side and the south Hegenberger Road
side—with the Oracle basketball arena and the stadium
situated in the middle. The RV parking is on the far eastern
end of the Hegenberger side. A canal surrounds the parking lot
on the northern and eastern side, as if the Coliseum is a castle
bound by a moat. Portable towers are strategically located on
game day, so Coliseum staff or law enforcement can monitor
what goes on throughout the parking lot.

Even by nine in the morning, barbeques have been fired up,
with tri-tip, chicken, or ribs. The skewers, hamburgers, and
sausages, requiring less cooking time, would be put on later.
Crock pots full of carnitas, beans, chorizo, or pulled pork are
put out on display. Chips, dip and salsa seem to emerge
somewhere from every vehicle.

Televisions hooked up to portable satellite dishes are
decked out under shaded canopies, airing pre-game shows.
Signs and banners extol the Raiders, berate their opponents or
display the clever name of the tailgating group. Footballs fly
through the air, in between the rows of vehicles. Games to
occupy tailgating hours are abundant, many involving the
sport of drinking. Giant Jenga, portable putting greens, beer
pong, ladder toss and flip cup are all well represented, with
cornhole being the most popular.

Blenders are connected to portable power sources and
mobile or makeshift bars are commonplace. Bloody Marys are
available in lavish quantities born from a spectrum of personal
recipes, along with tequila shots, margaritas, mimosas, vodka
cranberry or lemonade, red bull chasers, flasks of whiskey,
picklebacks, ice cold beer, beer bongs and grass. The Oakland
Coliseum might carry whiffs of weed throughout the lot and
even the stadium, more than any other NFL venue.

Fan jerseys represent every era of Raider history. From the
60's, and every ensuing decade, old player numbers and names
on silver and black or black and white shirts can be spotted.

But the jerseys in greatest supply are always the high profile players on the current team, particularly new acquisitions.

Customized vehicles abound in Raider Nation – from the home-painted silver and black campers that date back decades, to tricked out Cameros, Corvettes, Challengers, Chargers, brand new silver and black pickups, Harleys and even golf carts— are all adorned with Raider paraphernalia and logos. In the RV lot resides a tricked-out converted pop-up trailer, now an open air kitchen with two smoker barbeques.

But what truly sets Raider tailgates apart from other NFL tailgates, are the costumes. Some elaborately clad fans have dressed up in the same persona for up to twenty years, and have become minor celebrities in Raider Nation, commanding followings in the parking lot, signing autographs and posing for endless streams of pictures. Hours of preparation are required for some of the get-ups.

"The Violator" has appeared on television promotions for the team, and dates back to attending L.A. Raider games in the early 90's — with a zebra painted face, black skullcap, football jersey with "Violator" emblazoned on the back, and silver spikes rising out of the shoulder pads. "Gorilla Rilla" is donned in a full-length gorilla suit, with a black and white striped Dr. Seuss-style top hat, sunglasses and seriously oversized bling. "RaiderJuice" is one of the more colorful versions of Raider fans in 'Beetlejuice" style outfits slinking through the parking lot.

There is an endless variety of skulls presented as part of full-length costumes: skull heads; skull extra-heads for two or three-headed characters; skull necklaces large and small; skull helmets; skulls on top of helmets; skulls inside of helmets; skulls growing out of shoulder pads. Pirates are plentiful. Fans often are connected to large accessories, their heads emerging from Raider shields or weighted down by oversize chains.

There are Darth Vader Raiders, oversize Raider sombreros; Raider construction helmets – sometimes with silver plastic daggers bludgeoned into them; and basically any character from a Mad Max movie recast in silver and black. Then there are the female costumes – ladies in full-on football uniforms, cheerleader outfits, black cats, vampire temptresses, skin-tight spandex adorned with Raider accessories, plus plenty dressed in the same skull, pirate or apocalyptic gear that the men are wearing.

Perhaps the more recent decades of serious losing that followed the decades of serious winning, have led Raider fans to celebrate and party hard before the game has begun – before reality sets in – as there has been scarce opportunity to celebrate later in the day.

iPhone

Raymond was in the middle of his third unsuccessful call trying to find someone with a connection in the bay area, who he could start peddling his zombies to when Quon's phone went dead. Even the power shut down. Frustrated, Raymond flung the mysterious phone as high in the air as he could. He tried to catch it, but badly misjudged its return to earth. It landed on top of the cargo truck.

Raymond rubbed his hands through his crew-cut, loudly repeating the words "we're screwed." It was then he realized Brady was nowhere to be found. He ran to the truck cab, searching through it for Brady, as if his partner was a set of car keys. He jumped back out of the cab, leaving the driver door open, running a full circle around the vehicle. He called out Brady's name twice, before stopping abruptly, remembering their names were being broadcast all over the news.

Raymond sat down cross-legged on the crumbling parking lot asphalt behind the rear of the vehicle. A voice in his head listed just exactly how screwed he was at the moment: the Chinese bailed on him; his three best prospects for connecting him to black market buyers were of no help; Quon's phone quit working; he was afraid to use his or Brady's phone; Brady had disappeared; and he was the subject of a national search with his name being broadcast all over the news.

Think – what to do, the voice in his head started to command him. "Alright, I got it," he finally exclaimed out loud. His plan was to make the best of the situation. There were now tens of thousands of people in the parking lot. He would obtain someone's phone to keep making calls. Or, if he was lucky, he would run into someone in the lot with shady connections, whom he could talk a little business with. The question was, where should he start?

The answer arrived at his nostrils. The aroma of weed arrived in full force. Raymond rose up, following his nose.

Moments later, he was in the midst of an eclectic group of almost thirty young men and women getting stoned, hanging out in between their vehicles, parked just west of the oversized vehicle section. Several narrow rectangular tables were positioned behind their cars, with a very hastily thrown together tailgate spread of chips, store-bought guacamole, takeout burritos cut in half, and paper plates.

Raymond wandered in, introduced himself, and helped himself to each joint being passed around. He felt more confident with each toke, even though the anxiety remained. No one in the group seemed even remotely related to anyone with black market possibilities. He was just in the midst of a very wasted college and post-college age kids with enough money for a whole lot of weed and some decent rides. Still, he should have no problems relieving somebody of their phone, especially with the condition they were in.

But the pot was more than enticing, and he was starting to get high again. Ten minutes later, he was feeling it. He picked his target – an annoying clean-cut white kid in a Warriors basketball jersey and tattoo, who had made jokes about Raymond's crew cut. He motioned the young man aside, asking him if he wanted to go back to Raymond's truck and try out something with a little more kick to it.

The two exited the weed-fest and headed straight to the cargo truck. Raymond had his new companion wait by the back of the truck while he headed to side panel, pressing the button to open the back. Raymond repositioned the Glock in his pants pocket, concealed by his untucked shirt.

Raymond assured his new friend that that smorgasbord of drugs in the cargo bay would be life-changing. They climbed up onto the tailgate and inside the cargo bay. Classic rock music was blaring from within, drowning out Cassie and Bruce's pleas for help. Raymond asked – having to shout over the music — if he could borrow his companion's phone to check a sports score. He was quickly handed an iPhone 6.

Raymond explained that they needed to close the overhead door, so they could party hidden from view from any law enforcement. "What the hell is all this?" Raymond's new friend exclaimed, standing in the small opening, surrounding by modular walls with four separate doors. The young man started to feel a little uneasy, picking up some strange sounds and smells, from behind the walls.

Raymond pushed the button on the interior control panel to auto close the overhead door to the bay, and then pressed the cell door lock release, using the iPhone as a flashlight. "These are the party rooms, my friend. Open door number one, and let's see what you won," Raymond pointed to the first door to the left, using the light of the phone. Raymond's plan, now that he had the phone, was to shove the man inside, after the door was opened, and proceed to pull it shut.

The promise of exotic drugs lured the young man to step forward to the door. There wasn't a traditional door handle, just a vertical metal bar attached to the door. The man pulled it forward, stepping into the loud darkness. A second later, screaming competed with the din of the music from the first cell. Raymond rushed forward to shut the door.

Unfortunately, Raymond's motor coordination had diminished, as a result of his weed session. He dropped the phone, and with it, his source of light as the phone fell face down. Raymond reached out blindly for the door.

It was too late. Several zombies pushed their way into the small corridor. Raymond rolled quickly toward the control panel, hoping to escape. First he pressed the wrong button, switching the speakers off in the cargo bay. He next pressed the correct button, activating the overhead door. The door made it all the way to the top, the light from outside enveloping the corridor, blinding the zombies that had been encased in darkness for almost a day. The zombies from the first cell — three kidnapped staff from the Bruce's research facility plus a lady zombie from Black Rock City – abandoned the bitten prey that had been thrust into their room. They bypassed Raymond, who pressed himself against the edge of the interior, next to the control panel. The zombies rushed outside into the blinding light, falling off the edge of the truck and onto the ground.

With the back of the truck now bathed in light, Raymond could see his new drug companion moaning on the floor, inside the first cell, bleeding from the neck. Raymond considered that the cat was now out of the bag – there were zombies on the loose. He hadn't intended it that way, he was just hoping to jump out the back, and close the overhead door.

Raymond decided there was just one thing to do. Since some of the zombies escaped, he might as well let them all loose and give the world what it deserved. He would downsize his plan. He impulsively opened the second cell door and then opened the third cell. Seven zombies – six ladies plus Quon, emerged from the second cell, and eleven zombies – the ten from the research facility plus a guard came from the third cell.

Raymond didn't stick around to watch them make a beeline for the outside, falling off the tailgate just as the ones from the first cell had done moments before. Raymond opened the fourth cell door, rushed inside the cell containing Bruce, Cassie and Tess, and closed the door behind him before the zombies from the other cells took notice.

Raymond pulled the Glock 23 from his pants, equipped with the Silencerco Osprey 40 silencer, and raised it in the darkness – announcing his presence and possession of the firearm, and that he was taking Tess hostage. He couldn't see anything, his eyes not adjusted to the darkness. He had taken a chance entering, given he had placed a zombie into the cell with Bruce and Cassie, but felt it was worth the risk. He had, after all, placed Quon in with her back in the Black Rock Desert and Quon had emerged without being further damaged. Raymond was now going to pin his hopes on the z that Bruce had talked up a day earlier in the desert.

Everyone in the cell was struggling to see. Raymond was blinded by the darkness. Bruce, Cassie and Tess were blinded by recent sudden surge of light that momentarily assaulted the room. None of them were witness to what was starting to go down in the parking lot.

Halloween Riot

The zombies rose up, one by one, after falling off the cargo truck bay into the parking lot. Twenty-two Zs scattered in every direction. Soon, a twenty-third fell out of the truck to join them. As had happened in Burning Man two months earlier, those with drugs in their system took minutes instead of hours to expire and re-boot after being infected. The young man Raymond lured over, just to steal his iPhone, joined the ranks of Zs in the lot.

The special return of the Raiders to the Coliseum happened to fall on Halloween. As in past Halloween Raider tailgates, this brought the portion of the crowd in costume, and the elaborateness of the costumes, to a peak. Initially, the zombies in everyone's midst didn't merit a second glance.

The zombies were equipped with an extremely heightened sense of smell. A number of the Zs were immediately attracted to the nearby party still enjoying their weed. Another z group made haste to the nearest bank of porta potties. The remainder was content with attacking anyone who crossed their path.

The weed party positioned themselves as obscurely as possible from the line of sight of the nearest observation towers in the B lot on the Hegenberger side and from parked law enforcement vehicles. They congregated mostly in between their cars, shielded from view while passing around joints. They were equally shielded from view when the Zs arrived.

At first, those in the weed group noticing the four approaching zombies were bemused – thinking the Zs had outdone themselves with their makeup and special effects but were perhaps a little too much in character. The first z to arrive slipped in between a Toyota pickup and new Chevy Impala, to be offered a toke by the three men and two women, all in their twenties. The two ladies were bitten before it dawned on the men what exactly was going on. The three guys moved forward, trying to separate the z from their two lady friends. During the struggle each received multiple bite wounds.

The five were all slumped against the two vehicles, weakly trying to push the z away as it moved from person to person, biting and gouging around each neck and shoulder. Their cries were muffled by the music blaring from the Toyota's speakers. A second z – a shapely topless female captured the morning before in Black Rock City, was invited by three enthusiastic guys to take a hit with them. They soon regretted offering the invitation. The other two Zs entering the weed party arrived at different points, each taking down more partiers.

Those in the remainder of the party, standing behind their cars next to their folding tables, didn't immediately notice the zombie incursion in their midst. Several ran to see what was happening to their friends – only to suffer the same fate. Several more froze in their tracks, looking on the scenes in between the cars in horror. They were mowed down from behind, by a fifth z that joined the fracas.

The nearest bank of porta potties was situated on an island raised several inches above the asphalt, three rows of cars north, and over a hundred feet west, from the cargo truck. A group of Zs sniffed out the toilets – bypassing a sea of potential victims along the way – in favor of the outdoor johns.

Upon reaching the porta potties, the Zs encountered a long line waiting to use the facilities. They bypassed the line, ambling directly to the toilet doors. A porta potty door opened as a middle aged woman exited. One of the Zs – a larger male taken from the Sulphur research facility – bound for the outhouse, making it inside before the door shut behind it.

A number of the men in line for the toilets took umbrage at the cutting in line – four other zombies stood outside the porta potty doors, alternating between banging on them and pushing with their hands and wrists. A big burly fellow with a shaved head, goatee, and a left arm full of tattoo art – marched right up the porta potty door that the first z rushed inside.

The goateed man opened the outhouse door, ready to start a fight with whoever it was who dared cut in front of them. The z inside – not a small person either – was looking down into the toilet but glanced up when the door opened. The zombie grabbed the goateed man as he entered the john, biting him hard in the face. The door swung shut again. The z went to work on the goateed man from inside the porta potty.

Other men in line rushed at the other four Zs who had cut in front of them. Punches were thrown, but within sixty seconds every assailant had been bitten by the porta potty zombies. Others rushed in to help, only to be bitten as well. Gradually, doors would open to the other porta potty doors – causing the nearest z to abandon the biting and fighting in order to rush inside the open outhouse. Once inside, the z would unsuccessfully attempt to crawl down through the toilet hole, into the enticing ooze and muck below.

Other Zs wandered individually into nearby sections. Quon made his way over to the RVs. He arrived unnoticed at a rented unit at the south end, its occupants all outside underneath the canopy, playing a drinking game involved with the large flat screen television connected to their portable satellite dish. Everyone was taking a tequila shot each time Chris Berman, Chris Carter, or the other ESPN cast members said the word "Oakland" or "Raiders," as the game's change of venue was a big topic of discussion for the week.

Quon wandered inside the thirty-five-foot Fleetwood RV; the door above the attached steps was propped open. Quon was attracted by the odor. There was one person inside, a middle-aged man too wasted to continue doing shots with the others, after having done a number of lines of coke. The man's face was in his arms on the RV dining table. He was a little dejected. The others in the group had all chastised him for committing the cardinal sin of dropping a major deuce in the RV toilet, which hadn't flushed properly. It was the residual aroma that attracted Quon.

Quon paused indecisively, between the coked-out man and the RV toilet. Quon opted for the best of both worlds. He chomped hard into the man's right arm – barely eliciting a cry from his victim. Quon dragged him into the small bathroom. He sat on the floor next to the toilet, devouring the man's arm inches away from the smells wafting up from the RV potty.

From the observation tower in the southeast "B" portion of the Hegenberger lot, a number of flashpoints were spotted almost at the same time. Some kind of group altercation flared up by the outermost bank of porta potties; a large number of people in a group tailgate were strewn around on the ground with apparent injuries; several other spots were sighted with individuals hunched over and assailing multiple persons lying next to each other on the ground.

On-site Alameda County Sheriff's officers were dispatched to each location, taxing their available manpower. As all incidents were in the Hegenberger B lot, officers were called over from the 66th Avenue lot to assist.

A solo officer on foot, trotting over to the site of the former weed party, came across a single z. She was on all fours tearing away at the rib cage flesh of a fallen older man, partially obscured underneath an open tailgate of a Ford F150 pickup. The officer stopped, approaching the shapely female z in tattered clothing and smeared with dust and blood.

He called out to the female assailant, ordering her to back away from the man. She rose up – moaning – and slowly shuffled toward the officer. He had heard the briefing of the kidnapped zombies. He had followed ongoing news stories from the Black Rock desert since the Burning Man incident two months prior. There was no doubt in his mind he was facing an escaped zombie, who was now bearing down on him.

The officer brushed aside thoughts of the zombie protective legislation he had read about in great detail. He had just witnessed her gashing open a man, and was intending to inflict the same fate on him. He ordered her to stop several times – the last warning accompanied by a pointed revolver when she reached within ten feet. She continued, and he fired into her right thigh, which didn't same to faze her. He began to back up, placing a second shot into her upper right shoulder, still not slowing her down. When she was almost within arms' reach, he fired the kill shot into her skull.

A large crowd had gathered around during the previous fifteen seconds. The officer was alone when he first came upon the z ripping apart the older man's chest. The crowd only saw him confronting an unarmed, injured female, and shooting her down in cold blood. The crowd turned on the officer and a small riot began to ensue. Several bystanders took the officer's side, helping to turn the melee into a brawl. Additional officers arrived, escalating the situation.

Back at the porta potties, a number of the initial crowd was lying on the ground, bitten by the zombies who cut in front of them in line. All but one of the Zs were now inside the toilets – the remaining snarling z was surrounded by a large number of men who were tormenting it with a barbeque coal poker and other improvised implements. More than once, one of the crowd ventured too far in and was bitten on the arm.

The arriving officers divided their duties between dispersing the crowd, attending to the wounded, and – acting upon eyewitness statements – confronting the assailants who had taken refuge inside the porta potties. The officers found their commands issued to those inside the toilets went unheeded. Told the assailants had taken hostages inside the toilets, the officers' options were more limited.

Reassured by the eyewitnesses that the assailants carried no weapons, one of the officers stepped forward and opened one of the porta potty doors. A zombie bounded out and bit into the officer's neck. His fellow officer began firing away at the attacker, who was unfazed and took several more bites until a kill shot penetrated the Zs temple. The other officers decided to just wait out the other porta potties for the moment.

The weed party victims had already expired and re-booted. Most rose up and joined the nearby riot that started when the lone officer shot the female z. In the chaos of the riot, the attacks by the weed zombies were relatively unnoticed.

Meanwhile, Quon's coked-out victim in the RV also expired and rebooted – minus most of his right arm. One-by-one, members of RV's tequila shooting party went to check on him and check on the growing number of other disappearing tequila shooters, and didn't return.

Shut Up, Bruce

Immediately after bursting with his Glock into the darkened cell that contained Bruce, Cassie, and Tess, to announce that he was taking them hostage, Raymond realized that he wasn't going to keep control of the situation for long in an almost pitch black room. He waited less than a minute, while hollering at his captives to stay at the other end of the cell, before opening the cell door a crack to see if all the other zombies had vacated.

Only the partier Raymond brought inside the truck remained, bleeding out on the floor in the first cell with the door open. Raymond kept his cell door open a crack to monitor the partier and try to hear or see what he could from what was going on out in the parking lot.

More than five minutes passed uneventfully, other than Raymond's occasional commands for Bruce, Cassie, and Tess to stay where they were. Cassie tried to control her breathing. She tried not to think about how thirsty she was. She held Bruce's hand, while Bruce stared intently at Raymond. Tess seemed to almost be whimpering, while she held onto Cassie.

Finally, Raymond witnessed the partier rise up and stagger out of his cell. Raymond closed his cell door and waited more than another minute until he felt sure the partier exited the truck. He opened the door halfway, so that he could fully see the others.

Raymond's plan was to execute Bruce and Cassie once he figured out how to get control of Tess's movements. He ordered Tess to come across the cell, over to him. Tess remained where she was, clinging to Cassie.

"She doesn't understand words anymore," Cassie responded angrily. "You can't make her do anything."

"Oh yeah?" Raymond laughed. "We'll see about that." Raymond grinned while walking slowly toward them, his Glock pointed at Tess. He stopped at point black range, pressing the Glock against Tess's forehead. "Come on, you stupid woman.

You can't even seem to become a zombie right, you're so screwed up. Come follow me back or your lesbian lover here next to you is going to get her brains blown out." Raymond pointed the pistol at Cassie's forehead.

Tess bore a confused look. She clung to Cassie even more tightly.

"She can't talk?" Raymond asked Cassie.

"No," Cassie answered with a defiant tone.

"She doesn't understand what we're saying?" Raymond asked, still pointing the pistol at Cassie.

"No," she repeated.

"Alright then," Raymond started in a falsetto voice with a hammy southern belle accent, "why don't ya' all just be a darlin' and come mosey over with me to the other side of this here room, so your lady friend will follow us over?"

"Raymond!" Bruce interjected, "Come on – this is enough. When you sober up, even you will regret what you just did, letting these infected go out like this. You might be killing thousands of people, Raymond. Think about that — thousands. And if they break loose from this area, it could be unimaginably worse, Raymond. Even you can't want that. Let us go. Just get in this truck and drive off. Let us go to tell the authorities exactly what they're dealing with before it really gets bad. They'll be too busy handling this to go after you right now. I—"

Raymond cut him off. "Oh, Bruce. You sad little man. You don't know me. You don't know what I want. And I'm only too happy to tell you. I want a frickin' lot of money, after what I went through for the past day. These thousands of people dying that you're so worried about are my golden ticket. After what happens here today, everyone's going to want to check out why your friend got bit and didn't turn all the way into one of those zombies like all the others. And I'm selling her to the highest bidder. So just shut up, Bruce. Shut your damn, pompous-ass mouth. You know, I've wanted to say that to your face for the past month, every time you showed up and I had to listen to you going on like a big know-it-all up there at Burning Man."

Raymond turned to Cassie, again pointing the gun at her head. "Come on, lady. Walk with me over to the other side of the room, and let's see if your friend comes with us."

Cassie turned to Bruce, wondering what to do. He motioned his head forward. Cassie proceeded slowly across the room, while Raymond kept pace. Tess inched along with them. Half a minute later, the three made it to the other end.

"There, that wasn't so hard, was it?" Raymond asked calmly. He lifted his Glock 23, equipped with the Silencerco Osprey 40 silencer, pointed it directly at Bruce, and shot him. Cassie screamed. Bruce dropped to the ground.

The Fog of War

The Alameda County Sheriff's Office for many years had contracted with the Oakland Alameda County Coliseum Authority to provide law enforcement services on the Coliseum grounds. Never before on a Sunday, in all the years the Raiders played full seasons in the Coliseum, had the sheriff personally been contacted by his staff to escalate handling of an incident.

At nine forty-nine Halloween morning, the sheriff was on his way to church services with his wife and eldest daughter when he pulled over to be debriefed. He was advised that in the span of the last twenty minutes or so, rioting, altercations, fatalities, and bizarre incidents were taking place in a widespread number of locations within the southeast quadrant of the coliseum parking lots. A number of officers were under attack.

The sheriff requested a unit pick him up from his current location and take him to the Coliseum. He handed the keys to his wife, apologized to his daughter and spouse, and stepped out of their car. He stayed busy on the phone, getting further debriefed while waiting for his ride. What caught his attention was reports from several officers of behaviors similar to those reported of the Burning Man population.

The sheriff was well aware of the Black Rock City kidnappings. He ordered staff to contact Homeland Security and alert them of the situation. As his ride pulled up, he gave orders to staff to give the highest priority to confirming whether or not there were persons infected with Gorman's disease on the premises. He followed that with a command to coordinate shut-down of all access points to the Coliseum, at least temporarily. Next, he told staff to set up a conference call with contacts from the Coliseum Authority and the NFL to discuss the possibility of cancelling the game.

Clearly, something unprecedented was going down, but initial reports from the lot were sketchy. Those engaged in the flashpoints were too busy to discuss confirmations of

Gorman's disease. Reports from officers on the periphery of any action, and from security in the observation towers, were short on details or any actionable information. The added dimension of all the Halloween costumes made matters more difficult in ascertaining the actual facts on the ground.

Traffic around the stadium was already in gridlock conditions, as the main lots had just sold out. Long lines were being navigated to the gravel "M" lot on the Hegenberger side or to the BART parking lot or private venues. Even with sirens blaring, the sheriff's escort couldn't penetrate Hegenberger. Oakland City police provided a motorcycle officer to give the sheriff a lift the rest of the way, cutting in and out of traffic.

The sheriff ordered a command center be set up on the 66th Avenue side of the lot, where no incidents had occurred. He was extremely frustrated by the time he arrived. Little progress had been made. Traffic had not been shut down, the access points were still available. He watched a large group crossing the overhead bridge from the BART station to the Coliseum.

Homeland Security administrative aides had fielded their call, but no one in authority had replied as of yet. Requests for all available backup and for available emergency medical services, were still pending on-site response. His conference call time with the Coliseum Authority and NFL was still being scheduled.

Reports from officers and security on the Hegenberger side of the lot were still too sketchy to determine or confirm a root cause for the sudden flare up of so many incidents. He commented to staff surrounding him, that they were truly experiencing the fog of war.

On to BART

Raymond stood at the edge of the cargo truck bay, surveying the parking lot in front of him. A strange low-volume roar was sweeping through the crowd in waves – a crowd noise he had never experienced before. It began to unnerve him.

Cassie and Tess stood to Raymond's right; he continued to press his Glock directly against Cassie's left breast. Raymond took delight with placing it there. Raymond couldn't help but notice the growing police presence, and a rising level of panic in some of the surrounding tailgaters.

Raymond was angry and frustrated. The past day had spun out of control. He no longer felt connected to much of anything. He wasn't sure if it was the drugs or his bipolar condition, but everything seemed to be tingling. The world was surreal. What he did from this point forward seemed not to be of much consequence.

People tailgating by several cars, just north of the disintegrated weed party, hurriedly scrambled into their vehicles, attempting to flee out the Baldwin gate. A line soon formed. Raymond watched them get turned away, informed that gate was closed.

Raymond had previously been considering Brady's original plan, to exit the parking lot in the cargo truck before the game. Seeing that option was no longer available, he decided the best option was fleeing up the BART ramp, through the overhead bridge, and taking BART to a quieter locale.

Minutes before, he had escorted the ladies back to the first cell to gather the stolen iPhone he had dropped earlier. He decided he had been waiting far too long; they needed to get moving that instant. Cassie refused to leave without checking on Bruce, who lay unmoving in the cell. Raymond hadn't allowed her near since shooting him.

"Sweetheart, if you aren't going to come along willingly, you're going to suffer the same fate as your boyfriend Bruce," Raymond threatened Cassie, "and after that if I can't get your half zombie lesbian lover to come along, I'm going have to shoot her too – so her fate in in your hands." Cassie acquiesced, without answering Raymond.

The three began threading their way toward the BART ramp. Tess would only move at a reasonable speed if she was holding onto Cassie, so Raymond was positioned on the left end. His Glock was concealed from view underneath a Raider giveaway black towel he found lying on the ground in the lot, still pressed into Cassie's breast. Tess was to Cassie's right.

The Hegenberger parking lot had become a chaotic jumble, particularly in the "B" lot. The costumed crowd was no longer relaxing in front of barbeques with beers in hand – they were either craning their necks to see what is going on in other spots in the lot; frantically packing their tailgate gear back into their car; scurrying somewhere else; or in various hotspots – engaged in frenzied activity in the presence of one or more nearby Zs.

Raymond, Cassie, and Tess passed by a group of costumed ladies in black nun outfits with skeleton masks, oblivious to the emerging panic and passing around a bottle of Jägermeister next to their two vehicles. Next to them was a muscular, handsome young man in his twenties with neatly groomed facial stubble and a singular small tattoo on his bicep, trying to catch the nun's attention while passing the football back and forth with a buddy a dozen cars east, down the same row.

Cassie witnessed the man's buddy make a spectacular catch – saving the ball from careening into the cars – only to be sideswiped by a zombie that emerged from in between the vehicles, taking the buddy to the ground with the football.

Cassie kept a watchful eye out for law enforcement, hoping to attract their attention. Her heart raced as she saw a swath of sheriff's officers, decked in riot gear, two-deep, descending the BART ramp. Unfortunately, Raymond spotted them too. He cursed several F bombs, before pushing at Cassie's breast with his Glock and ordering her to veer right. He decided to try his luck reversing course to the RV section and see if they could sneak through any gaps in the fence in the far corner, south of the Baldwin gate, beyond the cargo truck.

The northern end of the RV section seemed removed from the madness. People were still partying. The first group they passed by were almost to a person clinging to ice-cold bottles of microbrews, pulled from metal troughs placed in front of two RVs. Everyone seemed to be immersed in deep conversation as Raymond, Cassie, and Tess passed through, including a silver-man group – painted up with great similarity to the Blue Man Group, including latex caps.

As they made their way down the RV row, the crowd seemed increasingly more uneasy. A frenzied group was loading their silver and black camper, a man in a full body football suit removed his Darth Vader helmet, barking orders at his son to hurry up.

Two RVs down, an altercation was taking place. Three men were going at each other in a three way fisticuff brawl, each taking on the other two. One was wearing the opposing team jersey, one in a Raider jersey, one a ripped and tattered shirt. A crowd had gathered around. At the edge of the fight was a bloodied z, sprawled on the ground, a switchblade embedded in its temple. Nearby, several bitten people lying on the ground were being attended. The fight seemed to have arisen as a result of the zombie stabbing.

Raymond pressed on through the crowd, keeping Cassie at his side. The last two RVs seemed scarcely populated. As they reached the end of RV row, Raymond stopped in his tracks. Another two-deep row of sheriff's officers in riot gear were marching toward the RV section from the Baldwin gate.

Raymond yanked Cassie back toward him. He motioned with his head to the left. They would duck into the RV next to them with the open door. Raymond stood behind Cassie. "Hey sweetheart, you and your pet zombie can go inside, and I'll follow," he ordered her. He followed up the steps, only to hear Cassie gasp.

Inside, bloodied people were strewn about on the beds, sofa, and dining table bench seats. Blood and grime were streaked across the floors, appliances, and upholstery. A terrible stench filled the vehicle – a mixed aroma of excrement, blood, and body odors. Members of the group were either passed out or moaning for help. Tess, who had been timid and compliant up to this point, stiffened up and sprang to life. She forcefully grabbed Cassie, then pulled her back behind Raymond, retreating from the RV in an instant, almost falling backwards in the process.

Two snarling Zs almost instantaneously emerged in front of Raymond – one with a right arm almost completely devoid of flesh with only bone and a few dangling tendons and veins remaining. The other zombie Raymond recognized. Raymond pulled out his Glock to dispatch Quon once and for all. Raymond squeezed the trigger, aiming almost point blank at his forehead.

Raymond let loose his last F bomb as the Glock misfired, undoubtedly a result of the dust from the Black Rock Desert, and a day of packing it around carelessly in the cab without cleaning or checking it. In an instant, Quon was on top of Raymond, followed by the partially armed man.

Raymond's last coherent thoughts were that Quon didn't seem to recognize him, as he tore with his teeth through Raymond's shirt and into his chest. Raymond screamed; the pain was unbearable. He weakly dropped Quon's Glock pistol next to its rightful owner. Quon and his z companion made quick work of the left side of Raymond's chest. Minutes later, Raymond bled out. With the drugs in his system, it didn't take long for him to join Quon's ranks, along with others in the RV.

Cassie and Tess were already long gone, weaving their way through the crowd, on their way back to check on Bruce in the nearby cargo truck, fearing the worst.

No One is to Leave
the Lot. Period.

Sunday, 10:10 a.m., October 31st

The sheriff hung up his smartphone to take another call. He couldn't connect and complete the calls fast enough. Homeland Security was flying someone in who would eventually take control of the incident, but for the next couple of hours, the Oakland Coliseum continued to be the sheriff's concern.

During the past twenty minutes, he became satisfied that the Hegenberger Coliseum lot was experiencing an active outbreak of Gorman's disease, undoubtedly originating from the hostages taken from Black Rock City. Upon telephonic advice from the CDC, Homeland Security, and the Air Force Commander who had overseen the Black Rock City siege, he shifted his resources to securing the perimeter of the Hegenberger lot. The mantra the sheriff passed along was that, until he gave the order, no one from this point forward was to leave the lot. Period.

The NFL and Coliseum Authority representatives had just agreed to cancel the game. They agreed to delay notice to the media until the sheriff communicated that the perimeter was secured and announcements were broadcast to the attendees in the Hegenberger lot. The concern was to minimize the level of panic and prevent a stampede to the gates. The NFL representative also obtained agreement that the teams could receive notice of the cancellation now, without providing the reason, to allow any staff already at the stadium the opportunity to quickly exit on the 66th Avenue side.

The specific plan just approved by the sheriff involved immediately starting to clear the 66th Avenue parking lot, one section at a time, in order to make room for a processing area. The angry 66th parking lot tailgaters weren't provided the full story – only that they had to clear the area due to an emergency situation, and that an announcement would be forthcoming that the game was being canceled. There was a deep concern from the sheriff's staff that a riot might develop on the 66th Avenue lot as well, in reaction to the evictions being initiated.

Attendees from the Hegenberger lot were going to be instructed to stay inside their vehicles if possible, until further notice. Those without access to vehicles would be advised to proceed on foot, up the BART ramp or up the ramp next to the Oracle basketball arena, and then take the down ramps to the 66th Avenue lot from either passage.

Entry to the processing areas would be secured by the officers. In the processing area, persons would be screened to confirm they weren't infected. After clearing the processing area, they could exit via the 66th lot via shuttle buses to be arranged, their own cars, or by foot.

Homeland Security informed the sheriff they had procured two experts on Gorman's disease, who had been on the cruise ship that just entered the bay, after suffering an outbreak that was all over the morning news. They were currently being brought to his command center via chopper, to be at his disposal for consultation.

Traffic all around the stadium was one clustered, chaotic, choking gridlock. While the Coliseum paved lots sold out by nine a.m., there was still an endless stream of vehicles seeking to get into those lots, to park in the BART and private lots in the area, or were just part of the general traffic patterns for a Sunday morning. Emergency and law enforcement vehicles called to the scene were having extreme difficulty reaching their final destination.

The media hadn't been officially notified by the sheriff's office, but social media was already starting to blow up with videos and posts from hotspots in the Hegenberger lot. Most of the initial viral discourse was focused on rioting and bizarre behavior versus any zombie incursion.

The officers called out to secure the perimeter were to a person nervous about three scenarios: 1) the crowd stampeding into the fences and gates, 2) persons slipping over and through the fences, which were poorly maintained, and 3) riots and subsequent looting after the game cancellation was announced and the crowd ordered into their cars.

There wasn't a lot of discussion among the officers ordered to guard the perimeters, about the threat posed by those already infected inside the lot – none of them had seen the impact of the infected up close and personal.

Inside the lot, it was another matter, for the small number of officers situated in the southeastern "B" section of the Hegenberger lot. Those stuck in the hotspots were too busy to file reports. Their only communications were pleas for backup, which weren't being adequately heeded, as resources had been re-directed to securing the perimeter, and reinforcements were delayed in traffic on their way to the scene. A number of the hotspot officers were already taken out of the fight, bitten by the growing number of Zs.

Outside the hotspot areas, the majority of the attendees were still oblivious to any zombie outbreak. Many could hear a buzz of crowd noise in the distance, and some had heard rumor of rioting, but tended to shrug it off when everything seemed peaceful enough in their little corner of the parking lot.

Ice cold beer was still being passed around. Tequila was flowing. Barbeques were still in the middle of sizzling. Tortillas were being heated. Weed was still being passed around. Footballs were being tossed. Fantasy Football lineups were being adjusted on smartphones. Costumes were still in full force. It was, after all, Halloween.

Tess's Moan

Cassie and Tess set out for the cargo truck at a brisk pace. Cassie started to run, but realized Tess didn't seem capable of doing so. It didn't occur to Cassie at that moment to seek out law enforcement and let them know what had transpired. She was focused first on returning to Bruce.

Cassie and Tess cut through the line of cars stuck trying to reach the Baldwin gate. With the gate closed, the vehicles were trapped by those that had rushed in behind them and from both sides. Many stayed inside, frightened by what they were witnessing through their windows. Others fled, sprinting on foot toward the gates on the western side.

As the cargo truck came into view, Cassie stopped mid-stride, letting loose a rarely used expletive. The cargo bay was surrounded by three snarling zombies. Cassie and Tess inched closer. They spotted Bruce – he had survived the gunshot to his upper right chest, at least so far. 'Bruce!" Cassie called out, but he seemed too preoccupied to notice.

Bruce had managed to crawl out of his cell out into the open part of the bay. He was on his knees, holding a zombie rod with collar that had been left in the cargo bay and was using it to push back the three Zs in an effort to keep them from climbing up inside.

Cassie scanned the area, seeing if there was anyone who could help them rescue Bruce. She spotted several more Zs shuffling around the cars in the area where the weed party had been rollicking just an hour before. She could see people scattered around the vicinity, lying on the ground, bloodied and writhing in pain. What she couldn't see, was anyone nearby who might help them out.

Suddenly, Tess grabbed ahold of Cassie with her left hand and pulled Cassie in tightly behind her. Tess began to advance, while reaching back and clutching Cassie with her left arm, keeping Cassie pressed into her shoulder blades. Cassie was more than frightened, but she decided to place her trust in

Tess. Soon they were close enough to command the three z' attention.

One of the zombies peeled away from the cargo van and stepped towards the two ladies. A second z quickly followed suit, and finally the third. Tess didn't flinch or back down. She continued forward, grasping Cassie even more tightly.

Inexplicably, the Zs stopped in their tracks. Tess began to emit a sound – a low, almost guttural tone with resonance. Tess turned to her side, shielding Cassie from the three zombies while the two women inched towards the truck. Once Tess passed them, she turned around, walking backwards so that she was still between the Zs and Cassie. The zombies stayed put.

Cassie rushed up to the truck tailgate, climbing inside. She crawled over to Bruce. Tess stayed on the ground, her back to the truck. The three Zs slowly shuffled toward her. Tess resumed her low resonant moan.

Cassie leaned over Bruce, who was lying on his left side. Several tears streaked down her cheeks. She stroked his goatee, then his short, jet black hair. "I saw you go down. I thought you had died."

Bruce clutched at the bullet wound just below his right collar bone. "Believe me, I feel like I did." Bruce coughed. A slow flow of blood dripped out of his mouth.

Cassie noticed how pale Bruce had become. "We need to get you an ambulance," she told him calmly. But as she glanced out the back of the truck, noting the number of bodies down on the ground in the periphery, she wasn't so sure how that was going to happen anytime soon.

The three Zs closed in on Tess. The zombies didn't seem quite sure what to make of her. They didn't attack her but didn't back off, either. She stood her ground, emitting her low-pitched moan, while a standoff developed. Cassie took notice of the three Zs. One wore shoulder pads and a Raider jersey, his shaved head painted jet black from the neck up, other than a billiard- ball white circle with the number eight painted near the crown of his skull. Another was wearing a Stabler jersey, sporting a silver- and black-streaked beard, just as old number twelve once donned decades before. The third was one of the Black Rock City lady zombies, wearing nothing but a collection of tattoos.

"Oh, God, no," Cassie pleaded out loud as she spied several more Zs that had been wandering nearby, now focused on the cargo truck. "Tess, get up in the truck," Cassie hollered at her friend. Tess didn't respond. Cassie, still on her knees, reached out beyond the tailgate, grabbing Tess's shoulder and pulling her back. Tess turned around. Cassie grabbed at her hand, pulling her up toward the cargo bay. Tess lifted herself inside.

"The control panel on the wall," Bruce called out, before stopping to cough. More blood dripped from his mouth. "There's a button to close the door, but I never got the chance to get to it."

Cassie rose up. With Tess occupying the zombies, she was at the panel in an instant. The door button was labeled. She pressed it. A mechanical buzz sounded, the door jerked for a second before stopping. "Oh, God, no," Cassie pressed the button again, to no avail. The three Zs had their hands on the tailgate. Behind them, more were on their way.

The Neighborhoods in the Lot

Sunday, 10:34 a.m., October 31st

Conner and Alan's helicopter landed in the one, clear spot in the complex – the football field. They were quickly escorted by Coliseum staff to the command center in the 66th Avenue lot. The sheriff took advantage of the Coast Guard chopper, placing an officer onboard to be his eyes in the sky, as well as to repeatedly broadcast a warning over the Hegenberger lot.

The chopper was soon doing just that, hovering low, with a recorded voice booming: "This is an emergency. Stay in your vehicles. If you are outside, get in the nearest available vehicle. Remain there until further notice. Do not attempt to drive. Remain calm and turn on your radio for further instructions."

On the 66th Avenue side, where there was no visible sign of trouble, many tailgaters had been compliant, and were patiently waiting in line to leave in an orderly manner. This was taking considerable time, given the snarl of traffic outside the complex. Large numbers of vehicles continued to head toward the coliseum complex, either not listening to the news and still headed to the game, or well aware of the news and wanting to get a personal viewing.

Two separate, large contingents of tailgaters had coalesced on the western ("D") and eastern ("A") sides of the 66th Avenue lot, in near riot mode and were refusing to leave. The two 66th Avenue mobs were unwilling to believe any explanations offered as to why the game was canceled or why they had to vacate the lot. They began chanting, continued drinking, with a mood growing uglier by the minute. Beer bottles began flying.

The sheriff's officers were seriously outmanned – most of their ranks were guarding the perimeter or were attempting to protect those in the Hegenberger lot. Reinforcements were still slow to arrive due to the snarl of traffic.

On the Hegenberger side, the neighborhoods in the parking lot had very different tales to tell. Virtually every bank of porta potties was overrun with Zs. In a number of stalls, zombies were trying unsuccessfully to climb down below but were unable to fit through the receptacles. Mostly, the Zs just repeatedly circled around the outside of the toilets.

The far southeastern corner was becoming eerily quiet – large numbers of wounded, infected persons littered the ground. Terrified tailgaters locked themselves in their cars. Occasional Zs wandered between the cars.

Sheriff's officers concentrated their forces in securing the BART ramp and the passageway by the Oracle arena. They began escorting small nearby groups that were stranded away from their cars, taking them up both walkways and over to the 66th Avenue side. The overhead bridge to the BART station wasn't being used, as the sheriff had ordered it locked, to prevent anyone else from entering the complex or anyone infected from exiting.

The site of the initial riot on the Hegenberger side, just to the west of the weed party, was now littered with infected on the ground, but the riot had morphed. The group continued to gravitate west and grow in size, as tailgaters would venture in to find out what was going on. There was no longer law enforcement trying to control the crowd; those officers had all been taken down by Zs or hooligans in the initial riot. Now the mob was simply behaving badly – fighting, damaging vehicles as they progressed, throwing beer bottles indiscriminately.

Chaos reigned throughout the mob; there were several zombies in their midst, randomly attacking participants. There was too much going on, too quickly, for those in the swarm of people to register that they were under attack.

Other pockets of the Hegenberger lot were still relatively calm. Many in the lot were doing exactly what they were told – staying locked inside their cars, finding and listening to news stations on the radio that were now focused on covering the incident. Some tailgaters were venturing through the lot, looking for missing loved ones, or seeking to help anyone in need. Others somehow continued to ignore the growing storm, as long as their neighborhood in the lot remained calm. They cracked open more beer and partied on.

Knock Yourself Out, Conner

Conner and Alan stood before the sheriff and his aides. The sheriff and staff were seated at folding tables commandeered from nearby 66th Avenue lot tailgates. The sheriff stood and shook their hands. "I understand you two must have had quite a day or two on that cruise ship. And now you've jumped from the frying pan into the fire, gentleman, so I appreciate you making yourselves available to help us out. I'm sure you can imagine I don't have time to even fart right now, so I'm hoping you can just take sixty seconds and tell me anything really big you think I need to hear, and then just make yourselves comfortable, and we'll call on you for expertise over and over in the next few hours, I am sure."

Alan spoke up. "Thank you, sir. We've been briefed on your setup and your plan. I guess the perspective we need to bring you, given we just went through this on the ship, is you need to take the infected into consideration. Some of them turn quickly – because they have drugs in their system or they experience some kind of trauma. But most of them lying out there in the parking lot aren't causing you any problems right now, so they've not been your highest priority. Within a couple of hours from the time of infection, they will turn. Judging from what we saw flying in and from our briefing, the numbers of infected lying on the ground are going to simply overwhelm you when they turn. You have too many people that have been bitten in too short of a time out in that parking lot."

The sheriff briefly laughed. "Well aren't you the bearer of good news. I don't suppose you have any advice I haven't heard already on what we're supposed to do about that?"

"Actually, I do," Alan continued. "Conner here suggested it – after we commented on how surreal it was to land in a chopper on the fifty yard line. You have an empty stadium at your disposal. You've got all those luxury suites with elevator access and doors that lock. Use the Coliseum employees stuck here at the stadium and volunteers from the lot if you must, to help your officers start retrieving those infected people off the parking lot and get them locked up in the suites."

The sheriff nodded. "That's good. That's very good. I like that better than what my guys out in the lot keep suggesting when they radio into us, which is to shoot them all. I'm trying to remind them about the zombie laws but they're feeling a little up to their asses in alligators right now, while we're talking about draining the swamp." The sheriff turned to an aide to his right. "You heard what this man said – and by the way – you know we're talking to the man they named this damn disease after don't you? This is Dr. Gorman. So go put Dr. Gorman's idea into motion right now."

The sheriff turned back toward Alan. "Speaking of zombie laws, I'm having trouble pinning anyone down so far at Homeland Security about rules of engagement. The regulations, as I understand them are pretty unworkable for our situation, so I haven't been aggressively reining my officers in, if you know what I mean. I must say, Tasers have been as worthless on them as solar powered night goggles. How far have I been sticking my neck out, here, Dr. Gorman?"

Alan smiled. "Sheriff, we heard that question asked a lot during the past day on the ship. There is no good answer. The law was clearly written for infected who are contained in a secured area. Direction came late, but eventually the Coast Guard on the ship was told to defend themselves at all costs.

"Well, that won't work, it makes too much sense," the sheriff replied, laughing. The sheriff turned away, getting ready to take another phone call.

"Excuse me, sir," Conner broke in. "We need to know if the kidnapper's vehicle with the Gorman's disease cases has been found or if anyone from the vehicle has been located. We were just with two of their hostages the night before."

The sheriff looked impatient. He had an endless queue of phone calls to get through. "Son, we haven't. And there is nothing I would rather do than catch those S.O.B. terrorists this minute and shove them up the asses of these zombies they brought with them. We've just been buried in rescue and crowd control and securing a perimeter. We're waiting on Homeland Security to bring some manpower and resources to sort through the lot and nail them."

"I think Alan can provide all the expertise that you need for consultation here, sir. I would be able to spot the two hostages if they're somewhere in the lot, and I would have a good idea as to what their transport vehicle would entail. I know you're short on manpower, sir, for the time -being. I'd like to volunteer to go out into the lot and locate them."

The sheriff let loose another short laugh. "You want to go out into that lot? My own officers don't want to go out into that lot anymore."

"Sir, I just spent a day and half on a ship that was the equivalent of that parking lot, and two months ago I was inside Burning Man. I know what I'm asking to do, here," Conner responded, looking him straight in the eye.

The sheriff smiled. "Oh, wait a minute. You're the guy. Now I get it. I saw you on television two months ago. You're the guy who fought his way out of Burning Man, in a Star Wars costume, to rescue your girlfriend." The Sheriff again let out a short laugh. "Alright, fine, you want to help us look for those terrorists and your hostages until Homeland Security gets here, you go knock yourself out. We'll even set you up with credentials and a radio unit so you can tell someone here what you're up to."

The sheriff turned to a different aide, instructing him to set up Conner with a radio and a lanyard with credentials to get him access to the Hegenberger lot. Conner asked the aide if he could spare some any protective gear as well.

Conner turned to Alan, looking sheepish for asking permission after the fact. "I'm sorry, Alan. I hope you're okay with my going."

Alan shook his head. "I think you're nuts. We need to learn to leave this sort of thing to the experts. But, as the sheriff said, knock yourself out, Conner. Just come back alive. And unbitten. And find our friends, while you're at it."

The Search for
Cassie and Bruce

Conner stood in BART plaza, the concourse intersection of the east side entrance. He pulled the lanyard over his head, and tightened the flak jacket, shin guards, helmet and utility belt with radio the sheriff's aide outfitted him with. He slipped his own sat phone into another container in the utility belt.

Conner grasped the baseball bat the aide donated to him, freshly brought in by one of the officers, taken from one of the 66th Avenue lot rioters who was just apprehended. He approached the officer policing access at the top of the BART ramp descending to the Hegenberger lot. Conner flashed his lanyard. "You really want to go down there?" the officer asked, not looking for an answer.

Conner considered his two friends from Parker Creek, perhaps the only links to his past and his future. He pictured both Bruce and Cassie then and now. He smiled. "I do," he answered. All he wanted was another chance to get things right with Cassie. He was not going to think the worst. Bruce was with her. They would watch out for each other. They were going to be okay.

Conner passed two officers escorting a group of around fifteen shell-shocked looking individuals up the ramp. Two women in the group were crying hysterically. One of the men in the group had twisted his ankle and was leaning on a friend for support.

Conner stopped as the ramp rounded the corner slightly, and scanned the parking lot while he still had a higher vantage point. He spotted the RV and oversize vehicle section straight ahead, underneath the power lines the traversed at the southern end of the "B" lot. Conner figured whatever transport carried the Zs inside had to be parked in that section, if it was still on the premises. He continued down the ramp, which curved inward as he descended, so that he had to veer left by the time he reached bottom.

Conner came across twenty or so bloodied, unattended, infected individuals lying neatly in three rows behind the first set of cement barriers near the start of the ramp. Whoever placed them there was long gone.

After the first set of barriers was a curb and access drive, followed by another set of cement barriers. An equal number of unattended wounded were lying next to these barriers, this time in one long, winding row.

Between the second barriers and the start of the RV section was a bank of porta potties with a number of Zs milling about. They were preoccupied with the toilets enough so that the sheriff's officers were able to sneak their escorted groups along the walkway next to the stadium and up the ramp without interference. Conner decided to follow that longer route and not risk drawing the porta potty Zs attention.

Conner cut south from the stadium walkway, keeping low and running between vehicles. Through his helmet visor, he could see people ducking down inside over half the cars. One rolled down their window, imploring Conner to get in and hide with them. Conner just shook his head and moved on.

After clearing several rows of cars, he sprinted out in the open, up to the two long rows of RVs. He began to scan the vehicles, looking for any that might have been modified for transporting a load of zombies. Looking down the row, it seemed like a ghost town, save for a few scattered people shuffling around toward the other end who were most likely Zs, and a large number of bodies strewn around on the ground, mostly at the far end.

As Conner ventured past the first RV to the left, the second door opened. A man popped his head out – a shaved, completely silver head at that – asking if Conner was with the police. Conner explained that he was not a policeman, but was working with them to find the vehicle that brought in all the people infected with Gorman's disease. The man said that he didn't know what that meant, but he had friends inside who needed help, and their whole group was frightened and panicking. He pleaded for Conner to come inside to check on his friends and explain to everyone what was going on.

Conner sighed – not wanting experience delays – but stepped inside the RV. There were at least five other men with shaved silver heads dressed in Raider jerseys, women in faux Raider cheerleader outfits, a few teenagers not in costume, a man and woman in Frankenstein makeup, and several bloodied men on the floor draped in blankets.

Conner was always taken back a little when he encountered people who weren't familiar with Gorman's disease or what had transpired at Burning Man, given he had lived it personally and talked about it now for a living. But the group in the RV had not heard about the Burning Man zombie invasion two months ago. They were having difficulty getting their heads around what was going down.

Conner did his best to give them an abridged zombie 101 primer. He confirmed the three men covered in blankets had been bitten and insisted the group carry them outside the RV, and make them as comfortable as possible away from the vehicle. Conner impressed upon them that those who were bitten were infected and would progress to the more deadly stage within a couple hours. The group could offer Conner no insightful intelligence that might help him locate Cassie and Bruce. Conner wished the group good luck and continued down the row.

Conner had similar conversations with several other RV groups. No one had actionable information that might help him locate Cassie or Bruce. One trailer did provide Conner with a hunting knife, which he attached to his utility belt.

Halfway down the row, Conner started to encounter the zombies pacing around outside the vehicles. Rather than engage them, Conner ducked in between the next two RVs, into the next row, which turned out to be a major mistake. The second row at the southern end was infested with Zs shuffling around listlessly. They seemed to snap to attention upon Conner's arrival. While the majority was outfitted in Raider jerseys or costumes, Conner spotted a couple that were more tattered and sporting playa dust.

Conner retreated between the recreational vehicles, back to the first row, with the second row Zs following him. Conner scanned the area, considering his choices. A half-dozen zombies were scattered in front of him, starting to close in. A stream of zombies was on his tail. He didn't want to take refuge in any of the RV's, or he might get trapped there for the duration.

Conner decided to press ahead. He shifted his hold on the baseball bat so that he was grasping the handle with both hands. He swung away at the forehead of the first zombie in front of him, a pathetic looking skinny man in a short-sleeved Raider jersey with his right arm mostly chewed off, exposing the bare skeleton. Conner's blow knocked the z backwards several steps, while Conner moved past him.

Conner managed to simply race past the second and third Zs, but his path took him directly in front of a large, tall Samoan zombie in an oversize Raider jersey, who looked like he should be playing for the team. Conner couldn't get leverage to effectively swing upwards at the Samoan's head, so he decided to swing hard directly at the Zs nuts, something he had never tried before.

Conner connected his swing on target, but the blow didn't seem to register with the Samoan. The z reached toward Conner, lifting him off the ground by the shoulders, pulling him close in order to begin biting away. Conner tried to run or push off with his feet, but they were suspended in air. With his right hand, Conner used his bat to whack the side of the Samoan's head. That blow didn't register either.

The Samoan z lunged forward, gnashing its teeth, trying to tear into Conner. It connected only with helmet and flak jacket. Conner dropped his bat and reached for the hunting knife he had been given. He clutched the handle with his right hand, reached back, and thrust it into the zombie's forehead. Without his feet touching the ground, he lacked the leverage to quickly finish the z off. The knife penetrated only part way.

Conner reached up with his left hand as well, pressing into the zombie's skull with both hands as hard as he could.

Slowly the Samoan lowered its arms until Conner's feet reached the ground. With the added leverage, he pierced the knife far enough into the brain for the Samoan z to collapse to the ground, the knife still embedded in its skull.

Conner could feel the two Zs he had just passed grabbing at his back. Conner spun to the side, eluding their grip. Seeing the bat just below him, he kicked it to his left, providing some separation between the bat and the two zombies. He sprinted to the bat, lifted it up, and swung away at both their heads. He connected with consecutive swings, sending each backward, toward the mass of zombies from the second row that were pouring in from in between the RVs.

Two zombies remained in front of him, standing just outside the last RV's doorway. Both had residual playa dust on their clothing. Both were about five foot seven inches. One was a Chinese z with smoky black hair. The other was a crew cut Caucasian with multi-colored tattoos of serpents on its right and left upper arms.

Conner surmised that neither Zs clothes were tattered enough for them to have been Black Rock City zombies the past two months. They had to have been part of Bruce's research crew or perhaps they were the hijackers. Conner looked over his shoulder and realized he had no time to figure that out. The wave of zombies was close behind. Conner also decided he no longer had time to retrieve the knife from the Samoan's forehead.

He sprinted all the way to the RV opposite the two Zs. He could see a number of persons poking their heads up to the RV windows, watching him intently. Conner witnessed a bloodied body crawling headfirst out of the RV behind the two Zs, the door partially unhinged and propped wide open.

Conner thought better of tangling with the Chinese and the crew-cut zombies, with so many z reinforcements just behind him. He had the angle on the two Zs. He raced out of the RV row into open space not far from the Baldwin gate.

In front of Conner was a hodge-podge of cars that had cut each other off, trying to exit through the Baldwin gate. They now formed a small sea of vehicles in complete gridlock. Nearly all passengers remained inside their cars, listening intently to the radio. Conner cut through the lines of cars wherever he could. He unfortunately brought the wave of second row Zs following behind him, who spread out amongst the vehicles, pounding on the windows at the people inside.

Conner scanned the area and spotted the cargo truck near the fence, well right of the gate. Another large group of zombies were milling around the back of the open cargo bay. Someone was standing at the edge of the cargo bay, fending off the zombies trying to get in the truck, with their bare hands. Conner wove through the reminder of the chaotic line of cars, until he reached open area.

He was close enough take a good look at the lady pushing back the Zs as they tried to climb into the truck. She had the tell-tale zombie skin pigmentation, but seemed to be behaving in a much more human manner. The lady sported a film of playa dust on her clothing and seemed oddly familiar.

Suddenly it dawned on him. "Tess?" he called out.

Running Over Z's

Conner stepped closer to the cargo truck. More than a dozen zombies gathered around the back, their attention focused on the cargo bay. Conner could make out two shadowy figures up in the bay behind Tess — one lying down, the other kneeling. They looked like Cassie and Bruce to Conner, but it was hard to tell, given the angle of the sun overhead and the shadows in the back of the truck.

Conner glanced around the area. There were isolated Zs in the periphery, stumbling toward the cargo truck from every direction. There also was the herd of Zs that followed him out from the RVs, who were currently occupied harassing those inside the jumble of cars behind him but might find their way over to the cargo truck at any time.

At the moment, Conner didn't feel as bound by the zombie laws as perhaps the sheriff's officers did. He had been through this before in the cruise ship and at Burning Man. He no longer felt any hesitation, if zombie blood needed to be spilt. Conner was hesitating, however, at what to do about the current situation in front of him.

The thought finally occurred to Conner that perhaps there was something useful in the cab of the truck, assuming it was unlocked. Whoever had kidnapped Cassie, Bruce, Tess and the zombies must have brought weapons with them. Hopefully, the kidnappers still weren't in the cab.

Conner kept some distance from the truck, trotting up to the fence. He caught the eye of a couple of the Zs, who broke from the pack and headed toward him, but most of the zombies stayed focused on the cargo bay. After reaching the fence, he sprinted to the driver door, beating the two Zs by a good distance.

Fortunately, the door was unlocked. He placed the baseball bat in his left hand, opened the door, and climbed in. He slammed the door shut as the two Zs arrived, pawing at the window. Conner removed his helmet. The radio was blaring

AC/DC's Highway to Hell. He turned the volume off and surveyed the cab. He spotted several water bottles. It dawned on Conner that Cassie and Bruce had probably been locked up in the back, probably without water for a day and a half.

Conner next spied the second Glock – the one Raymond left behind in the front bench seat. Conner was not an expert on guns, and wasn't even sure if the safety was on or if there were bullets in the pistol. Not wanting to wait to find out when he really needed to use it, he decided to try some target practice. He grabbed the Glock and scooted over next to the driver window.

Conner lowered the window a little – providing enough space for the pistol. The Zs reached toward the window opening with their arms outstretched. Conner aimed the Glock directly at one of the Zs foreheads and squeezed the trigger. The zombie dropped to the ground immediately. Conner quickly rolled the window back up. Conner wondered why the gunshot wasn't louder — not recognizing the gun was equipped with a silencer.

Conner gingerly set the Glock on the floorboard for the moment. He wasn't sure how to work the safety. He continued to scan the cab. He spotted Cassie's purse on the floorboard on the passenger side. It had been rifled through. Their two Raider tickets lay on top of the purse. He considered the irony that they had indeed made it to the Coliseum in time for the game, just as they'd planned. Conner opened the glove box, finding a first aid kit. He pulled the kit out – deciding it might be useful, given he didn't know what condition Cassie or Bruce were in.

Conner looked in the back seat of the cab and noticed a weighted net. Bruce had shown him similar nets used to bring capture zombies in Black Rock City to bring back to the research facility. Conner wadded up the net and placed in in the front seat.

Conner looked at the dashboard. "Oh, yes. Yes, yes, yes," he exclaimed out loud. The keys were in the ignition. He got behind the wheel and turned the switch. The truck fired up. He had a plan, but he had to hope that his passengers in the back would figure it out. The truck was positioned so that there was twenty feet of clearance behind it.

A number of non-RV oversize vehicles were parked against the fence. Behind them was a lane for traffic, and then the first row of cars. The traffic lane to the east had filled with vehicles unsuccessfully trying to leave via the Baldwin Gate, but the lane was still empty directly behind the truck. Conner planned to back up the truck with a little acceleration and hopefully mow down some of the zombies behind them. He could pull forward and repeat the exercise several times.

Conner considered how he was going to transport the goodies he found in the cab back to the cargo bay afterwards, given there would assuredly still be Zs to contend with. Glancing around, he saw am empty daypack on the back floorboard. He stuffed the netting, water bottles, first aid kit and Glock inside, and strapped the pack on his back – no easy feat given the flak jacket he was sporting. It was awkward to drive with the daypack on, forcing him to lean way forward.

Conner donned his helmet, and grabbed the automatic transmission gear shift. He began jerking the vehicle back and forth a few inches at a time, increasing the distance and acceleration each time, hoping it would provide a signal to his passengers to hang on. For good measure he honked the horn a couple of times.

Conner drew in his breath, hoping he was not sending anyone flying off the back end, and floored the truck in reverse. He could feel the bumps of zombies underneath the tires as he backed up. Watching his path in the rear view mirror, he braked before getting too close to the cars parked behind him.

Now most of the zombies stood in front of him, staggering toward the truck. Several were on the ground after having been run over. Conner floored the truck forward, mowing the Zs down that stood in front of him. He repeated this process several times, until none were left standing, as he parked back against the fence, leaving the keys in the ignition.

Conner realized that most of the Zs he ran over were still functioning – they were on the ground with broken bones or had just been temporarily knocked over. Only a few had been taken out of the game for good, their heads having been squished under the tires. Surveying the surrounding area, Conner could see a number of isolated zombies wandering toward the truck and the activity it was generating.

Conner decided this was his window of opportunity. He turned his thoughts to Cassie, hoping to motivate him to survive long enough to see her in the back of the truck. He opened the driver door with his left hand– his daypack strapped on over his flak jacket, his helmet nestled over his head, his baseball bat gripped in his right hand.

Conner's feet hit the ground. He sprinted to the back of the truck. Several Zs had already risen from the ground and were staggering back toward the vehicle. Conner reached the tailgate. He rolled his bat into the bay and lifted himself up. Tess reached over to push him back.

"Tess, it's me!" Conner exclaimed.

Cassie gasped and then screamed his name, before pulling Tess back and allowing Conner to scoot all the way in. He rose up on his knees, pulled off his helmet, leaned forward and hugged Cassie, who crawled forward to greet him. Conner quickly peeled off his backpack while glancing over at Bruce, who was lying uncomfortably on his back, his right shoulder area soaked in blood.

"Has he been bit?" Conner asked, fearing the worst.

Cassie and Bruce answered almost simultaneously that he had been shot.

It was clear to Conner that all of them were parched. He zipped open the daypack, pulled out the three water bottles and rolled them over to Cassie. "Here," he offered, "I brought you these." Conner didn't have time to appreciate how grateful they appeared. While Cassie frantically opened each bottle, Conner picked up the bat and stationed himself above the tailgate, and began swinging away at the handful of zombies that had staggered back up to make a nuisance of themselves again.

Conner glanced further out, pleasantly surprised to see that most of the Zs were stuck on the ground with broken legs or other ailments after being run over, preventing them from rising up to return to the truck.

While Conner fended off three zombies still in the fight, Cassie held a bottle up to Bruce's lips, while he slowly sucked down the warm water. Tess managed to figure out how to grasp the bottle that Cassie opened for her and gulped down the entire amount in seconds.

Conner landed a mighty head blow on a z dressed in a full body skeleton costume, sending the zombie to the ground for the count. Conner then proceeded to bash the fingers of the two other Zs trying to climb up, until their digits and wrists were broken beyond functionality. The two Zs stood at the tailgate, unable to grab onto anything, flapped their arms up and down in apparent frustration.

Conner could see that other surrounding Zs were slowly making their way over. They had maybe a couple of minutes of respite. He turned to notice the four cells immediately behind the central area in the cargo bay. "Should we retreat into one of these rooms, or can Bruce get up and move with us up to the cab of the truck?"

"I don't think he can go anywhere," Cassie answered on Bruce's behalf. "There is no exit wound, and he's not looking so good. And we can't get into the cells behind us anymore. Something went haywire with the control panel over there." Cassie pointed to the interior panel. "We can't get it to close the overhead door to the back. Even worse, playing with the buttons, we accidently locked the cell doors and now we can't get them to open. Bruce says there is an exterior panel too, but we haven't been able to get outside to check it out."

"Okay," Conner answered, and promptly hopped out of the truck, pushing the broken handed Zs aside. He ran to one side of the truck and then the other, with the two Zs following him. He located a panel on the passenger side that contained a button to open the overhead door, but no controls for the interior doors. He pushed the overhead door button with no results and returned to the cargo bay.

Conner again shoved the two broken-handed Zs out of the way. He climbed in to report he'd had no luck only to find Cassie stroking Bruce's hair and picked up a vibe that discomforted him a little, but he decided to not dwell on. Tess leaned over and hugged him, causing Cassie and even Bruce to laugh.

"She never did that to me," Bruce protested, before coughing again.

"You never brought her a bottle of water," Cassie laughed. She then studied Conner's face. "Where have you been and how did you find us?"

"You won't believe the past day I had on a cruise ship full of zombies. When we reached the bay this morning, they flew us here. But I have, like, a million questions and I don't think we have time for too many of them," Conner began, nervously scanning outside. Conner received the sixty second version from Cassie of how they encountered Tess, how special she appeared to be, how they were kidnapped, trapped in the back of the truck, and dealt with a psychotic captor.

Conner turned his attention to Bruce. "You don't look so good, buddy," he said, smiling as he leaned over his friend. "Let me call Alan and see if we can get some help for you." Conner chose not to use the radio he had been provided and instead pulled his sat phone from his utility belt. He reached Alan and quickly explained the situation and Tess's presence. Mid-conversation, Conner had to cut-him off. "I'll have to call you back, Alan. See what you can do. We've got more trouble coming."

Conner put his phone back in the belt, before leaning down to pick up his helmet and bat. Several new zombies had arrived on the scene.

The Second Wave

Conner stood at the edge of the cargo bay, swinging his bat down on the Zs hands, which were grasping at his feet. He was reluctant to swing the bat from side to side, as Tess stood next to him in the middle of the bay.

Conner took a brief moment to admire Tess's ability to push the zombie in front of her away from the truck without the z attempting to bite her and with enough force to send it to the ground. Conner instructed Cassie to pull the weighted net and Glock pistol out of the daypack, and leave them near Bruce. They could use both when things got desperate. Cassie then picked up the rod to the zombie collar that they had used before Conner arrived to ward off the Zs. She positioned herself to Tess's left, and began to shove the nearest zombie away with the rod.

Bruce lifted his head enough to watch the three fending off the Zs. He experienced a moment of deja vu. The four of them had spent hours fighting through the same scenario in the Alamo at Burning Man, two months before. "Seems like old times, doesn't it Connerman?" Bruce weakly called out.

"Hah," was all the response Conner could muster. He glanced out into the parking lot. A growing number of isolated zombies from different points in the lot were staggering in the direction of the cargo truck. He realized it could be difficult to gain the opportunity to get back on the phone with Alan to try and arrange a rescue.

Conner stepped back long enough to grab his phone out of the belt and slide it over to Bruce before returning to the fight. "Bruce, I'm sorry to ask you to do this, man. I need you to dial the last number called and see what you can work out with Alan to get you out of here."

Conner, Tess, and Cassie continued to repeatedly push the same small group of zombies away from the truck, including two with broken hands that Conner had already disabled. All were in Raider jerseys, except one in a Darth Vader costume, complete with mask and cape. Conner continued to bash away at the hand and arms of the newer arrivals, hoping to render them useless as well.

But time ticked on. In their area of the parking lot, there wasn't much else going on. There were plenty of infected tailgaters lying on the ground, and many more frightened uninfected ones safely locked in the cars – but not many ambulatory targets for the zombies lurking through the area. The Zs in the southeast "B" quadrant of the Hegenberger lot began gravitating toward the cargo truck – if for no other reason than they were following other zombies already headed in that direction.

Bruce had several conversations with Alan Gorman about attempting bring in an armed crew with a gurney to retrieve them. The problem was, the sheriff's officers were still overbooked and overwhelmed; there were countless flashpoints of major trouble with promised reinforcements slow in arriving.

Bruce reminded Alan that with them was the Black Rock City infected woman who never progressed to stage two after two months, and that they possessed the truck that the hijackers had used and could personally identify their hijackers. The best Alan could get from the sheriff was to pass along encouragement to Bruce to hang in there.

For each z that Conner successfully battered a pair of hands into a useless mulch of broken bones, two new zombies arrived on the scene. Cassie and Tess were successfully keeping the zombies closest to the truck from climbing up, but the task was growing more endless and overwhelming. Conner began to tire from the constant swinging of the bat.

Soon, a half-hour had elapsed. Bruce began to lapse in and out of consciousness. Cassie and Conner were running out of steam. Only Tess seemed indefatigable – in a zone of her own, she pushed every z within her five-foot radius, away from the edge of the truck.

In scattered conversations, Cassie and Conner learned of each other's past thirty-six hours. Cassie came to understand

and appreciate that Conner had been through this same zombie siege scenario on the cruise ship for many hours, only to be rescued and taken to the Coliseum by helicopter, where he could have remained in safety at the command center but instead chose to search and come to her aid.

By a quarter to noon, as Cassie and Conner started to feel fairly pessimistic about their prospects, they began to sense something consequential was starting to occur in every corner of the parking lot. They could hear almost a humming sound radiating throughout the lot. They could see blurs of movement in every direction. A zombie tide was forming.

The sheriff had heeded Alan Gorman's advice and deployed officers to begin retrieving the infected from the Hegenberger lot, up the BART ramp and into the east side suites entrance. The problem was, they simply couldn't retrieve enough infected, fast enough.

There was not an accurate head count available to Alan or the sheriff regarding how many total tailgaters had been infected by the original zombies, and how many were still in stage one versus already in stage two. The stage two infected up to this point, beyond the original zombies from the cargo truck, included the infected with drugs in their system and those that experienced an accidental death.

From where he stood, Conner roughly guessed that the stage two numbered somewhere around two hundred, and there was easily more than a thousand stage one infected on the ground – perhaps as much as two thousand spread around the lot.

The majority of them had been infected more than two hours ago. They were starting to progress to stage two in big numbers. The second wave was beginning to arrive.

All Hell Breaks Loose

Sunday, 11:45 a.m., October 31st

Media helicopters swept around the complex like vultures, continuously being chased off by the two sheriff's department helicopters that joined the Coast Guard chopper on site. Traffic around the complex remained snarled, although the Homeland Security liaison and entourage made it to the stadium – taking the airport BART train after their charter flight arrived, and then having the sheriff's officer specially open the BART bridge to let them through.

Slowly, reinforcements from all available law enforcement agencies leaked through the gridlock of traffic. The sheriff's two helicopters began ferrying in small crews into the stadium as well. Still, the forces on-site were overwhelmed.

The riots in the 66th Avenue lot continued. The lot was far from emptied, and continued requiring crowd control. Securing the perimeter was taxing their resources, particularly as spectators from the outside continually tried to the sneak in, and some individuals without cars from the Hegenberger lot tried to sneak out. Troops were assembled with gurneys to transport stage one infected up to the east side luxury suites. There were also the patrols sent into the Hegenberger lot trying to restore order and offer assistance.

The sheriff's teams had already retrieved as many as one hundred fifty infected into the luxury suites, when the stage one cases began to convert in big numbers. Around ten infected turned while being transported up the BART ramp, taking down and infecting a number of officers and support staff up near the BART plaza.

The Homeland Security liaison's arrival on-site brought on a transition of power that further confused the situation at the worst possible time. As reports began to pour in about the second wave in the Hegenberger lot, with direction on how to process being sought from all corners of the complex, the sheriff and his aides were tied up with the Homeland Security entourage, going over matters relating to their assuming control of the incident management.

A palpable buzz could be sensed throughout the Hegenberger lot, as the stage one infected turned and began to rise up and join the other zombies in great numbers. Cassie, Conner and even Tess took measure of it from the back of their cargo truck as they fought off their attackers.

The buzz of the second wave began to unnerve, and then panic the thousands of tailgaters, who up to this point had patiently and obediently waited in their vehicles for an all-clear signal. Many started to flee their car on foot, causing others to see them and decide to do the same. Even more began to try to extricate their vehicles from their confined positions in the parking lot, ramming their cars and trucks into each other, hoping to clear enough space to break free.

Those in the far western end of the Hegenberger lot, in the "C" section – who remained outside their vehicles up to that point – caught the buzz of crowd noise and the initial thrusts of zombies into their areas. More than one barbeque of hot coals spilled over, rolling underneath running cars. A series of fires and explosions erupted in that end of the lot.

A growing number of people were fleeing on foot - which hadn't been a major issue until this point – as the second wave of Zs pursued them. A number of persons were trampled in the process. Some of those on foot began to climb up the middle observation tower in the B lot to escape the Zs on their tail. Even more tailgaters sought out the tower as a refuge when they saw others before them taking that route. The structure soon became seriously beyond capacity. It didn't take long for the tower to tip over, sending bodies flying everywhere, scattered amongst the zombies gathered below. A plume of dust rose from the tower's collapse. Several cars were partially crushed underneath the fallen structure. Z's began picking through the numbers that had tumbled off the tower as it went down.

A surge of tailgaters fled up the ramp in between the Coliseum and Oracle arena. A number of Zs were mixed in between them, attacking and biting the panicked masses as they progressed. The line securing the perimeter wasn't deep enough to hold back the crowd. Homeland Security had just radioed all law enforcement on site, advising that kill shots were authorized for all stage two infected when clean shots could be taken. But the zombies were too mixed in with the surging group for any of the officers to fire. Z's had now penetrated the 66th Avenue lot.

From the command center, Homeland Security decided to order the main stadium entrance to the lower level on the Hegenberger side opened to allow a safety valve for the panicked masses in the lot. A number of officers were placed inside, to direct those seeking refuge down to the field, where they would be secured and protected. The other entrances were to remain closed. Few tailgaters were taking advantage of the opened entrance to the stadium, unaware of its availability or too scared to give it a try.

Small numbers of the tailgaters had weapons in their cars, which started to come out as the panic spread. A few of the tailgaters took the fight to the zombies. A group of three men in vintage Los Angeles Raider tee shirts flanked each other, each armed with pistols and extra ammunition clips, shooting at anyone resembling a z as they marched toward the Hegenberger gate.

They mistakenly shot more than one non-infected tailgater as they continued toward the gate. Not knowing to aim for the head, the men mostly just shot up Zs without taking them down. The men eventually made it to the Hegenberger gate, where the line of officers denied them access outside, directing them instead to go to the 66th Avenue lot where they could get processed and cleared to exit. They were also asked to surrender their weapons.

The men were having none of it. They huddled and decided to charge the gate, assuming the officers wouldn't fire on them. They were wrong. A short gun battle ensued, which ended badly for the three men. A number of tailgaters near the gate, witnessing the incident, emerged from their cars and advanced on the officers. Angry confrontations began to flare up, tailgaters shouting at the authorities who had fired on people just trying to get out. A potential riot began to brew at the Hegenberger gate.

Those who had been content to ride things out in their cars saw increasing numbers of other vehicles attempting to drive away. Many decided to join the fray. A growing mass of vehicles in the parking lot began to move their cars around in the chaos, with no open lanes or clear paths forward. The Hegenberger lot began to resemble a crowded demolition derby — one in which pedestrians get run over.

Around the Coliseum complex, all hell had broken loose.

The Reverse Mohawk

Brady eyed the security detail at the 66th Avenue gate nervously. The crowd around him had been ordered to disperse and get in line to be processed through the gate, either on foot, or in their cars. The unruly group's mood had shifted. Their beer had run out. There was word that some Zs had made it over to the 66th Avenue lot. The group hadn't believed the zombie stories circulating the lot until everyone's smartphones started filling up with news alerts and even video from the Hegenberger side.

Three hours earlier, Brady walked away from the cargo truck, assuming Raymond was soon going to exit with the hijacked Zs in his mad hopes of selling them to his imagined bidders. Brady made it to the BART plaza, intending to take BART into San Francisco, where he could blend into the crowds and try to come up with a plan.

But a number of BART police were milling around the entrance to the overhead bridge to the station. Brady wasn't willing to risk walking by them, so he kept his head lowered, proceeding down the BART ramp into the 66th Avenue lot.

Once in the lot, he decided to work his way to the 66th Avenue exit. It took some time to maneuver through the buzz of activity of tailgate parties getting underway in every direction. As he closed in on the exit, he stopped in his tracks. There were two squad cars parked by the gate. The officers seemed to be surveying the crowd in the parking lot.

Brady lost his nerve. He turned around, eventually striking up conversation with several revelers in a large party underneath a row of canopies. Brady was offered a beer. Then another. Then a burrito. He continued to eye the squad cars in the distance, which just wouldn't leave.

After that, everyone in Brady's party began to notice frantic activity in the periphery – law enforcement, stadium security, ambulances, and paramedics scurrying around. The level of law enforcement stepped up. The 66th Avenue gates were closed. Soon announcements were being broadcast throughout the parking lot. Brady was trapped. He remained with the party – hoping to keep blending in with the crowd.

Brady kept an eye on the gate. He noticed it eventually was re-opened for exit only. There appeared to be a process requiring screening persons as they left, manned by numerous law enforcement. Brady chose to stay in the lot. As sheriff's officers began to pressure the parties to disperse, pack up, and make their way to the exits, Brady gravitated to where one of the riots was starting to percolate. He was able to bide considerable time drifting through the chaotic crowd.

Brady refrained from participating in the riot. He kept moving, careful to keep his distance from the law enforcement on the periphery. Brady soon realized they were encircled. The officers were outfitted in full riot gear. They began pressing in – compacting the crowd. Brady knew he was ensnared.

Suddenly, the officers retreated en-masse, sprinting toward the ramp in between the stadium and Oracle arena. Looking back, Brady could see some kind of major flare-up was occurring at the top of the Arena walkway. Some of the rioting crowd followed behind the officers, wanting to see what was happening, and remain part of the action.

Brady stayed behind. A large, muscular man with a shaved head and goatee, wearing a Bill Romanowski jersey tapped Brady on the shoulder and handed him a bottle of beer. He offered a bottle opener. They both sucked down several gulps. "You hear the news, man?" the Romanowski fan asked Brady before continuing, without waiting for an answer. "I was just listening on the car radio before things got out of hand here. Two terrorist dudes brought a car load of those people infected like zombies from Burning Man into the parking lot here. They've overrun the parking lot on the other side. And now, people are saying they're coming over the walkway over there to our side. I think it's time to get the hell out of Dodge, man. I'm calling it a day and my advice to you, man, is to do the same. Can you believe this? What kind of sick dudes would do this to other regular people? What kind of twisted shit-heads would do such a thing? I hate cops, man, but I hope they find these low-life shit-heads and crack their skulls open and feed 'em to the damn diseased zombie folk. They said on the radio they think these terrorist shits may still be in the parking lot and they're looking for them right now. I know if I found 'em, what I'd do to 'em, that's for sure. Damn shit heads got our Raider game canceled and now people are dying and rioting and getting infected. I sure wish I could get my hands on these two." The Romanowski fan stopped his rant, tilted his glass up, and chugged down the rest of his beer.

"Yeah." Brady smiled and nodded. "I know what you mean."

The Romanowski fan set his beer bottle down in the asphalt. "Yeah, well, keep an eye out for them. Raider fans have to stick together." He turned, peering toward the gate. "My friends are following the crowd up there, but not me. They got the car keys, so I'm just gonna run over to the gate and get out of here on foot while the getting's good. Want to come?"

Brady smiled and shook his head. "I have to wait a little longer. Good luck, man." The Romanowski fan fist bumped Brady and then began trotting toward the gate. Brady stared up at the sky, reflecting on his situation. He felt considerable remorse – not for his own actions, but for Raymond's. Brady cursed a series of expletives conjoined with Raymond's name.

In Brady's mind, everything that transpired during the past day that had gone south was solely attributable to Raymond. Brady viewed himself as a victim of Raymond's lunacy as well. He wasn't about to sit idly by and suffer the consequences for Raymond's sins. Brady was determined to extricate himself from the web that Raymond had spun.

It occurred to Brady that if pictures of them were being flashed all over the media and law enforcement, he needed to quickly change his looks. The Romanowski fan with the shaved head inspired him. He would find a way to shave his short curly hair and soul patch, and change his shirt from what might have been caught on video up in the Black Rock desert. Then some silver face paint would really do the trick.

The parking lot was full of discarded boxes and bags from fleeing tailgaters. All he needed was a sharp knife, a half-full water bottle, and some cleaning soap. Within a couple minutes, he found what he was looking for in an abandoned box of barbeque provisions. Brady continued his scavenger hunt. He came across an entire box of "Back in the Coliseum" tee shirts that had been abandoned by an unlicensed seller. It took a few more minutes, but a can of aerosol silver face paint with a small quantity remaining, presented itself near the top of a garbage can.

Brady felt a wave of relief. After his transformation, he would mix in with a crowd, and head for the 66th Avenue exit. He maneuvered in between a row of cars with his knife, water, soap, shirt, and paint. He stooped down to get eye level with the driver side mirror. Brady dumped some of the water on his head, and then lubricated his hair with the liquid soap. He pulled out the knife, slowly and carefully scraping the hair in the middle of his scalp, starting his haircut with a reverse Mohawk. Brady smiled at the thought of how he'd look if he stopped there.

Brady raised the knife to start scraping a second row from his forehead back to the base of his skull when he spotted movement in the side mirror. "Drop the knife and raise your arms slowly," a voice commanded. Brady turned to find himself face to face with a sheriff's officer pointing a pistol at him. The officer issued a request for on his shoulder radio for backup. Another officer arrived in seconds, flanking him from the other side of the car, cutting off any hope for escape Brady might have been thinking of.

Brady dropped the knife and raised his hands. "This just seems too suspicious – somebody shaving their head in the middle of all this," the first officer hollered over to the second. "He sure looks like he matches the description to me," he added, while continuing to point the pistol at Brady's head. Another officer arrived.

A minute later Brady was cuffed and escorted over to the command center.

Conner's Last Stand

Sunday, 12:05 p.m., October 31st

Conner's mind began to wander as he methodically swung his baseball bat at the zombies below him. He glanced to his left at Cassie, trying to refresh his memory of her freckles, her strands of soft brown hair, and the curve of her shoulders, so he could picture her in his mind while he continued beating back the Zs.

His took the luxury of dwelling on a single moment — during the early spring of their freshman year in high school in Parker Creek – when Cassie decided to join the Junior Varsity girls' softball team, and had Conner pitch a whiffle ball to her for over a half hour in her front yard, while she practiced swinging away.

Conner wasn't sure exactly when the situation became hopeless. He just knew, as he scanned out into the parking lot from the back of the cargo truck, that it had been so for a while. All they could do now was hang in there as long as they could.

In the distance, the Hegenberger parking lot was filled with brawls; fires; cars ramming into each other; panicked pockets of people running through the lot with zombies in their midst; officers firing at isolated Zs when they had a clear shot, which was seldom; and stretches where zombies dominated the asphalt.

The area around the cargo truck was one such place where the Zs where in charge. In the foreground, it seemed to Conner there was an endless sea of zombies trying to climb up into the truck. They had been defending themselves since he arrived almost an hour before, and he was exhausted. He remembered from Burning Man that swinging a piece of wood didn't seem too difficult at first, but to do it repetitively for an hour at full force, with muscles you weren't used to using, would eventually drain you.

Early on, Tess and Cassie traded positions, so that Cassie was in the middle, poking back the Zs with the rod attached to the zombie collar. It was a much less effective tool than Conner's bat or Tess's ability to simply intimidate and push back the zombies with her bare hands without fear of being bitten.

Conner some time ago instructed Cassie to grab the Glock from his daypack, and start using it whenever a zombie not being attended to by Tess or Conner managed to start lifting themselves up into the cargo bay. Conner wasn't sure how many bullets were left to work with.

Bruce was not in good shape. He had difficulty even re-positioning himself a matter of inches. He no longer was capable of initiating a call. Alan phoned a number of times, but on each occasion, the call was cut off or Bruce wasn't able to answer before the call went to voice mail.

Conner continued to bash at the heads and hands of the Zs that forced their way to the front of the swarm. Almost all were in black Raider jerseys. Those that weren't were in a full menu of costumes, with a scattering of Zs in normal street clothes. Now and then, Conner would connect an awesome blow to the skull that sent a z to the ground. Occasionally, Conner would break enough digits, wrists and forearms to render a Zs upper limbs useless. But most of the time, all he could manage was to knock a zombie back a ways into the crowd.

Tess was the reason they had survived this long. The Zs on her side didn't seem to aggressively contest her pushbacks when they advanced to the front. They simply shifted around to regain their balance, then shuffled back forward, trying to shove themselves into the front row again.

Time seemed to slow down for Conner. His own movements — and those of his friends and the attacking Zs — seemed to regress to a few frames per second. He watched Cassie lower the rod in her right hand, lift the Glock in her left, step forward and fire a kill shot into the forehead of a zombie in a referee's shirt and black pants that had managed to lift itself up into the cargo bay enough to land its knees inside the bay.

Conner swung his bat down hard on the zombie hands clutching at the far edge of the cargo bay. He lifted up and repeated the process down the row until he was encroaching on Cassie's space. He darted forward to smash his bat into the nose of a z at his corner of the truck, which had managed to start crawling inside on its stomach. He smashed the bat into the Zs nose several times, until the momentum sent the zombie backwards into the crowd. The broken nose started to ooze the trademark green-gray oily zombie blood, before quickly coagulating and just leaving a cake of dried z blood on the lower half of its face.

Conner glanced over at Tess, calmly focusing on her business at hand. Suddenly, Tess turned sideways, as if she sensed Conner's gaze, and shot him a reassuring smile.

Another zombie in a full football uniform, including helmet, slipped past Cassie's initial thrust with the rod. It placed its palms on the edge of the truck, thrusting itself forward until its hips rested inside the cargo bay. It then pushed off the floor with its hands, and to stand upright, next to Tess. Tess stepped back and shoved it against the side of the truck, in front of the control panel. Cassie lifted the Glock, took a step forward, so that Tess was not in the line of fire, and fired the pistol.

The shot pierced the Zs neck, exiting the z and blasted into the control panel. A number of sparks erupted. A clicking sound could be heard behind Bruce. The football uniformed zombie advanced toward Cassie, but Tess stepped back again, grabbed a hold of the z, pushed off with her legs and sent the zombie airborne out the back of the truck.

Conner hoped the sound they just heard were the cell doors unlocking, after the control panel sparked. He also realized that they had few or maybe even no bullets left in Cassie's pistol. When the ammunition was gone, Cassie wouldn't stand a chance very long with just the rod, which would mean some Zs would get inside the bay, bringing everything to an end.

Conner beheld Cassie for just a split second, who was taking the time to glance back worriedly at Bruce. Conner just wanted her to be happy. More than that, he just wanted her to live. He felt a sharp pang of sadness that he would never get the chance to win her heart back after the glow of their relationship dimmed in the aftermath of Burning Man. His sorrow engulfed him at the thought he would never get the possibility to grow old with her.

Conner turned around and reached for the weighted net at Bruce's feet, which he had held in reserve. "Cassie, grab an end of this net," Conner called out to her. After he did so, he motioned for them to step forward and toss it over the front rows of Zs pulling themselves up into the truck. "Now!" Conner yelled and they tossed the net together over the entire mass of Zs surrounding the tailgate.

Buying them a little time as all the Zs near the tailgate became ensnared in the net; Conner turned around and checked the third cell door. It opened. "Bruce, baby, forgive me if this hurts, but I'm going to get you inside here," Conner hollered to Bruce. He reached over and began dragging Bruce to the door.

Bruce let out several weak moans. "Conner, don't bother. Just let me be and help Cassie." Conner ignored his pleas, pulling him all the way inside the cell.

Conner emerged back into the cargo bay, tugging and pulling Cassie into the cell with Bruce.

"Conner, damn it, what do you think you're doing?" She objected angrily, as he got her into the cell.

"I've got a plan, Cassie," Conner reassured her, standing in the cell doorway.

"Conner, the door doesn't lock anymore. We can't keep them out." She yelled unhappily.

"Look," Conner replied calmly. "Tess will be just outside the door, keeping them from getting in. They won't hurt Tess. Just keep the door shut, sit next to it, pressing your feet against the side wall. And use your last bullets if any Zs make it through."

Cassie realized there wasn't time to argue. "Well then, get in here too," she commanded Conner.

"Sorry, Cassie," Conner apologized. "I'm going to climb out on up to the roof and get down to the cab. Then I'm going to drive the truck around to get rid of some of these zombies." He closed the door.

"Conner, that's nuts," Cassie shouted, pounding on the door from the other side.

Conner grabbed Tess's hand and yanked her back with him. He motioned for her to guard the door in front of Cassie and Bruce's cell. Conner then turned around to make his way to the tailgate and lift his way up to the roof.

He never got the chance. Several zombies had already managed to work their way around the Zs trapped underneath the net. Two crawled inside the bay, then two more. They advanced toward Conner and Tess.

Conner looked at Tess and smiled. He lifted up his bat for the last time.

A Wave of Sadness

Conner thrust his bat against the face of the approaching z. He knocked it back several feet, but didn't disable the zombie. A second z reached in, gnashing its teeth unsuccessfully into Conner's helmet and flak jacket.

Conner gripped the bat with both hands in front of him, holding the bat horizontally, extending it into both Zs to push them back. As he thrust forward, another z latched onto the bat, then another. The initial zombie bearing the brunt of Conner's thrust managed to grab on as well. Conner became engaged in a bat tug-of-war – a battle that he was losing.

And then he lost. The zombies stumbled backwards with the bat as Conner lost his grip. Tess slipped into the vacated space between Conner and the Zs. She placed her left hand behind her, guiding and pressing Conner into the angled corner between the third and fourth cell doors. She pressed him forcefully against that corner with her back, attempting to shield as much of him as possible with her own body.

Tess began her low pitch moan, as she repeatedly pushed back the advancing Zs. The open area of the cargo bay filled with zombies – their arms outstretched. Conner was mystified, as the zombies wouldn't simply reach out and pull Tess away from him. The Zs would try to reach through her, to latch onto Conner, but didn't seem willing to physically tangle with Tess.

Zombie fingers kept prying through the gaps of space around Tess's body – between her arms and torso, and between her legs – trying to connect with, and grasp Conner. They were managing no more than pinches into his flak jacket or tapping on his helmet.

Conner was more concerned that some Zs would crawl down onto the floor, reach in and bite into his ankles, which weren't protected below his shin guards. But so far, the zombies were all upright, seemingly at an impasse with Tess.

Conner's view was largely obscured by Tess. He was taller and was able to see over her frazzled, dust-coated hair. He

328

could count the heads of more than a dozen zombies packed into the small cargo bay, their arms outstretched towards him. He just couldn't see below their necks. Unfortunately, Conner knew that the Zs were a very patient lot. They would shuffle around, grasping at him, until sooner or later, Tess shifted her position exposing him, and that would be that.

Tess didn't possess a vocabulary anymore, but she remembered the name 'Cassie' after hearing the word spoken repeatedly the last day and knew it was attached to the woman behind the cell door. Tess knew that Cassie was her best friend in the world, and had been so before whatever happened to Tess to make her the way she was now. Tess began to recall the faces of the man with Tess behind the door, and the man she was protecting behind her. She knew they were special to Cassie, which made them special to her.

Tess had never been in a direct confrontation with the others up in Black Rock City. They were indifferent to her; she did her best to avoid them. Tess had not come to understand that the others were at war with the machine men until this day. Tess had feared and mistrusted the machine men much more than the others until now. But the others were at war with her friends, her friends were at war with the others, and her friends got along with the machine men – at least some of them. Tess knew she was very far from the only home she could recall with certainty. All she had left were her friends in the back of this truck. She was going to protect them from the others, or any more of the bad machine men, at all costs.

Tess tirelessly kept swatting away the Zs outstretched arms and pushing at their chests. The zombies kept poking and prodding, trying to grab Conner. Minutes passed. Conner began to have difficulty seeing; his helmet visor fogged up from his labored breathing in the confined area behind Tess. More minutes ticked away. Conner's nerves were getting the best of him, knowing that at any second, one of the Zs might break through, and sink their teeth into him.

Sure enough, a zombie hand managed to grasp Conner's upper arm. The grip was unusually strong. Conner could feel himself begin to separate from Tess. His visor still heavily fogged, he could only make out a blur, but he could hear a buzz of activity in front of him. Then he began to hear voices.

Gunshots followed next. Zombies began to fall to the ground. More gunshots rang out. The zombie with the vice-like grasp let loose of him. Conner only now understood they were being rescued.

"Hey," Conner called out to their rescuers through the confusion and tangle of bodies in front of him. He could hear Tess whimpering in fright. It occurred to him they were going to shoot her as well. "Hey," he yelled again. Still partially blinded by his fogged helmet, he pulled her back and stepped forward, hoping to shield her, as she had done for him.

Unfortunately, Conner's valor proved to be necessary. The force of the two bullets from different weapons knocked him backwards, sending him and Tess against the door of the third cell. Conner slid down to the ground, pinning the terrified Tess behind him. She could see all the others were lifeless on the floor. She clung to Conner, although he felt just as lifeless.

A strange feeling came over Tess. The cargo van fell eerily silent, as the machine men with guns watched in awe as tears streaked down the face of the zombie hugging the man in the helmet slumped against the door.

The cell door pushed opened. Cassie's head emerged from behind the door to find Tess, working herself into a full-fledged sob, holding onto Conner, who wasn't responding. "No," was all Cassie could collect herself to cry out. She thrust herself down to the floor of the cargo bay, hugging Tess and Conner at the same time.

Cassie could sense a wave of sadness rolling through her, it seemed physical and tingled. It wasn't just because Bruce lay gravely injured close by. It occurred to her, she had just lost her chance to get her relationship with Conner back on track. She had seemingly lost the chance to grow old with him. "Conner," she called out, breaking the silence in the cargo bay, as she held onto him.

The Guardsmen

Alan Gorman was informed the truck was secured and was quickly briefed on what had just transpired. "Damn it," he yelled out to no one in particular. "This wasn't that complicated — don't shoot the infected lady they are protecting and secure them. So you shoot at her and drop the guy you're supposed to rescue. Damn it, anyway."

Alan had convinced the Homeland Security liaison of the value of securing the cargo truck after Bruce's initial call. But Alan was emphatically told the mission had to wait until reinforcements arrived.

Finally, the National Guard showed up from Camp Parks in Dublin. Alan received the green light to accompany a paramedic with field medical supplies, hop in one of the guard trucks with an armed escort and drive outside around to the Baldwin gate. The gate security quickly allowed them inside, on foot, where they shot their way to the cargo truck, parked exactly where Bruce had described it over the phone.

Alan sidestepped the zombie bodies littering the asphalt around the truck. He slipped in between the National Guardsmen with their rifles pointing outwards into the lot, their backs against the tailgate. He climbed up into the cargo truck, squeezing by the guardsmen dragging out the last of the zombie corpses from the cargo bay.

Alan sighed as he took in the sight of Conner slumped against the interior wall and doors inside the cargo bay – Cassie and Tess on each side of him, still crying. Cassie was unfastening his flak jacket, and was trying to check for a pulse. Alan did a double take upon viewing Tess for the first time. "Conner, what have you done?" Alan asked quietly.

"Where is Bruce?" Alan asked Cassie. She pointed to the third cell door, which was ajar. Alan poked his head inside. The paramedic was kneeling over Bruce with a flashlight. The paramedic guardsmen informed Alan that Bruce's vitals looked promising, but Bruce was in shock. He confirmed that a single bullet hadn't exited after entering just below the collarbone.

"Let's get him out into the light and stabilize him. If it looks like the bullet isn't lodged anywhere critical, we'll leave it, at least for now," Alan responded. Alan didn't receive permission to transport Bruce to a hospital. The area was under strict temporary quarantine with no exceptions allowed, no matter how dire. They would treat Bruce in the back of the truck.

Alan turned his attention to Conner.

"Don't you die, Conrad Zimmerman. You can't die on me." Cassie pleaded, while her forefinger and middle finger were pressed together on his neck. She noticed Alan standing over her.

"Alan, I can't tell if I he has a pulse or not." Cassie began sobbing.

"Here, may I?" Alan responded, motioning her to the side. "I think you just had her fingers in the wrong place. Alan eyed the two bullet marks in Conner's now unfastened flak jacket, and lifted up his shirt, examining the red raised welts in Conner's chest. Alan gently took Cassie's right hand and placed it on a different spot on Conner's throat. "See, Cassie? Feel the pulse now" he asked.

Cassie's face lit up, which caused Tess's face to light up. Cassie emitted an unintelligible sound of joy.

Then Conner's eyes opened, blinking repeatedly. "Conner, you truly are a cat with nine lives, although you have used up your credits pretty fast during the past day." Alan grinned, shaking his head. "It appears these flak jackets really do work. But you're going to have some nasty marks that are going to turn bright purple."

Cassie and Tess began covering Conner with kisses. Tess watched Cassie and began mimicking her, kissing Conner's chest as well. "Ladies, Conner, I'm sorry to break this up already, but I'm going to need you to slip behind another door, so you can stay protected while we make room to treat our friend Bruce, here."

Cassie protested. She had spent too much time in the dark behind the cell walls during the past day. "Alan, can we please, pretty please, stand outside the truck, if it's safe? I don't know if I can sit inside those cells another minute."

Alan looked down at Conner, who was rising up off the floor. Conner flashed a smile. "Well, okay, if the guardsmen will let you stand next to them. But at the first sign of trouble, you need to get out of their way and hop into the truck cab, assuming it's unlocked, okay?"

Cassie happily said yes, as she turned around to help Conner get off the floor of the cargo bay. He rose gingerly, wincing from the pain of where the bullets impacted the flak jacket against his ribs.

The guardsmen helped Cassie, Tess, and Conner down. There were eight of them lined around the back of the truck, all staring at Tess in awe. "She's okay? She's not like the others? She won't bite?" one of them asked.

Cassie laughed, feeling like she was being queried about her dog. "No, she won't bite." Cassie turned to survey the parking lot. Her smile melted. "Oh, no," she exclaimed, taking in the carnage. She reached to Conner next to her, grabbing his hand and not letting go.

They both glanced nervously back into the cargo bay. Alan and the paramedic had already moved Bruce from out of the cell into the bay so they could examine him. They could see the paramedic hooking up the I.V. and the pain medication drip.

The sound of gunfire in the distance could be heard from multiple directions. The smell of smoke and dust filled the air, along with zombie stench. The lot looked almost like bombs had been dropped. Cars littered the Hegenberger lot, pointed in every direction – none organized neatly in rows or lines.

The newly arrived reinforcements were making their presence known. Law enforcement and National Guard could be seen starting to file through the lot in tight formations, gunning down Zs as they progressed. Teams followed them, sorting through the bodies on the ground, stacking zombie corpses into piles, collecting stage one infected into designated spots.

A group of uninfected still on foot was spotted being escorted inside the stadium. Another group was being escorted over to the 66th Avenue lot. Other uninfected were visible, confronting and arguing with their rescuers.

Zombies were still wandering throughout the lot, but with each round of gunfire, their numbers diminished. A guardsmen standing next to Conner — after long bursts of rounds sounded not far from the cargo truck, in the RV area – turned to him with a wry smile. "It's kind of a catch-22, a paradox, a circular argument, don't you think?"

Conner smiled, amused that the young guardsmen would explain the dated phrase 'catch-22' to a man almost twice his age. "What's that?" Conner responded.

"We can shoot all we want– mow down all these stage two infected while the area is considered unsecured," the guardsman explained. "Then, as soon as the area as classified secured, the Gorman's disease laws apply and we can't touch them. It's like we have to shoot the zombies in order to save them."

Piling on Raider Fans

Alan, Conner, Cassie, and Tess stood over Bruce in his gurney near the fifty yard line inside the Oakland Coliseum. Behind them stood four national guardsmen, assigned by Homeland Security to keep Tess under guard, plus an FBI agent assigned to Bruce and Cassie – as the only witnesses to the zombie hijacking.

During the past hour, the Coliseum complex had been secured. The majority of the stage two infected had been taken down with kill shots by the National Guard, sheriff's officers and other law enforcement. The remaining zombies were collared and temporarily contained inside the Oracle arena.

Conner and Cassie glanced upwards into the Eastside luxury suites. Even from the field, they could see the stage two infected pressed up against the windows – having been locked in the suites earlier in the day when they were just stage one.

The football field had literally become a field hospital for treating injuries to the non-infected. Several rows of patients on gurneys and blankets were set up covering close to the length of the field. The preceding hours had produced a full spectrum of mishaps for tailgaters and law enforcement, from the riots, zombie encounters, car accidents, the fallen observation tower and friendly-fire.

Conner and Cassie held hands as they gazed around the stadium from the field. Tess had taken to mimicking, so she held onto Conner's other hand, while standing in front of Conner so she could be as close to Cassie as possible. Tess was clearly uneasy with the four armed guardsmen and FBI agent hovering over them, let alone the buzz of activity all around her.

It occurred to Conner how surreal it was to be standing on the football field at that moment. "You know," Conner commented loudly to everyone around, "right about now is when the football game should be ending, right here on this field. It's damn awful to think, but I'm guessing that Cassie and I are the reason this whole mess happened at the Coliseum."

"What?" Alan reacted skeptically. "How's that?"

"Well," Conner responded, "when I jumped into the cab of that cargo truck, while Cassie, Bruce, and Tess were trapped in the back by the infected, I found Cassie's purse sitting out. It had been rifled through, with our Raider tickets lying out in plain sight. I have to think they got to Oakland, panicked about where to lay low when their names were all over the news, saw the tickets, and decided to park here. And who knows where they might have ended up had they not seen the tickets?"

Conner turned to the FBI agent, who was listening in. "At least, that's the scenario you ought to check if your guy in custody would confirm," Conner advised him.

"Leave it to these Oakland fans to pour gasoline on this fire," cracked one of the guardsmen behind them, who were all listening in. "All of the rioting, and fighting, and running people over. That's why I'm a Forty Niner fan, man," the guardsmen continued, shaking his head.

Conner was having none of that. "Listen," Conner turned toward the guardsmen, angrily. "You think for a minute if you let loose those infecteds in any other stadium parking lot, trapped everybody inside, without any good information about what was going on for a long time, you'd have any different result? You don't need to answer, because I'm telling you, this is what is going to happen anywhere, anytime these things get loose in a crowded area. Don't be piling on these poor Raider fans. Can you imagine, they come back for one game to the Coliseum, and then this happens?"

Conner didn't want to argue the subject with the guardsmen. He noticed Bruce working his right hand in his mouth, while lying on the gurney in front of them. "Bruce, are you okay, buddy?"

"Man, I evidently bit my tongue hard when I got shot. I guess I scared poor Cassie with all the blood coming from my mouth. It still feels pretty weird, but Dr. Alan here fixed me up," Bruce told the group.

"Yeah, he had a decent tongue laceration," Alan explained. "Fortunately, we had the supplies and we wrapped it in four percent lidocaine-soaked gauze for ten minutes. I'd be more worried about that bullet that's still lounging around inside your shoulder there, Bruce buddy, if I were you."

Alan previously explained to Bruce that not every bullet had to be removed, and they certainly would have endangered him more trying to do so in such primitive conditions. He could be re-evaluated when he was cleared to go to a hospital, but for now, Alan had pronounced him stable and improving.

"So, how long do you think I have to stay here on this gurney?" Bruce directed his question to Alan.

Alan smiled. "Bruce, what's your hurry? The FBI here is going to be grilling you and Cassie for a good while when you're cleared to go. I don't think you're leaving the Coliseum anytime soon. And when you do, that doctor just down the row here is going to want you taken to a hospital for radiology to check out that bullet."

"Great," Bruce responded sarcastically.

"Alan," Cassie implored, "if I have to stay for questioning, you need to find out what happens to Tess while that's going on, as well as longer-term. I'm afraid to leave her, but if they're taking her up to the lab at Bruce's, I won't be there. I have to be with my daughter."

It was clear to Alan that Tess was firmly attached to Cassie. She also seemed taken with Conner, at least for the time being. "As you know, Bruce's lab personnel are all dead, and the facility is going to need some repairs. Tess isn't a danger to anyone, so how about I see if I can convince Homeland Security to set up something in San Diego? Conner, you could take some time off and go there to if you want. I know people at UCSD. I think we could get a lab established pretty fast."

"That sounds good to me," Cassie replied, pleased, while squeezing Conner's hand.

Alan lowered his voice. "But there actually is a danger you both need to be thinking about at all times if we get her to San Diego. Tess is still infected with stage one. It didn't kill her, but we have to assume that if she expires due to any cause – accidental or otherwise — she's going to reboot to stage two."

Conner and Cassie were silent after that sobering thought.

A small Coast Guard helicopter hovered over the stadium for a minute, catching everyone's eye. The chopper then shifted position to the immediate east of stadium and began carefully maneuvering down into BART plaza.

Alan stepped up to Conner, lightly punching him on the shoulder. "Come on, Conner. They've brought the infected subject from the cruise ship. It's time for us to roll."

Cassie released Conner's hand. Alan had already discussed the situation with them. Cassie had to stay put, under guard, until their full statements were taken – as did Bruce, who wasn't cleared medically to leave yet anyway. Tess, of course, had to stay as well.

Tess didn't want to let Conner go. As Conner pulled away to accompany Alan, Tess released his other hand but grabbed onto his arm, yanking hard to keep him from leaving. Cassie had to gently hold onto Tess and soothe her, until she relented.

Cassie and Conner exchanged smiles. Conner bid Bruce goodbye with a promise to return shortly. Then, he and Alan strode briskly toward the east side of the stadium, where security helped usher them up into the seats. They hurried up the stairs, past the tunnel and the enclosed vendor area and stadium exits, working their way to Section 137. They continued into the next level of seats, stopping at the final row just beneath the Plaza Suite windows. Five zombies had been shuffling aimlessly around the room, but rushed over to the windows when Conner and Alan appeared, pawing at the glass that separated them.

Incompatibility

The stage two infecteds were spread in several locations in the Coliseum complex. The largest numbers were locked inside the Oracle arena, consisting mostly of stage one infecteds gathered during the afternoon. There were also a few hundred in the stadium Eastside luxury suites, who had been stage one infecteds brought up from the Hegenberger lot in the late morning.

The Hegenberger lot also still held a number of Zs that were stuck inside vehicles – the result of someone bringing stage one infecteds inside their car – which the authorities hadn't dealt with yet. A rough estimate was the complex now held fifteen hundred active stage two infecteds, plus over two thousand zombie corpses.

Across the bay, the cruise ship held another seven hundred active stage two infecteds. The dilemma confronting the Homeland Security liaison at the Coliseum command center was where to consolidate and store the infecteds, who were now all meeting the conditions subjecting them to the laws protecting those inflicted with Gorman's disease.

Alan had convinced the liaison that before making plans to consolidate the infecteds from the two sites, they needed to test them for compatibility. Alan commented on the subtle differences he and Conner had noticed in the infecteds on board the cruise ship, compared to those from Burning Man.

A test was hastily arranged. The Coast Guard sent a chopper from the Alameda base, small enough to land outside the BART plaza entrance to the Eastside suites. It picked up a heavily restrained single stage two infected from the cruise ship, along with four Coast Guard specialists. The plan was to introduce the cruise ship infected into a Plaza Suite containing multiple stage two infecteds and observe any unusual behaviors or physiological reactions.

Conner and Alan were considered to be the expert observers to render an opinion on compatibility. Right after they reached the windows outside the Plaza Suite room, the liaison, sheriff, and an officer from the National Guard joined them.

The liaison arrived conversing on his phone. He stopped to announce to everyone that it would still be a couple minutes until the subject was brought into the room. The Coast Guard personnel were taking their time to be extra careful in their protocols as they transported their subject.

The liaison handed Alan the phone. "Here, the director wants a quick word with you." Alan stepped down a few rows so the talk could remain private.

"Alan, my goodness," the director began, "have you guys gotten around today or what? Now you can tell me first-hand how this little test of yours goes while we're on the phone, but while we're waiting, we need to set some things straight."

"Such as?" Alan asked warily.

"The preliminary statements from this Bruce Kepner and Cassandra Barton won't do at all, and neither will the statement we took from this Brady fellow that we apprehended. They just don't fit the narrative," the director complained.

"The narrative?" Alan wasn't sure where the director was going with this.

"Terrorism, Alan. Terrorism," the director explained. "ISIS has already taken credit on the Internet for both incidents. We can easily fit this Brady's profile as some disaffected outsider that got lured into ISIS' web. We can keep him buried from the public for some time easily enough. What we don't need right now is any talk of the Chinese or some drug-crazed lunatic co-conspirator. Things are delicate enough with the Chinese without bringing them into this. So for now, I'm pulling the request for formal statements from your people. We can always do that later if we have to. And I expect you to get a detailed, off-the-record briefing from them, which you can verbally share with me."

Alan sighed loudly in the phone, signaling his displeasure. "Why do you do this? The evil that these terrorists do around the world is bad enough and stands on its own, without you having to embellish things. I don't see the point of this."

"Alan, let's not go over this again," the Director cautioned.

"Fine," Alan sighed and responded. "Well, I assume you've heard we have a subject personally connected to our group, who maybe, just maybe, might provide a key into some level of immunity to the disease. I want to coordinate the arrangements with CDC for her to be studied by a team at UC San Diego. Also, the subject is highly attached to this Cassandra Barton. The only way we're going to effectively conduct the tests is to make Cassie available to the subject on an ongoing basis."

The director seemed distracted. "Okay, whatever, as long as I am first to know about material developments."

"And listen," Alan continued, "I have to get access to whatever your people have done with that fish from the charter boat we commissioned, and whatever they've found out so far. I hope you have some foggiest notion of how big this is and how bad it could be. We could be facing scenarios like the cruise ship on a daily basis, and that's assuming that just one of these meteor objects landed in the ocean. Who knows how many more might have hit other spots in the ocean around the globe?"

"Yeah, we'll let you in on whatever is going on with your precious fish," the director placated him but in an annoyed tone. "But pardon me if we reserve judgement for the time being on all your doomsday and alien meteor talk, Alan."

Conner called out to Alan. "Hey, they're letting the cruise ship subject into the room."

Alan told the director to hang tight. He hustled up the stairs in time to see a Coast Guard specialist just inside the door wearing a heavily padded protective suit and helmet release the cruise ship infected's collar at the other end of the rod he was holding. The specialist withdrew the rod and hustled back into the hallway, slamming the door shut behind him.

Collective jaws dropped outside the windows. The liaison, sheriff, National Guard officer, and Conner all fell silent. A zombie brawl ensued. The cruise ship zombie charged across the room toward the five Hegenberger parking lot Zs. The Hegenberger Zs immediately turned their attention from the windows to their attacker.

The brawl was quick and brutal. The cruise ship z seemed stronger and faster, quickly breaking the arms of two different Hegenberger zombies, and biting the ear off a third. But the Hegenberger zombies had the numbers. They piled on the cruise ship z, savagely tearing into him, not stopping until intestines, kidneys, colon and skin were all sent flying toward the window in small pieces. Greenish-gray blood was splattered everywhere. It didn't stop there. The Hegenberger Zs continued decimating the remains of the cruise ship z.

"Well?" Alan could hear the director on the other end of the phone, seeking a status report.

"Sir, it appears we have another problem," Alan responded.

www.ingramcontent.com/pod-product-compliance
Lightning Source LLC
Chambersburg PA
CBHW060934120726
47910CB00002B/330